BLOOD OF THE TITAN

VANESSA JOYCE

Blood of the Titan by Vanessa Joyce

Published by Vanessa Joyce

For permissions contact: vgarland89@yahoo.com

Book Cover Illustration by Angie Liu
Editor: Jasmine Barry
Allison Johnston-Crosier

ISBN: 979-8-31248165-5
ISBN: 978-1-7635600-1-7

First Edition.

Genre: Fantasy, Adult Romance.

Summary: One Titan family stands between a ruthless king and ultimate domination.
But his reign is not yet absolute—one final piece remains before he can cement his rule forever: Aliera.
Hunted for the power she carries, Aliera must escape across the fractured world, seeking to unite the last of the Farklı, Titans, Fae, and Dragons before Rael can claim her for himself.
She has only a handful of allies she can trust—including Beau, the enigmatic warrior who walks the fine line between salvation and destruction.
As desire tangles with deception and loyalty is tested in the shadows, one question looms—who will stand beside Aliera when the final battle begins, and who will betray her before it even starts?

FOR ALL THE BOOKTOK GIRLIES,
HERE'S ANOTHER BOOK BOYFRIEND
TO FANTASIZE ABOUT.

Special Thanks

Taylor Melnychuk

Ashley C Smith

Pronunciation Guide

NAMES:

Beau: Bo

Aliera: Ah-lee-ehr-ah

Rael: Rail

Astrid: As-trid

Zac: Zak

Kieran: Keer-an

Eleanor: El-uh-nor

Torin: Tor-in

Draven: Dray-ven

Thane: Thayn

Teresina: Teh-reh-see-nah

Starlette: Star-let

Cleo: Clee-o

PLACES:

Varsili: Var-see-lee

Creed: Kreed

Farkli: Fark-Lee

Antoli: An-toh-lee

Orman: Or-man

Lexia: Lex-see-uh

Tecrit: The-krit

OTHER:

Durgun: Dur-goon

Drake Hoca: Drayk Hoh-jah

Sonsuz: Son-zooz

AUTHOR'S PLAYLIST

From one mood reader to the next…

Let's Listen Together!

FJORD
INN
SONSUZ FOREST
TORIN'S
THE
ANTOLI REALM
LEXIA
ISLE OF KORSAN
I
ORMAN

RUINS OF TITANS
FARKLI
THE OLD OUTPOST
ECRIT
CREED
SWAMPLANDS
INN
WAR CAMP
WAR CAMP
DENIZ
VARSILI KINGDOM

BLOOD OF THE TITAN

CHAPTER ONE

ALIERA

My world had always been different—small, structured, and carefully contained, hour by hour, day by day—it never changed. Each day blended into the next, measured not by time but by tasks—washing, sewing, sweeping, tending to the small garden my mother kept behind the house. It was a life confined within walls, a life where movement was dictated by routine rather than choice. Sometimes I was allowed in our private garden where our mother would teach me how to grow and germinate fruit and vegetables with the limited space we had. The scent of damp earth and crushed leaves clung to my hands, the only reminder that something living could flourish in this confined world. It was the only place I could taste fresh air, feel the sun on my skin without the burden of secrecy pressing against my ribs. Even then, the stone walls loomed high, a reminder that I was still caged.

I was never allowed outside. That was for my brothers, all four of them. They would often come home tired, laughing among themselves, smelling of saltwater and smoke, stories spilling from their lips of adventures I would never know.

My parents had masked the truth by telling me I was privileged to be a girl, that I should be happy I didn't have to work at the forge, or in the vineyards, or even in the bays scaling and gutting fish like each of my brothers. I had nodded obediently each time, yet my heart ached, longing desperately for even a glimpse of the world beyond these walls. They said it with such certainty that, for a time, I almost believed them. Almost. But privilege didn't feel like being tucked away while the rest of the world moved on without me. Privilege wasn't a life condemned to silence.

In truth, I wasn't allowed to be seen; I was to be kept a secret.

All my life my parents and my brothers told me I was special, they whispered it like a prayer, like a promise meant to keep me from asking too many questions. But I didn't feel special. What was so special about a girl who had never touched the world beyond her doorstep? What was so special about a name that could only be spoken in whispers? It was a banishment from a life I should have never had. But here I was.

Late at night, as I lay awake listening to the wind whisper through the trees, I wondered, over and over again: what was special about me?—I felt afraid of who I was, where I was, and the consequences if I were to be caught. My brothers would reassure me gently when they saw the fear in my eyes, telling me they'd protect me no matter the cost, but their words only made me feel more trapped. We weren't the ones fighting in the war against the Fae in the Westerlands, not yet. But deep down, hidden beneath the layers of fear, I wished we could. At least then I would have a chance to finally discover who I truly was.

My family were the last remaining Titanborns. A part of a past the world had long since tried to erase. We were the blood of the Titans, watered down by generations passed, but still, some of us possessed magical abilities we were doomed to hide.

The Titans once ruled the north beyond the mountains of stone and ice, far past the forests of the world. They had been warriors, conquerors, forces of nature that bent the world to their will. They were riders of dragons, commanders of the skies, sea's, wielders of the elements. But unified they attracted jealousy around the Dunya.

Hiding wasn't in our nature, yet here we were. As we became the last of our kind, we also found ourselves living in the city of the King whose ancestors had laid waste to our people. We were ghosts of the past living among the very people who had tried to wipe us from existence.

My parents lived by the motto that being closer to danger made us safer. I had never understood that. How could standing in the mouth of a wolf be safer than running from it? But my father believed it. And my brothers followed his lead, they never questioned his orders.

My father had eventually assumed a General position in King Rael's army. It was the only freedom he could grasp. A carefully constructed disguise, one that let him move among the very people who would have gladly strung us up if they knew what we were.

He had demonstrated his worth within the army with his unmatched fighting skills. He was faster, stronger—deadlier— than any ordinary man, but he had learned to dull his edges, to pretend that his victories were the result of training and not bloodlines. This kept him in the King's good graces. He had worked his way up the human ladder of command and swore allegiance to Varsili. His only real goal was to keep our family safe.

And so followed my older brothers, Edi, Mason, Zac, and Wren.

They were all born with the same power as my father—inhumane strength, speed, and stamina—on top of their own unique abilities to conjure an element. A secret they carried like a second skin, always hidden, always restrained.

My mother was also enlisted as a physician due to her unique healing abilities. To the King's court, she was simply an expert in medicine. To those of us who knew the truth, she was something far greater. She had extensive knowledge in sorcery and apothecary thanks to her Farklian roots. Her magic wasn't loud like my father's, but it was just as powerful. She was a hearth sorceress, better than any doctor, but a fact she had to hide. She had the ability to save a mere human soldier or spare them pain during death, but she never let on too much more for fear of being caught with powers.

I had grown up watching her walk that fine line, never stepping too far into the shadows, never revealing too much in the light.

But me? I was more of a burden—I was kept hidden, and that was a job in itself when I was younger. A restless, caged thing that had to be reminded, time and time again, that the world outside was not for me.

I was no Titan or sorceress. I wasn't godly with outstanding abilities. I was just a girl in a big city with the wrong last name. I had been alone in the world by the age of ten. That was how old I was when the King found out who we were.

The King had taken my whole family to fight in the ongoing war that had flared on and off for centuries. They hadn't even been given a choice. The decision had been made for them, the pieces moved before they even had a chance to resist. With their lives at risk, they had no choice but to submit. The greater secret was me.

My family was special—magnificent even.

Each of my brothers had the strength to fight multiple men at once, masking their sight with hallucinations or their elemental abilities. They were valuable beyond measure in a war this old, a war that had forgotten its purpose except to breed hate against beings who were anything but human.

The Fae had powers of their own—regeneration, heightened healing, flight, and strength that no human could ever combat. But my family? They could challenge any Fae; they could challenge an army of Fae—They were weapons of war now.

So, here I was—an orphan in a kingdom of perpetual summers, a rich fishing city where the scent of salt and brine clung to the air.

And that was how I survived.

Fifteen years had passed. Fifteen years of silence. I wondered if I'd ever see their faces again. Would I recognize them? Would they recognize me? Did they think I was dead? Were they dead?

I had been kept a secret, even as an infant. My existence had been closely guarded from every person in Varsili.

My mother had given me tonics to keep me quiet, and any questions from others were quickly snuffed out by my father in a violent way. I had never been given the chance to be someone. To be my own person, to have a personality of my own. I had been molded this way.

My life had been lonely as a child. My brothers were much older, and they spent their days working. Mason would play cards with me when he could, Zac always made me laugh with his ridiculous pranks. But it was a laughter I could barely share, but for small moments my cheeks felt hot, and they reached my eyes as the climbed my face in happiness, and I felt alive in those seconds, but the loneliness when they left me was an unbearable pain that constantly ached in my chest—It never faded. It never softened.

In her final moment with me, my mother had hidden me in the bathroom of our home, as they boarded up all the doors and windows. She spelled the home into silence and enchanted the doorways so only I could use them—the house stayed that way for the next fifteen years.

Silent. Empty, and so did I. I remained silent because silence was all I knew.

It had become a part of me, woven into my skin like an unspoken law. Silence meant survival. It meant not drawing attention, not existing in the eyes of those who could take everything from me.

We had been over this scenario repeatedly, hoping it would never come to fruition, but that was a fool's hope. My mother had rehearsed it like an incantation, my father like a battle plan. If they came for us, we would be ready. We would know what to do, but knowing didn't make it easier. Deep down, they knew the King would come for them.

And if he found me? My fate would be more terrifying than anything we could dream up.

When it happened, my brother Zac was caught wielding flames in his hands as he worked in the forge armory.

It had been a careless mistake—too brief for most to notice but not brief enough. The wrong pair of eyes had seen, and rumors spread like wildfire until the guards of the King descended upon the forge, it took 30 men to restrain Zac, that's what Mason told me. He wouldn't go down without a fight, he was fiery and fierce, just like his gift.

The Fae were powerful, yes. They could heal, they could fly, they were stronger than men—but even they could not conjure fire from nothing.

And so, the whispers about our family's origins, about our bloodline, suddenly had weight to them.

My father had no choice. He offered my brothers into service quickly after that incident in an effort to protect me and keep me hidden. He was willing to sacrifice all of them—for me.

A bitter choice. A desperate one. His position in the army was now more important than ever. He began serving at King Rael's side, his Titan puppet, an insult to our family. But with me as a threat that lingered in his mind, it was the only thing keeping him compliant.

The King didn't need loyalty. He only needed obedience. So, my father did everything Rael said in desperation to keep me hidden—to erase me from the world so completely that even the King's shadow could not find me.

Rael already had my brothers. My father had already lost.

Our world was no stranger to chaos. Violence had always been the currency of kings, and war had stained the streets long before I was born. Peace was just a fairytale that oracles told small children.

But who would bother a little girl when the stirring of the city was mixed with constant anarchy? That was what kept me safe. Not my father's sacrifice. Not the magic hidden in my bones. Just the sheer indifference of men too preoccupied with their own battles to notice a shadow slipping through their streets. I had managed to slip through all the cracks. I was small enough to be overlooked, small enough to take only what I needed. I stole food—just enough to keep me alive, never enough to make anyone notice.

But as I grew older, I needed more.

I busied myself with collecting clams, mussels, and any seafood I could find in the shallows of the sea. The work was cold, but predictable. The tides followed their own rules, there was a low tide, then a high tide. At times plentiful, others not so much. It was a work that came easy to me. I would sell my catch at the markets on the far side of the castle, where the wealthy men drank and whored with the more expensive and sober women at the House of Red. They tipped better than the rest—at least on good days, when my catch was heavy and my oysters fat with meat. Oysters always fetched me a good price.

Six of them could buy me a whole chicken. A meal that meant I wouldn't go hungry for days.

I regularly saw Rael whoring in the same market where I sold the seafood. He was a man who craved indulgence. He always appeared rugged, as if he were trying to fit in amongst his guards or go completely unnoticed altogether. But he wasn't hard to miss. He had a salt-and-pepper beard with a full silver head of hair and brown eyes, a scar under his left nostril that deformed his top lip into a little hook big enough to spot from a distance.

He had more bastards than he could count on all his fingers and toes.

Three sons with a legitimate claim to the throne, but none had any interest in claiming it. They all spent their days rotting in whorehouses, drinking and eating until they were sick. And each day, the pattern repeated.

Rael didn't like this, and he made it obvious with how he treated them in public spaces.

Every month, when the townsfolk asked where his sons were, Rael would scoff and ignore the questions. A king with no promising heirs, a throne dangling by a thread. He was desperate now to make a statement, to set his reign above that of the Warmaker's. His last hope, his bastards. But anyone could claim to be one of those.

The people were growing restless, but no one dared to say it.

My kin were slaughtered in one of his father's wars. The Warmaker, they had called him. His name was lost to history, but his destruction was not. His jealousy tore the Dunya world to shreds.

The Fae, who once traded and lived amongst human cities, were now their enemies. The Titans were gone—erased.

Our city now lay in ruins, overrun by the effects of time. I had never seen the ruins, I wanted to more than anything, I wanted to stand where *they* had stood, to feel the echoes of the past in the stones beneath my feet. It was the one thing I desired. To feel close to the place I should call home. Between the ruins and Farkli.

I had made it to twenty-five years old and hiding had become so much harder. The population of the city grew, and every time guards roamed the streets to collect taxes, they attempted to break through the doors of my family's abandoned home. They never got through the magic spelled on the house—Not yet, it was just a matter of time.

My mother was not Titanborn, but her mother was a sorceress born in Farkli. Farkli was a dark, mysterious city that only the bravest of humans would explore. They never returned. Not whole. Not sane. Anyone entering Farkli had to be mindless, or they would risk leaving half-witted.

I knew my time here was limited. I could feel the walls closing in, the weight of years pressing against my chest. I couldn't evade them forever. I wanted to leave. I wanted to find my family. I wanted to live.

I had a single friend in this city. A small boy named James, no older than eight. He was a wiry thing, all sharp angles and restless energy, with a mind that worked faster than his words could keep up with. He had a fidgety way about him, a desire to complete tasks to their completeness, and if not done correctly, he would suffer from meltdowns and completely shut off from everyone except his mother. But he was clever. Sharp in ways most people ignored, but he was kind. Kindness was rare in Varsili. Rarer still for someone like me. We traded together often, his fruit for my clams, or sometimes his father would give him vegetables to sell. He took his work seriously, haggling with an intensity that was almost comical for a child. But I never laughed. Because this was his survival. Just as mine was the sea.

On the days I caught enough mussels, I could trade ten for a few potatoes and carrots, which I could then sell for a loaf of bread— or, on the rare occasion, eggs.

James never asked where I came from. He never pried. Maybe because, like me, he had learned that asking questions led to trouble.

Life in Varsili was repetitive and boring and I longed for something more. I longed to live in a place where I didn't have to hide who I was. Where I didn't have to be a shadow. Where I didn't have to lower my gaze or avoid speaking to strangers for fear of being noticed. The weight of it pressed against my chest more heavily with each passing year.

I had heard of other cities—places that felt more like stories than real places. Isles with no rulers. An outpost so large it could see the whole continent from its highest peak. There was Orman, the Fae capital King Rael was continuously at war with.

But there was also Lexia…

Lexia, the name itself sounded like an answer to a prayer I had never dared to say aloud. Sailors described it as the most beautiful, magical city on the continent. A trade capital for the isles.

A place where different races of beings were welcomed. It was protected by ancient Antoli magic, and even though the population was largely Fae, its roots were of Titans. The last remnants of my bloodline, hidden not in the shadows, but in plain sight.

That's why the sailors said the city was so large and vast that it went deep underground, where the Moles mostly resided.

The Moles were the keepers of all the meaningful histories in the world. They were not creatures. Not vermin, as some called them. They were scholars. Guardians of knowledge. Deep in the underground was a library large enough for a thousand lifetimes. The Moles themselves never left the library. They became so pale and dependent on the darkness that the sight of sunlight would blind them forever. So that's how they gained the name of the Moles.

Nobody ever saw them, they were the servants of time. They lived their lives in service of the past. And yet, the thought of them stirred something inside me. If history still had its keepers, if records of the Titans still existed—then maybe, just maybe, I could find something of my own past among them.

It was always safer talking to sailors. They were rarely from Varsili and had an abundance of interesting stories to share. They had seen the world beyond the city walls. They had touched the places I had only heard of in whispers. They were never reluctant to answer my questions and entertained my curiosities. To them, I was just another street vendor, another nameless girl selling what she could. It was the safest way for me to have a social life. Even if for a fleeting time.

Today, I had caught nothing. The sea had been cruel, withholding its gifts, leaving me empty-handed.

I would pass by the store I frequently traded at one last time on my way out of the city.

The decision had been made. I had decided this would be the last day I waded in the waters for oysters, mussels, and clams. It would be the first time I saw the gates from the outside. The first time I would walk beyond them, no longer a prisoner of my own making.

I had never lingered longer than a moment, sometimes stopping for a glimpse as soldiers poured into the city, hoping—just hoping—that I would see one of my brothers among them—but they never came.

The land outside the gates was green. Orchards and vineyards sprawled for miles down a flat brown path. A road that led to somewhere. Somewhere I had never been. Somewhere I was finally ready to go.

I headed into the back alley of my family's abandoned home, my hands tightening around the straps of my empty basket.

I didn't look back. I had nothing to look back on, so I packed a bag with a change of clothes, spare boots, all the food I had, all the money I had—three silvers. Three silvers wouldn't get me much more than a night at an inn. Not nearly enough for what I needed, I'd have to find work along the way.

Somewhere. Anywhere. As long as it was far from here.

Chapter Two

Beau

I had returned to Varsili the night before last. King Rael had sent me on a mission to an eastern war camp to eliminate a spy in their company. The target, an older woman from Farkli. An alchemist working for the King of Creed, likely in alliance with Farkli and the Fae. She came disguised as a healer under the guidance of the mages, but instead, she had become a silent assassin, poisoning her way through the camp's hospice of already wounded men. I recognized her immediately, not just from stories whispered among soldiers, but from her husband—a soldier I knew, one with his own agenda. The kind of soldier who only followed enough rules to keep his head down. She knew who I was immediately. Unlucky for her, I understood exactly the danger she posed. Her knowledge and pity of me for being Fae was an unwelcomed feeling.

There had been no words exchanged between us, no room for mercy, revenge was the taste in my mouth when I cut her down, to my surprise she didn't fight back. She could have, but instead she looked at me like she owed me this, right up until the moment my straight blade crossed her throat. I granted her the mercy of my less terrorizing sword, but the moment breath left her body I didn't feel whole the way I thought I would.

But I couldn't afford to have my identity exposed—either identity. Even if she was serving the right side, any side was better than the one I was on. If there even was a right side anymore—I doubted it more each passing day. I was trapped in a web spun by Rael, bound to serve a ruler I despised, each mission chipping away at what remained of my soul. What Rael had cooking in the depths of the castle and in those camps could only be explained to those who knew the chaos a mage could bring to the world. He was playing war in a twisted new way now.

A fairer ruler governed Creed. King Nixon was young and wise in his new role and had made several attempts at peace over his brief time in power. Not that it mattered. Creed was a small farming city blocked off from the rest of the world by a strong outpost and dangerous swamplands. Creed had an impenetrable outpost and on the other side, a single bridge out, and nobody took it—not if they wanted to return.

But Rael would never yield unless the entire world bowed to him. A pathetic human king riding off the back of his grandfather's succession in eliminating the Titans. He milked the crap out of that, stretching the victory across generations as if it had been his own accomplishment. The remaining bloodline worked in his armies, some sent to Farkli where they could be contained. There was still active magic in the ruins, and Farkli was across the river, the perfect distance to keep eyes on any movement. The people of Farkli were unfriendly, often hostile, and targeted outsiders for sport. Few could enter and also be granted leave.

I was awake but lost in my thoughts when the knock clambered at my heavy wooden door.

"Beau, you are summoned to the great hall." A servant knocked. They knew better than to barge in and wake me.

"In ten minutes. GOT IT!" I yelled in response. My voice carried irritation and resignation—I'd done this dance too many times.

I slipped my pants on, pulled my boots up and laced my shirt. Every motion felt heavy, weighed down by the years of reluctant obedience. I brushed through my hair with my fingers and tied it back as neatly as I could, then splashed my face with water from the bowl left in my room. I wrestled my old leather jacket on and in a second, I was racing down the three flights of curling stairs. I met the doors that led to the extravagant great hall. The doors opened and in the middle of the room King Rael was seated on his oversized throne large enough for two others, it wasn't uncommon for him to take women on his throne, the pig that he was.

"Your Highness." I bowed as I approached.

"Ahh Beau! I have an important task for you." He gushed with excitement. Too much excitement that it set my nerves on edge, so I listened intently, and spoken with caution.

"How can I serve you, my King?" I asked.

"There's a peasant girl I want. She sells the clams and mussels at the House of Red. Bring her to me." His lip curled into one of his filthy smiles.

"A whore?" I asked plainly.

"She will be when I'm done with her." His chuckle was grotesque as his look intensified, a look that ordered the other men and women in the hall to laugh with him—or else.

My jaw tightened in disgust as I sneered inside but kept my composure and nodded in agreement.

"What is the bounty?" I questioned.

"Bounty? Oh, name your price." He smiled his yellow, toothy smile, his scar stretching across his top lip.

"Two hundred silvers." I didn't hesitate and my brow raised as I waited for his response. The bounty was high, I had never asked for this much before.

"Done." He tossed me a bag so heavy that it continued to jingle as it hit the tiles of the floor before my feet.

"That's four hundred, have some *fun* with her if you wish—I wouldn't mind having more of your bloodline around if they were as good at killing as you." He snickered maliciously.

I grabbed the bag and bowed as I stepped out of the hall and went back up to my quarters. Standing before the mirror, I stared bitterly at my reflection, questioning how many more insults I'd endure before something inside me finally snapped. Below, the city's streets bustled innocently, oblivious to the evil within their walls. I slipped my knives into my belt, the money into a satchel, and wore my two swords in a cross over my back—one jagged for extra torture, slicked with poison, the other clean and straight.

I made my way into the city through the rear tunnels that only soldiers and servants used. I kept to the shadows, my movements stealthy and practiced, invisible to those who walked openly. Blending easily into the crowd near the House of Red, I approached the seafood market where I had been led to believe she would be.

"Any clams today?" I asked the shopkeeper.

"My girl will be along shortly." He assured me anxiously. "Would you try an oyster while we wait for her?" He offered me the shell, within it a fat oyster, a squeeze of lemon, and a sprinkling of salt.

"Or would you prefer vinegar? I have a bottle fresh from the vineyards, it's a special wine vinegar. Three years shelved, perfectly tangy." He spoke proudly of the product.

"Your own recipe?" I asked.

"Oh, I should only hope to be so talented in fermentation. No, sir. My hands are for shelling, not the hands of a cook." He opened his hands before me. Scars from cutting himself too many times, broken skin from sharp shells.

"You shell them well." I took the offering of food, and he gave me one of each now.

"Thank you, sir." I could tell he was nervous about losing me as a customer. I slurped the oysters down one at a time, ensuring I took a moment to savor each flavor. They slipped down my throat with ease and I cleaned the shells with my tongue. It was the best vinegar I'd ever had. I placed two nickels on the table as thanks and he gleamed at the coins in delight.

"You're in luck, here she comes!" The old man pointed to a young woman. Instantly, an unsettling sense of dread churned within me.

"Dear!" The old man shouted.

"Oh, Darius. I don't have anything for you today. Apologies." She bowed politely but distantly.

"No bother." I stepped closer, studying her carefully.

"Have a good day." she murmured nervously.

I followed her, my instincts sharp, focused entirely on the would be enemy before me. She moved with practiced ease through the streets, clearly intent on avoiding attention, but I knew the city too well.

She walked through gates, but not before being stopped by guards with questions. She explained that she desired to forage for mushrooms and patted her bag on her hip. They foolishly took the bait, a nod to her pleasant looks. I didn't need such an explanation. Any man carrying weapons generally meant they were on a king's mission. I hung back a little as I watched the woman reach high into the apple trees. They were almost too tall for her as she stood on the tips of her toes.

"You shouldn't be this far out alone." My voice startled her sharply.

"Oh! You frightened me. I'm just collecting apples." she smiled falsely.

"We both know you lied about mushrooms. What else are you lying about?" I questioned, narrowing my eyes.

She ignored my presence and continued picking the apples, tossing them down onto the ground to bag later.

"Why are you following me?" she demanded. No fear in her voice now. Just caution and strength.

"You've caught the interest of King Rael." I let the words sink in. Let them settle in the space between us like a trap waiting to be triggered.

She flinched. "Why?"

I moved closer, watching her carefully. Then—the flicker of something. A calculation. She was assessing me now, just as I was assessing her. Her fingers twitched. Then, quick as lightning—A knife.

Small. Dull. But still a blade.

She held it steadily, pointed directly at my throat, her knuckles white from the force of her grip.

"I don't want any trouble." she said beneath her breath.

She dropped the apples.

"I was leaving. Please just let me go." She spoke softly now.

"Relax." I replied, unbothered by her pitiful blade. I did not move toward her, but I did not step back either. "Put the knife down." I added.

She hesitated. Her breath was shallow, her pulse flickering wildly in her throat, but she didn't lower the blade, and I exhaled calmly to let her know I was unbothered by her weak threat.

"Do you even know why they want you?" I said as I pulled out a length of rope from my bag.

Her hands trembled now, the kitchen knife glinting in the faint light that slipped through the trees.

"No." Her voice was quieter this time. Maybe a lie, maybe confusion. Her golden eyes puddled with nervous tears, but she held firmly.

Her beauty had been my first assumption. The kind of beauty that drew attention. The kind that made men like Rael hunger for ownership. But now? Now, I wasn't so sure.

She ran, taking the opportunity while I lost myself in thought. She was faster than I expected. She weaved through the trees, leaped over bushes, darted between the thick trunks like she had done this a thousand times before. But I had been here a thousand times more than her. I knew the land. I knew how it would betray her. So, I let her run. Let her chase an escape that would never come.

Until—She was right back where she started.

The trees had played their trick. The repetition of them cascading down the farmland, twisting the world into an endless maze.

She staggered, panting. Blinded by the futility of it all. And that was when I struck. I sprung from the brush, catching her in my arms, pressing her down into the dirt. Her breath left her in a sharp, panicked gasp as she fought— Clawing at my face. Punching, kicking, thrashing beneath me.

"Please, let me go!" Her voice broke, but her fists did not stop.

I gritted my teeth, wrapping the rope around her wrists as she continued to struggle. She bucked, twisted, thrashed, her dress tangling in the dirt, her hair wild with leaves, but it was pointless, I was too powerful for her fight off.

"Nooo!" The cry left her lips, raw and desperate, as I secured the knot.

And just like that—She was caught. Leashed like an animal, but I knew what would happen if I took her back. She would be raped over and over again. By Rael. By his commanders. By his sons. She would not survive a week. And for what? For beauty? For sport? If that was all they desired of her, she didn't deserve the violent future they intended for her.

She tried to fight me again, but I held firm. She tried to run, but she was bound. I sighed as she slipped in the dirt and mudded her clothes over and over. She never gave up.

She didn't make it easy. She kicked my knees out from under me, sending me face-first into the ground. Threw herself over me, grappling at my belt for a knife. But I was larger. Stronger. I threw her beneath me, pinning her down. She panted as I forced my thighs onto her chest.

"STOP IT!" I growled. Her golden eyes burned into mine.

"Why aren't we going back to Varsili?" She glowered. She turned her head, staring at the city in the distance. I stood up, releasing her from the weight of my body. She scrambled up, fists clenched into one.

Then—A handful of dirt. She hurled it at my face. It didn't touch me. Her face fell in disappointment.

I laughed. "WALK." I shoved her between the shoulder blades, guiding her into the deeper woods.

But she resisted and continued to protest. "I haven't done anything wrong."

"I know." I sighed.

Her lips parted at that response. "Then why are you doing this?" She pleaded.

Something in her voice—something more than desperation.

"Keep quiet!" I snapped.

"I will not!" she snapped back.

"Tell me what you want with me!" She fought the rope again, her wrists red and raw from the attempts at loosening the tie.

I gripped her by the throat. Lifted her just slightly—just enough to silence her.

Her hands flew up, fingers splayed across my wrist.

Begging suddenly, no longer fighting as she submitted to me. The wriggling stopped.

"I don't know who you are." I said. My voice was a low dangerous growl.

"But I know if I take you back there, you'll be raped until you carry a child with Rael's blood. And when he's done with you, he will pass you around like cheese at a feast." I loosened my grip.

She gasped, rubbing her throat.

"They know." The words barely escaped her lips.

I shook my head and pulled her along by the rope, deeper into the forest. We had a long way to go. We walked for hours; she fought me at every turn. Dragging her feet like a child. Twisting the rope, tugging at it to stall me. She was refusing to listen. But she was bound, and she would go where I led her. Even if she despised me for it. Even if she wanted me dead. Even if I had to carry her, I was taking her away from Varsili.

"Where are we going?" Her voice was sharp, accusing.

"To Creed." I answered.

"No! Take me to Lexia." She stopped abruptly, yanking against the rope as if she could command her own fate.

I exhaled sharply, my patience thinning. "Lexia? Lexia is on the other side of the Dunya."

She had no idea what she was asking. No idea what it would take to get there.

"You're an enemy now." Her voice was quieter this time, more dangerous. She was starting to play my way.

"If they find out that you helped me, you'll be killed." She met my eyes.

And there was something new in them now. Calculation. A challenge.

"You'll be safe in Lexia too." She was trying to sway me.

Trying to make me believe we could be anything but what we were. I was her captor. She was my prisoner. That was all.

"I'll think about it." I grunted, tightening my grip on the rope.

"Seriously?" She was suddenly surprised.

"Yep." I replied.

I reached into my satchel and pulled out a long, dark sash.

"Not getting kicked again." I muttered as I tied the blindfold around her eyes.

The first night, she tried to run. Of course she did. So, I tied her to a tree with a trunk so large she couldn't reach around it to untie herself. I bound her legs, gagged her mouth. And when she still fought? I tied her tighter.

Then the second night, she fought again. Her legs had the strength of a horse, but I had far more experience in abduction than she gave me credit for. She remained blindfolded most of the time—unless she was eating. We had been gone for two nights now. And we had been lucky not to cross any other travelers, or wildlife. But luck never lasted.

It was still dark when I woke. The lake at our side was covered in a delicate fog. The sun had not yet broken the horizon, but the sky was streaked with grey, enough that I could see her still asleep, curled beneath her tattered cape. She was shivering. Her arms wrapped tight around herself, her breath uneven—I sighed.

She wouldn't survive like this for long. We needed food, we needed shelter.

I crouched beside her, shaking her shoulder. She groaned through her gag, trying to rub her face against the dirt to move her blindfold.

I loosened it, and she closed then once more as she looked up at me.

"Damn, still you." She narrowed her sleepy eyes at me.

"Still too lippy for your own good." I grunted back.

"I need water." she rasped.

I pressed my canteen to her lips, tilting it gently. She drank slowly, her lips catching the water, careful not to spill a single drop. I waited until she had enough, then lowered the canteen.

"I don't suppose you have some food?" she asked.

"No." I admitted.

Then, with a smirk I added. "Bet you wish you hadn't dropped those apples right about now." Her nostrils flared at me, her eyes dark.

"Blame yourself for that." She hissed.

"Get up." I rolled my eyes.

She twisted her hands, shaking the rope in the air.

"My legs, you idiot!" Her words venomous.

I sighed dramatically, untying her ankles.

"That attitude isn't helping your cause." I muttered.

She stood slowly, rolling her shoulders, flexing her fingers.

Then, suddenly—She darted for a log. Aimed. And hurled it straight at me. I dodged it easily, laughing as it landed harmlessly at my feet.

"Stop throwing things at me." I snickered.

She glared, unrepentant. "If I had a better aim, I'd have split your skull."

I grinned. "Oh, sorry, were you aiming for my head?" I laughed aloud.

She huffed, crossing her arms. I turned and started walking.

She hesitated at first and then called out. "Wait for me." She yelled.

I smirked. "Oh, so now you want my company?"

She scowled, picking up her pace into almost a run until she was beside me.

"Do I have a choice?" she muttered.

"If we're stuck together, you could at least tell me your name." She froze as she said it.

Like she had only just realized that she didn't know.

I turned my head slightly. "Beau."

She let out a breath. "I'm Aliera." she said quietly.

I nodded once. "Can you promise you'll stop throwing things at me, Aliera?"

She bared her teeth, her expression vicious. "If you stop tying me up, maybe."

I laughed under my breath and pulled the length of rope from my belt. I tossed it to her.

She blinked at it.

Then, slowly, wrapped it around her fingers, twisting it in her palm, her wrists still bound together, but she had the leash now.

"Happy now?" I asked, starting to walk again.

She nodded as she stumbled over a root, then a patch of uneven grass, falling slightly closer to me each time.

"A hot meal is currently at the forefront of my mind." I sighed.

Her stomach rumbled and she pressed a hand to it, trying to silence the sound before nodding in agreement.

I was starving, that was true. I hadn't eaten since we left Varsili. She had already eaten through her food on the first day—a sign she had no idea what kind of journey she was in for. She had no idea what it meant to travel— to survive.

She had this vision that someone would offer her a free ride on a ship to Korsan without payment, that they would feed her and give her a warm bed to sleep in. She wasn't like any other Varsilian woman I had known. She wasn't soft, but she wasn't hardened either. She had been hiding in the seafood stalls for years. Right under Rael's nose and yet, he had never ordered me to collect a street vendor before. Not for this kind of bounty, not for four hundred silvers.

There had to be more to her—And I was going to find out what.

The road ahead was long, winding deeper into the untamed lands at the tip of Varsili's borders. Aliera walked beside me in uncomfortable silence, then I stopped her.

"There's nowhere to run, remember that." I said as I cut the ropes from her wrists." She still wouldn't trust me—Good, she wasn't supposed to.

I wasn't her rescuer; I was her captor. And I had no plans to let her forget it.

"Where are we stopping for food?" she asked, breaking the silence.

I glanced at her from the corner of my eye. She wasn't asking because she was curious. She was weighing her options. Testing me.

I exhaled slowly. "There's a village a half-day's walk from here. We'll find something there. If we don't cross it, there are Inn's also." A partial truth, there were Inn's, but the villages were more like war camps.

She narrowed her eyes. "That's a long way." she muttered.

Too long for someone who hadn't been preparing for a journey.

She thought I wouldn't notice the slight hitch in her step, the way she was already shifting her weight to ease the growing ache in her feet. I did—I noticed everything.

"Keep up, then." I said smoothly.

She shot me a glare but said nothing.

She walked in silence for a few minutes before speaking again. "You don't have to take me anywhere." One final attempt at honest freedom perhaps. But the softness in her tone was almost convincing.

I smirked. Was she giving up so soon?

"You could let me go." She sighed.

I gave her a look. "And then what?" I asked.

She hesitated, then lifted her chin. "I can disappear. You don't have to be a part of this." She exhaled, as she tried to catch her breath.

I scoffed. "You think you can survive on your own?" I crossed my arms over my chest and waited for her next comedic answer.

She stiffened. "You did." She thrashed her arms up.

I chuckled under my breath. "You're not me. I was born into this life."

She glared, her hands curling into fists, but she didn't throw anything this time. She just kept walking.

She didn't try to argue again for a long while, but she was thinking about it. I could see it in the way she walked, the way her eyes flicked from the trees to the path ahead, always looking for an opening. She was planning. So, I let her think she had a chance— She didn't.

By midday, the sun had risen high, casting long streaks of golden light through the leaves. The road had turned rough, uneven terrain slowing our progress. I could tell she was getting tired. She was gritting her teeth, fighting through the ache in her legs, refusing to show weakness. I almost respected it—Almost.

"How do you live with yourself?" she muttered suddenly.

I raised a brow.

"Excuse me?" I paused.

She turned her head slightly, her eyes filled with fury.

"You take orders from a monster. You steal people. You kill them. And you act like it doesn't mean anything." Her words were heated.

She took a breath. "And for what? Money? Power?" She ranted.

I exhaled through my nose. Here we go. "You think I have a choice?" I asked, my voice dangerously low.

She laughed, but there was no humor in it. "Everyone has a choice." She growled.

We both stopped walking now and stood there frozen in the moment. The air between us went taut. And I swear the trees stilled to hear our words. Aliera held my gaze, daring me to argue, but I didn't.

Because she was wrong, she knew she was. She turned slowly, like she was preparing for something. Her muscles coiled.

And then—She ran. Again.

I sighed heavily, already moving before she had even taken her third step. She had no idea how easy she was to catch. She barely made it past the treeline before I grabbed her by the arm and yanked her back. She flailed, kicking and fighting like a wild animal.

"Stop." I growled, but she continued to fight me.

She drove her heel into my shin, twisting violently in my grip. "OUCH!" I Growled.

I shoved her against the nearest tree, pressing an arm to her chest.

"ENOUGH!" I ordered. She paused. Her eyes teary. Her breathing now in ragged, uneven gasps, her golden eyes locked onto mine with pure hatred.

She wasn't afraid of me, that was a problem. She should be afraid.

"Go ahead." she spat, her voice shaking. "Drag me back to Rael. Let him do whatever he wants to me. You're no better than him." She hissed.

I stiffened. Her words were a challenge, sharp as any blade, but she didn't know what she was asking for. She had no idea what I was doing for her. What I was saving her from, and I wouldn't tell her. She was my enemy, not my responsibility, and I owed her nothing. I released her roughly. She staggered, rubbing at her wrists.

"Walk." I ordered.

She hesitated, but there was no fight left in her now. She turned, muttering something under her breath as she walked ahead of me. I didn't ask what she had said because I already knew. She was testing me. Pushing me—Trying to find the limits of my cruelty.

She thought she had me figured out. She thought she knew what I was, but she didn't, if she did—She would hate me more than she already did.

She would fear me, and that would be the smart thing to do.

CHAPTER THREE

ALIERA

We had been walking for days, and we still hadn't made it to a filthy war camp or an inn. The landscape had begun to shift, the vast lakes fading into the distance behind us, replaced by dense trees and uneven ground. The silence between Beau and me had grown thicker with every passing mile.

We were barely past the larger of the lakes when wolves appeared from the tree line, moving in eerie silence, their bodies low to the ground, stalking forward as they licked their snouts. Their wicked red eyes narrowed on me first—then on Beau.

Four of them of them in varying sizes. Their leader was massive, easily the size of a full-grown stallion, his black fur sleek and bristling with tension stood on end as he stepped forward into the clearing.

Beau stepped in front of me, his shoulders so broad they completely shielded me from view.

His hand moved over his shoulder, fingers curling around the hilt of the massive, jagged sword strapped to his back. He unsheathed it in a slow, deliberate motion. A warning, but the wolves didn't care for warnings.

"Give me a knife, I can help!" I yelled.

Beau didn't move. "Shut up, Aliera." His voice was sharp. Controlled, but I could hear it, the catch of fear that lurked in the back of his throat.

His head moved slightly, scanning back and forth as the wolves crept closer, their bodies tensed, ready to strike.

Then—I noticed it, the way Beau's shoulder blades shifted. Not like a human's. Not like anything human at all. His muscles tensed unnaturally, his spine curving for a moment in a way that no ordinary man's should. I stared. My heart hammering.

"Beau…" I stuttered his name, but he didn't turn, didn't react. He didn't even seem to hear me.

"You go left; I'll go right." he commanded. Like nothing had happened. Like I hadn't just seen something monstrous.

I moved hesitantly, stepping out towards a small baby wolf, she was barely grown, the smallest of the pack. Our eyes met, and I shuddered with fear. She was a young pup. Her frame was lean, her paws too large for her, her fur patchy with the awkwardness of growth. Too young. Too small. Her eyes locked onto mine, uncertain. The small knife burned in my hand. It was meant for the softest part of her neck, but I wasn't sure which of us was more afraid of the other.

I should have lunged. Should have slashed at her throat before she had the chance to attack me. But she just stood there watching me—Terrified. As if she knew that she didn't belong in this fight. As if she was just as afraid of me as I was of her. The first growl split the air, then—Chaos erupted.

Beau lunged for the largest wolf, his blade carving through fur and flesh like water. Blood sprayed, painting the ground in thick, dark pools. His sword was merciless. It was a jagged beast of a weapon. Designed not just to kill—but to ruin, destroy and maim. If the blade didn't rip you into a grim, impossible puzzle, the venom would finish you. The blade itself was porous, the tiny divots along its surface housing a venom so deadly that no cure existed for it. One touch was enough—the wolves never stood a chance.

The pup flinched as another wolf, one of her own snapped at her, forcing her to the ground. A command—fight or die.

She hesitated and then the larger wolf lunged, sinking its fangs into her throat just enough not to draw blood.

I didn't hesitate as I drove my knife into its ribs. It snarled in agony, whipping its head toward me, it's jaws snapping inches from my face. I straddled it, gripping the blade tighter.

And then—I drove the knife up into its jaw. Into its skull and twisted. The wolf went limp and I stepped away from the body.

The pup staggered backward, trembling. She was alive because of me. Her eyes flickered between fear and something softer. I nodded at her as she blinked slowly in return.

And then—Beau was there. His body covered in blood. His chest rising and falling unevenly, his shirt torn open, revealing the massive wound across his torso.

"You're hurt." My voice came out softer than I intended.

His gaze darkened. "No shit." He didn't look at his wound, he didn't care —He was staring at the pup. Rage twisting his face in disgust.

"You missed!" He pointed his sword at the pup.

I followed his gaze, and I motioned for the pup to stand behind me—she did as ordered.

"Oh, come on! She's a baby, she won't hurt us. She had the chance, and she didn't!" I argued.

Beau's fingers curled around the rope at his waist. "Give me your hands."

I gaped at him. "You're kidding?" I protested.

"If I could trust you, they'd all be dead." His eyes were still on the pup.

I exhaled sharply. "At least let me clean that first before you get an infection." My eyes locked onto the bleeding wound on his stomach.

Beau hesitated then glanced down at his torn flesh. "Fuck."

I moved quickly, digging through his bag for anything I could use. Water, a cloth, something clean. I raised a brow as I pulled out an old shirt and wet it with what water we had left.

"Do you even know what you're doing?" He grunted.

"No. But I'm the best you've got." I pressed the damp fabric to his wound.

He flinched violently and I didn't ease my touch. I wasn't feeling particularly merciful.

"It needs to be sewn." He huffed. Beau's jaw locked and his expression changed now.

But I had nothing to stitch it with here, so I tore a strip from my dress, wrapping it tightly around his torso. He leaned into me, his weight heavy and unyielding, I let him rest there —for now.

The pup whined softly at my feet.

Beau sighed, rubbing a hand down his face.

And then—Instead of binding my wrists, he looped the rope around the pup's neck and handed me the free end.

"I want to trust you, Aliera." His voice was rough. "But can I?"

I held his gaze. The anger was still there. The exhaustion. The distrust.

"We're all each other have." I sighed at the truth of it all. He was all I had known outside the walls of my home.

His jaw softened slightly as the pup settled against my legs. Beau looked at her, then back at me.

"She has no family now." I exhaled.

"Why do you think I leashed her for you?" He softened just a little.

I knelt beside the pup, smoothing my hand over her fur.

"You can come with us now." And for the first time in days, I didn't feel completely alone.

We had been walking for at least an hour now, and Beau's strength was fading. I could see it in the way his steps became slower, heavier. His body was working against him, the wound still bleeding beneath the makeshift bandage, but he wouldn't say it. He wouldn't admit he was getting weaker. He wouldn't dare to acknowledge a wound, even as it stole the fight from him with every step.

We couldn't take too many breaks. The longer we waited, the worse it would get. The inn had to be close—It had to be.

"She needs a name…" I pondered aloud trying to lighten the mood. "How about Raven?" I looked at her.

"Woah, so creative, she's black." Beau laughed at me.

"You really are a dick!" I nudged him in one of his smaller bites.

"OUCH!" He growled. "Okay, what about Luna?" He added as he rubbed his chest where I jabbed him.

"Luna? I like that." I agreed.

Luna was sniffing towards something, hopefully food. My stomach was growling.

"The Inn must be close." Beau's eyes lit up.

"See, she's useful!" I widened my eyes.

Beau narrowed his eyes at me. "She's coming along, isn't she?" His tone sarcastic.

My stomach was beginning to gnaw at itself, the aching emptiness clawing through me like a slow-burning fire. Beau's eyes flickered with something unreadable as he watched her.

"It can't be too far away now." he muttered. I grinned in hope.

In the distance, a warm flickering light appeared. Lanterns swung gently on their iron hooks in the light breeze, casting a golden glow over the dirt path. The first sign of civilization we had seen in days. An inn. Relief flooded through me like a final surge of strength, pushing away the exhaustion that had weighed me down for so long.

I picked up the pace, reaching for Beau as I wrapped an arm around him. He didn't resist as I guided him up the steps, and together we pushed open the doors.

Inside, heat wrapped around me like a long-forgotten embrace. The scent of roasted meat, spiced ale, and burning wood filled the air. Laughter rumbled from the fireplace, where drunken soldiers crowded together, their voices thick with ale. Older men and women sat at the dining tables, their plates piled high, their faces warm with food and drink. Behind the bar, a large burly man poured pints from an oak barrel, his keen gaze already taking us in.

I stepped forward, keeping my voice steady. "Sir, can we please have a room for the night?" I said politely.

He wandered toward us, his shrewd gaze flickering to the blood on Beau's torn shirt, the exhaustion on my face, the silent shadow of the wolf at my side.

"I've got one room left." His tone was smooth, practiced. A businessman who knew when he had the upper hand.

I hesitated. "How much?" I fumbled with the last three silvers hidden in my dress pocket, the weight of them suddenly feeling far too light.

"One silver… each." I stiffened at his answer.

Beau slapped five silvers onto the counter without hesitation.

His voice was unwavering. Commanding as he spoke now. "Meals brought to the room. Fresh water. And we take the linens when we leave."

The innkeeper arched a brow, eyes gleaming with amusement. "What about your pet?" His gaze drifted to Luna.

Beau's jaw tightened. "A nickel."

A slow, greedy grin spread across the innkeeper's face. "Done." He scooped up the coins, motioning for us to follow.

We climbed the narrow wooden stairs, the creak of the old boards beneath our feet the only sound as he led us to a room at the very end of the hall. The innkeeper swung the door open, stepping aside to let us pass. Beau barely took two steps inside before his eyes landed on the bed.

"One bed?" His lips twitched into a smirk.

I clenched my teeth as the innkeeper shrugged. "Like I said—last room."

He clapped Beau on the arm, a jest meant for amusement. Beau winced—I scowled.

"I'll have some meals sent up soon. Let the girl know if you need anything else." The burly man said as he walked away.

And then he was gone, leaving us in the quiet suffocation of our shared space. Beau lowered himself into a chair, his movements slower now, more deliberate. I watched as he leaned back, exhaling sharply, his body sinking into exhaustion. His fingers hovered over his side, where the blood still seeped through his ruined shirt.

I inhaled deeply as I moved toward him. "We need to clean that." I said, already reaching for his shirt.

He tensed. "I'll live."

"You'll get an infection." I said sternly.

Beau exhaled through his nose, his jaw clenching like he wanted to argue—but he didn't.

Instead, he reached for the hem of his shirt and pulled it over his head.

I didn't mean to stare, but I did. His torso was littered with scars, some pale and faded, others darker, deeper. A body carved by war, death, and survival.

I forced myself to look at the wound. It was worse than I thought.

A deep, jagged bite, swollen and raw, blood still seeping from the torn flesh. I turned toward the door just as a soft knock echoed through the silence. The girl from the bar handed me a small tray with a needle and thread.

I didn't thank her as I took the tray. Didn't speak. Just shut the door.

And turned back to the man I was supposed to hate. Beau had already shifted onto the bed, an arm draped over his face as he prepared for the pain. "Just get it over with." He begged.

"This is going to hurt." I exhaled sharply, kneeling beside him.

He didn't respond, he didn't flinch. Not until the needle pierced his skin and his entire body went rigid, but he didn't move, he didn't make a sound.

I worked quickly, my fingers steady, my focus sharp. The wound was deep, but not fatal. It would heal. I finished the last stitch, tying off the thread before sitting back.

"Finished." I exclaimed as Beau released a shaky breath.

His body was damp with sweat, so I pulled a blanket over him as I stood upright. My actions weren't out of kindness, but because I needed him alive—For now.

Beau released a shaky breath, his muscles still tensed from the pain. I should have stepped away. Should have put more distance between us now that his wound was taken care of. But I didn't, something kept me there. A strange pull. A hesitant curiosity. For the first time, Beau didn't feel like my captor. He felt like something else entirely.

I adjusted the blanket gently over his shoulders, not out of obligation. Not because I had to, but because—for the first time since I met him—I wanted to.

The knock at the door startled me, I turned just as a young girl shuffled inside, her arms full of plates. Hot meals, fresh fruit, bread, thick with butter. Jugs of water and milk. My mouth watered instantly at the sight of it.

Beau barely reacted. He was still half-dazed, his chest rising and falling in slow, steady movements.

"Five silvers." he muttered, voice hoarse.

I hesitated, still overwhelmed by the sheer amount of food in front of me. I had never seen a meal like this. Never smelled food this rich. I reached forward slowly, my fingers brushing over the warm, golden crust of the bread. It was soft and fresh. I had never had bread that wasn't stale.

Beau's voice broke my trance. "You've never had this before." It wasn't a question.

I swallowed, keeping my face carefully neutral. "No." I didn't know why I admitted it. Didn't know why I allowed the truth to slip out so easily, to be so vulnerable.

But Beau didn't laugh, didn't sneer. He just watched me. His eyes warm, and unreadable.

"What did you eat?" he asked quietly.

I shrugged, ripping off a piece of bread and chewing slowly, savoring the taste.

"I stole. Fished sometimes. But I was awful at it." I offered him a weak smile, trying to brush it off like it didn't matter.

Beau's expression didn't change. I expected him to scoff, or to mock me. To tell me I should have learned better, but he didn't.

Instead— "You stole food?" he murmured, his voice softer than I had ever heard it.

My response was a mere nod, it was all I could muster as I thought back to a time when I had nothing, nobody.

"That's how you survived?" He asked. But I just swallowed, suddenly uncomfortable with how much he was staring at me now.

"I did what I had to do." I exhaled trying to shake off the hitch in my voice.

He said nothing, but his jaw tightened slightly, like he was trying to keep himself from speaking. The silence stretched between us, heavy, uncomfortable.

Beau turned his attention back to the plate in front of him, tearing off a piece of turkey with his teeth. I let out a slow breath, finally allowing myself to relax slightly. He was different now, quieter, less dangerous. And I couldn't decide if that made me more afraid—or something else entirely.

Luna rested her head on my lap, her fur warm against my legs as I absentmindedly stroked her soft ears. For the first time in days, I felt like I could breathe. Like I wasn't just running for my life. Like maybe—just maybe—I had found the smallest sliver of safety.

Beau pushed his plate away, leaning back against the headboard, one arm draped over his chest, his other hand resting over the bandage on the side of his stomach. His fingers brushed against the fresh stitches, a flicker of discomfort passing over his face. I studied him for a moment. The hard set of his jaw. The way the firelight flickered against the strong angles of his cheekbones, his broad shoulders, his lean, sculpted torso. I wasn't blind. Beau was…Strikingly handsome.

I hated the thought the second it entered my head. Hated that I had noticed. Hated that I was still looking. I forced my eyes away, pretending to focus on my plate.

But my voice was quieter when I spoke next. "You said Rael paid you four hundred?"

Beau stiffened and I regretted asking immediately, but I couldn't take it back. I couldn't swallow the question now that it had slipped into the space between us.

"What does he want with me?" I added.

Beau's fingers tensed against the bandage. He didn't answer right away, he didn't even look at me.

"He never told me." Beau admitted finally.

His voice was low, careful, too careful.

I narrowed my eyes. "You're lying."

Beau finally met my gaze. I didn't flinch, nor did I blink, because I knew. I knew he wasn't telling me everything. And he knew that I knew.

For a long moment, neither of us spoke. The air between us grew tight, thick with something I couldn't name. I hated him. Didn't I? He was my captor, my enemy, and yet—There was something different in his eyes now, something I hadn't seen before, not mockery, not amusement, something else.

I turned my head, swallowing back the questions burning at the tip of my tongue.

"I'm tired." I murmured, pushing away from the table.

I climbed into bed, turning away from him, but even as I closed my eyes, I could still feel the weight of his gaze. I could still hear the quiet rise and fall of his breath, and I didn't know if it made me feel more at ease... or more afraid.

"Goodnight, Beau." I whispered softly.

"Goodnight, Aliera." His voice was sleepy as he dozed off with ease.

Sleep didn't come easily for me, even though I desired it. Not because the bed was uncomfortable—it was the softest thing I had slept on in years. Not because the blankets weren't warm—they were thick and heavy, cocooning me in much-needed heat, but because of him. Because even though Beau was stretched out beside me on the enormous bed, a full arm's length away, I could feel his presence. Every shift. Every slow inhale—I was too aware of him.

The way his breathing had steadied, the sheer size of him, even as he lay beside me. Even the way his voice had changed tonight—softer, less cruel. I turned onto my side, staring at the wooden planks of the wall. This shift between us was dangerous, I needed to remember who he was, what he had done, what he had been sent to do.

And yet, no matter how many times I told myself to hate him, to ignore him, to push away the warmth I felt in his presence, to go to sleep...I still wasn't sleeping.

The first crack of light seeped through the window, cutting across the bed in long golden streaks. Luna stirred first, shifting near my feet with a low huff before nuzzling her cold nose against my ankle. I groaned, curling into the blankets as the warmth of sleep threatened to pull me under again. I realized I had managed to fall asleep, but it felt far too short.

Then— The door creaked open.

My eyes snapped open instantly, my body went rigid at the sound of footsteps, soft, deliberate steps that inched closer. I turned my head just enough to see a shadow moving across the room. Not an intruder, not a threat, Beau. He had returned from…wherever he had gone.

He moved around the room with a quiet ease, the scent of cold morning air clinging to him. Then—he reached over the bed, extending something toward me—a bundle of clothing.

"These might be more appropriate." he muttered, his voice still rough with sleep.

I blinked at him, caught off guard as I sat up to accept them.

The Beau I had met days ago wouldn't have done this, he wouldn't have thought to find me clothes that fit, that protected me against the cold.

I hesitated, then took them from his hands. "Thank you." I murmured.

His eyes flickered with something unreadable. Then he turned away, giving me privacy to inspect them.

I stepped behind the privacy sheet and quickly washed with the cloth and bowl of water provided. I worked quickly so I didn't freeze and dried off. I began inspecting the clothes now, the pants were thick, brown leather—sturdy, warm, clearly made for travel. The shirt was an oversized black tunic, simple but soft, its fabric lighter than I expected. I pulled it over my head, cinching it at the waist with my belt.

When I stepped out from behind the sheet, Beau was already sitting at the table, eating a handful of fruit.

His eyes flickered toward me, studying me for a moment before nodding in approval. "Much better."

I rolled my eyes, but I couldn't help but agree. For the first time in days, I felt strong, not exposed, not weak. And I hated that he was the reason why.

Beau pushed himself to his feet. "I need to clean up." He disappeared behind the privacy sheet now as I stepped out.

I turned toward the window, trying not to listen to the rustle of fabric, but then—I saw it. The sunlight cut through the room at just the right angle, casting his silhouette against the thin sheet. I froze. My breath caught in my throat.

He was magnificent, broad, powerful shoulders, defined muscles carved by years of battle. His biceps flexed as he ran the damp cloth over his chest, wiping away the remnants of dried blood and sweat. His torso—thick and strong, a latticework of scars sprawling over his body.

I should have looked away, I should have ignored the sudden, unwelcome heat that licked up my spine, the slow ache curling in my stomach. The way my breath quickened—not in fear, but in something far more dangerous. It was primal. Raw. My body betrayed me, caught in the carnal allure of a warrior stripped down to his most human form.

Strength. Power. Hunger. And gods help me, I felt it too. That restless stir deep inside me—the kind of hunger I had never felt. The kind I had never allowed myself to feel. I clenched my hands into fists, forcing the ache away, forcing my mind back to reality. This wasn't a moment to admire him, this was my captor. My enemy. And yet, my body didn't seem to care.

"How's the show?" He chuckled.

My face flushed instantly; my body went taut as I snapped my gaze away.

"I didn't see anything." A lie.

Beau chuckled. "If you'd like a proper view…"

The sheet shifted slightly, teasing me with the barest glimpse of his hip, the smooth cut of his abdomen, the thickness of his naked thigh and his eyes peeked over the top, watching for my response.

I whipped my head toward the door, mortified. "Stop it." His laugh deepened.

Then, suddenly he was quieter—almost curious—"Have you ever been with a man before?"

I swallowed hard. "No." There was an unnerving silence now as the truth stirred in the air of the stagnant room.

"No wonder he paid four hundred." The amusement was gone from his voice now, replaced with something tighter, something heavier.

I turned slowly, watching as he stepped out from behind the curtain, now fully clothed. His hair was still damp, his skin still flushed from the cold water. But his eyes—They were different. The tension between us shifted.

"Four hundred what?" I whispered.

Beau's gaze didn't leave mine. "Rael paid four hundred silvers for me to bring you to him." He answered.

I inhaled sharply. I had known there would be a bounty on me.

But hearing the number—the sheer amount—It made my stomach twist, I wasn't just a prize, I was an investment. And I had known why.

Beau turned away, pulling on his boots, securing his weapons, like this conversation didn't matter, like it wasn't changing everything.

"What does he want with me?" A stupid question, but I knew the answer. I was just in shock at the amount.

Beau stilled, but he didn't look at me, didn't answer.

I took a step closer to him now. "Beau." His jaw tensed.

Then he spoke—"He never told me."

I exhaled. Slow. Controlled. "You're lying."

Beau finally turned, his eyes locking onto mine. For the first time since I met him, I saw it, the hesitation. The part of him that was holding something back.

My stomach tightened. Whatever King Rael had planned for me…I was sure Beau knew, and he wasn't telling me.

I took another step forward, my body moving before my mind could stop it. Beau's broad shoulders lifted slightly with his breath, tension running through him like a silent warning. He was watching me too closely now, like he expected me to run, to fight, to do something. And maybe I should have. Maybe I should have turned, put space between us, reminded myself that this was a man who had dragged me from that field, who had tied my hands, who had been paid to deliver me to a fate I still didn't understand.

But I didn't move.

Because even as my mind screamed at me to run, my body was reacting to something else entirely. The way his lips parted slightly, like he had something to say but held it back. The way his fingers curled, the slightest twitch in his stance like he was resisting the same pull that I was. The way the air felt heavier between us now, thick with something I couldn't name. I swallowed hard, forcing my breath to steady.

"I wouldn't believe you anyway." I murmured at his ongoing silence, barely recognizing the sound of my own voice.

Beau's jaw flexed. "Then don't."

I clenched my fists, that wasn't an answer, he sensed my frustration, my growing desperation. And for the first time, I saw something that almost resembled guilt flash across his face. He didn't want to answer my next question, but I asked it anyway.

"You're still taking me to him, aren't you?" My breath airy.

Beau hesitated just long enough for me to feel the answer in my bones. Long enough for the ember of heat I had felt toward him to snap into something colder.

Just long enough for me to remind myself that no matter how I felt when I looked at him, no matter what pull existed between us—He was still the man who would sell me to my fate.

Beau exhaled slowly, like he was choosing his words carefully. He wouldn't lie, but he wouldn't tell me the truth either.

"I don't have a choice." The words were quiet. Measured.

They should have made me furious, desperate. But all I could focus on was how tired he sounded. Like the weight of his decision was crushing him just as much as it was crushing me. As if maybe, just maybe, he didn't want to do this either.

I hated that it made my stomach twist. Hated that I even cared. Because it didn't change anything. He was still my enemy. No matter how much I wanted to believe he wasn't. Beau turned, grabbing his weapons and slinging his pack over his shoulder. The muscles in his back shifted fluidly, a movement so smooth and precise it should have been forgettable.

But it wasn't, because my traitorous mind wouldn't stop noticing things about him. The shape of him, the sharp angles of his jaw, the way his fingers flexed against the hilt of his dagger as if some part of him was always prepared for a fight.

I knew I needed to stop looking at him like that. I needed to stop feeling things I shouldn't be feeling. Because the moment I let my guard down, the moment I forgot who he was—That would be the moment I lost everything.

The tension between us had changed. Before, it had been sharp, jagged, edged with hostility, but now, it was something else entirely, something heavy. There was something unfamiliar in the air between us, electric like the sky before a storm.

I didn't know if it was anger, or something more dangerous, something that made my skin burn when he got too close. Something that made my stomach clench every time his eyes flicked toward my lips. It made my body react before my mind could remind me of who he really was.

I hated it.

I hated him.

Beau stopped at the door, glancing over his shoulder. His expression was unreadable, but his fingers tightened around the strap of his pack, like he was holding something back, he wanted to say something—but wouldn't.

I took a step toward him before I could stop myself. The movement was small. Subtle, but he noticed.

His eyes flickered down at my small frame from his enormous height, catching the shift in my stance. For a moment, we just stared at each other. My eyes should have been level with his chest, but I gazed up at him in absolute silence. The air between us felt too charged, too *something* I didn't have the words for.

And then—His fingers brushed against my wrist with intent. A fleeting touch, so light, so quick, I almost thought I imagined it— But I didn't, I felt it. And I wanted more.

The warmth of him. The strength beneath his calloused hands. The way my pulse excited at the contact. Beau's gaze dropped to where his hand had touched my skin.

And then he was gone, the door closed behind him with a soft thud, leaving me alone with the feeling of his touch still burning against my wrist. The room felt colder the second he left. I flexed my fingers, staring at the spot where he had stood, willing away the lingering sensation of his touch. And yet—I could still feel him.

I turned toward the window, pressing my forehead against the glass, my breath fogging up the cold pane.

I should have been thinking about my escape. I should have been calculating the distance, weighing my options, finding a way out, instead, I was thinking about him.

The way his voice had sounded when he said he didn't have a choice, the exhaustion beneath the reluctance of his rasp, the struggle behind those words.

They meant something more, and I hated that it mattered to me. I hated that I could still hear the quiet hesitation in his voice. The way his fingers had twitched before he touched me. As if he regretted it.

And for some stupid, reckless reason…That hurt.

A soft whimper pulled me from my thoughts.

I glanced down, finding Luna watching me, her eyes wide with quiet understanding. She shifted closer, pressing her cold nose to my knee before resting her head against my lap, she was a welcome, silent comfort, a quiet reassurance.

I sighed, threading my fingers through her thick fur, feeling her warmth seep into my skin.

At least she was constant. At least she didn't make me question everything—Not like he did.

I shouldn't have cared. Caring was the most dangerous thing of all. Because if I wasn't careful…If I let this grow, if I let my body forget what my mind already knew—I wouldn't just lose my freedom. I'd lose my life.

I packed what little I had, adjusting the strap of my bag across my chest. Beau hadn't come back, I should have been relieved, but instead, I found myself restless. I pressed my lips together, shaking off the thought, this wasn't about him, this was about getting out. About figuring out what I was supposed to do next. Luna stretched beside me, shaking out her thick fur before trotting toward the door, she was ready. I wasn't sure I was, but it didn't matter. We had no choice but to move forward.

The inn's wooden floorboards creaked under my boots as I made my way downstairs. The tavern was still alive with the remnants of last night's drinking. Men slumped in their chairs, some passed out against the bar, their snores rattling against the walls. The smell of ale and damp wood clung in the air—Beau was nowhere to be seen.

I exhaled, adjusting the weight of my pack.

For a moment, I thought about running. Just walking straight out of here, disappearing into the early morning mist, but the moment the idea solidified in my head, I felt it, a familiar warmth brushing too close.

And then—His voice. "You're up early." I turned sharply, but he was already there. His words came naturally as if he forgot our encounter already.

His body radiated heat from just inches away, his voice low and edged with something unreadable. He looked different. Not just because he had cleaned up, but because something in his expression had changed, he had spent the morning thinking about something he didn't want to, maybe he had felt the same pull that I had.

I swallowed hard, trying to keep my voice steady. "And you're late."

His lips tipped slightly at the corner.

Not quite a smirk, but close. "You thinking of running?" His tone was calm, but there was something beneath it. Something taunting. Testing. Like he already knew the answer.

I lifted my chin. "No." A lie.

His eyes flicked down, scanning my stance. He could see the tension in my body, he knew exactly how close I had been to making that choice.

His voice dipped lower. "Good." For a moment, neither of us moved.

The sounds of the tavern faded, the murmurs of drunken men becoming background noise to the weight that settled between us, something unspoken. Unwanted, and dangerous.

I should have stepped back, I should have put distance between us, but I didn't, and neither did he. Beau's gaze held mine for a second longer than it should have. Then, just like that, the moment shattered.

His voice was sharp again, back to business. "Come on."

He turned, walking toward the door without waiting for me to follow. Like he already knew I would. And that irritated me more than anything. Because he was right. With a final glance at the tavern, I exhaled and followed him out into the morning mist.

We moved through the dark parts of the woods, past the road that led to Varsili and still towards the north, past the places I had once known. I was confused, but I wouldn't correct his misdirection, if it were misdirection at all. Every step forward was a step away from everything we had been.

Beau walked beside me now, not leading, not pulling. Just there and it unsettled me because I didn't know what it meant. I didn't know what came next.

We stopped near the edge of a creek, the soft murmur of water filling the silence between us. Luna padded ahead, drinking from the stream, her dark fur blending into the night.

Beau didn't move. He stood at the edge of the clearing, his hands loose at his sides, his gaze fixed on something I couldn't see. Then, after a long stretch of silence—He spoke.

And I didn't know what to say. I swallowed hard as I thought long and hard and he watched the calm leave my body.

"Are you sure you're ready for this?" He spoke.

"I think so. But why the linens?" I asked curiously.

"The bridge will be watched; we have to go around it. It'll be cold, especially going north." He sighed.

"Around to where exactly?" My eyes widened at the revelation we weren't going back to Varsili after all.

"The bridge past Creed isn't guarded." He explained.

"That's awfully close to the ruins near Farkli. How exactly do you mean to get us into Creed, it's a fortress!" I shuddered.

"We're not going to Creed. We're passing through Tecrit. We'll be careful, there's only us we'll likely go unnoticed if we go through the swampland." He replied.

"The swamp! The swamp the sailors say is impassable, not because of all the debris from the ships who have tried to pass it, but because of the victim's waste from the Dwellers that devoured them." I yelped in fear.

"You listen to too many fairytales. It's shallow, we'll wade over slowly. I've seen it. There's one crossing not too far in distance, we can make it." He pressed his brows together commandingly.

"What are you running away from?" My eyes narrowed.

"Who said I was running?" His eyes locked on mine.

"You're the king's assassin, his most favored. What risk do you have?" I asked.

"I'm his bastard. If more people knew, I'd be beheaded in the square by my older brothers the instant they found out it was public knowledge. I hold too much power at court for their liking already. If they knew I had even an ounce of a right to claim the crown, they'd take me out. None of them are warriors, they are weak men. They can't afford the competition. What's fucked is none of them even want the throne and they know I won't fund their lifestyle. If I go back… it's more risk every day." His voice was low, edged with a bitterness that ran so deep it felt carved into his very being.

"Who was your mother?" I asked, my voice softer now.

"A courtesan. She came here from the Isle of Korsan for a summer." He exhaled. His gaze drifting, as if reaching for something that had long since slipped through his fingers. "She left me at the steps of the House of Red when I was only days old. King Rael frequented the House daily and took me in. He loved my mother, I guess."

"I'm sorry." I whispered, unsure if my words held any real weight.

"So am I." His expression hardened, shutting out whatever emotion had flickered there before. "Neither of us chose our unfortunate births."

"Then he raised you to be his assassin?" I asked carefully, watching the tension as it tightened in his jaw.

"When I was younger, I would go with the huntsmen to busy my days." He paused, his tone distant, almost hollow. "I have the gift of killing." A sad truth, spoken plainly. "Rael was told about this, and from then on, I was placed into war camps. I learned from the best warriors Varsili has to offer."

His confession settled between us like a blade driven into the earth—unchanging, inescapable.

"Since we're sharing secrets… Your father sent my family to war." I sighed, hoping that trusting him with my truth wouldn't end terribly.

His head tilted slightly, his eyes narrowing in quiet realization, the weight of recognition pressing into the space between us. "You're General Gray's lost daughter?"

I swallowed hard. "I thought that was just a rumor."

"You knew my father?" My voice wavered, uncertain of what I wanted his answer to be.

"We've met." His sigh was controlled, careful—but something flickered in his expression, something deeper, something he wasn't ready to share.

The light of the sun crept through the trees, illuminating the forest in a golden hue as the flowers stretched open, their colors coming alive with the warmth of the sun. Another stream shimmered in the distance, its surface reflecting the shifting morning light. As soon as she spotted it, Luna rushed forward, eager for a drink, her tail wagging in excitement. We followed, settling by the water's edge while she splashed and played, her sleek coat quickly becoming soaked as she chased the darting fish and tadpoles weaving through the shallow currents. Lily pads bobbed gently, sheltering tiny frogs that leaped away from Luna's playful pursuit.

Beau appeared more at ease here than I had ever seen him. He reclined against his pack, eyes closed, his body basking in the dappled sunlight filtering through the canopy. I mirrored him, allowing the warmth to settle into my skin, feeling, if only for a moment, the illusion of peace.

Luna eventually trotted over and flopped beside me, her damp fur pressing against my side. She had something dangling from her mouth, her latest discovery, though I wasn't sure it was anything remotely edible. Smirking, I tore off a wedge of cheese and a piece of bread, sharing it with her as my stomach let out a low, demanding growl. Hunger had been gnawing at me since we left the inn—I had barely eaten this morning, too distracted by my own shameless staring.

Beau had been the sole object of my curiosity, the only man I had ever seen so exposed. And what a fine specimen he was. Shoulder-length dark hair, light brown eyes that carried the weight of unspoken experiences, and a sharp contrast between the clean-shaven face I first met and the stubble now gracing his jaw. His frame was formidable—thick and tall, his thighs like tree trunks, broad shoulders, and arms carved with ripples of strength. He was nothing like the soft, pampered men I had known. Beau was something different entirely. He was built for war.

Beau didn't move. He stood at the edge of the clearing, his hands loose at his sides, his gaze fixed on something I couldn't see. Then, after a long stretch of silence—He spoke.

"What now?" I turned to him as he spoke the words.

His voice wasn't sharp, it wasn't a demand—Just a question. A quiet, open-ended thing that made my stomach twist.

And I didn't know what to say. I swallowed hard as I thought long and hard and he watched the calm leave my body.

"I told you…" I said softly.

"Lexia?" He confirmed.

I nodded silently.

"Lexia then." His words were a promise as he held my eye in his.

CHAPTER FOUR

BEAU

A full day had passed before we finally emerged from the dense forest. The air was thick with dampness, the scent of earth and stagnant water filling my lungs. Ahead, the terrain shifted—what had once been solid ground gave way to the sprawling expanse of the Swamplands. We stood at the very edge of Varsili, east of the bridge, perched on the furthest western point before the wilds of Creed. The only way forward was through the unusually clear waters ahead, a mirage of waters that I knew were deceitful, but there was no other choice.

We would have to cross twice—first from Varsili into Creed, then further up the shore before wading from Creed into Tecrit. Each step forward would take us deeper into uncertainty. These were the safest routes, but even they carried risks. The water was shallow enough to walk through in some parts, yet still treacherous. As long as we moved carefully, disturbing the surface as little as possible, we might just slip through unseen. But I knew better than to rely on luck alone.

I hoisted Luna onto my shoulders, she shifted her weight instinctively, ears twitching at the strange, unfamiliar environment. The wind carried an eerie silence, broken only by the distant croak of unseen creatures and the occasional ripple in the water—evidence of life beneath the surface.

Beside me, Aliera hesitated, her body rigid, tension built through every inch of her as if bracing for an unseen force to drag her under. She stared at the water as if it might consume her whole. Her breath hitched, her hands clenching into fists at her sides. Still, she inhaled sharply, forcing herself forward, the icy water biting at her ankles like a warning. A visible shudder ran through her body, but she pressed on, forcing herself forward despite every instinct telling her to turn back.

I watched her for a moment, her jaw clenched in determination. She was afraid, but she wasn't stopping.

Good, we would need that stubbornness to survive this crossing. Her boots sank into the soft, slick mud beneath the water, and I could see her slump, panic set in her eyes as she tried to pause her movements. Her breath shuddered as the cold hit her skin, sharp enough to make her shoulders twitch.

She didn't stop, she pulled in a deep breath, steadying herself. Then, against every better instinct she had—She kept moving. The warm weather had stilled the surface, allowing the dirt and debris to sink to the bottom of the Swampland. We could see everything beneath us. And I wasn't sure if that made me feel better… or more afraid.

"You're doing good." I whispered to Aliera.

"Don't distract me." she exhaled, keeping her eyes forward, her movements slow and controlled.

She waded carefully, her hips shifting as she moved through the water, doing everything she could not to disturb what lurked beneath. We were meters from the bank now. Close, almost safe. And then—I saw it.

A shift in the water, a flicker of movement just to my left, like it was teasing me, luring me into the deepest parts, waiting to strike—Aliera noticed my hesitation.

"Your knife, now." I kept my voice low, sharp, urgent.

In one swift movement, I peeled Luna off my shoulders and tucked her under one arm—Panic set in and pup became limp as she allowed me to fling her wherever I needed her, her whimpers a sure sign she was just as terrified as I was.

Aliera didn't hesitate, she grabbed Luna and my pack from me, lunging for the bank in a frantic rush to escape. I barely caught her knife in the exchange before she fled, just in time, because then—It struck.

The creature lashed for me, twisting around my body with terrifying speed. Its head was that of a fish, its body slick and unnatural, covered in slimy, malleable scales. Red spikes ran down its neck in jagged ridges, its mouth gnashing hungrily, revealing rows of needle-like teeth—I barely had time to react.

I drove the knife deep into its side, feeling the blade sink into the soft tissue beneath its scales. It shuddered violently, its body convulsing in pain. I gritted my teeth, gripping its skull and slicing downward, tearing through flesh and bone.

But the second it went still, I saw it—Another one.

Lurking just beneath the surface…Waiting.

I had seen them before, but only as a story villain in stale books—Dwellers. That's what they were called, predators of the swamp. They had hundreds of long, thin, razor-sharp teeth, red fins that covered their backs in overlapping rows.

The second one came faster. I barely had time to recover from the first kill before the next one was lunging, its teeth snapping at my arm, missing me by a hair. I twisted, barely avoiding the bite, the knife still in my grasp. Then the water erupted around me, churning as the creature thrashed forward, its long body moved like a serpent beneath the surface.

It was bigger than the first—and it was hungrier.

I lashed out, but this Dweller was faster than the last, it used the weight of its body to lunge and strike at me, like a threat before it barred its teeth. The first one's body still drifted beside me, blood bloomed in the water like red wine on a fine carpet.

And then I realized that was the problem. The scent of blood was drawing them in. I could already see the ripples further out, barely visible, but there, twisted and calculated—More were coming. I had no time to spare. I adjusted my stance, steadying my grip on the knife. The Dweller lunged again, its body moving in an eerie, fluid motion beneath the surface.

But this time, I was ready. I caught it by the throat, my handout stretched barely covering even half the width of it. I forced the blade deep beneath its jaw, twisting hard.

It screeched, a wet, guttural sound, its body convulsing violently against me, blood soaking me. The moment it went still, I hurled it aside—and that's when I saw the third one.

Bigger.

Faster.

And it was heading straight for Aliera, she was almost to the bank, pulling herself up onto the muddy shore with Luna still clutched in her arms—she didn't see the shadow surging toward her from beneath the water.

I lunged, moving faster than I should have been able to in the water, wrapping an arm around her waist and hauling her backward just as the creature struck. Its teeth snapped inches from her leg. Aliera gasped, clutching onto me instinctively as if we were about to be torn apart.

I barely had time to react before the creature whipped back around, its red fins flaring, preparing to strike again, it's teeth gnashing at me. I threw the knife, putting everything I had into the throw. The blade impaled right into its skull. It let out a shrill, bubbling screech before it sank beneath the surface, motionless.

For a long moment, neither of us moved. The water was still, and the ripples faded, the only sound was our ragged breathing. Aliera's fingers were still clutched around my arm. Her chest rose and fell in quick, uneven breaths. I didn't let go of her—she was shaking. I could feel her pulse was still racing, her body trembling slightly as she pressed against me. Finally, she exhaled, her breath warm against my chest.

I swallowed hard, forcing myself to step back.

"We need to move." I said, my voice lower than I expected.

She nodded, her hands still gripping my arms, like she hadn't realized she was still touching me. Then she let go. Without another word, we climbed up onto the shore. The bodies of the Dwellers floating behind us.

Some were more serpent than fish. Others were more fish than serpent, with long, muscular tails that propelled them forward with terrifying speed—The smaller, the faster, the more lethal.

Then another Dweller broke through the calm of the surface and tore me from her arms and wrestled me violently back into the waters. I barely had time to react before I saw Aliera move. She pulled my sword from the bag, the weight of it heavy in her grasp. She raced into the water, no fear attached now.

Luna's bark were muffled by the water as it beat against my ears, the Dweller dragged me down further, then teased me with a glimpse of the surface. Luna howled wildly from the shore, pacing frantically, but Aliera didn't hesitate. She whipped the sword in every direction, the steel catching the dull light as she cut through the water, freeing me from another Dweller before it could strike.

The force of the blow sent a thick spray of blood across the surface. We stood back-to-back, blades raised, chests heaving. Then the largest one appeared, it didn't lunge or rush towards us. This one was calculating. It moved slowly, deliberately, the water shifting around its massive frame. It was bigger than the others. Its red fins flared along its spine, its slanted, black eyes fixed directly on us. It came for Aliera first, she responded and struck out, her blade finding its mark.

The Dweller let out a horrible, piercing shriek, thrashing violently as dark blood stained the water. Its long body snapping upward in and out of the water like a snake ready to strike. It wasn't done, and it was angry.

"RUN!" I shouted.

We didn't hesitate, we ran.

The water slowed us, dragged at our legs, but we pushed forward, racing toward the bank where Luna growled and snarled, pacing wildly.

The Dweller was still pursuing us. I turned just in time to see Aliera had fallen behind. She was slower than me, struggling to keep up. I couldn't let it reach her, then the Dweller lunged for me, but it was too big for my sword and soon it's body was wrapping around me, it's slime coated my skin as it tightened its grip around me. I was locked down, my breathing slowed, and my vision blurred.

Aliera rushed for the Dweller without hesitation now. She thrust her blade deep into its neck, twisting hard. Its body jerked, its mouth snapping at me one final time, it loosened now as it tried to strike at Aliera. But Aliera slashed at the neck one more time.

And finally— It's head tore free with the final jerk of its body. The severed head flipped through the air, landing with a sickening thud beside me.

"BEAU!" Aliera's voice was sharp, panicked as she raced to catch me.

I turned, barely managing to stumble toward her as the weight of the fight caught up to me. My breath was ragged, my body burning with exhaustion.

I collapsed onto the shore, taking in deep, shaking breaths. Aliera sank down beside me, her chest rising and falling in heavy gasps.

"Please tell me that's it." She heaved, brushing her tangled hair from her face.

She had a thin scratch along her arm, no deeper than a hair, but she wrapped it quickly with a torn strip of fabric. I swallowed hard, pushing myself up on my elbows.

"I want to say yes." I exhaled, my pulse still hammering.

"But I'm pretty sure that wasn't fully grown." I puffed heavily.

Luna whined loudly, licking at Aliera's face, pawing at her with soft, insistent nudges.

"There has to be another way." She gasped, still catching her breath.

I sighed, rubbing a hand over my face.

"There is." I admitted. "But you aren't going to like it." She narrowed her eyes with suspicion.

"Does it have a bridge?" she asked.

I hesitated. "Umm, yes." I coughed, glancing away.

Technically, I wasn't lying. The bridge over to the old outpost still stood, barely. But the mountains had been uninhabited for years.

Aliera straightened. "What's the catch?"

I exhaled, my breath coming out rough. "We have to go through the ruins." Aliera didn't react immediately. Her lips pressed into a thin line.

"And how do we get to Lexia from there?" she asked, her voice flat.

I didn't blame her. I rubbed a hand over my jaw, glancing toward the distant peaks, jagged shadows against the horizon.

"We have to reach the Fjord, by going over the mountains." I said, nodding toward the dark monstrous peaks.

I looked back down into the water. The blood-stained swampland was still again, deceitfully calm, waiting for its next victim.

Aliera shuddered slightly, then pulled herself up. She hesitated for only a moment before turning toward me, her expression unreadable. Then, slowly—she offered me her hand, I took it. Her grip was warm, firm—but her strength did little to help me. Still, for a moment, I let her believe it did.

"Any more questions?" I asked, raising an eyebrow.

Aliera huffed in frustration.

"What's the point." she muttered, but it wasn't a question, it was a statement. "I've never even left Varsili, I barely even left my home, Beau. I don't know what I was thinking." She sighed.

I stopped and watched her, but she didn't look at me when she continued to speak.

"That day you kidnapped me…" she exhaled, rubbing at her temple.

"That was the first time I'd been outside the walls. Ever. I had never even been to the farmlands or seen an apple tree. I thought they grew on vines like the grapes that adorn the city walls. I know nothing of this world, Beau. I am completely at your mercy." She let out a small, bitter laugh, shaking her head to mock herself.

I stared at her. I hadn't thought about it. I didn't even realize I had reached for her until she stepped back, swiping a hand over her face.

"I didn't mean to mock you." I muttered, raising my hands slightly.

"It's fine." She exhaled.

"Can I ask why?" My curiosity peaked and the words slipped out before I could think about what I was saying.

Panic set into her eyes. "I… I wasn't allowed out, my family kept me hidden." Her tone changed into a low vibration now. Her eyes still as she focused on the blades of grass.

"Why would they do that?" I was angry for her.

"Because I'm not like everyone else. I'm…" She stuttered and her breath hitched before she could finish the sentence.

"You're a Titan…" The realization washed over me as I looked her over. She didn't look like someone from Varsili. Her radiant hair, those golden eyes that pulled me in. She was well spoken, and she had been taught the basics if not more about fighting.

Of course she was a Titan, she was Gray's daughter. Why did it take me so long to put this together? And I was about to take her through her ancestral homes.

"Let's just do this." Her voice cracked as it fought an internal sadness that brewed inside her.

She turned away, quickly, keeping several paces ahead of me. Luna followed close at her side, her ears twitching toward Aliera as if sensing the shift. I let her go ahead. Creed was nothing like Varsili, the air felt cleaner, the land wider.

The people were better, kinder. They simply wanted to live their lives. There were no war camps. No tyrant king, just a place untouched by Rael's hunger.

Aliera was quiet for most of the day. She walked inland, putting as much distance as possible between herself and the swamplands.

Luna kept her occupied, darting after mice, rats, and rabbits, leading her through the wild as if she had been made for it.

And Aliera simply followed and watched after Luna, letting her explore the forest. They were both seeing the world for the first time.

I watched her from a distance, the way her gaze flicked from tree to tree, the way she hesitated at every new sound, every unfamiliar scent. I had spent my whole life in the open. She had spent hers trapped behind walls.

And for the first time since I had taken her—I wondered what that must have been like, to grow up isolated from the world, never being allowed outside your own front door.

CHAPTER FIVE

ALIERA

We had walked through the trees for the length of the coastline, the rhythmic crash of waves against the distant shore a constant companion. A full day had passed when we finally spotted the bridge. It loomed ahead, battered by time, plastered with weathered warning signs that flapped weakly in the breeze. Gaping holes marred its structure, entire planks missing, leaving treacherous gaps that threatened to swallow anyone foolish enough to attempt the crossing. A slick layer of green moss and mold coated what remained, glistening with dampness under the fading sunlight.

From here, the old outpost was colossal—far grander than I had ever imagined. Built of dark stone, it was now a grave of its former self, swallowed by creeping moss and tangled vines. And bones. So many bones. I had only ever heard stories of how its towers once speared the clouds, a fortress unrivaled. Now, it stood as a monument to ruin. Even in its decay, it was taller than any structure I had ever laid eyes on, its jagged remnants clawing defiantly at the sky. The tower, though crumbling, still loomed over the mountains that encircled us like silent sentinels, watching the past fade into dust.

We stood at the outer edges of an ancient nameless Titan city, its ruins charred black by the wrath of Fae fire. The destruction had been absolute. The magical flames had come from Emberleaf arrows, a force so relentless that as long as there was fuel, the fire would devour it. Not even dragons could withstand its scorching grip. King Rael's ancestor had deceived the Fae into using that same Fae magic to decimate my ancestors, erasing them from history with an inferno that consumed not just the city, but the very land itself. The mountains bore scars of that devastation, their once-mighty peaks now hollowed-out husks, painted in layers of lifeless grey, frozen in time by an unnatural stillness.

Nothing green had grown here since. Nothing except the moss. The land was so dead, so utterly drained of life, that no root dared to take hold in its cursed soil. Fae flames left no survivors, no rebirth, no second chances. The only thing that had ever been able to counter them was a Titan—a fire-wielding Titan.

But there had been none here when the destruction came.

Then Zac was born. The first flame wielder in centuries. Even with our blood watered down—diluted by Farkli and human lineage—our family had somehow managed to bring fire back into the world. It had been unexpected. Flame wielders were known to be volatile, reckless, completely unpredictable. And Zac was all those things.

He was cocky, arrogant at times, but also playful. And, despite everything, he was a good brother—most of the time.

Slippery moss covered every inch of the structure, making even the idea of crossing treacherous. Below, the river churned, dark and unwelcoming.

"We go one at a time." Beau instructed, testing a plank with his boot before stepping forward. It creaked under his weight but held. I swallowed hard, my palms began to sweat as I followed. The bridge swayed violently with every step, the rotted wood shifting beneath our feet. Luna whined; ears flattened as she hesitated. "Come on, girl." I whispered, trying to coax her forward. She darted ahead quickly, her small frame barely making an impact. My foot slipped on a patch of moss, my stomach lurching as I barely caught myself on the remains of the railing. Beau was already ahead, moving with practiced ease, his balance unwavering.

Then, the unmistakable sound of wood cracking split the air. I barely had time to react before the plank beneath me gave way, splintering into nothingness. My hands grasped wildly at the edges, my feet dangling above the drop. "Beau!" I gasped, struggling to hold on. He was there in an instant, his strong hands gripping mine as he hauled me up effortlessly. "Told you to be careful." He muttered, but there was something softer in his eyes. A flicker of something unspoken.

We made it across, breathless, adrenaline still pulsing so hard I could hear and feel it in my ears.

"We need to be quiet." Beau pressed a finger to his lips, his gaze locking onto mine with a warning edge.

I nodded, exhaling slowly as we crept into the ruins—a silent graveyard of what was once a magnificent megalopolis, built by Titans and those who had stood beside them as equals. Even in its desolation, the city still held a haunting beauty. The marble walls, once pristine, were now blackened from smoke, their surfaces crystallized over time, shimmering faintly beneath the moonlight.

Towering figures loomed in the distance—headless Titan warriors, frozen in stone, remnants of the past carved by the unforgiving heat of the Emberleaf. They stood motionless, silent sentinels watching over what remained of their lost empire. Their sheer size was humbling, making even Beau seem small in their presence. Beside them, Luna was barely the size of an ankle. To call myself Titanborn felt like a lie. I wasn't like them at all. I was nothing compared to the giants who had once ruled these lands.

"Let's make camp here." I murmured, my voice barely above a whisper, as I stepped toward a structure that had once been a home. Centuries old, it had long since been reduced to little more than ash and soot, the echoes of its former life lingering in the scorched remains. It was smaller than the homes across the street, more humble, more human. Planter pots sat outside; their soil long dead, blackened by fire. An old milk churn remained by the door, untouched by time, a fragile reminder that life had once thrived here.

We stood at the threshold, peering into the darkness beyond the broken windows, uncertain of what ghosts might still linger in the ruins of the past.

"You sure?" He asked me.

I nodded as I looked around the empty street we were on and felt an eeriness of safety amongst my ancestral grounds.

Beau went into the house and found a room for us in the back of the house away from any windows. He laid out the blankets and I followed him in as the day turned to night.

"Big day." I sighed, my words few.

"You can say that again." Beau yawned as he lay on the bed, and I moved towards him.

I reached for his shirt and pulled it up to see the wolf bite. He peered down to see what my expression would give away.

"You're fine, it needs another clean but it's a miracle you didn't tear it this morning." I smiled.

He handed me his canteen of water and I tipped a little onto the wound and I wiped it clean with the end of the pillowcase we had carried our food in.

"You should eat." He said handing me an orange he had pulled from the bag.

"So should you!" I tore it in half and climbed to sit in the remains of what was once a bed beside him. It was far too big for us, we weren't the size of Titans, even the smaller ones who had lived here.

"Get some sleep." I rolled over and tried to rest, my eyes were heavy, and the exhaustion was now punching me in the forehead, but my mind was alive, I couldn't stop tossing and turning.

Beau turned and grabbed me to hold me still. "Shhh, it's okay." He hushed me.

"It's not." I said with my eyes still closed.

"What is your big secret Beau?" I said as I sat up.

"What do you mean?" He asked.

"Surely you wouldn't risk your neck for some girl the king just wants to bang." I sighed.

"I told you, my claim as a warrior and bastard is too strong, if you knew, then my brothers must know too." He answered.

"There's something else…" My teeth chattered.

"Can we call a truce, I'll tell you anything you *need* to know, and you do the same. We need to trust each other. Especially now when we are all we have." He said softly, his arm tightened around my back as I rolled to face him, I wanted to trust him.

I sucked in a breath. "Well, you know my secret, I'm Titanborn, I assume your father found out and that's why he sent you to assassinate me." I let out a deep breath. I was terrified about what he might do with that knowledge.

"I knew your brothers then." He sighed.

"Knew?" I sat up so close our noses might touch.

"Wren and Edi, they were stationed at a camp with me." He explained.

"Where are they now?" I begged and my eyes locked onto his.

"They were sent a long time ago to Deniz, Wren and Edi's abilities were sending ships to the cliffs of Orman without any risk of shipwreck. Orman was battered but the Fae are strong and skilled with similar powers." He said. "It's been an ongoing and tiring war." He added.

"Then what happened?" I grasped his leather jacket and shook him as my eyes puddled.

"I don't know what happened after that. I was sent to another camp. I never knew the others. Except for your father. He's still alive." Beau said as he wiped tears from my cheeks.

"My mother?" my lips shuddered at the word and what the answer might be.

"I didn't have the pleasure." He softened as he moved his hands down my arms.

I was in his lap now, the cold of the marble made the hairs of my body stand on end. Beau removed his jacket and wrapped it around me and held me close to him.

"Where is my father?" I asked.

"He commands the training camps when he isn't close to Rael." He answered.

"Wren and Edi, they were stationed at a camp with me." He explained.

"Where are they now?" I begged and my eyes locked onto his.

The training camps— I'd heard stories of what they did to people who didn't comply at these camps. I'd never heard anything good, but what could be good about raising killers? My brothers and father were now a part of that legacy. And what I'd heard about the Mages at these camps made my blood run cold.

"I know I'll probably never see them again, but I want to know, I need to know, and now the reminder of it all makes it ache in my chest like the day they left me." I cried.

"I'm sorry." He squeezed me.

"No, I'm glad, sometimes it helps to feel. Thank you for the small ounce of closure you've given me." I whispered.

"So, you weren't just a really pretty whore." He laughed trying to break the sadness in the room.

"I'm not a whore at all!" I snapped. " I've never been with a man, I told you that." I confessed.

The room had darkened, and I couldn't see him now, but I felt his body relax and the sound he made when his expression softened, the way he touched me as his hands loosened around the small of my back.

"I'm sorry, I didn't mean to imply." He apologized.

"Let's get some sleep." I yawned once again.

I peeled myself off of him and lay beside him to absorb some of his warmth. He threw a blanket over us, and he tucked an arm under my head for me to use as a pillow. It was a closeness I had never felt with anyone else, was this what trust felt like? I didn't know, I had never trusted anyone with any secret, with my vulnerability. I was meant to take it to my grave.

Deep down I knew what people could do with this knowledge. It was a thought I rarely gave light to.

That much knowledge could have me murdered, enslaved, sold, raped, or all of the above.

Beau was sound asleep while I lay awake with thoughts I didn't often think. About my family, my future, what had they all done these past fifteen years?

Beau was no longer clean-shaven, he had a stubbly beard growing, his long wavy hair now messier than the first time I had seen him. He was a handsome man, with a striking jawline, and lips just the right size for kissing. His arms were thick and heavy, one slumped across my body. I wriggled beneath him and turned as I fitted myself into the nook between his shoulders and chest. He slipped a hand over my pants and squeezed the rump of my ass tenderly. His smile against my forehead, his hand left my pants and reached up to touch my cold cheeks.

"You're cold." He whispered.

I nodded against him as he called Luna to lay against my back. Together they warmed me up just enough to fall asleep.

When I woke the sun barely seemed to touch this place. It felt like later in the day than it was. Beau and Luna weren't here, but his jacket was on the end of the bed, and I grabbed it and pulled it around myself, still cold from the night before.

I climbed out of bed and looked around through the windows in the front room of the house, then walked out into the street and strolled through what I assumed would have been shops further down the way. Luna spotted me and raced to my side, Beau was still a distance away, in his hand, he held a decently sized kill.

Luna and I walked towards him, he had a shine about him today that wasn't there yesterday. He reached me with his long strides and leaned down to kiss my cheek and I blushed.

There was no denying the attraction between us, my stomach did somersaults as he acknowledged the same feelings with his gentle kiss.

"Where did you find that?" I asked.

"It was flying overhead and perched on a tower. Close enough for me to throw a dagger at it." He explained.

"I don't think we should risk a fire here. Farkli is close and if they see the smoke…" I panicked.

"Well, jerky then." He smiled.

I had never seen him smile before, I had felt it pressed against me, but this was a first, he was a withdrawn person until last night. I couldn't help but grin *too* wide at him.

"What?" He scrunched his brows and slackened his jaw.

"You should smile more." I said shyly.

"Give me a reason to smile." He teased.

"Beau, are you flirting with me?" I giggled.

"Hard not to when you're rubbing up against me all night." He dropped the duck and placed his hands on my hips.

"I was cold!" I shrugged.

"Yeah, it was. Your ass felt pretty good in my hands." He lowered one hand and gave my ass another gentle squeeze.

I reached for his neck and tugged him to me and our lips crashed together, his stubble tickling me as his tongue massaged mine and he rocked into me.

"I have to tell you something." He broke free of my grasp.

"Okay?" I nodded somewhat, afraid.

He unlaced his shirt exposing the bite wound, but he pulled the shirt all the way off. I hadn't seen him without it except for his silhouette the day he was behind the sheet at the inn washing. His perfectly naked silhouette.

"Please don't freak out." He exhaled.

He turned around and exposed his back to me. His muscular back had old wounds where he had been hacked of his identity, the only remaining evidence of who he could have been were nubs that were bored into his shoulder blades. Hatched scars on both blades all going halfway down his back where his wings would have once ended.

I reached forward and traced his scars with my fingers, and I kissed his back as our hands tangled together and pity swelled in me before I could register what this meant.

"Who did this?" I asked.

"King Rael ordered it." He didn't stutter at all, and I felt a wave of heat in him as his words came out rough, almost violent. "This is why I took you, I knew you were of value, but I had no idea *who* you were." He confessed.

"WAIT! You're a Fae! A FUCKING FAE!" I shrieked and pulled back at the sudden realization that *he* was my mortal enemy.

"I was!" He said with regret. He pulled his shirt back on and began lacing.

"How?" I questioned.

"My mother was a Fae." He answered. "I didn't get my wings until I was well into adolescence. Rael was there the nights I writhed in pain as they grew through, it's an excruciating process. He genuinely believed my mother to be human." He added.

"Did he butcher you?" I asked.

"Him and... General Gray." He glowered and our eyes connected. My throat went dry at the name.

"My father..." I choked.

"Relax." Beau slumped to a stone and sat down. "He didn't have a choice. Rael used him to do any and all his dirty work. He was the only one able to hold me down while Rael cut through the bone and membranes. Gray sewed me up. It took years to heal so Rael sent me away to camps to *toughen me up*. When I returned, I was a weapon. With all my Fae abilities, just no wings. Nobody could suspect me, I was just a real kickass assassin." He sighed.

"Why are you telling me this now?" I asked.

"Because when I was holding you last night and finally absorbing who and what you were, it occurred to me your father did *this* to me." He explained.

"And you want revenge? You're taking me back?" I felt the blood leave my face and the cold smacked me in the head.

"No, I thought of what this one man's greed has taken from just the two of us alone. How he's manipulated thousands to do his bidding because he has mages with the same goal as him." He sighed.

"If he isn't stopped, what will he continue to do?" I held his gaze, we seemed to have found another common ground.

"Lexia has stayed out of the conflict, but what if we can get them to help Orman?" He suggested.

"The leadership in Lexia is Fae? If they see you like this surely the outrage will be enough to stir a revolution. Rael is only a human!" I growled.

"A human with Titanborn leadership and mages more powerful than anyone in Farkli." He added.

"We need to be smart. Will Creed help us?" I asked.

"Maybe, they only want peace." He replied.

"Someone has to help, look at this city his family torched to the ground because they were more powerful and disobedient. His deceit knows no bounds. He will stop at nothing." I was beginning to argue with myself and Beau's expression turned from rage to admiration.

"Don't ever lose that passion!" He walked towards me and kissed me once more.

"So, we have half a Fae and a powerless Titanborn. Together we're whole." I spoke to his lips on mine.

"Light a fire!" He became excited.

"Are you insane, Farkli will see it!" I gasped.

"Wasn't your mother from Farkli. It'll be in your blood, they will sense it." He urged.

"You sure you want to do this?" I asked.

"If it doesn't work at least we get to cook the duck." He smiled.

We looked around for rocks and wood to start a fire. Beau had started without me and soon he was blowing at the kindling to ignite the embers below the few dry roots I had found.

I sat and plucked the duck of its feathers while Beau kept the good ones to use for other things.

"We need seasoning." He moped.

"You grew up with privilege." I laughed.

"I wouldn't call salt a privilege so much as a bare human necessity." He scoffed.

"You're talking to a person who thought potatoes were good raw." I shrugged.

"We'll fix that, one day when all of this is over, I'll cook you a really good baked potato." He teased.

"With salt, right?" I joked.

"If you're well-behaved, I'll even add butter." He laughed.

"You're ridiculous!" I smiled.

The fire began to smoke, and Beau added feathers hoping it would make the flames bigger.

"No turning back now!" He fanned the flames with his shirt.

"If it's the right thing to do, I'd like to do it." I nodded.

"I can get on board with that notion." He agreed.

The duck was cooking, it was fatty and rich. I'd never had duck before, but I know what he meant about salt. Just a dash would lift this immensely. I was gnawing off small pieces of a leg when the sun began to set and flaming torches began to walk in through a dark alley and Beau sat up on edge. I dropped the leg, and I rose up next to him, our hands locked together, and he looked down at me and his eyes spoke without his lips. *'I'll look after you'* they said with each blink.

Two men and two women approached. They glared between us and Luna and back at each other.

"You're either really stupid or you knew what you were doing lighting that fire." One of the women said. Her eyes were a dull shade of green, her hair a fiery vibrant red so luscious and thick it took over her tiny frame. She wore an ankle-length dress two shades darker than her hair with black boots.

"The latter." Beau said.

"A Fae…" The other woman said. She was taller than the other. Her hair was a mixture of white and brown, adorned with a crystal band, she had icy blue eyes, her skin tawny and she was dressed more practically, with pants and a cape covering her top half.

"How do you know that?" I asked.

She sniffed the air deeply and exhaled with satisfaction. "And a Titanborn woman." She gleamed as she looked at the tall man beside her. His eyes and hair were both the same shade of darkness, he was almost the same height as Beau and the words seemed to sink into him as he looked to their other male companion. Their eyes bulged at the same time they whispered my name. "*Ali.*"

"Zac…" I sputtered. I almost lost my balance. He raced to me and wrapped me in a hug and spun me around with an excitement I remembered only vaguely.

"You're alive!" He placed me down and held my face. "You're all grown up." His eyes welled with tears.

Tears cascaded down my cheeks as I took in the wrinkles of time at the corners of his eyes and he hugged me once more, as if he were afraid that I'd disappear into a memory.

"I'm here. I'm alive." I squeezed him back.

"We thought the worst." His chin sunk into his neck as his companions looked on.

"Where are the others?" I grabbed his wrists gently.

"I don't know, I was assigned to Farkli, but they took out Rael's army, once they realized what I was and I hadn't chosen to work for Rael, I had the option to stay." He explained.

"When was the last time you saw them?" I asked.

"The same day they took us all to Varsili. I was separated from Wren, Edi, and Mason." He sighed.

"So, Mason is the only one we have nothing on." Beau added.

"And our mom." I said.

"No, she was here in Farkli but sent to Creed. I haven't seen her again. I can't believe you're here! What are you doing in this place?" Zac stammered.

"We're heading to Lexia." Beau moved forward to shake his hand. Zac looked him up and down with hesitation but eventually shook his hand.

"He's okay, Zac. He's my friend." Beau's arm reached around my waist, and he looked down at me and smiled.

"This is Astrid." Zac pointed to the woman with the red hair. "My wife." He smiled.

"Eleanor and Kieran." He said as the other two bowed.

"Wife!" I gasped.

She smiled and came to hug me. She was warm and smelt of an intriguing blend of smoke mixed with flowers.

"You remind me of our mother." I smiled as I held her arm's length away.

"It's the sorcery." She winked.

"Flame wielder?" Beau questioned.

"How'd you guess." Eleanor laughed.

Her hair was a dead giveaway, and the smell of smoke wasn't from our fire, it was her. It wasn't an ugly or uncomfortable odor, it was quite pleasant and alluring even. Zac being a flame wielder also made sense for him to be with someone who could enhance his powers.

"Come to Farkli?" Zac asked.

Beau tightened his grip on me, and I rested my hand on him to cover his white knuckles and angst.

"Just come for a night, it's not safe here." Astrid added.

I looked up to Beau and he sighed and nodded with his eyes closed.

"And what kind of friend are you to my sister?" Zac asked Beau. "You seem awfully comfortable together." He raised a brow as he eyes closed the distance between us.

"A new development." I answered before Beau could.

Zac had always been an overprotective alpha male, and this moment was no exception. His stance was rigid, shoulders squared, his presence an unspoken warning to anyone who dared step too close.

Eleanor and Kieran were far ahead, their figures blending into the distance, while Astrid clung to Zac's arm with an easy familiarity. Beau and I lagged behind, our pace unhurried, as if neither of us was in a rush to reach what lay ahead.

We didn't speak, but our eyes did. Every glance a silent conversation unfolding between us as we stepped onto the bridge spanning the river into Farkli. His gaze held a quiet curiosity, laced with something heavier—concern, maybe even hesitation.

Zac and Astrid's home stood on the outskirts of the city, a solitary structure against the horizon. Built from weathered blackened stone, its silhouette was marked by several chimneys, releasing faint wisps of smoke into the evening air. Inside, a room was devoted entirely to Astrid's sorcery and potions, glass vials and dried herbs crowding the shelves. Another was stacked high with old, dust-laden books, their spines thick and ancient, too large for my hands to hold with ease. The sprawling kitchen exuded warmth, the ceiling lined with dried meats, fragrant herbs, and strips of fruit jerky swaying gently from their hooks. Out the window, the valley stretched wide, revealing Farkli in all its chaotic brilliance. Sparks crackled and danced through the air as residents wielded their magic freely, the energy pulsing through the streets like a living current. The buildings towered over the streets, their sharp silhouettes illuminated by the flickering glow of enchanted lanterns and arcane symbols etched into stone. The streets bustled with life, lined with stalls overflowing with shimmering potions, enchanted trinkets, and relics humming with dormant power. Cloaked figures wove through the crowds, their eyes glowing with the unmistakable mark of magic, their presence both eerie and mesmerizing. It was a city of pure magic, a world so far removed from my own that it felt almost like stepping into a dream—a life I had never even dared to imagine.

In Varsili, even a whisper of magic was enough to seal your fate. Anyone suspected of wielding it was dragged into the streets and put to the sword before they could utter a single spell. Of course, there were oracles, those who walked the fine line between secrecy and survival, their gifts overshadowed by the mages who held true power.

The oracles operated in the shadows; their hands stained with unseen deeds. Seemingly unassuming, they moved unnoticed through the streets, listening, watching, and whispering secrets back to Rael, their loyalty bought and paid for. For their service, they were rewarded handsomely, living in quiet luxury—better than the common folk, though still beneath the nobles who ruled the court.

Zac opened a door to a bedroom and inside was a fireplace, a lounge chair, and a bed. "Do you need a separate room?" He winked at me.

I hesitated to answer, but Beau shook his head. "No, we'll be okay together." He said.

I could sense that Beau wasn't entirely trusting of Zac.

"You're moody." I said as I shut the door behind Zac.

"I'm worried about how Rael let a fire-wielding Titanborn slip through his fingers. And what that means if he's lying to us." Beau sat on the lounge and his expression filled with worry.

"We're here now, this is what we're doing. Let's just be cautious and stick together." I exhaled as I sat beside him.

"Do you trust him?" He asked.

"Honestly, I trust her more." I dropped my chin. "But he's always been a reckless rebel, the black sheep. Zac is how my family got caught in the first place, he's careless." I confessed.

Astrid knocked at the door and came in with freshly roasted ham and a loaf of bread. "I wasn't expecting visitors." She said with embarrassment.

"Are you kidding! This is amazing." I stood up to thank her.

She smiled, turned, and headed out the door to give us time to eat alone. Once we were done eating, I went looking for a washroom and stopped in the kitchen to ask Astrid who was preparing a pie.

"Could we wash somewhere?" I asked.

"Of course." She smiled as she led the way to a wet room. There was a tub with hot coals beneath it and she helped me tip buckets of water into the tub. It was made of stone with embers of magic I could see from the sparkle when the water hit it.

"Zac made it." She smiled. "Some of his better work." She giggled.

"What was the bad stuff?" I smiled.

"Check the armory after." She laughed.

"Oh, he's never been able to master that, he thinks cause he wields fire he can magically turn out weapons, he needs to understand the fire isn't his, it's borrowed, he can't control it like that." I sighed.

"Sounds like you get it more than him." She laughed.

"It's what mom always told him, it makes sense." I added.

Beau appeared in the doorway and looked over at the tub and began to help us dump water in.

"You'll be washing each other I assume." Astrid smiled as she reached for extra towels.

"I like you, Astrid." Beau smiled back as he took the towels.

"Even if I am a Farklian, Fae?" She teased.

"Being Fae means nothing to me." he confessed.

She raised a brow and caught my eye, and I shook my head for her to caution on the topic.

Astrid smiled politely and left the room. Beau locked the door and removed his shirt. His bite was almost fully healed now, and I began to remove the stitches while he rested against the tub.

"Clear something up for me?" I asked.

"Sure." He replied.

"What is this?" I flicked my hand between the both of us as I pulled a thread from his wound, and he sucked in a breath.

"What do you want it to be?" He pursed his lips as he winced in pain as I yanked on another thread.

"BEAU!" I grunted.

"The truth is after you saved me in the swamp, I just want you all the time." He laughed with embarrassment.

"Aww my damsel in distress." I teased. "Really though?" I chuckled.

"Really, I've never met a woman who'd risk her neck for me, especially not a woman I had kidnapped. It's hot." His voice heated and a smoulder appeared on his perfect stubbly face.

"I like you with a beard." I smiled.

"That's it? Just when I have a beard?" He sighed.

"I didn't mean for that to be my final answer. I like you too, there's something about us both being fucked up that I can't ignore. We've bonded since then." I grinned.

He pulled me into him, and I rose onto my toes, my fingers brushing through his beard before reaching up to untie his hair, letting it cascade down his shoulders. His hands traced softly along my cheeks before threading into my hair, drawing me closer as I melted into the warmth of his touch.

"Beau." I whispered against his chest.

He was undressing me now, his hands exploring my bare skin with deliberate slowness, each graze igniting a fire beneath my flesh. Every touch sent ripples of pleasure through me, his fingers tracing the contours of my body as if committing them to memory.

His lips followed, pressing soft, heated kisses along my collarbone, down the curve of my breasts. His palms cupped them gently, thumbs circling before his warm tongue flicked over my hardened peaks, drawing a gasp from my lips.

Beau sank to his knees before me, his grip firm as he guided me onto the edge of the stone tub. His breath was warm against my skin, anticipation pooling deep in my core. Then his mouth found me, and a sharp inhale left my throat as his tongue traced up and down, teasing, tasting. He moved with precision, circling my bud in slow, tantalizing motions that sent waves of pleasure rolling through me.

My thighs tensed around him, the overwhelming sensation making me arch backward. He held me steady, his strong hands gripping my hips as he devoured me, his tongue relentless, pulling me deeper into the abyss of ecstasy.

I pulled him up from the ground and pulled his pants off and he sprung out for me.

"Are you sure this is how you want to do this?" He asked gently, knowing I was a stranger to the intimacies couples shared.

"It's not, but I want to satisfy you too." I smiled and wrapped my hand around his girth and tugged back and forth as his eyes fell back into his head. I wrapped my lips around the tip and lashed my tongue all over him, one of his hands now in my hair guiding me tenderly over him. The other now holding my neck supporting me as he gently raked himself in and out of my mouth. Soon he was pouring out of me, and he lifted me up and plunged me into the tub and he climbed in with me.

"*Now* we've bonded." He pulled me on top of him and kissed me as his hands rubbed up and down my back and I ground myself against him wanting more.

"Not here." He slowed and brushed the hair off my face.

I nodded to agree, I lay over him in the warm water as he ran suds over my body, the pulse still pounding hungrily between my legs.

"You were unexpected." I smiled.

"So were you, but here we are." He smiled back as he pulled at my chin, and I kissed his lips greedily.

Chapter Six

BEAU

We lay in the tub long enough for Aliera to drift into sleep against me, her body warm and weightless in the water. She was perfect in so many ways, and yet, a deep, gnawing fear grew inside me. I was Rael's blood. No matter how much I tried to deny it, it was a truth I could never outrun. If we ever took this further—if we gave in completely and she bore my children—he would win. Our children would be the first of their kind, both Fae and Titanborn, bound by the blood of a sorceress and a human. A union that would be both a miracle and a weapon in the wrong hands.

I could never allow that. I couldn't do that to her. To us.

She had spent so long hiding, fighting, desperate to escape Rael's grip, and if I let this happen, I would be delivering her straight into the very fate she feared most. A betrayal far worse than any blade to the back.

So, I held her closer, pressing my lips softly against the crown of her head, committing this moment to memory, knowing that no matter how much I wanted her, there were some battles even I couldn't afford to lose.

"Aliera?" I whispered as I tried to wake her.

"Hmm." She sighed.

"We should dress for bed." I pulled her up slowly, her breasts perfectly pointed at me, a little freckly from the cold.

She stood rubbing her eyes as I wrapped a towel around her, and I lifted her from the bath after wrapping a towel around myself.

"Can you feed Luna?" She yawned.

"I will." I nodded.

I carried her into the room where Astrid had laid out clean clothes for both of us, the warmth from the roaring fireplace instantly easing the lingering chill in the air that came with the darkness. The soft glow of the flames danced across the walls; casting flickering shadows that made the space feel as otherworldly as I knew it was.

I draped a gown over Aliera's shoulders, the fabric melding against her skin as she shifted. She climbed into the bed, curling into the pillow with a weary sigh, her exhaustion pulling her under almost instantly. Her breathing steadied, her features softened in sleep. For a moment, I simply stood there, watching the way the firelight traced her face—one of the rare times she looked truly at peace.

I pulled on the clothes left for me and went out to see where Luna was and what Astrid had so that I could feed her. I found her playing with Zac in the dining room and he poured me a beer and tapped the table for me to sit with him.

"So, you're banging my baby sister…" Zac scoffed.

I didn't answer him, what we did together was between us.

"So can you help us over the mountains?" I questioned.

"You don't go over the mountains." He laughed.

Astrid entered the room and settled beside Zac, seamlessly joining the conversation. I turned to her for an answer, sensing her calm and measured nature. She was far less sarcastic and childish than Zac, and for a moment, I wondered how she managed to tolerate him.

He carried himself with an air of self-importance, his humor more self-indulgent than actually amusing. His ego was unmistakable—bigger than the room itself—but as I studied him, I decided then and there that, while he might be a jerk, he was ultimately harmless.

"You go through them." She sighed.

"Why does that sound bad?" I sat back and sipped the beer to taste it.

"Cause it's pitch black, and nobody has ever come out the other side and bragged about it. It's definitely worth bragging about." Zac's eyes widened.

"You wouldn't go back through the human lands?" Astrid asked.

"Too risky, Rael is looking for me by now, especially if she's gone too." I sighed.

"What are you to him?" Zac questioned.

"I was his assassin." I fumbled over the words knowing there was so much more to that sentence than what I had let out.

"You don't sound sure?" Zac pressed.

"It's my business." I firmed.

Astrid looked between us as she noted the tension and our growing dislike for one another. She patted his leg as if it would calm him down and Luna came to sit beside me.

"If you're going to take my sister through those tunnels I'm coming with you." Zac announced cockily.

Astrid laughed, her gaze locking onto Zac with sharp amusement, her eyes narrowing as if she could see straight through whatever excuse he was about to conjure. He sank slightly under her scrutiny.

"If he's going, I'm coming too." she stated firmly, her voice laced with defiance. Her lips pursed, anger simmering just beneath the surface, making it clear that there was no room for argument.

"You really don't need to." I said.

"You're a flightless Fae and she has no ability other than the fact she can breathe and claim to be Titanborn, I honestly wouldn't have believed her if Zac hadn't recognized her." Astrid added.

"Offensive!" I scolded. Luna whimpered at my raised voice.

"You can come, but don't slow us down." I sighed. A fire wielder and sorceress would be handy if we were going through dark tunnels even if I didn't like Zac much.

"Get some rest, we leave tomorrow." Astrid clapped at Zac to move him to the bedroom.

"What about Eleanor and Kieran?" Zac asked.

"They will come past in the morning, we'll discuss with them then." Astrid sighed.

I pulled myself off the chair and downed the remainder of the beer, the bitterness lingering on my tongue. With a nod of gratitude to Zac, I pushed away from the table and headed back to the bedroom where Aliera lay asleep.

The room was dimly lit by the soft glow of the fire, casting long shadows along the walls. I eased myself into bed beside her, careful not to disturb her, but the shift in weight made her stir. She rolled over instinctively, pressing herself into my side, her breath warm against my skin. Without hesitation, she nestled into the crook of my shoulder, her body molding against mine as if this was where she had always belonged.

I exhaled, pressing a lingering kiss to the top of her head, allowing myself this fleeting moment of peace.

We slept well and comfortably for the first time together but were woken by a disturbance at the front of the house. It was Astrid yelling at someone.

"I guess it's time to get up." Aliera yawned as she brushed a pile of her hair off her face.

I pulled her to me, and she quickly submitted to a few more moments in bed together. I tried to lock these moments in my mind before they were stripped from me. I'd never liked anyone as much as I liked her, but I wouldn't deceive her or trap her into a life with me.

"Penny for your thoughts?" She brushed through my beard as I looked into her eyes.

"Nothing, just tired." I lied.

"When did you go to sleep?" She asked.

"I had a beer with Zac and talked them through our travel plans. We've gained some companions." I winced.

"Ohhh…" She sighed.

"I didn't invite them, Zac insisted, and then Astrid also insisted." I explained.

"Well, there goes any peace. Zac might be my brother, but he's a pain in the ass." She laughed.

"I'm so glad it's not just me who thinks that." I laughed back.

"He means well, but he's an egomaniac." She added.

"I got that vibe when he handed me a beer, I don't normally drink but I felt like he was trying to prove something by the way he tapped at the table for me to sit down and slid me the cup." I shrugged.

"Ughh, he's trying to intimidate you. I guess he's trying to make up for past grievances." She sighed.

"Possibly, I'll give him the benefit of the doubt." I nodded into her forehead.

"Thank you. I guess you know what Wren and Edi are or were like?" She asked.

"Only a little, I liked them though. What few interactions we did have were good ones, they were nice guys." I smiled.

"You wouldn't feel that way about my dad though…" She sighed.

"He was following orders. I can imagine his fate wouldn't be a good one if he wasn't doing what he was told to do." I said with understanding.

"He'd never do that to someone by choice." She sighed.

"His hands were tied. I'd have done the same to protect someone I loved." Whatever that meant.

She looked at me and smiled from one corner of her mouth and whispered, "Thank you."

"I guess we should rise to the occasion and see what's going on out there." I grunted.

Aliera slipped to the side of the bed and pulled on her pants and boots, and I did the same. We left the room together and in the front room, Kieran was arguing with Zac while Eleanor and Astrid were packing vials of potions and satchels of other dried supplies.

"You're either coming or not. We aren't letting them go alone." Eleanor turned and snapped at Kieran giving him an ultimatum.

"You're all going to die in there, what lies in those tunnels does not sleep!" His face was white as he stood there shaking.

"What's in there?" I moved into his space to sit him down.

Aliera was helping Astrid pack food now.

"KIERAN!" I shook him.

"Fire breathers…" He squeezed my arm so tight *my* skin went white now.

"Dragons?" Zac scoffed.

"That's impossible, dragons were the puppies of the Titans. They went extinct with the Titans." Astrid argued.

"Umm, HELLO!" Aliera wavered her arms in the air and Zac did the same.

"I guess it's possible, but why would they retreat to the mountains?" I asked.

"Nowhere else was safe for them." Kieran spoke.

"How do you know this? Why have you never said anything to me?" Eleanor was mad, her arms crossed in front of her with an insulted look on her face.

"My family wasn't always from Farkli, we served the Titans, tending to their animals." He explained. "And you never asked." He turned to Eleanor.

"How am I supposed to know to ask a question like that?" Eleanor scolded.

"Okay, breathe everyone!" Aliera threw her hands up and ordered the room. When her hands went up so did Eleanor and Kieran as if she were lifting them herself.

"PUT ME DOWN!" Eleanor screamed.

"Well, fuck me!" Zac's jaw fell open at the same time they hit the ground, and Kieran crawled backward out of the drop zone.

Aliera fell back also into the kitchen table, her hands white and blotchy like a storm cloud with blood.

"What just happened?" She cried.

"You just got your power." Zac cheered.

"How?" She asked.

He shrugged his shoulders highlighting my original thoughts of his stupidity. "It just happens when you're ready. Guess you weren't ready till now." He said.

"How the hell do *you* have yours then." I couldn't help myself and the insult lit up the room.

Zac's eyes narrowed on me and his fingers flamed as he moved closer to challenge me. I stood upright and pulled my blade in front of me. I'd cut his fingers off if he so much as threatened me again.

"STOP!" Astrid yelled. Her voice was like a loud bang that flashed hard enough that we all felt a jolt from her.

Zac listened and blew out his flames as I tucked away my sword.

"If you're all finished, we have to decide. Kieran, are you coming or not?" She barked.

"I'm coming." He said sluggishly.

"Everyone back here by dusk. We leave at nightfall. Get some rest and pack only what you need. Food, water, warm clothes. We are walking into the winter." She ordered as we all started moving around.

"*She* chose you?" I gawked at Zac.

"Shut up fairy boy." He punched me playfully.

"FAE!" Aliera walked over and corrected him. "And I chose him." She smirked as she climbed on my lap and kissed me.

"Ughh, gross." Zac got up and left the room.

"Hey fairy boy, wanna finish what we started." She kissed down my neck as she pushed my hair away.

"We should be packing." I kissed her.

"We might die in that tunnel… I'd like to experience you before that happens." Her eyes softened.

"Don't think that way, I'll protect you." I rubbed her back.

"I know." She smiled.

I stood up and carried her to the room we had been staying in, Astrid had given us some bigger backpacks and a bunch of new clothes to bring.

"She's honestly ninety-five percent of their relationship." Aliera laughed. I laughed too as I agreed with what she had said.

We finished folding our clothes, the quiet rustling the only sound between us. I double-checked my weapons, ensuring everything was in place before handing Aliera a blade to wear at her hip. Then, I slipped a spare into her boot and another into her bag, my movements swift and practiced.

She stared at me, her golden eyes narrowing slightly, as if I had conjured the weapons out of thin air. "How many of those do you have?" she asked, disbelief laced in her voice.

I smirked, sliding another knife into my belt. "Enough. Assassin by trade." I shrugged.

"Are we done?" She asked as she bounced her eyes between our bags.

"Let's get some food." I grabbed her hand and pulled her through the doorway.

"What is that noise?" Aliera asked as we heard a slapping coming from down the hallway.

"The other five percent." I laughed. She hit me playfully and cringed as we walked into the kitchen, so we didn't disturb them.

"Looks like Astrid already packed all the food." She smiled. "Maybe we can have some time together too." She walked towards me with seductive eyes, and I wasn't sure how I'd get out of this except for complete honesty.

"You're not worried about pregnancy?" I asked.

"I was more worried about it being my first time." She grunted.

"I've killed the mood…" I slumped into a chair.

"No, I just wasn't being that responsible." She plopped herself next to me.

"It's been bothering me for a while." I explained.

"You don't want kids one day?" She asked.

"If we were to have kids Rael wins. His grandchildren will be Titanborn." I confessed.

"So, you don't want to touch me because of him." She sighed. "He never has to know if we live in Lexia, our kids, if we *choose* that, never have to know what a monster he is." She added.

"Astrid will have a potion to make sure it doesn't happen before it's time." I knew we were headed for our first fight, so I tried to deflect it.

"Forget it." She got up and walked away and I didn't know if I should follow her or give her space.

"I'm no expert but I think you should go after her. You don't want to embark on this journey and not have a clear head." Zac stood in the doorway with a towel around him and a heartfelt expression on his face.

I stood up and nodded a thank you his way and went after Aliera.

I tried to open our door, but it was locked so I banged continuously.

"What?" She opened the door, her face wet with sadness.

I pushed my way into the room and backed her into a corner.

"I've never felt this way about anyone, and I've been with a lot of women. None make me feel alive the way you do. So, I won't waste this." I pulled her into my arms, and she wrapped herself around me as she ripped at my clothes to undress me.

"I don't care about kids." She said flustered.

"Let's not talk about that. It's you and me right now and that's all I care about." I pulled at her clothes and threw her on the bed where I climbed over her.

She stroked over the broken bone fragments that stuck out of my back and down the long-hatched scars as she pulled at me to enter her.

"You ready." I asked before I plunged into her.

She gulped and sucked in a deep breath as I kissed her plush lips. She nodded and pulled her legs up and locked them around me.

I held her thighs and slowly entered, her warmth relaxing me immediately and she gasped as I filled her with every motion. Her hands on the bedframe behind us gripping the bars as she tightened around me and rocked her body against mine.

"I think I might explode." She gasped.

"Good, cum with me." I sped up a little and she groaned and pulled at me as I pulled her on top of me and we came together.

We sat there panting with each other as we caught our breath, her body still locked on me, and I could feel her body pulsing around my length, squeezing my girth.

"You're amazing." I kissed her.

"That was perfect." She smiled.

We rolled off of each other and lay in bed naked for a while, we didn't speak, we just played with each other's bodies and enjoyed what it was like to be this simple. Tonight would be different, we were opening our arms to hardship and struggle, but Rael had to be stopped.

The day began to darken, and I held Aliera while she slept in my arms taking in what might be our last comfortable nap for a while to come.

"Time to get up you two!" Zac knocked at the door.

I wanted to tell him to fuck off, I wanted the world to fuck off. For the first time, I was happy, and it was because of another person, this person… my person.

Her eyes opened and she stretched. "Time to go." I kissed her cheek.

She sighed loudly and rolled out of the bed and we both began to dress. I armored us both with everything I had and holstered our weapons to our bodies.

"A real warrior princess now." I snickered.

"Oh shush." She laughed.

"Come on!" Astrid banged at the door.

We slipped our packs over our shoulders and headed down the hallway. Astrid, Eleanor, Kieran, and Zac were in the front room ready to go. Luna was also ready, She had something of a saddle that had small bags on each side presumably carrying her own food.

"Let's go." Zac nodded. We all followed him out, Astrid was the last and they stopped in the threshold as they kissed through a shared sadness. "One day we'll come home." He pulled her into a sweet embrace, and they kissed. Together locked the front door and turned into the street.

We walked away from the city lights, swallowed by the darkness as we approached the old bridge—the only route leading back into the ruins. The air grew colder, thick with the weight of history and the whispers of those long gone.

As we moved forward, we passed through a massive graveyard sprawled behind the outpost, its silence eerie. The graves stretched endlessly. It was a city of the dead, trapped between two smaller mounds, their slopes littered with crumbling stones and remnants of lives forgotten.

The mountains beyond loomed in the distance, their blackened peaks still bearing the scars of old magic. Under the moonlight, they shimmered in their crystalized state, a haunting reminder of the destruction that once raged through this land. Shadows stretched long across the path ahead, a warning.

"There's a small cave entrance at the back of the ruins, towards the lonely forest." Kieran whispered as he led the way with an old city map.

Luna was afraid, she was on edge and listening to all sounds the wind whipped and whistled through the unnatural breeze.

Aliera raised her hands in a calming gesture, her movements deliberate, measured. She wanted to test her control, to see if she could command the chaos rather than be consumed by it. Sure enough, as her fingers splayed, a faint glow flickered along her hands and wrists—a soft mix of white and red hues pulsing like embers beneath her skin.

The wind, once a raging force, suddenly stilled as it obeyed her movements. A heavy silence settled over us, thick and unnatural. Even Luna, ever watchful, pressed her head against me, her warmth grounding me in the unsettling quiet.

The absence of sound was deafening, as if the world itself was holding its breath, waiting for what would come next.

"We'll travel through the night." Astrid pressed on as she saw the entry to the cave and picked up her pace. Zac was never far behind her, always keeping her in his sight.

The cave smelled stale. A lingering fog clung to the atmosphere, curling around the soot-covered walls like ghostly tendrils. The air carried a damp chill, laced with the faint scent of something ancient—ash, decay, and something else I couldn't name.

Old, broken scales littered the entryway, their edges dulled by age, yet still whispering of the beasts that had once shed them. I stepped forward cautiously, my fingers grazing the rough stone, tracing grooves worn by creatures long vanished. Each step felt heavier, as though the past itself pressed down on me.

This place held the echoes of a past long forgotten, where dragons—the most powerful beings to ever soar the skies—had once reigned. And yet, something had driven them into these mountains, forcing them to retreat into hiding, cowering from their own undoing.

Aliera grasped my hand firmly, she was holding a scale as big as her head. "No turning back now." She sucked in a breath and exhaled hard.

"Can you clear the air, it stinks in there." Zac said to Aliera.

"I'll give it a go." She shrugged.

Aliera raised her hands once more, summoning a gentle breeze that whisked through the cave, carrying away the lingering dust and stale air. The movement was careful, controlled—she didn't dare risk too much.

Zac entered first, his hands raised in cautious readiness, his every step measured. Something about the air here felt different—older, watching.

"Should we risk fire?" Aliera asked.

"We have to, I can't see a thing, and if we step on something or someone…" Astrid's eyes widened.

Zac flamed up and his hands glowed with a raging fire flowing beneath his skin.

"Does that hurt?" I asked.

"Nope." He smirked. He was at the height of his cockiness now as he lead the way through the tunnel. It was one straight path, and it had been carved out. You could tell by the scratch marks on the walls.

Astrid looked around beside Zac as he allowed a little more fire and held his hands up to the walls at least ten feet taller than me.

CHAPTER SEVEN

ALIERA

There was no telling how long we had been in the cave or how far we had walked. The darkness stretched endlessly ahead, swallowing the light of our torches as if the tunnel had no end. My eyelids were heavy, each step growing heavier, the ache in my legs settling deep into my bones.

Beau kept glancing in my direction, his eyes tracking my exhaustion. Finally, he exhaled sharply and came to a stop, his voice firm yet gentle. "We need to take a break."

No one argued. The moment the words left his mouth, we all dropped where we stood. Zac dulled the flames, allowing the cavern to settle into a dim, flickering glow. Astrid moved silently, pulling out food and passing it around. The scent of dried meat and bread filled the air, mingling with the damp earthiness of the cave.

Luna was ecstatic for the rest, her tail thumping against the ground as she nestled against me. Kieran had carried her part of the way, letting her sleep draped across his arms, but now she was awake, content to share what little food I had left. She curled up beside me, her warmth soothing against the cave's cold floor.

Beau shrugged off his jacket and draped it over us, his warmth lingering in the fabric. Then, without hesitation, he settled beside me, slinging his arm over both Luna and me, his presence steady and grounding.

I allowed my eyes to close, letting the exhaustion pull me under.

We all slept for what felt like days—perhaps it was days. Time had lost all meaning inside the tunnel, swallowed by endless darkness. There was no way of telling whether it was day or night. We rested when exhaustion took hold, and when our strength returned, we walked—hard and fast, pushing ourselves as much as we dared.

But something about the darkness drained us, more than mere fatigue. The tunnel was never straight, twisting and curving unpredictably, winding in ways that made it impossible to judge our distance. A gnawing fear took root in my chest: what if there was no end? What if we had miscalculated? Days, weeks— months could pass, and we might still be here, walking toward nothing.

We rationed our food with careful precision, stretching it as far as we could. Hunger gnawed at our stomachs, but we ignored it. We had to. Every crumb, every drop of water had to last, though none of us knew for how long.

Only Luna seemed immune to the weight of it all. She moved ahead with boundless energy, trotting confidently as if she knew the way. The constant darkness seemed to sap the life from the rest of us, but she remained unaffected.

Then, at last, we stumbled upon something new—something different from the endless emptiness of the tunnel. The first true sign of dragons. Not just old scales littering the ground—those had become almost expected, scattered throughout the tunnels, their metallic sheen catching in the dim light Zac provided. But these weren't just remnants, these were bigger, stronger scales.

Beau knelt beside one, running his fingers over its surface. It was as hard as steel. He drew his sword and pressed the edge against it, testing. The blade met resistance, unable to cut through. Kieran crouched beside him; eyes gleaming with realization.

"If we can carry enough of this back." Kieran murmured, "we can have it fashioned into armor."

Beau nodded, already gathering what he could carry, the weight of the task ahead momentarily forgotten in the face of newfound purpose. For the first time in what felt like forever, we had something worth holding onto.

Zac had stumbled across a clutch of eggs. They were still warm, their shells slick with a strange, iridescent liquid that made my stomach twist. Had they just been laid? If so, their mother couldn't be far. And if she was near, she wouldn't be pleased to find us here.

There were five eggs in total, each varying in size and color. When Zac illuminated them with his flames, their surfaces shimmered, casting a mesmerizing dance of colors as if tiny galaxies were trapped beneath their hardened shells. The sight was breathtaking—until movement flickered behind them.

A pair of glowing eyes emerged from the shadows. Then, the rest of her followed.

She lifted her head over the eggs, her massive form protectively around them. Even in the dim light, I could see the sheer scale of her—those teeth alone were the length of my entire leg. If she decided we were a threat, we wouldn't stand a chance.

She hissed, her gaze flicking between us, assessing, measuring. My heart pounded, my muscles locked in place, waiting for the inevitable strike.

Then, she sniffed at Zac. Her sharp pupils dilated, and almost instantly, her posture shifted. Recognition flickered in her massive, ancient eyes. She knew what he was—Titanborn. His fire-wielding abilities marked him as kin, and she liked him immediately.

Slowly, she turned her attention to Kieran, slithering closer. Her wings remained folded—there was no space for her to extend them in this narrow tunnel, but even restrained, her presence was suffocating. She inhaled deeply, and whatever she sensed in him seemed to satisfy her. He bowed to her, a silent acknowledgment of what they both understood.

Astrid and Eleanor were next. They didn't hesitate, raising their hands and calling forth their magic. Their sorcery shimmered in the air, their voices slipping into an ancient tongue I couldn't understand. The dragon tilted her head, intrigued, her curiosity outweighing her aggression. Then, ever so gently, she nudged her eggs toward them, as if testing—waiting to see what they would do.

"She wants us to take the eggs." Astrid was crying. She knew this was an honor and the trust between them was clear.

She slithered toward me next. I held my breath, my pulse hammering as she studied me. There was intelligence there, something deeper than mere instinct. She was testing me.

Slowly, I raised my hand and summoned the wind, letting it swirl around my fingers, a soft whisper of power in the still air. She watched, unblinking, before extending a massive claw toward me. Tentatively, I reached out and touched it, my fingertips pressing against the cool, scaled surface. The moment our energies connected, a rush of something indescribable passed between us—a current of recognition, of understanding.

"You're a wind wielder." Astrid murmured, a knowing smile playing on her lips. "You're sisters."

"How?" I asked.

"You command the wind she flies upon." Astrid replied.

The dragon whipped toward Beau, a deep, guttural growl rumbling from her throat. Her muscles taut, ready to strike, but before she could, I threw myself in front of him.

"You can trust him." I said, my voice steady despite the tension that lurked in the air. I could see it in her eyes—the raw, seething anger. The Fae had played a devastating role in the near extinction of the Titans, in the slaughter of their kin, in the forced exile of the last remaining dragons. Her hatred was justified, burned into the marrow of her being.

And yet, Beau was not them.

The dragon hesitated, her piercing gaze flicking between us, weighing my words, testing the truth in them. The air between us crackled with unspoken history, with centuries of betrayal and bloodshed. But trust? Trust was a fragile thing, and it would take more than words to earn it.

"Please…" I begged as fire enveloped her throat and I shut my eyes, I backed into Beau, and he spun me out of the way.

We ducked as the flames roared through the tunnel behind us, engulfing a pack of Dreadwolves in an inferno of burning flesh and shrieking howls. Their twisted forms writhed in agony, their grotesque, malformed bodies silhouetted against the firelight.

They were hideous—each a nightmare born of cruel experiments. Their teeth jutted at unnatural angles, their faces deformed beyond recognition, a grotesque fusion of wolf and bat. Their black and red transparent wings, veined with something unnatural, oozed malevolence as they flapped in vain against the consuming fire.

There was something deeper, something darker lurking within them. I could feel it—the unmistakable pull of corrupted magic.

They were not merely beasts. They were puppets, vessels of something far more sinister, possessed, and controlled.

Only the mages of the Dunya could wield such power, and all of them served Rael.

The Dreadwolves pulled back from the scorching heat, their grotesque forms momentarily hesitating as the flames fanned against them. Their glowing eyes flickered with renewed rage before they lunged forward again, their snarls reverberating through the cavern.

The dragon let out a thunderous roar, igniting another surge of fire that cascaded through the tunnel, illuminating the space in a searing amber blaze. The heat was suffocating, the force of it sending waves of energy crackling through the air.

Zac stepped forward, his palms ablaze as he seized control of the fire itself. He twisted the flames, bending them to his will, channeling their fury into blistering strikes. Each Dreadwolf that dared charge was met with an unrelenting inferno, their monstrous shrieks swallowed by the raging firestorm.

The cavern walls trembled as the battle raged, the scent of scorched flesh and burning fur enveloped the air. The Dreadwolves faltered, writhing in agony, their malformed wings curling as the flames consumed them.

But there were still more lurking in the shadows, waiting for their moment to strike.

"You saved our lives." I gasped as Beau, and I pulled ourselves up from the ground and looked to the dragon. She bowed her head as she wiggled backwards to her eggs still nudging them at Astrid.

"Those are Rael's dogs." Beau gasped.

"Grab the eggs. We need to move!" I said to Eleanor.

"He's just a human!" Zac laughed.

"A human with an army and mages, our brothers, our mother and father fighting on his side. He has more than us Zac!" I scowled.

Mages were darker than the sorcerers of Farkli. Sorcerers were born with their abilities, their magic woven into their very essence from birth. Mages, however, were different. They were taught, shaped by rituals and incantations that demanded unwavering dedication. They committed their entire lives to the pursuit of power, often straying too deep, delving into the forbidden arts, and serving anyone willing to fuel their relentless hunger for more.

They had been human once, just like the rest of us. They could come from any race, any background, but once they tasted power, it was never enough. It consumed them, twisted them, turned their ambition into an insatiable craving. And no matter how much they took, how much destruction they wrought, they always needed more.

"Keep moving." Beau growled at us all.

The dragon had surged ahead, disappearing into the darkness of the tunnel, but her presence was impossible to miss. The sound of her claws raking against the stone echoed through the cavern, shaking loose dust and debris as she widened the passage for herself. The air was thick with swirling grit, and I gritted my teeth, doing all I could to summon a gust strong enough to push it toward the Dreadwolves.

They never traveled alone. There would be more lurking in the shadows waiting. Perhaps human soldiers, if we were lucky. But more likely, there would be mages—ones who weren't just controlling the beasts but embedding themselves into their very minds.

The others pressed themselves against the walls, shielding their faces with their clothes as the dragon carved deeper into the mountains, her relentless digging shaking the very foundation beneath our feet. Each scrape of her claws sent a fresh wave of dust billowing through the tunnel, choking the stale air as we braced ourselves for whatever hunted us in the dark.

"Astrid help her!" Eleanor yelled.

Astrid's powers could conduct anything with the spark of a flame. "Zac, give me a fireball. Everyone else, stay down!" She ordered as she stepped in front of the dragon and halted her efforts.

With Zac beside her, she strengthened his flames, pulling them into her own hands and weaving them with fury. Orbs of white and red light crackled as they collided, growing hotter, brighter, until she sent them hurtling through the mountain. The explosion rocked the tunnel, sending shockwaves through the stone.

I raced to her side, throwing my arms up as the flames roared higher, hotter, igniting with a power I had never summoned before. The weight of the collapsing rocks pressed down, but I caught them within the cyclonic force that surged from my core. The energy vibrated through my veins, raw and untamed.

With a sharp inhale, I flung my hands to my sides, and the mountain groaned in protest. The earth split apart, the cavernous walls tearing open as the rocks cascaded into the ravine below, swallowed by the abyss.

Daylight poured through the gaping exit, a stark contrast to the darkness we had fought through. My eyes burned from the sudden brightness, but there was no time to hesitate. We raced forward, breaking free onto the jagged edge of the mountain, the wind whipping against our faces.

Behind us, the dragon unleashed another inferno into the heart of the mountain. The fire burned so hot that the peaks steamed, thick plumes rising into the sky like smoke from a dying beast.

"I think we got them." I smiled at her. She bowed her head.

"It's just you isn't it, there's no other dragons left?" I asked.

She shook her head from side to side with sadness as if she didn't know the answer to the question. She looked to Eleanor who had bagged the eggs, and she seemed to sigh.

"We'll look after them, we're going to Lexia, the moles will know what to do. She growled at the idea, and I remember she wouldn't like the inclusion of Fae being near her eggs.

"You don't need the moles. The eggs need to go to Antoli." Kieran explained.

"But there's nobody there." I questioned.

"Then to the tree of life in the Sonsuz forest. The eggs aren't fertilized but if they are left to complete their growth beneath the tree, like everything, they will grow there." He looked at the dragon and smiled, and she nodded.

"Friggin dragon whisper!" Zac joked.

"I'm not dressed for Antoli." Eleanor shivered at the idea.

Antoli was the Titan capital, nestled deep within the ice mountains, a fortress sculpted from frost and stone. When Rael's war ignited the eastern city, the west answered the call, emptying their castle to come to its aid. But the Fae had been waiting. Watching. They anticipated the counterstrike and lay in wait at the old outpost. The last Titans were not just defeated—they were captured, slaughtered, and beheaded without mercy.

The Warmaker had promised the Fae their spelled castles in the east in exchange for their allegiance, but he had betrayed them. His mages, relentless and cruel, tore through their magic, breaking enchantments that had held for centuries. They didn't conquer the strongholds—they obliterated them. A city built by Titans could only be rebuilt by Titans, but there were none left.

Now, Antoli was letf abandoned, a graveyard of lost history, all the magic of the worlds trapped inside.

We were stranded on the wrong side of the river, and scaling the ice mountains was suicide. The only choice was to go around. That meant cutting through a dense forest I had only ever seen in the town square's painted map. Somewhere within it, a bridge stood—heavily guarded by the Fae. There were no guarantees they would let us pass, let alone allow these eggs to hatch.

Fae and Dragons were sworn enemies after the ambush at the ruins, but it hadn't always been that way. Once, they had been allies. Antoli's magic had kept Lexia protected for generations, their shared dominion over the skies unchallenged. But time had turned that alliance to dust. Now, all that remained between them was bloodshed and broken oaths.

"Will you come with us?" I asked the dragon. She shook her head, then she looked back to the tunnel.

"She's afraid." Kieran placed his hand on her face.

"If she's found there'll be no more dragon eggs, she needs to stay hidden." Astrid sighed.

The dragon parted the rubble with ease and climbed over and into the maze of mountains. Her long-scaled body was a mirror for the sunlight, it was like a golden rainbow. She disappeared into the mountains without looking back.

"She'll go to the ruins, she'll be safe there." Eleanor added.

We all sat on the mountainside trying to catch our breath. The air here was cold as the breeze blew over from the ice-capped mountains. Below us was a village at the foot of a large waterfall that flowed clear blue water into an icy stream. Across the river was another village but it was blanketed in snow, the only visual hope was the smoke coming from the chimneys.

"How do we get across?" Zac asked.

"We swim." Astrid replied.

"Let me rephrase that, how do we get across alive?" Zac said sarcastically.

"We could go around, there's got to be something beneath those falls to cross over.

"I don't like either of these ideas." I whispered as I looked up to Beau. He nodded his head to agree with me and we sat back to listen to the others bicker over the best means of getting to the other side.

"Let's get down to that village, maybe someone has a boat?" Eleanor intervened.

We slid down inch by inch, the jagged rubble biting into our skin, sharp edges tearing at our clothes. My hands burned from the friction, raw and stinging as I struggled to hold on. Then, in a split second, I lost my grip. Gravity seized me, yanking me down the slope in a freefall. The world blurred as I tumbled, my body colliding against debris.

I hit the ground hard, my back slamming into a mound of rubble that formed a makeshift wall at the edge of the village. Stars burst behind my eyes, pain stung sharply in my skull as I lay there, momentarily dazed. Warm blood trickled down from a fresh gash on my forehead, the metallic tang filling my nose, but I forced myself upright. Compared to the others, I had gotten off easily.

Beau hit hardest, he was the largest in build and groaned as the rocks dug into him from every angle.

"Is everyone alive?" Zac asked as the cloud of dust that followed our landslide threatened to choke us.

Everyone made some sort of grunt or groan to let us all know they were okay. I stood up first and helped the girls as Zac helped Beau and Kieran.

The village before us was wrapped in a fence protecting it from the onslaught of rubble and to one side was a gate with a broken latch. I pulled myself up and stumbled over to Astrid, she wasn't as deep in as the others.

"We need to find an inn." Kieran coughed.

Kieran emerged unscathed, moving with ease as he began helping Eleanor to her feet. Astrid and I pulled Beau free with Zac's help, each of us wincing as the adrenaline wore off and the sharp sting of our scrapes and bruises set in. We were all bleeding superficially, scratches tracing lines across our skin, but for the most part, we were intact.

The eggs, to our relief, were as solid as stone, unmarked by the rough tumble. Whatever magic had forged them had made them impervious to harm, a reassuring thought as we gathered ourselves.

Brushing off the dirt and debris, we moved forward, stepping through the splintered, worn wooden gates and into the village. The first signs of life greeted us in the form of a rowdy tavern, its golden glow spilling onto the street, the sound of clinking mugs and raucous laughter escaping into the cold night air. Beyond it, a narrow strip of homes lined the cliffside, their windows glowing softly with lantern light.

The lamplight illuminated the cascading waterfall in the distance, its waters shimmering as they tumbled down the mountainside. Occasionally, sharp icicles broke free from the rocks above, crashing into the pools below with a muffled crack. Overhead, the moons loomed large, bathing the world in silver, their light trickling down the mountain tiers into the fjord below, painting the landscape in an ethereal glow.

We walked along the cliff edge, across the water was the other village covered in ice, equally just as lit up hidden in the shoulders of the Antoli mountains.

"We need to cross the river." I said to Beau.

"Not at night. We'll freeze." He replied.

"Speak for yourself." Zac snickered from behind him.

"Shut up!" Beau sneered playfully.

Astrid was on the steps of the tavern and tilted her head to call us all over. We entered and the room became silent. She walked to the bar where a woman was pouring beers, and she smiled at Beau and Zac in a flirty tone.

"Do you have any rooms available?" Astrid asked.

"Depends on what you want to do in those rooms?" She grinned.

"Ughh, just wash and sleep for the night. Perhaps some food." Astrid's brows knitted together as she waited for a response.

"You can have two rooms, one for you ladies and one for you boys. I'll look after you." She grinned as she adjusted her breasts and pulled her dress down just before her nipples became exposed.

"Miss, I think you've misunderstood. We're married to each of these men." Astrid lied.

"What's the price of a good night's sleep though?" She winked playfully.

Zac turned his nose up at the woman, she was blonde with vibrant blue eyes, and she hadn't pulled them away from him or Beau since we walked through the door.

"Maybe we should take our business elsewhere." I exasperated.

"There's nowhere else." She laughed.

"I'm not fucking her." Beau whispered in my ear.

"I don't think you have a choice." I laughed.

Her vibrant eyes latched onto me, and she raised a brow and looked between me and Beau. "Maybe I can look after the both of you." She winked.

"Maybe you take the money and give us THREE rooms." Beau slammed a handful of silvers onto the bench and her eyes lowered to his clenched fist as she turned it over and peered at how much he held.

"Oh, well! Why didn't you say you could pay!" She laughed.

Astrid smacked herself in the forehead with her hand and Zac exhaled hard as he pulled her close to him.

"Three rooms, come along." The tavern busied once more, and we followed the woman up the stairs and down a hallway full of empty rooms. "Now we only have pie, and the pastry didn't really work out, but it'll fill you up." She smiled.

"Thank you." Eleanor smiled softly as we all waited for her to walk back down the stairs.

"You were almost her dinner." Astrid teased Zac.

"I don't ever want to feel the way that woman just made me feel, ever again." He laughed.

"Like you would be better than the pie we're about to entertain?" Beau snickered.

"I'm not eating that." Kieren gulped. The rest of us nodded to agree.

Beau and I went to our room and looked around the old unclean space. The sheets were yellowed from multiple uses from strangers, they stunk of sweat and drool and there were broken mugs and plates in front of the old, chipped basin.

"I'm sleeping on the floor." I stepped back away from the bed.

"The cells in the Varsili palace are cleaner than this." Beau angered.

I grabbed his hand "Let's just be grateful we have a room with light and some food, at least we have our own blankets, the others don't." I said, even though I knew they were likely just as dirty by now.

His hand glided over my cheek and down my neck as he pulled me into him. "At least the water is clean." He added his small note of positivity.

"That's right! Let's wash." I began to unlace his shirt.

As Beau pulled his shirt over his head, he revealed a plethora of bruises and cuts from the fall we all took from the cave tunnel. "You're hurt." My eyes widened with every new wound I found.

"I'm used to it." He pulled at my clothes.

"No, You're really hurt, Beau. You need to stop and rest for a few days." I felt my eyes become glassy at the idea of everyone being injured because I demanded to go to Lexia. "We should have gone through Tecrit." I averted my eyes.

"Tecrit is a dense jungle, and even if you managed to navigate the jungle, the people aren't like those from Varsili or Creed. They have disassociated with the rest of the world." Beau grunted. "We can't delay, the mages won't be far behind us." He added soap to a large bowl and set it on the only table in the room.

"Luna." I called.

Luna sighed and rolled onto her back then rolled back over onto her front and licked her lips hungrily as Beau gave her a bowl of water to drink.

I was lathering Beau in soapy suds when Zac knocked on the door and then he burst in without an invitation. Nothing had changed with him.

"You're lucky I wasn't the one being washed." I squinted at him.

"Shit, you took a few hits." He said to Beau.

"Can we help you?" I sneered.

"Pie?" He pulled out a large soggy pie from behind his back and barely held his composure as Beau's expression turned into nausea.

"Luna?" He offered her the pie. It stunk of offal and wet dough and even Luna refused to make eye contact with him or the pie.

Zac quickly got the hint that he was intruding and left the room without a word as I continued to help Beau, a lot of his bruises were large welts. Purple, almost black in color surrounded by swelling and redness, I was thankful the wolf bite had healed now, but he was left with an impressive scar.

"I just need to lay down, they'll be gone soon." He sighed as he watched my expression closely.

I nodded as he walked towards the bed and threw our blanket over it, he laid down and Luna lay beside him. As a Fae, he should have enhanced healing abilities, but my thoughts were that since he had been clipped of his wings, that might not be so strong anymore, but I didn't want to speak it into existence.

I cleaned myself as quickly as I could. This place was cold, and the water was its equal. I wasn't accustomed to such weather. Once I was done, I dressed in the warmest clothes I had. Beau was asleep and I pulled the other side of the blanket over him after I had pulled on my boots. I took four silvers from his pouch hoping that I might find some food if I took a walk.

Luna was stirring but tired enough not to disrupt Beau. I slipped out of the door and down the hall to Eleanor and Kieran's room. Eleanor was awake and I could hear her stomach growling.

"Shhh..." She pointed to Kieran asleep in the armchair.

I smiled and stepped back as she pulled on her boots. She met me in the hall, and I showed her the money. She smiled as she circled her hand over her stomach. Astrid shut her door behind her as she also stepped into the hall, and we all shared a look of hunger and exhaustion.

"I can't sleep hungry." I whispered.

"Same." Astrid laughed. Eleanor used her hands to shush us. We all took the stairs down into the tavern and out into the streets.

"Left, or right?" I asked.

"Right, there's so many houses, there's got to be some food around." Astrid said pulling a hood over her flaming red hair.

"Who are you trying to fool?" Eleanor laughed.

"We're a long way from Farkli, hopefully, everyone." She growled.

We started walking up the cobblestone paths as snow fell at our feet. Over the water, the other half of the village was being blanketed in more snow as it fell hard. The river between them had small boats and docks, ladders to climb up and out. Some homes were built into the cliff faces of the mountains that enveloped the small village.

Ahead of us, we found a small stall of older women cooking hot soups. There were meats on sticks cooking over an open fire and vegetables boiling.

"Can we eat here?" I asked as I held one silver coin out.

The grey-haired woman smiled and took the money and gave me some change as we took the last remaining seats, she placed empty plates before us. Another woman gave us bowls of broth with crusty bread. We all began to feel the warmth as we ate each dish they served us, the vegetables were perfectly salted, the meat tender, and just the right amount of fattiness.

"Do you know where we might buy some clothes?" I asked one of the women.

"Just around the corner." She smiled.

"Thank you." I said.

Eleanor would have licked her plate clean if Astrid hadn't reminded her about her manners. They were an interesting duo, polar opposites in a very literal sense. Eleanor was gentler and more playful whereas Astrid was all business. I still couldn't understand what she saw in Zac either, they were such an odd match.

We walked around the corner and found a small shop with the town's old bits and pieces. Old clothes, shoes, weapons, bags. "Perfect!" I said as I picked up a fur coat and pulled it over me.

Eleanor and Astrid picked out pieces for themselves and the others also. We paid and began to walk back to the Inn when the snowfall became heavier.

"It's so beautiful." I looked up and smiled as I caught snowflakes in my hands.

I stood still in the moment with the fur wrapped around my shoulders and I felt the magic of the cold as it freckled my skin but sent a buzz of life through me.

Snow began to fall down the mountains in a light flurry and then it became heavier as wings batted down and a shrieking howl flooded the fjord.

"RUN!" Astrid screamed.

Looking ahead there were already Dreadwolves on the roof of the Inn where Beau, Zac, Kieran, and Luna slept.

Astrid stopped and her hands stole the flames from the oil lanterns in the streets. She blew into her hands to grow the fire and hurled it into the pack of Dreadwolves, but they weren't alone. These wolves weren't possessed, I couldn't count how many there were now, but they were violent and ruthless as they attacked and terrorized the people who walked the streets.

"WE NEED TO GO!" Eleanor shouted as she pulled at Astrid.

Astrid forced her feet through the deepening snow, Eleanor not letting go of her. I kept tightly behind them until I felt the pull of a bite snap at my cape.

I screamed as I turned and with my hands, I flung the beast into the air with all the power I could wield and dropped it into the river impaling it with the candle stick that coated the waters.

I pulled the blade Beau had given me from my boot and sprinted to catch up with the girls, my heart hammering in my chest as they reached the doors of the inn. The scent of blood and charred wood hit me first, thick and suffocating. Inside, a massacre unfolded—Dreadwolves tore through the bodies of the once-living patrons, their snarls drowning out the distant echoes of music that had played earlier. What had been a place of warmth and revelry was now a slaughterhouse.

Eleanor raised her hands, her eyes darkening as she tapped into the earth's power. With a single flick of her wrist, the splintered remains of wooden chairs lifted into the air, hovering for the briefest moment before she sent them hurtling into the beasts. The jagged stakes impaled them mid-lunge, their howls of pain cutting through the chaos. The Dreadwolves writhed in pain, their glowing eyes flickering as they clawed at the wooden spikes lodged deep in their flesh, but Eleanor showed no mercy.

We had no time to waste. More of them would come, drawn by the scent of death. We had to move—now.

"WOAH!" I exhaled as I tried to catch my breath.

"Show off!" Astrid reached for the flames in the fireplace and raised the building with one flick of her arms.

Beau was carrying Luna down the stairs. Zac and Kieran not far behind him.

"There are too many!" I shouted as the pack outside stormed slowly towards us, some in flight hovering over us, others still with flames engulfing them.

"THE EGGS!" Eleanor yelled.

"I've got them." Kieran reached her and handed her two of the eggs.

A hooded figure approached as the building around us began to collapse and the Dreadwolves stood still at his command—a mage.

"Hand her over." His voice was dark and heavy, husky even.

There was no way out of this, there were at least a hundred Dreadwolves around us. I stepped towards the mage.

Beau pulled his long-jagged poisonous blade from its sheath and put himself between me and the mage.

"Careful Fae." The mage whispered in a low growl.

The mage raised his hands, his eyes glowing with an unnatural light as he locked his gaze on the ground beneath us. With a slow, deliberate squeeze of his fingers, the earth trembled violently. Cracks spiderwebbed outward, deep fractures splitting through the ground as the cliffside groaned under the pressure. The once-solid earth buckled as, chunks of stone broke away and tumbled into the abyss below.

From across the ravine, villagers gathered outside their homes, watching in silent terror. Some stood frozen in horror, while others scrambled frantically to load their wagons, their desperate hands shoving belongings into place as they prepared to flee. The air buzzed with panic, the distant cries of frightened children blending with the low rumble of the collapsing land.

Dust billowed into the air, thick and choking, as the mage's power continued to twist the very foundation beneath our feet. Time was running out—we had to move before the earth swallowed us whole.

"Beau." I pushed his hand down, my eyes begging.

"He can kill us all right now." My eyes welled. "Take my brother to Lexia, he can win this war. Protect him." My lips trembled.

"One wrong move and you'll all be dead, Fae." The mage uttered as he backed my plea.

"You're mine to kidnap and protect." Beau's eyes watered.

I brushed his stubble once more and he kissed me gently as he snuck a secondary blade into the waist of my pants.

"I'll be right behind you." He whispered so only we could hear.

"ENOUGH! GET HER!" The mage ordered.

The largest of the Dreadwolves loomed behind me, his breath hot and rancid against my skin as he hooked his claws around my waist. He was monstrous, towering over me with a mass twice my size. His jagged talons, sharp as razors, pressed into my sides, and his drool—thick, putrid, and laced with the blood of the villagers he had just slaughtered—dripped onto my shoulder.

With a powerful beat of his wings, he launched us into the air. The force of it wrenched the breath from my lungs as the ground plummeted away beneath me. My companions became little more than dark specks, swallowed by the distance, and then, within seconds, even the village's light disappeared into the abyss below.

CHAPTER EIGHT

BEAU

She was gone before I could blink, the other dread wolves right behind her. The mage was still before me and the temptation to kill him was stronger than ever.

"Where are you taking her?" I growled.

"Varsili, where she belongs." He sneered.

The last Dreadwolf picked him up and they flew south.

I turned to the others. Zac's head was steaming now and he let out a growl so violent flames almost appeared. I walked forward and punched him in the face.

"You coward! You let them take your little sister!" I scowled. "And she told me to protect YOU!" I yelled.

"Beau…" Kieran's jaw was open as he looked into the darkness behind me.

A low growl filled the atmosphere and soon a thundering roar shook the ground.

"She wants to help." Eleanor smiled as the dragon came into the light and the villagers screamed in panic.

"We'll take the eggs to the eternal forest. Meet us there with my sister." Zac pushed me into the dragon, and she snarled at him.

I turned and looked up at the dragon. Her eyes were hardened, colder than the last time I had seen her. The thick scales forming a brow above them cast deep shadows, making her fury all the more menacing. A low, guttural snarl rumbled from her throat, her massive jaws snapping as rage coiled within her, ready to erupt.

She couldn't have gone far—not with all the fighting that had erupted around us. But this wasn't just our battle; it was hers too. Rael and his ancestors had stolen everything from her—her life, her family, the future of her kind. If her eggs never hatched, she could be the last dragon left in existence.

Dragons lived for hundreds of years, and she had likely been young when the war began. That's how she survived—small enough to vanish into the caves, to slip through the cracks where others fell. She had slithered, stalked, and crawled through the ruins, but never once had she taken to the skies.

She was large enough that she didn't have to fly over what would seem like a short distance for her.

I put my hand on her scaled face, and she rested her neck on the ground, permitting me to mount her. I climbed up using her scales as steps, gripping tightly as she shifted beneath me. She wiggled, adjusting my position until I was nestled securely between the spikes along her back.

"Hold on!" Kieran shouted up at me, his voice barely carrying over the howling wind. I nodded gruffly, my fingers tightening against the rough ridges of her hide.

The dragon flapped and fanned her undergrown wings, the sheer force of it kicking up a whirlwind of snow and ice. She crouched low, muscles jerking with raw power, and then launched forward. Each mighty step sent tremors through the ground, triggering avalanches that roared down the mountainsides in thick, blinding waves. The cliffside beneath us crumbled, massive chunks of ice and rock plummeting into the freezing water below.

She reached the edge of the village and ran out of room. Without hesitation, she leaped—her massive form tilting forward in an almost clumsy lurch. For a breathless moment, it felt like we were plummeting, not soaring. The world tilted, the sensation of falling consuming me before, with a powerful snap of her wings, she steadied. The rush of cold air slammed into me, stealing my breath, but we were no longer falling.

We were flying. And then, my own fear set in.

"FUCK!" I shouted as we plummeted to the ground.

She growled at my incredulity and steam bellowed from her nostrils. I felt her throat fill with fire as she panicked, we were getting too close *to* the ground now and I held on to whatever was closest to me—nothing but spikes and scales.

"YOU CAN DO THIS!" I yelled at her.

Flames evaded her mouth and the sheer power from the blast lifted us back into the air as the thrust from her flames gave us the pressure we needed to combat the air.

"FLAP YOUR WINGS!" I yelled once more.

She listened and flapped hard and fast, now tucking her legs higher. She was flying, and it was clear this was her first time in flight.

"Well done girl." I patted her.

She was smug and thrilled all at once and then we caught the scent of the Dreadwolves. She sped up as we flew over Tecrit, and the dread wolves could be heard howling as they turned to face us, still suspended in the sky, their smaller wings flapping harder and faster than the dragons. One dragon and me against all of them.

"Don't get cocky." I said to the dragon. She exhaled steam at my remark and whipped us closer and I was thrust forward from the jolt of her speed, she seemed to chuckle from the hitch in her throat that rumbled loudly.

"Easy!" I growled.

She inhaled deeply, her entire body vibrating with the intensity of the heat surging through her veins. The scales beneath me radiated blistering warmth, forcing me to shift uncomfortably to avoid burning my ass. Then, with a single, powerful exhale, she unleashed an inferno.

The fire erupted in a sweeping arc, scorching everything in its path. She turned from left to right, carving a line of destruction through the sky, and soon, the only thing filling the air was the nose tingling stench of burning fur and flesh. The Dreadwolves howled in agony, their monstrous forms writhing as the flames consumed them. Their wings flapped desperately, but the more they fought, the worse the fire raged.

One by one, they plummeted, their charred bodies tumbling from the sky, crashing into the trees below.

"Where is she!?" I demanded as the dragon flew us closer to them. Her throat was full of fire, her smile even more unnaturally smoldering.

And then I saw her, she was passed out in the clutches of the largest Dreadwolf, he juggled her from arm to arm and then the mage appeared sitting atop the back of another larger wolf.

They flapped effortlessly before me and the mage spread his arms and I felt a cocky smile building beneath his hood. I never saw his face completely, just his hideous grin, his pale hands and nails too long, veins sickeningly dark.

"Give her to me or I'll end you!" I growled at the mage.

"I'm almost tempted to believe you, Beau." He sneered, my name on his lips shocking me. "Oh, don't be so surprised bastard. You knew there was more than army training going on at the war camps." His voice was grisly and hoarse as the words left his lips.

"These are the soldiers?" I looked between the dreadwolves and the mage.

His smile widened. "Some of my best work!" He smiled.

"That woman wasn't trying to kill them, she was trying to fix them." The realization smacked me hard in the chest.

"Kill him!" I whispered.

The dragon raged once more, circling the mage in relentless fury. Her flames never ceased, yet they did nothing—the mage and his Dreadwolf remained untouched, immune by some dark magic that defied even the dragon's wrath. Frustration boiled within her, and she shifted tactics, abandoning fire for the raw brutality of physical combat.

With a deafening roar, she dove at them, claws bared. Her talons raked down the Dreadwolf's thick hide, sending sparks of resistance against its unnatural flesh. The impact sent tremors through my body as I tightened my grip, bracing for the next strike. Seizing the moment, I yanked my sword free and leaped into the air, lunging straight for the mage.

We collided midair, the force of the impact sending us both spiraling downward. He thrashed wildly, clawing at me with razor-sharp nails that felt like steel, piercing through my armor and into my flesh. Pain flared through me, but I refused to let go. We twisted and tumbled, locked in a brutal struggle as the wind howled around us.

Then, suddenly—I was no longer falling.

The mage plummeted beneath me; his screams swallowed by the wind. I blinked, disoriented, until I realized—Aliera was on top of the dragon now, she had caught her. Her body was weak, battered, barely holding on, but her hands were raised, her magic straining against exhaustion. With the last remnants of her strength, she kept me suspended in the air, refusing to let the mage determine my fate.

"LOOK OUT!" A Dreadwolf was gunning for them and the dragon dropped her wings so they would miss but she had trouble getting them back out again.

"SHITTTT!" Aliera screamed.

We all dropped now, and we were headed straight for the trees, and we were going down hard and fast.

"JUMP AWAY FROM HER OR SHE'LL CRUSH YOU!" I shouted to Aliera. I prayed to the gods she would hear me, and she did. She threw herself with all the energy she had towards me.

The concentration in her eyes was broken as she whipped past me, then larger gusts of wind until she crashed into me and then we were pulled apart once more.

Down below I could see the city awake and stirring from the chaos that had erupted from the Dreadwolves dropping out of the sky. Others were still on fire, some were rife with madness and attacking the humans in their treehouses. We had awoken the city of Tecrit.

We were about to hit the trees, then I crashed hard into a house, shattering the roof. People around me scattered and screamed, but they came to my aid when they realized I wasn't a Dreadwolf.

I looked up through the roof and Aliera was plummeting for the same house I grounded my feet as best I could, and I attempted to catch her.

She screamed the whole way down and her elbows buried into my ribs as we landed in a heap on the floor of the broken home. This time the villagers looked through the roof for another body to fall, but all they saw was the dragon finally flying again and biting a Dreadwolf in half.

"DUCK!" I yelled. A leg bounced off the roof of the house and into the village.

"What is going on?" A man asked.

"So sorry about this." Aliera pulled herself up sucking in a painful breath.

"Blame Rael!" I coughed as I pulled myself up.

We ran out of the house along the tree-top walks, there were bridges everywhere. Most with missing planks, and lines of rope for swinging from tree to tree.

"Are you okay?" I pulled Aliera into me.

She nodded as she wiped blood from her brow. Her shirt was ripped and there were cuts over her ribs from where the wolf had grabbed her ruthlessly.

"Are you?" She pulled my eyes back to hers.

"I'll see another day." I kissed her.

The mage stood behind her on another bridge, his presence looming like a specter in the chaos. Below, the rocky stream ran red with blood as the surviving Dreadwolves clashed with the villagers, their snarls and screams in violence.

I didn't hesitate—I jumped the bridge, landing hard among the fray, my swords already unsheathed. Behind me, Aliera's voice rang out, raw with desperation as the villagers dragged her back, pulling her from the ropes before she could follow.

I had no time to look back. The Dreadwolves had noticed me. Their bodies were ruined—exposed flesh glistened where the fire had seared through fur, their bones jutted at unnatural angles, and their wings, burnt and tattered. And yet, they did not falter. They honed in on me, their bloodlust unshaken, as they surged forward.

To my surprise, some of the villagers rushed in to fight alongside me, armed with axes and crude woodcutting tools. They were outmatched, but they were brave and stood their ground.

One, a man nearly as large as myself, took my back, holding the line beside me. The others followed suit, forming a makeshift defense, their expressions grim but determined.

Then, the Dreadwolves struck.

They latched onto whatever human they could reach, tearing, raking, dragging them down into the blood-soaked earth. I thrashed my swords into them, cutting deep, carving through them with brutal precision. The air filled with the stench of burnt flesh and the sickening crunch of bone on blade.

But no matter how many fell, more came. And soon, I was on my own. My human partner had been forced back, disappearing behind a wall of snarling creatures. Between us, the Dreadwolves still prowled, blocking the path, their eyes gleaming with hunger.

I tightened my grip on my swords. This wasn't over.

"DRAGON!" I yelled.

I needed her fire, I needed her help.

Aliera pulled away from the humans, raised her arms, and opened the trees with the power to command the wind. Moonlight and stars shone as a wind tunnel blew through the village and soon the dragon was hovering above us.

"RUN!" The humans screamed.

And they did, but the Dreadwolves stayed put. I had only done it once in my life and only when fear was at the forefront of my mind. I blinded them with hallucinations, the village wrapping around them to confuse them, it was nothing fancy, but I didn't have the power to concoct anything too complicated. But it was enough to give the humans a head start.

"NOW!" Aliera yelled.

The dragon perched her massive claws on the thickest of the trees, her wings stretching wide as she surveyed the burning village below. The air shimmered with heat, the sky painted in hues of red and gold as flames raged through the wooden pathways. Everything looked like autumn set ablaze. Then, with a deep inhale, she opened her mouth, and an inferno erupted, engulfing the Dreadwolves in a firestorm so intense that the very ground beneath them cracked from the heat.

She didn't relent this time. The blaze roared unchecked, wrapping around them like a living creature, devouring fur, flesh, and bone alike. The sickening sound of marrow sizzling and bursting filled the air, the creatures' final shrieks swallowed by the roar of the flames. The fire burned so deep that their skeletons glowed before crumbling into nothing.

And yet, the Mage stood unscathed.

Unbothered. Unmoved.

The dragon turned her fury on him, unleashing another torrent of fire, so hot it melted the very air around him. His clothes disintegrated, his hair curled into embers, his nails and skin blackened and peeled away, falling into heaps of ash at his feet. But still, he remained. Standing. Breathing. Alive.

The firestorm receded, leaving behind only a figure stripped of everything but existence itself. The dragon let out a frustrated snarl, her wings flaring as the realization set in—this was no ordinary man. He was something worse.

"What magic do you possess that a dragon can't end you?" A villager resembling a witch stepped forward and brushed past me.

"A dragon cannot decimate its ruler." He snickered.

"A mage is no ruler." She argued wildly.

"I'm not just a mage." His lidless eyes bulged at Aliera and the color drained from her face.

"Mason…" The words fell from her lips, and she dropped to the ground.

"HE'S A TITAN!" I yelled. Everyone ran for cover as I ripped Aliera from the ground and dragged her as fast as I could away from him.

The witch and the male who had helped me in the battle worked swiftly, guiding us through the chaos while Mason took his time toying with the villagers. Every step he took was a promise of destruction, a slow, deliberate drumbeat of thunder against the trembling earth. The ground cracked beneath his weight, splitting like fragile glass under his wrath. The trees quivered, their leaves rustling in fearful submission.

He drew the very forest to himself, absorbing its essence as if it had always belonged to him. Layers of earth and moss clung to his body, forming a living armor of soil and decay. Leaves fused into his flesh, dirt and bark wove together until he was something beyond human, beyond beast—something ancient and primal. Dead vines coiled into a thick, twisted beard, while gnarled branches twisted into jagged horns atop his head. His eyes, once mere embers of fury, now blazed with the raw, unrelenting fire of a dragon, casting an eerie glow against the darkness.

"Little Aliera, mommy's favorite. Don't you want to come and play with your big brother? I was always your favorite." He teased as his voice carried through the trees.

"Leave me alone!" Her voice was loud like a bang as she welcomed in her true form and stood at the edge of a doorway ready to fight him.

"You can't!" I pulled her arm.

"I'm the *only* one who can!" She fought me.

"I can too. I'm a Fae." I answered.

"Then let's kill him." Tears cascaded her puffy cheeks as the wind around her tangled her hair and whipped violently at Mason.

"I'll do it, you shouldn't have to kill your own family." I said softly.

"He'll kill you alone." She sighed.

"I'll help. I'm Luca." He said and offered his name.

"It's been nice knowing you, Luca." I shook his hand.

I pulled Aliera into me and whispered in her ear. " Get to the dragon, she's loyal to you. If I don't make it, she'll get you back to Zac." I brushed the hair from her wet face as she leaned into me, and I kissed her one last time. "Go!" I added as I walked away with Luca into the direction where Mason was still shredding the landscape.

"Fae, right?" Luca asked.

"Sort of…" I replied.

"Any special abilities?" He looked hopeful.

"Excelled healing, I can make bigger waves in the sea. Nothing that's going to help us here." I answered.

"But you can fly?" Luca quizzed me.

"Not even that, but I am a damn good assassin." I smirked as I stalked forward into the clearing where a stream ran through, and towers of stones had been made by children.

On the bridges above us families watched on as Mason threw a cloud of dust in our direction.

"How exactly do you kill a Titan?" Luca asked.

"We have to separate their head from their body." I exhaled.

"Really?" Luca gulped.

I nodded as I flung my swords around and exercised my arms. Mason would be harder to break now, the stones, roots, and vines had him wrapped and armored so well I questioned the integrity of my blades against him.

I threw Luca my straight blade, his second weapon a large axe, the blade as long as his arm, curved, it was obvious it had been kept extremely sharp.

Mason threw spears of wood at us but the families from up above blocked the majority with an old door tied to the ropes.

The door dropped to the ground beside us, sending a cloud of dust into the air. I barely had time to react before I grabbed a spear and hurled it at Mason with all my strength. He deflected it with a single flick of his finger, the force of his magic sending the weapon spinning harmlessly into the dirt.

A second figure descended from the bridge, moving with the precision of a predator. He leaped from rope to rope, landing effortlessly beside Luca. He was leaner than Luca, but there was no mistaking the sheer speed and confidence in his movements. Fearless. Calculated. A fighter who knew his own advantage and planned to use it.

"Let's kill this creepy fucker." I sucked in a breath and walked towards the earth that was in a whirlwind protecting him.

Aliera appeared behind him, she slammed her hands into the ground ripping away his defensive shield.

I ran first with my blade, and I was surprised when I made contact and actually landed a hit on him, but Mason wasn't just a Titan, he was a mage. Mages studied and learned all the power of the earth, forbidden and beyond. Our eyes locked as I sawed my jagged blade through his branch-covered arm. Before I could remove it, Luca was on him too. Soon his smaller friend was trying to hack his other arm off. Mason's disadvantage was his size now, he was slow and unable to move like a human would.

"FASTER!" A woman yelled from the treetops.

Another man leapt down to help and soon others came to help too.

It took all but one swipe of his hand to throw us all off of him, most of us winded and aching from the hard impact.

"STAY BACK!" Aliera approached. She divided the trees above her and the wind tunnel welcomed the dragon into view. Mothers held their children as they shrieked in fear of her.

"BURN HIM!" Aliera commanded.

The dragon let out an inferno of fire and Mason was now on fire.

"You'll never beat me, I'm too powerful for you sister." Mason coughed through the smoke his new body created.

She moved in silence, her approach deliberate, her gaze locked onto him with an eerie stillness. As she closed the distance, her fingers wrapped around his throat, tightening with a force that sent cracks rippling through the air. His body tensed, his monstrous armor—once an extension of the forest itself—began to crumble away, disintegrating into piles of smoldering coal at his feet.

With her free hand, she lifted her palm before his mouth, swirling it in a slow, hypnotic motion. Wisps of ethereal blue mist seeped from his lips, unraveling from within him like smoke drawn from a dying flame. His breath shuddered, his body convulsing as the very essence of his power was siphoned from him, pulled away by an unseen force. The air grew thick, charged with an energy that crackled and twisted, as if the very world around them held its breath, waiting for what came next.

"WHAT ARE YOU DOING?" I yelled.

"I'm taking away his oxygen. HURRY!" She yelled back.

He was immobile from the lack of air. I ran over with my blade in hand and whipped it across the back of his neck, his head fell in a clean swipe into Aliera's hands, and she dropped to the ground cradling the head.

The dragon leaned into the forest and picked up the body in her mouth and flew away with it.

"Where is she going?" Luca asked.

"The remains can't be buried together." I explained.

"She'll take it to the ruins, where he'll petrify into stone." Aliera said glumly.

"The head?" I asked.

"It stays here. As a reminder a Titan fell here." She wiped tears from her face as she sat up and avoided looking at the burnt head of her brother.

The people around us began to sing a lullaby. I pulled Aliera up and brushed off the dirt from her.

"Are you okay?" I asked.

"I killed him, Beau. I killed my brother." She wept.

"You didn't have a choice, he would have killed you." I assured her.

I pulled her up, her body trembling against mine as ragged breaths escaped her lips. A woman hurried over, pressing a cup of water into my hand and laying a stack of towels beside us. I murmured my thanks and dipped the cloth into the water, gently wiping the blood from her face, my fingers careful against the bruises blooming beneath the dirt.

Behind us, the dull scrape of shovels against the earth filled the heavy silence. The men worked quickly, digging the hole where Mason's head would spend eternity.

"You're safe." I whispered, though I wasn't sure if it was true.

Her fingers tightened around mine, cold and trembling. "No one is safe." she whispered back.

"Come, you need rest." Another woman said.

"Mom, give them a minute." Luca grunted.

I smiled at her, she seemed too young to be his mother, but Luca couldn't have been much older than twenty. Although he was huge, his face was youthful.

"It's okay." Aliera began to walk and follow Luca's mom.

"Thanks for your help." I shook his hand.

"You must live such thrilling lives." Passion soared in his tone.

"The less uneventful, the better. Trust me." I sighed.

We walked behind Aliera and his mom as young children began to flock into their main center and adults handed them all food and blankets.

"Where to now?" Luca asked.

"We have to find Aliera's brother. The good one." I sighed.

"Can I come?" He asked.

The question shouldn't have shocked me like it did. Luca was so full of life, and he was eager for more excitement.

"You might never see your home again…" I said. "They'll need you to help rebuild." I added.

"They've already started without me." He pointed to men on the bridges with tools and planks already mending homes and walkways.

It was a city unlike any I'd ever seen. Lanterns swayed gently from the branches of towering trees, casting a warm, golden glow over the bustling village. Children laughed as they grasped thick ropes, soaring effortlessly through the air. Each home was expertly woven into the embrace of massive trees, their sturdy trunks serving as the hearts of the homes but into the trust of the branches.

Women worked tirelessly shredding fibers from branches to craft soft stuffing for bedding, while others braided intricate ropes. Older children moved skillfully among the lower branches, gathering ripe fruit that would be shared among the whole village. It was the most harmonious civilization I had ever encountered—every task performed with purpose, every individual contributing selflessly. They thrived as one, bound together by an unshakable unity, where everything was for everyone.

"I envy what you have here, Luca." I said as I looked around.

"You do? But it's so boring." He sighed.

"It's peaceful. Don't take it for granted. All that waits outside this forest is war and bloodshed." I put my hand on his shoulder hoping he'd rethink his decision.

Thoughts passed through him, his eyes puzzled for a long moment as he weighed his options, and he gazed around his home. "I still want to see it, if you'll take me?" He smiled.

"If that's what you want, you can come. But we have targets on our backs and when an army of Dreadwolves and a powerful mage don't show up back in Varsili it'll be a hell of a lot worse. That's not all Rael had in his arsenal." I grunted.

"I can fight, you know I can." He pumped his fists playfully.

I laughed at his movements and nodded. "Go and ask Aliera." I smiled.

He ran off to find her and I began to help the villagers pile the dead bodies of Dreadwolves, ready for burning.

"Thank you!" A large man smacked me on the back, his grip firm but full of warmth. His long, braided hair swung with the movement, and his scraggly beard barely concealed the laugh lines that crinkled at the corners of his eyes. There was a rugged strength about him, but also an undeniable zest for life, carried in the rich timbre of his voice and the easy way he threw his head back when he laughed. He had the air of someone who had seen much, endured more, and yet still found joy in every moment.

"I just made a big mess." I sighed.

"Those creatures were not of this world. Tecrit is usually left out of the troubles of the world, but I know an abomination when I see one. A Wolf with a bat's wings. This animal was created by mages, not gods." He glowered.

"I'm Beau." I offered my hand as I marveled at his words of wisdom.

"Elio." He shook my hand and smiled.

"You look like you might be in charge around here?" I pointed at his large chestpiece. It was a talisman of some sort, something ancient I hadn't seen before.

"I'm just the chief, my wife is in charge." He laughed as he pointed to Luca's mom.

"Oh, you're Luca's father?" I raised a brow.

"He wants to go with you?" Elio asked.

"He does, and I'm not sure he knows what he's asking." I sighed.

"He craves the world, he always has. Then it fell out of the sky." Elio laughed. He was so carefree and friendly, unlike anyone I had ever known in Varsili.

Elio was a tall man, dark skin with black and grey hair, and green eyes. Everyone here had green eyes.

"If you agree, I'll take him. But I can't guarantee his safety." I sighed.

"I have taught him all I can of Tecrit and all I know of the world, still it is not enough. He is ready now to learn from you, Beau." Elio placed his hand on my shoulder as if he were sending me on a quest.

I agreed and shook his hand, sealing our silent understanding. For the next hour, we worked side by side, piling the bodies with steady, unspoken determination. The flames roared to life, consuming everything until there was nothing left but ash and embers. The heat licked at our skin, and the scent of smoke clung to the air, but we did not turn away.

Around us, the villagers began to dance, their voices rising in song—not out of joy, but out of defiance, a celebration of survival. The rhythmic beat of drums pulsed through the night, a stark contrast to the destruction that had preceded it.

The feast stretched across a long wooden table, overflowing with rich meats, fresh fruits, and warm bread. I sat with Elio and Luca, the weariness of the day pressing against my bones, but the warmth of the fire and the hum of conversation made it easier to breathe.

Then, Aliera emerged, fresh and clean, but still with a lingering sadness in her eyes. The draping green gown hugged her waist before flowing in soft waves, just barely brushing above her ankles. Her mahogany-brown hair, still slightly damp, cascaded in glossy waves down her back, catching the flickering lantern light and reflecting deep red hues in its strands.

For a moment, the night—the loss, the fire, the weight of everything—faded away.

"You look beautiful." I stood up as she approached me.

She smiled and sat beside me as Luca moved down a seat to allow us to sit together.

"Did Luca talk to you?" I asked her.

"Yes, I think it's a good idea." She replied.

"Great, we'll leave in the morning." I said to them both.

"Where will you go?" Elio asked.

"North, if we're lucky we might find our friends as they head for the bridge to Lexia.' I explained.

"Be careful of the pass. There's a small settlement on the peak most east. They are not friendly." Elio explained.

"Is there a way around?" Aliera asked.

"Not unless you want to swim." Luca sighed.

"Do you have a boat?" I asked.

"We do, I can sail you over." Elio nodded.

"Thank you." Aliera smiled as she ate the food on her plate.

We spent the night reveling in the feast, laughter, and music weaving through the warm air as we danced beneath a canopy of stars that trickled through the trees. The scent of roasted meats and sweet fruit lingered, mingling with the crisp night breeze. For a brief moment, the weight of the past days lifted, replaced by the simple joy of celebration.

When it was time to rest, Elio guided us to a small, empty home, nestled among the others. Though more modest in size, it held the comforts we desperately needed. Water, buckets, and towels awaited us for bathing, and a collection of blankets and pillows lay neatly on the floor. Relief flooded me at the sight. Astrid and Eleanor had carefully wrapped the eggs in our blankets before our journey, leaving us to carry nothing but ourselves. Now, for the first time in what felt like ages, we could finally breathe, even if only for a little while.

"It's small, but I'm guessing you are used to most conditions." Elio said.

"It's beautiful." Aliera thanked him.

Elio turned and walked back to his own home, and I shut the door behind us. Aliera lay in the bed, and I went to wash the ash and dirt off my body.

It didn't take her long to fall asleep, she hadn't had a good sleep in weeks, and we felt safe here. Her bedding was plush and comfortable and after a little while she even began to snore lightly.

My excelled healing had started to kick in. It wasn't too fast, but it would stop me from bleeding out if that were to happen. My bruises would always linger but the welts would be gone within a day but anything more serious took a little longer.

The water washed off the blood and dirt and I could see the red flow through the stream below that the dirty water drained into. Elio had left me a change of clothes, a grey shirt similar to my now shredded one, leather pants, boots one size too big, and a fur cape. Aliera still had her fur coat from the Fjord market, but everything else was ruined.

 It was dawn when the village began to buzz again, and we readied ourselves to leave.

Chapter Nine

ASTRID

We watched as Beau and the massive dragon made skittish, fumbling attempts to take off, their movements were unsteady with inexperience. Again and again, she beat her wings as her legs scrambled. She ran and it was obvious her forelegs weren't used to being used upright. She lurched forward, part of her instinctual serpent-like behavior from living within the tunnels for so long. She was unaccustomed to the air, the breeze that blew within it, the one thing that would carry her if she just willed it, but she had lived her life as close to the ground as she could out of fear, and now she didn't trust her natural habitat—the sky.

It was the saddest I'd felt thinking about her. She should have been soaring through the clouds, feeling the wind over her wings. They were clearly not developed the way they should have been, what should have been majestic sails lashing as she beat them, were underdeveloped bones, skinny membranes, and scars layered the tips from years of scraping through tunnels too small for her, she was a ghost of what she could have been. While she was malnourished, she did have intensely overgrown nails from all the scratching she did to widen and deepen the tunnels to accommodate her size, they sunk deep into the ground leaving a firm imprint of everywhere she had been.

Finally, they were airborne, it wasn't graceful, but we all felt relief. We watched as they flew higher and then they staggered for a short time. We could hear Beau shouting commands and prompts hoping to guide her, teaching her to use the wind as her ally, to never fight against it. She could understand us, that much was obvious as she eventually found her wings and surged through the weightlessness of open air, they disappeared now into the distance. Beau's cries lessened and then the dragon known as Azra tilted from side to side as she became the predator in the sky.

Kieran and Zac were rummaging through the rubble of the Inn and then moved on to other establishments, desperately trying to pull together items that would be of use to us on our travels, we'd lost everything except the eggs in the battle. We'd need to take a boat down the river until we passed the cliffs and reached level ground to dock. There was one ladder left that looked sturdy enough for us all to make it down. Everyone else had fled to the west village once the dragon landed and lay slaughter on the Dreadwolves, some boated, some risked the dive, and others froze in the icy water.

Eleanor was packing the dragon eggs into hessian sacks with as much padding as she could find. We'd carry one each now, except for Kieran who had the two smaller more vulnerable eggs.

"What about food?" Zac asked as he peered into his bag.

"We'll hunt or fish." I groaned, forgetting the guys hadn't had a proper meal like us girls did on our walk through the town.

Kieran grabbed a fishing net that hung on the post where the ladder hung down the cliff.

"You go first." I said to Zac.

"Why me?" He argued.

"Cause you're the male and you're a fucking immortal, you'll survive some candlestick icicles if that's your fate. Plus, I can pass you, Luna." I huffed.

He grinned and shrugged his shoulders, then scaled the wobbly ladder with ease. Zac did everything with ease, but he was arrogant, cheeky, and a pain in my ass. But gods, I loved him so much. We weren't meant for each other, when he set foot in Farkli I should have killed him, nobody was allowed in Farkli, but he wasn't alone, he was with his mother. A Farklian, she had been changed by the world, by her husband, but she still possessed all her natural Farkli beauty. She crushed herbs and mixed our potions like the master she was born to be and in the little time I knew her, I had learned a lot from her. Zac's job was to take her to Farkli and collect ingredients that could only be harvested in our lands. The soldiers came back for her, but Zac got away. His firepower was too dangerous to combat any human, even mages wouldn't challenge a fire wielder, and certainly not in Farkli. So, he stayed on the outskirts and slept in the markets scavenging food.

We met one night at the fire festival, everyone with firepower was there showing off their tricks. He was there making fireworks for children in exchange for a piece of fruit. His humbler beginning.

"GET IN THE BOAT!" Eleanor yelled as I stopped daydreaming.

Everyone was in now and I climbed down the ladder and into the boat.

"Where were you?" Zac smiled.

"With you, in a memory." I smiled.

"Oh, the one where I do this?" He trailed his hand up my thigh.

I slapped his hand and giggled. "The one where we met at the fire festival." I answered.

He pulled me close and kissed me. "Best night of my life." He said and then he pulled my hair over my shoulders.

"Still don't get the appeal…" Eleanor rolled her eyes.

"He has a gentle side." I rolled my eyes back at her.

Kieran was rowing and Zac started to help once he found the paddles.

"I don't suppose one of you witches can make this thing go any faster." Zac grumbled.

"Sorceress!" I scowled.

"No, but you know that." Eleanor smiled as she sat back and watched as he and Kieran paddled hard and fast.

"What exactly is your power again?" He joked.

Eleanor, who we affectionately called Ele poked her tongue at him. Ele was a Hearth, a sorcerer who focused on their homes, they put magic into all the things they did, and they prospered well because of it, but they had no skill in elemental divinations, nor did they worship any alters. Hearth sorceresses were the most human-like of the Farkli. Ele was essentially a healer of the body and the home, but she never tangled with anything that could harm someone. We thought of her as our physician. Her focus had always been on healing and that's where she excelled.

Kieran was similar but also with his lineage to the dragons he had bountiful amounts of knowledge of the Titans, dragons, and any history that connected them all.

We took turns between rowing and sleeping until the morning when we reached a bank shallow enough for us to go ashore.

Ele and I landed the boat, the bank was icy and slippery, and we were out in the open in a large clearing with hills on the horizon and others to our left along the coastline. We woke Zac and Kieran. Luna was out of the boat before all of us, she was sniffing around near the trees and relieved herself multiple times.

"Which way do we go?" Ele asked.

"We follow the iced mountains, they'll lead us to the bridge over to Lexia." I replied.

"Is that smart?" Kieran asked.

"We don't have a Fae with us anymore, and we're carrying Dragon eggs. They aren't going to let us in." Zac grunted.

"Then we go to Antoli." Ele said.

"We can't get to Antoli without passing over the same bridge. The Fae guard it." I sighed.

"Why?" Ele asked.

"Because it's still extremely valuable, it's full of magical relics, doorways, books. Antoli is the gateway to other worlds, but nobody can get in without a Titan." My eyes darted to Zac.

"NO!" He growled at me.

"Just tell them who you are!" I snapped.

"If I tell anyone what I am do you really think they'll just let me go? The only reason I survived in Farkli was because there are fire sorcerers, I was able to blend in." Zac became frustrated.

"He's right, they'll never let him walk away, not with *his* powers." Kieran agreed.

"Then we are stuck here, between Orman and Tecrit with those *THINGS* after us!" I scoffed.

"Let's make camp, collect some wood for a fire, and try to find some food." Zac cut the conversation off as he headed into the trees.

"WAIT FOR ME!" I yelled.

"I guess we'll collect wood then!" Ele yelled after us.

"Okay!" I yelled back as I turned to where Zac was lengths in front of me already.

I raced after Zac into the woods and immediately I felt chills and a bad aura about the way the fog didn't move as we pushed through it, the air was stale and nothing moved, nothing made any sound.

"I don't think we should be in here." I finally caught up to him and almost fell as I tried to grasp his hand.

"It's fine. Look." He flamed his hands and as he did my worst fears became real. Above us were webs as thick as ropes suspending dead animals, Fae bodies, and human bodies. They were all skin and bones, the life had been sucked out of them, and nothing but rotting corpses remained.

"OH SHIT!" Zac panicked as he looked above us.

"We need to go!" I urged as I pulled at his arm.

"THEN GO!" He turned me around and we ran as fast as our legs would carry us.

We didn't recognize where we were now, everything looked different with the flames, and I couldn't see past the trees anymore in the repetitive forest.

"We're lost." I halted us before we walked into more webs.

"We'll be okay." Zac wrapped himself around me to protect me.

"You know I love you, right?" I shuddered as the chill of the forest pinched at my skin.

"Oh, that's why you boss me around all the time." He smiled.

"Something like that." I buried my face in his chest as I felt the presence of something dark and terrifying lurking around us.

"We've practiced this a thousand times, don't be afraid. I love you." Zac whispered as softly as he could.

We had prepared for the worst, in case Rael sent soldiers back to Farkli for him, but he never did.

Zac let me loose as I turned and skimmed the trees with my eyes from every angle until I saw it, a grey spider caked in dirt, dried blood, and glistening strands of drool escaping from its maw. Its fangs, grotesquely oversized for its face, gleamed as it glared down at us with dark red eyes, unblinking and hungry

The trees above the webs were snowcapped solid, but the ground was barely wet. The spider raced from side to side in silent fluid motions, almost gliding down the webs as it tried to outsmart us. Zac flamed a fireball and aimed it just in front of the spider. It lit up a fallen log and any dry debris as it tumbled down onto the ground and the flames ignited the silky threads of web.

The spider backed away but snapped its fangs at us irritated as it scaled a tree and attempted to come from above while the fire fizzled out as it scaled closer to the snow.

"Zac..." I became worried.

"I know!" He rushed to a tree with his excelled speed and shook at the trunk as I held a flame in my hand ready to launch it at the spider.

Zac unsheathed a dagger from his side as he leaped down from the tree, his landing swift and precise. The moment his feet touched the ground, he sprinted forward just as the spider dropped from above, looming before me. I hurled the flame into the coarse hairs on its back, and the creature let out a shrill, ear-splitting screech, its legs flailing wildly as it struggled to maintain balance. The stench of singed hair filled the air.

Zac didn't hesitate. With a fluid motion, he drove his dagger deep into the spider's head. The force of his strike, amplified by his Titan strength, sent a shockwave of blackened blood spraying in every direction. The spider twitched violently, its monstrous form jerking in a final, desperate struggle before it stilled, its lifeless body collapsing into the dirt, it had succumbed to death.

"That wasn't too bad." Zac snickered as he pulled his knife out.

Then the snow above us began to crack and fall into the forest. The trees started to move, and a hoard of more unnatural movements ravaged the treetops. Our eyes locked as we realized, there wasn't just *one* spider.

"RUNNNN!" Zac yelled as we spotted a whole family of spiders heading straight for us, babies and all.

I barely had time to look around before Zac gripped me by the elbow and yanked me onto his back and he raced us through the forest twice as fast as I could ever run, but still, the spiders were just on our tails.

In the distance, I saw the light from the fire that Ele and Kieran had lit.

"GET BACK IN THE BOAT!" I shrieked.

Luna was barking erratically now and soon howling as she became afraid of the trees moving so strangely.

"What is that?" Ele asked too calmly.

"SPIDERS!" Zac dropped me to the ground, and we grabbed Luna and hurled ourselves all into the boat. We barely made it into the water when the hordes of spiders stopped at the bank snarling and hissing as their eyes watched us move down river and slowly they crept and followed us in the distance.

"Row, please fucking row." I buried my face into Luna's neck as she whimpered, and her stomach growled.

"I'm so sorry, girl. I know you're hungry." A tear escaped my eye.

"I have some old apple peels, if you have some water, I can try to spin a spell to make her an apple." Ele sighed.

"I took a tomato when the Inn caved in. Will that help?" Kieran asked.

"YES!" Ele smiled.

She put the peels and the tomatoes under a piece of cloth and sprinkled some powders over them. She had a satchel full of all her own potions and ingredients.

A few minutes later the lump under the cloth grew and she revealed four apples and four tomatoes. They weren't large and they wouldn't fill our bellies, but it was sustenance enough for now.

"Oh, thank god!" I sighed as I held out an apple for Luna. She ate it in less than two bites, and she thoroughly enjoyed it as she looked up at Ele, licked her snout, nodded a little, and then turned to look at mine.

"Here, girl. I'll have your tomato." I smiled as I bit into the tomato like an apple.

We rowed further down the river and at every turn the spiders were racing through the shadows of the shore— they were stalking us.

"Look there!" Kieran squinted into the darkness.

A glimmer of light in the distance flickered as we rowed around a sharp bend. There in the privacy of the hills was a single castle. A small castle with only a tiny fishing dock. The spiders were still climbing the hills when we landed the boat, and we had a good amount of time to run to the castle.

"We shouldn't stop." Ele said cautiously.

"There's nowhere else to go, if we go straight, we land in a swamp full of Dwellers, if we go left, we end up on Creed's borders or at the old bridge, we'll be nowhere near Aliera and Beau. This is our best shot at getting to Lexia." Zac answered.

"Ok." Ele agreed as I helped her step off the boat and Zac carried Luna to the end of the bridge.

We all ran to the front of the castle and banged loudly on the door hoping whoever was inside would let us in. The first of the spiders could be seen creeping over the hill now. We pounded our fists on the door with all of our weight, then we fell into a heap on the ground as an older woman opened the door.

"What do we have here?" She smiled.

"QUICK! SHUT THE DOOR!" Zac yelled at her.

She pressed the doors closed and sealed them with a log and chains.

"Now who are you?" She turned and asked.

"We are just travelers from Creed, we are going to visit family in Lexia." I lied before any of the others could out us.

"And what were you running from?" She squinted at me now. The look in her eyes told me she knew, and she was amused by it.

"We were being chased…" I answered.

"By what?" Her eyes widened.

I couldn't say what, if I did, she'd know I lied about where we came from. And just as I was about to lie some more three men appeared from a long dark hallway.

"We have dinner…guests." She smirked at the men.

One smiled, then they circled us, their movements eerily synchronized. Together, they guided us down the dimly lit hallway, the flickering candlelight casting long, distorted shadows along the walls. The air was thick, musty, and held the faint scent of something metallic.

The dining room we entered was grisly, dark, and dirty. The wooden beams overhead sagged with age, and cobwebs draped over the corners like abandoned lace.

Before us, on the long, worn table, sat a single plate of meat— sliced and glazed, its surface glistening in the candlelight. A two-prong fork stood upright in a thick, larger cut, as if someone had left it there mid-meal. The table linens were stained, stiff, and crusted with remnants of old meals, yet the table itself was set with the formality of a royal banquet, an unsettling contrast to its grimy surroundings.

As we hesitated, the old woman gracefully laid a napkin over each of our laps, her movements precise, practiced.

"You must be starving." she said with a smile, her voice rich with warmth that didn't quite reach her sharp, watchful eyes. She settled at the head of the table, and the three men took their seats across from us. "These are my grandsons, Axel, Jasper, and Torin." She gestured to each of them in turn.

Axel was the only one who looked remotely healthy. His long, oily dark hair clung to his shoulders, and his skin was darker than I had expected for this cold part of the world. He carried himself with quiet confidence, more composed than the others, his sharp gaze assessing rather than idle.

Jasper, in contrast, was gaunt—so thin his cheekbones and jawline stood out in stark relief. His complexion was washed out, his skin almost translucent under the dim glow of the candles. Long, limp blond hair fell around his face, and his bloodshot eyes darted nervously between us. His clothes hung off him, too large, swallowing his already frail frame. He twitched as he sat, his fingers drumming anxiously on the tabletop, making poor eye contact as if the very act of sitting still was a battle in itself.

And then there was Torin. He had long blonde hair to the middle of his back, some in braids, a strong masculine man with bright blue eyes, but he was terrifying, beastly with an overwhelming presence about him that even I as a sorceress had trouble understanding. His beard was tidy in cut, his body chiseled, his teeth sharp as he exposed them just enough. He was a puzzle, one that I could see Ele was interested in solving.

"What are you looking at?" Torin's voice was directed at me, but his eyes were on Ele.

Zac's hands heated beneath the table, his fingers resting on my thigh. I flicked him gently to say no fireworks.

"Just trying to pick if you are all brothers or cousins." I smiled.

"We are brothers." Axel interrupted.

His gaze was poisonous as he stood and began to dump slices of the meat on each of our plates.

"A fine kill, may I ask what this is?" Ele directed her question to Torin.

Jasper laughed as he peered between his brothers. His snicker almost became a howl as his volume raised in a more chaotic tone. Kieran played with the meat on his plate a little before attempting to slice it, but Ele held his hand steadily as she listened intently to the sound of spiders encapsulating the castle.

Scratching could be heard over the roof, and the room grew silent, and everyone stopped cutting and chewing. The older woman pushed out her chair and listened at the walls with her glass and Jasper's eyes filled with panic as Axel restrained him to the chair with a rope and made an insidious moment of eye contact with Torin as if he were giving him orders, then he left the room, and Axel locked us all inside the dinner hall.

"What's going on?" I asked.

"Forest spiders. You wouldn't know anything about that, would you? They don't normally come this way unless they are chasing something?" Axel's eyes narrowed.

"Are they dangerous?" I played dumb.

"If their venom doesn't kill you where you stand, and they catch you? It's said you will feel every drop of blood drain from your body before you die." He explained.

"Where did Torin go?" Ele asked.

"Torin deals with these things in Torin's way." He smiled wickedly.

Jasper rocked back and forth shaking his head as he covered his ears, and a loud roaring could be heard ripping through the air as it echoed through every part of the castle.

"Was that Torin?" Kieran asked.

Axel all but smiled while Jasper's screams almost matched the pitch of the beast outside.

"He's a shapeshifter?" I asked.

"He's *something* gone wrong, but we don't hold it against him." Axel snickered as he squeezed Jasper's shoulders too tightly and he winced in pain, his eyes watering.

"DON'T DO THAT!" The older lady shouted, she smacked Axel with a broom to release Jasper.

Jasper was clearly triggered by Torin, and whatever he was experiencing wasn't new to any of them. The scraping against the roof did nothing to ease Jasper's anxiety. Soon, we could hear roof tiles being stomped upon, shattered, and hurled with force. The screeching of the spiders grew louder, an eerie, grating sound that rattled the cutlery and glassware on the dining table.

Jasper was frantic now. He had released his grip on his ears, but his body convulsed with panic. His head snapped back and forth violently, his eyes rolling into the back of his skull with each jolt. Their grandmother gaped in horror, frozen as she watched, her hands trembling at her sides, unable to look away.

A thundering boom of footsteps and fighting could be heard reaching down the hallway as it came closer to the door to the dining hall.

Axel became worrisome in the hysteria of the spiders throwing themselves against the doors, their black sludgy blood now leaking beneath the door and into the room.

"ZAC!" I warned as I backed into him, and he noticed the blood.

"Get behind me, all of you." He looked to Kieran and Ele— we did as he said. "When I say…" his eyes made contact with mine once more and I nodded as I registered his thoughts.

The door hammered over and over, but it didn't take long to weaken. Howls and growls could be heard, but they didn't belong to the spiders, they belonged to Torin.

"What is he?" I grabbed the old woman.

"A mistake." She whispered.

"That's not enough! TELL ME!" I took her by the throat now and Axel stalked closer.

"He was the first of those flying monstrosities.' Her eyes darkened.

"A Dreadwolf?" I asked as the doors rattled some more.

"He never held the form, they didn't do it right. He was a failed experiment. They didn't know he could turn on command, but he can't fly." She scowled as Axel hovered between us.

"So, he's tame?" I asked.

"Not always…" Jasper's voice was hoarse, and his eyes bulged in fear and the pounding now shook the table before him.

The doors blew open and the spiders crept through the arch and climbed up the walls and hung from the ceiling as Torin crawled forward, he'd been stung hundreds of times and it was taking its toll, Dreadwolves even of his making weren't invincible.

Torin was frozen still now, the poison had inflamed his veins, and they swelled as they heated from the venom, his cries excruciating to the ears. His grandmother ran to his aid, but he was still four times her size and he snapped and thrashed on the ground as she dared approach.

The spiders began to descend from the walls as they set targets on the rest of us. Axel threw an oil lantern into the swarm closest to him. Jasper was under the table now, his screams only drawing more attention, the sound making the spiders more frantic.

I could feel the heat from Zac's body now, his eyes were on fire as he tore his shirt off and revealed the flames that ignited his whole body.

"GO NOW!" He yelled at everyone.

I pulled Jasper from under the table. "We have to go!" I tugged harder as Kieran pushed the table off of him.

The heat from Zac's body was enough to scare the spiders away long enough for us to get him up. Axel's jaw hung open as he stared blankly as Zac's inferno began to turn the walls of stone red with burning heat. Soon the spiders began to sizzle and drop from where they clung to the foundations of the castle.

"HURRY! Or you'll die too!" I pushed at Axel.

Their grandmother was trying desperately to help Torin up from the ground, but he was spent. Axel was tugging at him, but the room was so hot now Torin's hair was scorched, his skin melting from the poison and flames, and he writhed in pain in the heat of the room. I projected a flame shield small enough to keep the spiders away but enough that Axel, Kieran, and the grandmother might be able to help him up. It wasn't my first time conjuring a shield, but it took everything from me to do it.

"You have to turn back! I can't carry you like this." Axel heaved.

Ele had managed to guide Jasper out of the castle, and she ran back in to find us.

"Ele, can you heal him?" I yelled over the sound of the heat cracking the stone.

"OUTSIDE!" She ordered. Axel strung a rope around Torin's shoulders and together we all dragged him outside while I kept the shield up around us. Zac followed, his fire setting a blaze to any creature that followed. He was cautious this time to make sure they were all completely dead.

We were all lying in the grass now at the foot of the mountains closest to the castle. Ele was working on Torin with all the potions she had.

"Can you change him back? For good?" The grandmother asked.

"I don't have the power to strip away a mages magic. I'm sorry." She apologized.

Axel and Jasper watched as Zac melted their home to rubble and ash. Ele was furiously mixing herbs and oils as she tried to milk the poison from Torin's veins.

"There's too much." She sighed as she worked over his limp body.

"If you give up, I'll kill you." Axel held a knife to her throat.

Jasper backed into his grandmother and wept as they watched on. Ele was running out of ideas now and I didn't have the kind of magic that could draw out a poison. The sting sites had already healed from the beast's excelled healing, the venom was trapped in the body.

"We need to puncture an artery, a big one." Zac had cooled and sat beside Ele.

"His aorta?" Ele asked.

"We can drain him and then replace the blood, but we have to work fast." Zac went on.

"Any volunteers?" Axel pointed his sword between us all.

"You're insane!" Jasper scowled as Axel's sword stopped and rested on his shoulder.

"You are weak." Axel tilted his head.

"AND YOU ARE MORE MONSTER THAN TORIN!" Their grandmother's voice was loud and commanding as the field went silent, even a breath couldn't be heard as we all felt her rage, it was as if her heartbeat was outside of her chest now.

"You are meant to be brothers, yet you would sacrifice one for another?" Her lips quivered as her rage became possessed by sadness.

"Look at him, you think he will thrive in this world?" Axel argued.

"Would you thrive in this world without Torin? Is that what you are really afraid of?" She scolded him.

His jaw slackened as she walked in circles around the three of them.

"I raised you from children, you took Torin to war and returned with a monster, and we have lived in fear ever since. Look what that fear did to Jasper, he wasn't always the ghost of himself!" She hissed.

"He kept us fed!" Axel hardened as he looked over Torin.

"He fed us Tecritians!" Jasper wailed. "He was feeding us other people because there is nothing to hunt in this part of the world, that's why this castle was abandoned by Creed." Jasper's nostrils flared amidst the rage, this was the first full sentence I had heard from his lips. I gulped hard as I thanked the gods I hadn't touched a piece of that meat.

"You brought him back because he served you as a weapon! That should be you, Axel. You are the real monster." Jasper spat at him.

Torin's body began to slowly change, he became smaller. More human by the second and soon he was as naked as the day he left his mother's womb, his veins still thick with venom, murmurs filled with the pangs of aching barely able to leave his body.

"He doesn't have long." Ele put herself between them all.

"Do what you must." Jasper stood, closed his eyes, and held out his hands in a sacrificial way.

And like a rouge gust of wind the older woman tore a knife across Axel's throat, and he lost all essence of life in a matter of seconds.

"Work quickly girl!" She ordered.

Ele took a blade from Kieran and winced as she pierced through Torin's chest and gushes of dead blood left his system, his body paled, and Jasper rested Axel's throat over Torin's mouth.

"DRINK IT!" He yelled.

"This is dark." My eyes narrowed at Zac as the words left my mouth in a whisper. He nodded as he agreed.

"That won't be enough." Kieran whispered to me. He wasn't wrong. This might heal him, but he'll hunger for more soon after and I wasn't sure I wanted to be here when that happened.

Torin's hand reached around Axel's body, and he gorged on his body more greedily. Ele pulled her hand from the cavity in his chest that was keeping his artery from self-healing. She stood up right now and began walking backward towards us, her eyes never leaving Torin. But Torin was up too, and he had sucked every last drop from Axel. His eyes were not human now, they were carnal and they were searching for their next target.

Luna was whimpering as the sun crept over the hills and she ran out into the field that led to the forest of Tecrit.

"LUNA!" I called. But she was gone, she was terrified, and rightfully so, she had seen too much.

We all stood around Torin as he glanced between all his possible victims and then his eyes narrowed on Jasper.

 CHAPTER TEN

BEAU

Luca said goodbye to Elio and his mother Hina as Aliera said farewell to the children and took gifts of food and supplies to help us on our journey. It was still barely light but travelling anywhere at night was discouraged no matter what part of the world you came from.

I loaded the supplies into the bags and Elio started lugging them to the small, lonely dock barely visible through a small clearing where you could feel the sea breeze cool your cheeks, the smell of the sand lured you to the shore. On the beach were children collecting seashells and tiny crabs and mussels. Aliera looked on fondly and a warm smile graced her face as she stood still to take in the scene.

"Penny for your thoughts?" I asked.

She sighed. "It just reminds me of Varsili. I know I can never go back, but it was home." She explained.

"When all of this is over, I will take you back and you can collect all the clams you like." I smiled.

"Can I be honest?" She whispered.

I nodded and listened intently.

"I never liked the taste of them." She laughed.

I turned and grasped her hand. "You never have to eat those again." I smiled.

Elio placed the last of the food into the boat. Luca climbed in, then Aliera while I untied all the ropes. Then I heard a familiar sound— Luna's bark.

"Did you hear that?" Aliera asked.

"YES!" I turned and ran towards the sound of her voice.

Aliera had leaped from the boat, she was soaked and struggling to keep up with me. I could see Luna now, she was still far away. But I caught a glimpse of her, she was a huge fluffy black cloud and as I came into her vision she barked louder.

LUNA!" I called her to me as I stopped to take a breath. She stopped, found me in the field, and tackled me to the ground.

This was a sign of hope that the others were okay and made it over the waters from the Fjord.

Aliera caught up after a few minutes and she slumped to lay in the long grass with us. Elio and Luca walked the distance and Luna sniffed them out.

"Where are the others?" Aliera asked Luna.

Luna whined as she lay in the grass, she covered her face with her paws and had a sadness about her.

"I need you to take me to them, girl." I patted her softly.

"Somethings gone wrong." Aliera's voice became shaky.

"We'll find them!" I assured her.

"I think I know where they are, with those devils." Elio spat at the ground, irate that he'd said the words.

"Father, no!" Luca's voice filled with worry.

"That castle is the first step out into the world, this is what you wanted. This is what you get." Elio growled.

Luca followed behind Elio. Luna followed too, but her head was down and her tail between her back legs, she was afraid.

"Stay here with her." I stopped Aliera and Luna.

"If she's that scared, I'm scared you might not come back to me." She shook her head.

I pulled her long hair over her shoulder and brushed her lips with my thumb. "I always find you." I pressed my lips to hers and she squeezed against me.

"What if you need me?" She asked.

She was right, what if we did need her? She was powerful in her own right, she wielded powers that nobody else had. She was formidable beyond measure.

We walked a distance until we saw the smoke from a castle in the distance and then we ran towards it.

"ZAC!" Aliera ran faster than I thought her legs could carry her. I raced to catch up. Elio and Luca are already at the scene.

"We're too late." Aliera cried.

A rustling from behind a small network of trees caught our attention as Kieran and Ele popped their heads out with their fingers over their lips hushing us.

Fear was laden in Ele's eyes as she pointed to the corner of the inside of the gateway that led into the castle's grounds. A beast three or more times the size of a man was feasting on a pale-skinned man, two more bodies piled beside him. An elderly woman and another man.

I covered Aliera's mouth and pulled her backward. I could see Astrid in the corner of my eye with Zac. His hands were red hot and ready to fight.

I drew my sword and stalked forward. But Astrid pulled me back.

"Let him turn back." She spoke softly. I raised a curious brow.

We waited and watched as he devoured the remaining body, not even a moment later and he sat back away from the bodies and looked at what lay before him, and the beast howled. Luna began to howl with him and his eyes darted around looking at all of us. Elio was ready to attack, this had been the creature who had killed so many of his people.

"His name is Torin." Astrid informed me.

"TORIN!" I shouted.

He whipped his yellow eyes at me and his body size shrunk dramatically as he found his human form. He was a regular-looking person once he was clothed— Kieran had thrown him a cape to cover himself.

"And you are?" Torin looked at me, his voice deep and raspy.

"Beau." I replied.

"This was my family." He cried as he wept over the bodies.

"They were your keepers." Astrid corrected.

"My brothers!" He continued.

"One feared you, the others only saw you as a weapon of destruction, a hunter. They were cruel, they made YOU cruel." Ele argued, unafraid of what he might do.

Elio approached him, fearless and with a fist ready to pummel. He landed it hard into Torin's jaw and Torin was unshaken, unbothered, and nonresponsive.

"Why did you do that?" Aliera asked.

"He's been murdering people in our village for months." Luca explained.

"Axel told me to." Torin explained.

"KILL HIM! BEFORE HE KILLS US ALL!" Elio raged.

"He could be useful, he can turn back from the Dread. He doesn't fly. Beau, think about it. He could be helpful." Zac nudged me.

Now this shithead wanted to be my friend.

"We all have to agree, does the risk outweigh the benefit?" I asked the others.

"What does he want?" Aliera stepped forward and examined him.

"Why don't you ask me." His voice was a low growl.

Ele stepped forward and smiled at Torin. "I think he just wants to feel like a man." She smiled.

"You want the job." He smirked at Ele.

"Maybe." She darkened her eyes.

I was confused and looked between her and Kieran.

"*They* aren't a thing." Zac laughed.

"WHAT?" Aliera was in shock.

"Have you ever seen them even hold hands?" Zac raised his brows. "They're just friends, but away from Farkli it's safer for Ele to pretend he's, her husband." Astrid added.

"I won't cause any trouble. I can control it, I hope." Torin sighed over all the chatter.

"Then why didn't you control it when you murdered our people." Luca was furious.

"I was providing for my family, you would do the same." He replied.

"You should be punished!" Luca hissed.

"And he will be." Elio pulled a length of leather from his clothing and approached Torin.

"If you can withstand the lashings without turning then I know I can trust you to go with them." He offered the deal.

"How many?" Torin asked.

"One hundred." Elio replied.

"Oh my god." Aliera covered her mouth.

"Come on Elio, if you strike him that many times, he'll be no use to us. Twenty?" I bid.

"Fifty!" Elio argued.

"Thirty!" Zac joined in.

"Thirty-five and no less." He said firmly.

"And what if I say no?" Torin argued also as he looked between us all.

"Then you die." Luca answered as he drew a finger across his throat in a demonstration.

Torin glowered at each of us, tore off the cape, and stood with his face towards the only remaining wall of the castle that still stood.

Ele blushed as she took in the view of his body and Astrid held her hand as Elio delivered the first lashing. Torin sucked in the air and planted his feet harder, his fingers tightening around the rocks that formed the wall.

Elio delivered another blow, and another blow, and soon Zac counted out thirty.

"How are you doing?" I asked.

"How the fuck do you think I'm doing?" He growled.

His back was a ruin of torn flesh and smeared blood, each wound deep and relentless. Strips of skin hung where the strikes had landed too many times, leaving raw, exposed muscle beneath. His grip on the rocks weakened, his fingers trembling as blood coated the jagged surface, making it impossible to hold on. The pressure had been too much—his nails had begun to part from the flesh, peeling away with each desperate grasp. Still, he fought to keep hold, even as pain threatened to pull him under.

"GET IT OVER WITH!" He growled once more.

Ele was sobbing as she sat in the grass, Luna nestled against her while Astrid wiped at her own silent tears. The raw emotion in the air was almost suffocating, thick with grief and a deafening understanding that this was a necessary evil.

I admired his commitment and his bravery. He had the power to rip everyone here to shreds, yet he chose not to. Instead, he fought to survive—with us, for us. That choice, that restraint, spoke louder than any words ever could.

"Maybe you should ready something to patch him up." I said to Ele.

"NO! No potions, he endures this like his victims endured him." Luca ordered.

Elio delivered the final blow—this one deeper, more ruthless, a jagged slash that tore from Torin's neck to his ankle. The force of it sent him crumpling to the ground, his body hitting the mud and stones with a sickening thud. No cry of pain, no last words, just silence as he lay motionless, the life drained from him in an instant.

Kieran moved without hesitation, stepping forward to cover Torin's broken form with the cape once more, a solemn finality in the gesture. The air was thick with the scent of blood and damp earth, and the only sound that remained was the distant rustling of the wind, whispering through the trees as if mourning the fallen.

"He did as you asked." Kieran stood over him in defense.

"Why do you protect this monster?" Elio asked.

"He's not the real monster, it was them! They used him for their own gain. They suffered at his hand the way he had suffered at theirs." Kieran looked at the pile of bodies.

"They must have been deserters. That's why they would have to live out here alone." I added.

"From Varsili?" Aliera asked. "They would have had to sail all around Creed." She added.

"Beats going through the swamplands." I said.

"They would have been stuck here, there's no way past that forest." Zac added.

"There's nothing to hunt here, except fish." Luca added.

"Jasper ate the fish." Torin coughed.

"That's why he was like that?" Ele asked.

"He refused to eat the humans I brought back, instead he weakened and ate the fish and poisoned himself. He was dying slowly." Torin explained.

Ele moved to his side and began to bandage his wounds and sew any gashes that were too deep, which was most of them.

"How was there nothing else to hunt?" I asked.

"The spiders." Astrid answered. "They're what drove us down here. We had landed the boat after the iced mountains, Zac and I went to find food in the forest. All we found were bodies suspended by giant webs, we were lucky we weren't eaten. We all jumped back into the boat, and we ended up here." She explained.

Everyone except Elio seemed satisfied with the explanations and Ele kept working to sew Torin's back. He was in and out of consciousness.

"If this goes wrong, you're dealing with it." I punched Zac in the chest.

"No shit!" He rolled his eyes and flames danced through them.

The day stretched long, and the sun hung high past midday, its heat unwavering, yet our focus remained fixed on the task at hand. Ele had finally finished stitching Torin's back and legs, her hands steady despite the tremors of fatigue threatening to set in.

To my surprise, it was Elio and Luca who stepped forward, bracing Torin as he struggled to stand. Their support was firm but careful, a silent acknowledgment of his endurance. With slow, measured steps, they guided him toward the boat. Each step weakened from the toll of injury and survival. It would be a long walk at their pace, but no one hurried. This was a moment of resilience, a quiet battle against pain and time, and they would face it together.

It was nightfall when we reached the boat, and we loaded everyone in. We sailed with only the light of the moons guiding us.

"Where are we going?" Zac asked me.

"There's a small human settlement up those cliffs, they are kind people. We trade with them often. There is an Inn, a whore house, hot food, and a tavern. Everything travelers need." Elio laughed.

Luca's eyes beamed with excitement, and he looked to Kieran hopeful he would enjoy all the settlement had to offer together.

"Whore's cost coin, boy!" Elio laughed at Luca.

I tossed him a silver, enough for a room and five women to entertain him and feed him handsomely.

"Really?" He smiled.

"You've saved my life more than once. I can buy you a fuck and a hot meal." I laughed.

"Ughh…" Aliera scoffed at me.

I pulled her closer to me and she landed on my chest. "You pig." She laughed. "You want me." I grunted. She blushed as she kissed me, but the guilt of our relationship still boiled in my stomach.

"I just really need a good night's sleep." Astrid's eyes were heavy as she leaned into Zac who held her affectionately. He was always attentive to her, I couldn't fault him for the love they shared. It was more real than any I'd ever witnessed.

Elio landed the boat at the dock, the water lapping softly against the wooden posts. It must have been after midnight by now.

Zac and I carried Torin up the worn stone stairs that led to the inn, his weight pressing heavily against our shoulders. The others followed close behind, burdened with the supplies Elio had provided. The inn was mostly silent, save for the distant clanging of dishes from the kitchen.

Luca was the first to step through the door. The moment he crossed the threshold, he was met by a dark-haired young woman in a dirt-streaked white dress and a saturated apron, a strand of hair slipping loose as she wiped her hands against the fabric. She had a quiet grace about her, her sharp eyes taking him in before shifting to the rest of us with measured caution.

Luca, however, was speechless. And with that silence came a sprout of sheer, unfiltered stupidity. Without thinking, he placed the silver on the counter in front of her and grinned as if that alone would suffice.

The woman arched an eyebrow, unimpressed. "You're either paying for a room or trying to buy my patience. Which is it?" she asked, crossing her arms.

Zac stifled a groan beside me, and I bit back a laugh. Luca, bless him, had no idea what he'd just walked into.

"He wants a room." Kieran couldn't help but laugh.

"He can get a little more for that." She giggled.

He nodded his head aggressively thinking she was offering herself to his service.

"Lana!" The girl shouted.

Another woman stepped around the corner. She was older, much older, and she wore bright red lipstick that had smudged from the evenings work and she gave a tired smile to Luca.

"Come on then." She grabbed his hand and walked him to a room. Elio was in stitches laughing at what had just transpired.

"Now what do we do with you?" Astrid asked Torin who was barely standing on his own legs.

"I'll stay with him. I'm the healer." Ele shrugged her shoulders. He gave her as much of a smile as he could muster, and she placed a coin on the table.

"Food and water too please, some bandages if you have them." She said politely.

"I'll see what we have." The young girl agreed.

"Same but no bandages." I place a coin on top of Ele's.

We all walked to our rooms and settled in. We placed Ele and Torin between ours and Zac's room just in case. Kieran had ordered her to keep the door unlocked.

"Can I have Luna?" Kieran shrugged.

"She won't cramp your style when your visit arrives?" Zac teased.

"I'm free if you want some company." The young brunette walked down the hall and dropped the bandages at Ele's door.

"Oh, if you're offering." Kieran went red.

"Luna, come!" Aliera called her back from his door.

"Luca is going to die!" I laughed.

Kieran grabbed her hand and they disappeared into the room and the latch clicked to let us know it was locked.

"I'm going to SLEEP. Don't even think about it." Astrid glowered at Zac. They walked into their room and closed the door behind them.

Ele came out, grabbed the bandages, and yawned goodnight in our direction.

I opened the door to our room, and we entered. Luna immediately made herself comfortable by the small fire that lit up the room just enough to see it was clean and there was fresh fruit on the table.

Aliera took off her pants and weapons and climbed into the bed after taking a sip of water from the cold jug that graced the table.

"Beau?" She called for me as I undressed and placed my weapons together.

"Yeah?" I answered.

"Could we just cuddle?" She asked with a shade of embarrassment in her tone.

"Of course." I climbed into the bed and pulled her into my arms. " You look exhausted." I observed.

"You must be too." She pulled herself closer to me. The shape of her body fit perfectly against mine like she was a missing part of me.

"Get some rest, tomorrow will be long." I kissed her forehead as she buried her face into the nook my chin and shoulder created.

CHAPTER ELEVEN

ELEANOR

I collected the bandages and closed the door behind me, keeping it unlocked as Zac and Kieran had ordered. Not that Zac couldn't burn it down in a second. He thrived on the illusion of control, the sense that people respected him. Truthfully, the only reason I tolerated him was that he had married my sister. Otherwise, I found him insufferable—an egomaniac wrapped in fire and self-importance.

Torin was lying face down on one half of the bed. There was hot food on the table, a stew of sorts, and fresh bread.

"You should eat." I said.

He turned his head and looked at me with sad eyes. "I'll bring it to you if you can sit up a little." I suggested.

Torin pulled himself up slowly, breath uneven with effort. His muscles trembled, but he kept moving. I stepped in, steadying him with an arm around his back. He didn't protest, just exhaled sharply, letting me help.

We eased him onto the bed's edge. He sagged against the post, head tipping back, eyes slipping shut. His grip on my forearm lingered before he let go, exhaustion settling over him.

I offered him spoons of the food and he seemed to enjoy the meal as he held the warm bread and smiled.

"This is good." He mumbled.

"Good, food will help." I smiled up at him. He was effortlessly handsome. He was less fidgety now than when I first met him. He was less scary. The things that kept him scary weren't haunting him anymore.

I puddled with tears unintentionally and I pulled away embarrassed as I wiped my face with the length of my dress. He watched me, I felt his eyes touch me like they wanted to comfort me.

"I'm okay now." He assured me.

"I'm sorry. I don't know what came over me." I blubbered as I continued to weep.

"You're a healer, which means you're an empath. You heal with your whole heart." He held my gaze, but I couldn't reply.

I walked back to him, wiping my face clean as I sat beside him once more. His eyes flickered over me, lingering just a little longer than before. Without a word, he lifted a spoonful of food toward me, a silent offering. I met his gaze, something unspoken passing between us before I parted my lips and took the bite. His hand lingered for a moment before he pulled back, watching me as I swallowed.

We fell into a slow, deliberate rhythm—him feeding me, then himself, the spoon passing between us like a quiet promise. Each bite carried an intimacy neither of us addressed, but it was there, woven into the wholesome, gentle exchange. His fingers brushed mine when he passed me a piece of bread, the brief contact sending warmth curling through me, deeper than the food could.

By the time the bowls were empty and the last of the bread was gone, the space between us felt different—closer, charged. Neither of us spoke, but the silence hummed with meaning, with something just on the edge of becoming. He didn't look away, and neither did I.

Whatever this was, it had begun.

"You should rest." I stood up and fluffed his pillow. I was trying to wipe the enchantment off my face, but I was bewitched.

"I will." He replied. The same smile captured his gaze as he watched me fluffing those pathetic pillows.

"Let me bandage you first." I murmured, gathering the cloth and kneeling before him. He didn't hesitate, he removed the cape and sat before me, bare, raw, and utterly vulnerable. I accidentally gasped as my gaze flickered downward, and before I could stop it, a warmth crept up my neck. I was impressed—but I wouldn't put him through unnecessary pain by acting on the thoughts racing through my mind. Still, a small, traitorous smile broke free before I could contain it.

He caught it, and his own lips curled in response, amusement dancing in his tired but sharp eyes. With an easy, knowing movement, he placed a hand in his lap, covering himself just enough to allow me to focus.

I steadied my hands and began wrapping the bandages around his torso, careful with every pass. The heat of his skin beneath my fingertips sent a slow current through me, but I forced myself to concentrate. I worked in steady circles, securing the cloth over the worst of the wounds, my breath measured, my focus absolute.

Then his hands moved—a soft, grounding touch as they rested on my hips, his fingers splayed, possessive yet gentle. A silent acknowledgment. A quiet pull toward something unspoken.

I didn't move away.

"Why are you helping me?" He whispered.

"You deserve a chance, what you had back there wasn't living." I sighed.

"You said you can't fix what I am, why risk your life with me?" He asked.

"Maybe you don't need to be fixed?" I answered.

"What do I need then? What can contain me?" He exhaled.

"Love?" I slipped the word out unintended.

"You?" He smiled as his hands traced up the small of my back now.

I cupped his face gently, my fingers trailing over the roughness of his jaw. His eyes—those piercing blue depths laced with flecks of gold—held me captive. There was something untamed within them, something raw and dangerous, a reminder that no matter how tender this moment felt, violence still lived inside him, just beneath the surface, waiting.

I nodded a little as he pulled me into him. "I think we can control it, if you're willing to try?" I questioned.

"If you're willing to take a chance on me, I'll do anything you say. I promise you can trust me, Ele." He whispered.

"Good." I brushed through his hair.

"You're a remarkable woman." He smiled.

A bang at the door set off a growl in his throat and Zac burst through the door.

"Seriously?" I grunted in Zac's direction.

"Just making sure you're alive. He looks like he wants to eat you." Zac joked.

"I do, but not in a violent way." Torin smiled.

"Eww! That's my sister-in-law." Zac laughed.

Beau appeared behind him and squared Zac with his eyes in a way only a Fae can. Beau was tolerant of Zac, but he didn't take shit from anyone.

"Let them sleep." Beau shuffled Zac into the doorframe.

"I was joking." Zac grunted.

"You know you make people really uncomfortable? You can't just barge into our rooms and disrupt the peace." Beau scolded him.

"You're lucky my sister likes you so much, I'd smoke you in a fight." He punched at the air in front of him.

"You think so? No powers? You really think you could beat me?" Beau was larger than Zac and he hovered over him, his shoulders broad, and Torin and I became invested.

"Yeah, of course I could." Zac's voice lowered.

"Tomorrow, out in the stables. I'm going to humble your Titan ass." Beau laughed as he walked away.

"Sweet dreams fairy boy." Zac laughed.

The door slammed behind them and Torin's eyes were wide. "So, they don't like each other?" He asked. I burst into laughter before I could answer.

"I've waited for the day someone would bring him back down off his cloud." I confessed. "He's a pain in the ass!" I blurted.

"But the power thing?" Torin asked.

"Beau is a Fae, but he's been clipped which took away a lot of his powers, he still retains the strength and speed but, Zac is a flame wielder, a Titan! He controls fire. He's insanely strong and fast, everything is elevated for Zac, but he can enter an agreement to fight fairly. And he just did." I smiled.

"Dinner *and* a show." Torin smiled.

I was still wrapped in his arms, my hands were on his shoulders now and I couldn't help running my fingers over his biceps.

"We should get some sleep." I stuttered.

"Yeah, we should." He nodded as he loosened his arms.

I climbed into bed beside Torin as he lay on his stomach off of the wounds and he turned his neck to face me. "I think you're remarkable too." I whispered as his eyes closed.

Sleep had come in waves—some moments restful, others haunted by nightmares. I was no stranger to them, but these were different. They bled into my consciousness, thick with the deep burgundy of spilled blood. I didn't know what they meant, if they meant anything at all. Still, they left a lingering unease in my chest.

I brushed my hair from my face and turned onto my back, exhaling softly. Torin was still asleep beside me, lying flat on his stomach. The dim light revealed the slight shift in his bandages, the white of them now marred with fresh oozing puss. Concern tightened in my chest. I reached out, resting the back of my hand against his forehead. His skin was too warm—much warmer than it should have been.

Frowning, I pressed my palm more firmly against him, hoping I was wrong, but the heat beneath my touch confirmed it. He was burning up.

"Torin!" I nudged him gently.

Torin lay as still as stone, his body tense beneath my touch. I worked carefully, peeling away the bandages, but they clung stubbornly to his skin, the dried blood fusing them to his wounds. My stomach twisted at the sight beneath—the stitches had inflamed, the surrounding flesh red and swollen, some areas already glistening with the telltale signs of infection. A thick heat radiated from his back, a fever brewing beneath the surface.

My jaw tightened. The thread I had used was likely contaminated, and time was not on our side. Dread or not, he was still part human, still vulnerable to the slow decay that sickness could bring. I needed to act quickly, or the infection would take hold, and no amount of strength or stubbornness would save him then.

I sharpened my knife tip to be as lethal as it could be, I'd need to release over a hundred stitches and time wasn't on my side.

"ASTRID!" I screamed hoping she'd hear me.

Moments later I heard feet pounding down the hallway and Astrid crashed into the door and threw herself through it in a panic.

"What happened?" She was nervous as she approached.

"The thread must have been dirty. I need you to help me cut it out. I handed her a secondary knife.

"WHAT! No, I'm not a healer." She stepped back and slammed into Aliera.

"Here, I'll help." Aliera leaned down beside the bed and started cutting the threads and pulling them out while I set to work cleaning the one mammoth wound it had all become.

Beau and Zac entered the room curious and probably ready to beat each other up.

Torin began to stir, but he wasn't aware of anything happening. I offered him a tea to help him sleep but he refused.

"No, I want to watch their fight." He looked to Beau and Zac with a lazy grin.

"You need to rest, I'm sure they'll wait for you to heal." I assured him as I stared between Zac and Beau and they both shrugged.

"WHAT FIGHT?" Astrid's eyes darkened and Aliera stood up and crossed her arms.

"Zac?" Aliera had fury in her breath.

"Why do you automatically assume it's me?" He laughed awkwardly.

"Really? You think we don't know you?" Astrid scowled.

"Let me beat his ass, he needs to be taken down a few levels." Beau laughed.

Aliera and Astrid whispered between themselves and seemed to nod.

"Fine, but only till the first blood is drawn, no powers, no broken bones." Astrid said firmly.

I continued my work on Torin and shook my head as I wiped away pus. Aliera was mixing salt with water so I could cleanse the area properly and Beau went to fetch more thread, this time to be boiled.

"Hang in there." I whispered to Torin. His hand squeezed mine.

Aliera stared between us and smiled her beautiful gentle smile, her eyes golden, her volumized mahogany hair draped romantically over her shoulder. She was beautiful, a strong woman, she was nothing like what I expected when Zac first told us he had a little sister. I had pictured someone entirely different—a cheeky, impulsive girl, spoiled by her status. A female version of Zac, brash and relentless. But Aliera was nothing like that. She carried herself with grace, with a resilience that spoke of battles fought in silence, of burdens shouldered without complaint. She was fierce without arrogance, kind without naivety. And in that moment, I realized just how much I had underestimated her.

"You care for him?" She sat beside me.

I nodded. "I know it seems stupid to you." I sniffed.

"It doesn't. You have a tenderness about you Eleanor, it's so rare. You never forget to be kind. I admire that about you." She smiled.

With a clean rag, I dabbed the saline mixture over Torin's back and tried to avoid wiping against the more shredded areas.

"Arghhh!" He groaned.

"Sorry, it needs to be done." I squeezed his hand and felt the calluses forming on his fingers and panic raced through my veins as I felt the bones in his hand cracking.

"Please don't turn." I whispered to him as Zac stalked closer.

"LEAVE!" I stood and straightened as I pushed Zac towards the door.

"BEAU GET HIM OUT!" I yelled.

Beau pushed Zac out the door and Astrid went with them. Aliera stayed.

"I hope you know what you're doing Ele." She huffed.

I soaked a fresh cloth in saline, wringing out the excess before carefully pressing it to the raw wounds on Torin's back. The heat radiated from him like a furnace. Beside me, Aliera worked swiftly, her fingers steady as she plucked the final threads from his torn flesh.

The moment the last stitch was removed, Torin roared. His entire body tensed, muscles rippling with the force of his pain. His back arched violently, and I heard the sickening crack of his neck as his head snapped back. The sound sent a chill through me, but I forced myself to stay still, to keep my grip firm.

Then, just as suddenly, he pushed himself upright. His breath came in ragged gasps, his chest rising and falling as he fought for control. When he lifted his head, his eyes were no longer the piercing blue I knew—they burned a feral, unnatural yellow, bloodshot and wild. A low growl rumbled in his throat, vibrating through the space between us, raw and untamed. I swallowed hard, keeping my hands at my sides.

"Torin?" My voice was careful and measured.

He didn't answer. He just stared, his pupils dilated, his entire body rigid with something far more dangerous than pain.

"TORIN! Control it, please." I begged.

"I can't bear the pain." He said through fanged teeth.

"Well, if you don't, they will kill you." Aliera stepped away towards the door trying to pull me away, but I swatted her hand from my shoulder.

"NO, I'm staying with him. You would stay with Beau!" I argued. Her expression saddened as she latched the door locked with the three of us inside.

"GET OUT!" Torin cried as his shoulders expanded and wounds on his back tore open.

I dropped to the ground, unsure if it was fear-driven or if I'd just given up.

"I don't want to hurt you…" Torin could barely push the words out as his face cracked and his muzzle appeared, all the things about Torin had disappeared into the body of a botched Dreadwolf.

Just like that, he was gone, he was different, formidable—he was a weapon.

"NOW, we have to go, Ele." Aliera didn't hesitate now. Torin wasn't moving, he was healing. The Dread had the power to self-heal but as a human, he was just a human. But Aliera was spinning her hands ready to blast him with cyclonic winds if he got too close.

"Wait…" I grabbed her wrist.

Torin's back was almost fully healed now, and he collapsed on the bed.

"ELEANOR!" Aliera shouted as I ran to him.

His body began to morph once more, back to his human state. I shook him as he came back to consciousness. He rolled over on the bed and stood up in front of me like nothing had happened.

My eyes scanned him as I forced him to spin around and show me every inch of his naked body. "You're okay!" My jaw dropped.

"I promised you could trust me." He smiled.

"You weren't too sure for a moment there." Aliera scowled. "And you're even luckier Elio left last night. He would have you whipped again." She added.

"I would have endured it all, I intended to. But someone tried to poison me with their dirty thread." He snickered at me.

"I didn't know I swear. I'm so sorry." I shied.

"You couldn't have known." He said forgivingly.

"You're okay now?" I looked over him one more time.

"I'm going to give you guys some privacy." Aliera stepped out of the room.

I walked to the door and locked it so nobody else could interrupt us. As I strolled back, Torin had laid back on the bed and he watched me with his intriguing eyes as I moved towards him. His hands covered his shaft even though he could have easily pulled the sheet over himself.

"You can safely hurt me in other ways now if you like." He grinned.

"You're going to get me in so much trouble." I smiled as I climbed onto the bed and sat on top of him, he peeled my dress off of my shoulders.

"I won't tell." He pulled at my neck and kissed me as I knotted my fingers in his golden hair.

He untied the laces of my dress and pulled it off over my head as I sat before him naked.

"About time I got to see *you* naked." His left hand stroked the small of my back, his right hand playing ever so gently with my breasts as I positioned myself over his erection and he slid inside me gently.

"UGHH." I gasped as he filled me effortlessly. I thrust myself gently up and down him as he rocked into my rhythm, his hands on my ass now as he sucked at my breasts while I pulsed my way to my first orgasm.

"Cum for me." He began to circle my clit with his thumb as he lay back into the pillows and he watched me get myself over the edge, rocking into him greedy for his body.

"FUCKKK!" I screamed as the warmth pounded inside me and everything became tender to the touch.

He flipped me over and kissed trails down my body, making his way to my clit. He sucked hungrily at my swollen lips as I wriggled into the tickling of his beard. He inserted two fingers and flicked softly with his thumb making me want him over and over.

"How does it feel?" He gazed into my eyes as I pulled him against me.

"I want you inside me." I breathed hard.

He pulled his fingers out and stroked himself teasingly as I rubbed my clit, still not ready to let go of this feeling. But he couldn't resist the urge as he slid between my legs and stretched me one more time.

"You feel so good." He kissed my neck.

"I don't ever want to leave this room." I ran my fingers over his strong arms and bucked to let him know I wanted him deeper. He was cautious not to go all the way, but I wanted to feel every inch of him inside me.

"Slowly, I don't want to hurt you." He became gentler as he watched his length sliding in and out of me, gauging how much of him I could take.

"Is that okay?" He asked as he pushed deeper.

"Mhmm." I mumbled as I craved him even more.

He slid in some more and I felt the crash of his thighs on mine now. "Am I hurting you?" He cautioned.

"I like it." I assured him.

"Keep going." I begged.

He pounded into me softly in ways I'd never been fucked before, I was no virgin, and I could tell he wasn't either. He lay over me now, the weight of his body warming my own and I felt double the joy as he ground against my clit and hit me deep inside where it counted most.

"Cum for me." He kissed me.

"I want you to do it with me." I kissed him back.

"I'm ready.' He quickened his pace, and our bodies collided over and over again as we exploded in euphoric efforts.

"Holy shit." I puffed as I squeezed my muscles greedily wanting all his juices inside me.

Torin climbed off of me and pulled out gently to lay beside me. He pulled me into his arms, and we tangled our bodies together as we caught our breath.

CHAPTER TWELVE

BEAU

Zac and Astrid had listened at Ele and Torin's door the whole time. At first, we thought he was going to attack her, but it turned out to be a very different attack.

"You guys done yet?" I glowered.

"You can't tell me you weren't worried too?" Zac asked.

"Of course, but we'd know, and we'd react accordingly. You don't need to stalk her door and listen to that." I shook my head in disgust.

"ARE YOU KIDDING ME!" Ele ripped the door open wrapped in a sheet, Torin lay on the bed with another sheet over him, sipping at a glass of water. 'You know these walls are paper thin? I heard all of that!" She said frustrated.

"You're welcome." I knew and that's why I said all I did.

Ele glowered at Zac and Astrid, but they were unbothered by her reaction. She was just another little sister to them, the same way Aliera was.

"Get dressed, we're leaving!" Astrid ordered both of them.

We dressed quickly and met outside our room. Once ready, we crossed the tavern to find Luca and Kieran. They were in a single room, each lying beside a woman—one older, one younger—both asleep in their beds.

"Surprised that we didn't hear you lot, too." Aliera poked her head in and grinned.

"Ughh, what time is it?" Luca rubbed his eyes.

"Time to go!" Aliera spun on her heel and went to the kitchen in search of food.

"Come on. Meet you outside in ten minutes!" I pounded my fist loudly on the door.

On the outside of the Inn were benches along the wall and tables to eat at, a small stable with about ten horses and a flock of chickens.

Kieran was out first, he gently placed the pack with the dragon eggs on the table.

"Have a good night?" I laughed. He rolled his eyes at me and nodded, and I smiled back in approval.

Aliera came out with a bowl of fruit and boiled eggs for everyone to eat.

"I'm no cook but I can boil eggs!" She said proudly of herself.

"You did good." I rubbed her back as she sat beside me.

Her eyes looked me up and down and she softened and slumped into my arms, and I wrapped myself around her.

Kieran went to catch a chicken to cook and now we were alone.

"Are you okay?" I rubbed her arm.

"I just want to be able to choose!" She was angry.

"Choose what?" I was confused.

"I want to choose you! I want you to choose me the way Ele and Torin did. Fuck Rael, fuck the bloodline. I want what I want, Beau I want all of you. Fae or not, Titan or no Titan." She gasped.

I stood up and stretched my arms behind my neck. I puffed out a breath and her face was down on the table now, her hands wrapped around her head.

"FUCK YOU!" She screamed at the wood. She meant me, I had been too delayed in saying anything at all.

"Aliera…" I started but I was caught off guard and Luna was whining now.

She raised her head, and the table flipped in my direction, her eyes white with the wind and I fell back and sat on my elbows.

"GIVE ME A MINUTE!" I yelled.

"Why do you need a minute? If it's not at the forefront of your mind, then it's not important to you!" She growled.

"It's *not* important right now, Aliera! It isn't, you forget we are trying to stop a war. We are trying to stop a dynasty that wiped out your whole race, not empower them by falling in love with each other! Stop acting like a teenager and think straight!" I scolded her.

Ele and Astrid stepped outside and soon the others followed behind them. Aliera's face was wet with tears, and I was desperate to comfort her, but I was the reason for her misery.

"What did you do to my sister?" Zac rushed over and pushed me.

"It's none of your business." I shoved him back.

Luca, Kieran, and Torin all took a seat on the benches while Astrid and Ele spoke to Aliera.

Zac pulled off his weapons, and his shirt, and pounded on his chest. "I'm going to kick your ass!" He growled.

I wasn't in the mood for this idiot's bullshit, and I wasn't going to stroke his ego. I dropped my weapons, and he immediately got in my face. He took a swing at my face first and I stood unrattled before him as he threatened a second hit.

"COME ON! You know you want to hit me." He teased.

I did want to hit him, but if I started hitting there was a chance I might not stop. I hadn't been trained to stop. I pulled off my jacket, and then my shirt, punched out my arms, and stretched my muscles. Till now only Aliera had seen my back. I could feel the tension rise as everyone stared and made small talk about the hatched scars I wore on my shoulder blades where I should wear large terrifying wings.

Zac stalked towards me once more and I thundered a mighty punch down into his face. Blood splattered over the table, and he dizzied and slumped onto the bench across from the others.

"Beau wins." Kieran announced and clapped.

Everyone else clapped softly and the chatter became silent as I pulled on my clothes and weapons.

"Time to go!" I growled.

I began walking without the others, the iced mountains in the distance were the only landmarks I needed to follow, they would take me to the bridge, and we'd be there in a day if everyone kept pace.

Torin ran to my side, he was faster than the others and kept up with me. He was the same height as me but a little burlier than I am. His blonde hair was in two twists that sat over his shoulders and a rugged beard two shades darker than his hair.

We slowed our pace so the others could keep up and we only stopped for breaks twice. Once, so the girls could go to the toilet and the second so we could all eat some of the food Elio had given us.

The girls all stuck together even though Ele and Torin's eye flirting was making the rest of us sick, and Luca and Kieran had some weird new bond after they shared a room with those two women.

I could see the bridge now, it was still well into the distance, but it was visible because of the large towers that protected it. "We're almost there." Astrid smiled.

"Then what?" I groaned.

Aliera rolled her eyes at me.

"We get permission to hatch the eggs, then we go back with dragons and convince Lexia to help Orman kill off Rael." She answered.

"Kill him off, and his sons…me?" I looked at her.

"You know what I meant!" She sighed.

"Can you two stop? One minute you're obsessed with each other and now you want to kill each other. What the fuck is the problem?" Ele put herself between use.

Aliera and I glared at each other for a long minute until she snapped. " Let's just get this over with, if we survive it might be worth answering." She paced forward ahead of us all.

An hour later we reached the bridge. Archers from the towers caught our attention and met us halfway across the bridge. Each of us was questioned and once Kieran showed them the dragon eggs, we were all escorted to Lexia by a horse-drawn carriage.

It was magnificent, larger than any city I'd ever seen, with the exception of the Titan ruins. Fae were flying everywhere, curious teenagers swooping over us to peer into the carriage. Each Fae's wings were different. Some would sparkle like rainbows and raindrops, others clear and small, others feathered. A lot were bigger than the body they carried, long and luscious, velvety feathers that never dragged but hovered just above the ground.

The city stretched toward the heavens, its towering spires piercing the clouds, their peaks lost in mist and golden light. Bridges of shimmering crystal arched between them, adorned with cascading vines that bloomed with luminous flowers, glowing softly like captured stardust. It was breathtaking—unlike anything I had ever seen. Judging by the awe in my companions' eyes, they felt the same.

The towers, each unique in its shade of pearl, gleamed with iridescent hues, reflecting the shifting light like mother-of-pearl kissed by the dawn. A vast river coursed through the city; its waters infused with silver streaks that glowed beneath the surface. It wound through homes and structures, its current whispering against stone and wood, before tumbling over the edges of the city in magnificent waterfalls. The cascades fed into the lower levels, their misty spray catching the light, weaving ribbons of water into the very heart of the city itself, providing life and magic to all who dwelled within.

"This is incredible." I smiled as I took in the tall ivory iridescent skinny towers, my eyes following the water as children played together and splashed guards and quickly swooped away.

"Lexia is a one-of-a-kind city." One of the guards agreed.

"Is Orman like this?" I asked.

"Orman has been battered, it was great once. Not anymore." One guard sighed.

We were brought to a large tower where nine large thrones together formed a circle in the large room. Through the floor-to-ceiling openings, a waterfall was visible. Fae swam in the falls and watched as we all sat in the middle of the room and soon, they perched on the stones to watch and listen.

Nine beings, all came to the room and sat on the thrones. Representatives from all of the corners of the Dunya and small Fae children brought them all goblets of wine.

"What an interesting company you keep." A female said to me. She was Fae, tall with dark hair like mine, her wings were large grey feathers, horned at the tip, her nails just as sharp.

"Titans?" She looked to Zac and Aliera as she sniffed the air around us.

I nodded. She looked at the others and coughed as she came across Torin. "Who brought their dog!" She scoffed. Luna whined at the comment and sat between Aliera's legs.

"Not you, pup." The Fae woman called Luna to her, and she ran over and licked at her face.

"You have dragon eggs!" The male Fae said excitedly.

"We have five eggs." Kieran answered.

"Where did you find them?" He asked.

"They were given to us by the female herself." Kieran was proud of this.

"Azra lives?" He stood up against his throne.

"That's her name?" Aliera asked.

"The last female, she hasn't been sighted in over a hundred years." The Fae explained.

"The last we saw she was flying back to the ruins after fighting the Dreadwolves." I explained.

"And none followed her?" He asked.

"They were all under orders from a mage." I answered.

"A mage? What happened to him?" He asked.

"He perished at my hand." Aliera replied.

"And his identity?" He pressed.

"Titan, Mason Gray. My brother." She dropped her chin.

"YOU DIDN'T TELL ME THIS!" Zac's hands flamed and his anger was set on Aliera.

Her power fanned his flames to nothing, and she didn't say a word more. But her body language was all I needed. What happened to Mason still pained her deeply.

"Orman wants peace with Varsili but that won't happen with Rael on the throne. We need a conqueror!" A human said.

"You need dragons. You won't conquer anything while Rael is turning soldiers into Dreadwolves." I argued.

"He's turning humans?" The Fae from Orman asked.

Torin put his hand up and sighed. "I was brought to his camps and experimented on, they've since been able to make the soldiers turn, once they turn, they can't turn back, and they can fly now." He explained.

"This can't continue, his mages have gone too far!" One shouted.

"What does Farkli have to add to this?" The Fae woman asked.

"Farkli wants to remain isolated. In order to maintain that the Dunya needs peace." Astrid spoke loudly as she stepped away from the group and into the circle closer to those who were speaking. "You are wasting time with this. Send us to the Sonsuz so we can hatch these eggs." She shouted and her voice echoed through the tower.

"You will need a Fae to get past Thane, he doesn't tolerate other species. Lexia embraces it, but not all do." The Fae woman stared at me.

"Why should we let you live? You are not Fae." The Fae from Orman laughed.

Zac's eyes flamed as he stepped forward, he circled me now and our eyes exchanged what might happen next, he had a plan. He pushed me forward, kicked me in the back of the legs, and ripped off my shirt in a dramatic scene that exposed the massacre on my back.

Dead silence, gasps, and disgust filled the room. Even those swimming in the falls shrieked in fear. He exposed my back to the room, my shoulders flickered the only remaining nubs below the hatched scars, the silence was numbing as I kneeled on the ground and each of the Fae took flight, hovered over me, and examined my old wounds.

"Who did this?" The Fae woman asked as she landed before me.

"Rael. Who else?" I said with sarcasm.

"I've never seen this before." The humans and Fae talked amongst themselves.

"Your powers?" The woman asked.

"Barely any." I sighed.

"That's not true!" Aliera stepped forward and knelt beside me. "Beau is the greatest assassin in Varsili, he has Rael's favor. He's the heir to the throne if you count bastards." She held my hand, and I felt all the tension between us diminish as she looked down at me proudly.

"And you were his final catch… what an epic love story." The Fae of Orman teased.

"We can't allow Rael to butcher Fae like this!" The woman growled loudly silencing the room.

"Why should I align with a Titan?" The Fae from Orman groaned back.

"We all have the same enemy now!" Zac sparked flames from his fingers.

"What do you gain?" The woman asked.

"We are the only ones who can access Antoli. If you want what's there, you'll have to trust us." He looked at Aliera and she sighed.

Aliera knew there was magic there, magic that was too strong for anyone without the protection of masses of Titans.

"We will fight with you if the Titans will fight with us." The Fae woman said to the Fae from Orman, and he looked to the other council members for approval.

"So, we begin the Dunya war." The humans of Creed sighed.

"Beau, you will travel to the Sonsuz Forest with the dragon servant and the Titans. The others will rest here and enjoy the comforts of Lexia." The Fae from Orman announced.

"WAIT! I can help." Astrid argued.

"The Sonsuz is a healing forest, Sorceress. I fear your blood is human, the forest will cleanse you of your powers." The Fae woman explained.

"I'll look after them." Kieran hugged her.

The rulers left the room except for the Fae woman who circled Aliera and me.

"Hatch the eggs, win the war. Become a king! With a Titan for your bride. An interesting turn in history. The moles would have never predicted this." She smiled.

I queried her thoughts with my eyes and lost my focus when Zac tried to confront Aliera.

"You killed our brother!" He threw her into a wall shattering the stone that stopped her, leaving her in a heap on the ground. Guards rushed in but were quickly stopped when she sent a gust of wind at them.

She pulled herself up and ran at him, catching him in a wind tunnel. Astrid used her powers to blind him.

"I didn't have a choice, he wasn't Mason anymore! You didn't see what he could do, Zac. It wasn't an easy decision, and I needed the help of a dragon to do it." She tried to explain.

Ele used her powers to ice his hands to the point of freezing and together they all put him down and one by one they released him.

"You didn't have to kill him." Zac sat defeated on the ground.

"He was too far gone, you were face to face with him in the Fjord and even you didn't recognize him." Aliera argued.

Zac's face changed, and his jaw slackened as the realization hit him. He didn't know him anymore, he hadn't known him or what Rael had done to him.

"I need time." He pointed at Aliera in a flicking motion.

She nodded her head to agree, and he walked out into the city streets where a horse and carriage waited for us all. We were being taken to the bathhouses.

We were led south of the city, where the land sloped gently toward the cliffs overlooking the Isle of Korsan. Here, nestled into the hillside, lay the bathhouse—not a structure of wood or mortar, but a masterpiece of ancient stonework, seamlessly woven into the earth itself.

The chambers were carved deep into the rock, each room a testament to the skill of its creators, etched with intricate patterns that seemed to hum with the whisper of old magic. Steam curled from the natural pools within, carrying the scent of minerals. The water shimmered under the soft glow of bioluminescent veins in the stone, casting an ethereal glow across the smooth surfaces.

It was more than a bathhouse—it was a sanctuary, untouched by time, a place where the weary could surrender to the embrace of the mountain itself.

Each room was a sanctuary, carved from smooth stone with its own private stream, the water crystal clear and flowing over polished pebbles that shimmered like scattered gems. A grand bed sat just feet away from the gentle waters, draped in soft silks that caught the flickering candlelight.

A large table was set with bowls of fresh fruit, warm bread, and golden honey, the scent of lavender and spice lingering in the air. Candles burned steadily, their soft glow casting dancing shadows across the walls. Above, through a hollow archway, the distant melody of a harp drifted down from a higher chamber, the notes weaving through the air like whispered magic, filling the space with an ethereal tranquility.

Servants brought in towels and white gowns, fresh selections of clothing, sandals, boots, scented soaps, jewels for Aliera to wear, and a note for us both to read welcoming us to the establishment.

"The bells will sound when dinner is ready." One of the servants informed us.

"Thank you." Aliera smiled.

The others had run off to find their own rooms. There was a common room for us all to share meals and a large stable inside with horses of cream and white shades. Simply stunning in appearance and nature.

"It's so magical here." Aliera smiled as she stroked the mane of the white horse.

"Shall we bathe?" I gently reached for her hand from the other side of the horse.

She nodded and we walked back to our room where the soaps were now beside the running stream on a silver plate, towels resting beside it.

"How deep do you think it is?" I asked.

"Not deep enough for you to jump!" She replied as she removed her clothes, sat on the edge of the smooth stones, and let her long wavy hair out, it glimmered a little more purple here under the sunlight.

I stepped into the water, the warmth enveloping me as I moved toward her. She watched me closely, her gaze tracing every movement as if etching the moment into memory.

Without hesitation, I pressed my torso between her thighs, the heat of our bodies mingling with the steam rising around us. She reached for me, her fingers threading through my hair, undoing my braids with slow, deliberate care. Her touch lingered, tracing the pointed tips of my ears, curiosity and reverence blending in her movements.

"Your ears aren't as pointed as the other Fae's." She said with observation.

"I'm only half Fae." I shrugged.

"They still think of you as one of them." She inched closer.

"I'm not so sure." I sighed.

"They are going to war for you." She slid her hand over my cheek.

"They have other agendas that the war serves." I whispered.

She gazed around the room and sunk herself into the warm water. Standing together, her head only met my chest, and she reached to pull me under with her.

"Come on!" She grabbed me to explore the stream with her. It led into a large pool with its own private miniature waterfall where the roof was hollowed, and the music sang through.

There were plants along the waterline of the stream, and I raced back to the plate of soaps.

"We should wash!" I floated the plate on the water as I ran the bar up my arms.

"Let me." She moved closer.

She lathered the rose-scented soap in her hand and with a sea sponge she rubbed it all over my body, paying close attention to my back and chest.

I crouched down for her after wetting my hair so she could use the shampoo bar on my hair.

"I don't ever want to leave this place." I melted into her hands as she scratched gently at my scalp with her long nails.

"I wish we could stay here." She echoed my thoughts.

I picked her up and we swapped positions, my hair still lathered, and I rubbed the bar of soap over her body, it didn't take as long as it took her for me, she was half my size.

I'd been fighting the urge to touch her like this for so long, resisting the temptation to meet her gaze and see the same hunger reflected in her eyes. But now, there was no more restraint, no more hesitation—just the warmth of her skin beneath my hands, the way she leaned into my touch as if she had been waiting just as long.

Her hair was thick, a cascade of silk even with the lather coating it, catching the dim light in soft waves. My fingers worked through the strands, slow and deliberate, savoring the moment, the intimacy of it. Her eyes fluttered closed, a quiet sigh escaping her lips as she surrendered to the touch.

I wanted her. More than that, I wanted this—the quiet trust, the way her breath stammered when my fingers traced the curve of her neck, the way she lingered in the space between us, not quite closing the distance but never pulling away. And when she finally opened her eyes, locking onto mine, I knew.

She wanted this too.

"I'm sorry for how I've acted." She dipped her chin.

"No, it's me who should be sorry. I've been unkind and ignorant of your feelings. I want this as much as you. I'm just afraid of what this means. I don't ever want to hurt or shame you." I confessed.

"You think I'd be ashamed of you?" She looked up.

"I don't know." I shrugged.

"Beau, maybe we need to strip back who and what we are and just *be* together, if it feels right then we conquer the obstacles as they come. We don't have to answer to Rael or Zac. You are not his heir, he never claimed you." She rubbed my arms.

"It does feel right, you're the only one it's ever felt right with." I pulled her to me and kissed her heart-shaped lips.

She clung to my body as she wrapped her legs around my torso, her tongue diving into my mouth with a sexual hunger I wasn't mad about.

"I want you now." She broke the kiss just long enough to say the words.

I walked us to the edge of the stream where the stones were smooth and gentle on her tender body as I placed her down. I spread her legs wide as I teased her thighs with my tongue and teeth, grazing closer and closer to her center. She was bucking against me ever so gently now, letting me know she was hungry for what I was just as desperate to give her. I stroked up and down her warm inner lips with two fingers as I watched how her body craved me, her nipples hard as she massaged them softly, her other hand on my wrist which was pulling her deeper onto me.

"Please!" She cried, pleading with me to give her what she wanted.

I dipped my fingers slowly inside her, but I couldn't resist her. I wanted to taste her, to feel her in my mouth and stroke at the place that made her the most unhinged. I lashed my tongue softly around her bud, my hands holding her in place, she rocked back and forth now, but she stopped me suddenly and sat up.

"Come to me." She said sleepily. I climbed out of the water and over her.

Her mouth gaped as she saw my excitement and she fisted me with both her hands as I knelt over her, she placed my shaft into her mouth and ran her hands over my large muscular thighs.

"Oh, fuck yes!" I gently grasped her neck, moving her up and down my length as she fought the urge to gag, her eyes watering, but she was still fixed on the task and bobbed her head, tantalizing her tastebuds with the first beads of excitement forming at my tip.

I pulled out of her mouth, and she pushed me to the floor, straddled me, and began sliding herself up and down along my length as my hands bounded her up and down and my eyes rolled back in my head as I approached climax.

"I'm not so good now." She sprung to her feet and squatted over me, her hands behind her on my thighs keeping her up. I used one hand to play with her bud as she adjusted to my size, and she winced a little with each deep plunge she took.

I sat up and she sat into me still rocking with her sexual starvation as I kissed trails down her neck, and she smiled at the tickles my beard gave her.

"Beau…" She whispered in a long note an octave lower than her normal drawl.

"Yesss, I'm ready!" I pounded into her harder as she went limp over me, dizzied from her orgasm and then we exploded together, and we landed in a naked heap on the ground covered in our wetness—the evidence of our lovemaking, we weren't just fucking now.

"I think I'm falling in love with you." I pulled her onto me.

"You think or you know?" She asked.

"I know." I kissed her.

"I love you too." She kissed me harder.

I had no desire to fight this any longer, I had longed for this moment between us, but still never knew I could have it. Rael would kill for her, and he would send armies to steal her from me, but now I had an army at my back. I almost let her go once, because of him. I wouldn't do that again.

CHAPTER THIRTEEN

ALIERA

I sat there a moment stroking the curves that built his chest, listening to how his heart raced for me, and as he ran his hands up and down my cool back, I shivered against his touch.

"You're cold." He squeezed me.

"We both are, we should wash. Properly this time." I laughed.

We slid back into the crystal-clear water and swam around eventually finding the floating plate with the soaps and then the dinner bells chimed and the music from the harp stopped.

"I'm starving!" Beau exclaimed.

"Please don't expect anything from me later, I plan to eat my weight in food." I grinned.

I stepped out of the water and dried off with the fluffy towel and dressed in the white gown provided for me. Beau was given a beige and white set of clothes that he pulled on with ease and he kindly sat by the bed and laced my sandals for me.

We walked down the long stone hallways till we found a room full of chatter and smelt like nothing I'd ever experienced before. As we entered the room all of our friends were seated and drinking wine. A long table was between them all, it was adorned with platters of different foods, fruit, cooked vegetables, pies, desserts, and meats. Everything I could wish for, everything I didn't know to wish for. Beau rubbed my back as he noticed I was overwhelmed by choice and hadn't made any eye contact with anyone or anything—except the food.

Draven, the lord from Orman, joined us with Cleo, the ruler of Lexia. There were others from the council, Jace from Creed and Starlette from Farkli. The lesser lords and ladies didn't attend after the gathering today.

Beau and I took the last two remaining seats between Jace and Starlette and Draven stood to make a toast as he struck his goblet with a spoon to get everyone's attention.

"Welcome to our new friends, I hope your welcome has been warm, we look forward to peace and a future shared with all. We thank you for the risks you will take to help us build a world without tyrants." Draven held up his glass and smiled as Cleo clapped and the rest of us followed her lead.

Warm bread was served with a plate of flavored medallions of butters. Beau and I tried each one, there was a sweeter maple and cranberry butter, golden and rich with whisps of red swimming through it. Then a savory flavor, this one was mixed with roasted garlic and freshly toasted herbs and my tongue danced in my mouth as I savored every morsel in my mouth. The final option was more colorful, roasted, finely diced red peppers with a slight bite to them, the heat intensifying all the flavors.

"Mhmm!" I moaned unintentionally aloud. My eyes sparked when Beau rubbed the inner part of my thigh.

"Sorry, it's just so good." I laughed to myself.

Beau smirked at me and rubbed the small of my back as I sat forward on my chair eager for the next tasting on offer as more food entered the room on larger platters carried by Fae women.

Salted meats and a stinky cheese were served next, one piece each. This was a tease. I ate them slowly trying to silence my hunger with smaller bites, but now that I was eating the true extent of how famished I had been over these weeks started to rear its ugly head and my stomach growled in excitement.

The kitchen staff came in shortly after and began slicing the meats presented on the table and Draven began to fill his plate, the rest of us did the same and I did my best to try every dish on the table. All of the meats were rich, tender, and juicy. The vegetables were salted just right. Sweet pies were served with dollops of clotted cream and sprinklings of powdered sugar.

Kieran was eyeing one of the servants and Luca seemed to be eyeing another. They had become quite good friends, both similar in age, mid to late twenties if I had to guess.

Astrid and Zac sat next to Starlette and Jace and for the first time, Zac seemed composed and well-mannered, not making people feel uncomfortable. Or maybe he was just happy he got to kick Beau without me sending him into the sea, or that he just talked his way into a war that would put him in a position to command legions of Fae, he'd be able to throw his powers around and raise buildings to flames, he would wreak hell on the Dunya, and a real fear began to swell in my stomach, Zac truly being unleashed is something that couldn't be contained. I'd never seen him completely let loose on anything.

I shook the feeling out of my head as I spooned more pie into my mouth and Beau poured me more wine, he could see thoughts rushing through my mind and raised his brow as if it were a stand-in for a question and I nodded that I was okay.

We sat around the table for hours more, filling ourselves with wholesome food until the candles burnt down and our eyes became heavy from the pointless small talk we were forced to make. Draven and Cleo retired together, Jace with Starlette followed. We walked them down the long stairway adorned with flowers and candlelight till they entered their carriage and journeyed back to the castle where we had first met.

"Does anyone else feel like we are getting the shit end of the stick?" Zac glowered as the servants departed and were left on the stairway alone.

"Do we have a choice?" Beau asked.

"Once we hatch the dragons…" Zac started.

"The dragons are minor in this, they won't be fully grown till Rael is on his deathbed from old age." Kieran added.

"But they can still ignite fires." Zac groaned.

"We aren't sending BABY dragons into a war with Dreadwolves and whatever else the mages may have mixed up in their labs." I interluded.

"Torin? Did you see anything else in there?" Ele held his arm tightly to her as if she were protecting him. Her eyes were soft and gentle as she waited for him to speak.

"A lot of failed attempts, there were some creatures kept in cages. I think the worst they could do is release all the failed projects. Hundreds of men that can't eat, won't eat but they remain alive, they're slow and easy enough to kill, but a lot of them, their veins are black and have basic fighting skills. The main threat is how many there are. I heard some of the mages calling them the Durgun." Torin explained.

"They don't have wings too, do they?" Luca cringed.

"They didn't at the time Axel broke me out." He replied.

We started walking back inside and ended up back in the banquet room sitting around the table once more.

"How did you end up there?" I asked.

The same way everyone from Varsili ends up there, at the king's command." He grunted sarcastically.

"All of you?" Beau queried.

"Axel was keen on the idea, Jasper not so much. I was young and stupid and wanted an excuse to throw my weight around. I was picked out during a *friendly* boxing match. A mage collected me from my tent to *heal* me, Axel had signed me up for all of it, right up to the boxing match. He's cunning, he thought it would earn him favor when it didn't, and he was given so much as the role of a medic, he broke me and Jasper out. Jasper's hysteria started there, constantly looking over his shoulder, and hearing things that weren't there. Then we found out I could change to and from the beast. That made it worse. The rest you know." He sighed.

"How many mages?" Zac asked.

"Four that I saw." Torin replied.

"There's a lot more than four." I muttered.

"I used to see them walking through the city to the street of oracles. I never counted but it was enough to line the streets, people would back against the walls as they passed. You never saw their faces, I guess that's why I never recognized Mason." I added.

The conversation took another direction when Kieran began browsing a map and looking over the area leading to the Sonsuz Forest.

"Let's just get in and out as fast as we can." Beau said.

"We have to pass through another forest." Kieran said as he looked over a map.

"Tell me there are no spiders." Zac bounced his knee.

"There's nothing here to say what we might encounter." Kieran answered.

"We could sail up. There's an inlet, we'd have to start after the bridge, and we'll pass more guards but that's going to be easier than another forest." I said as I looked over the map.

"That would be better, if we are carrying supplies and the eggs, paddling it sounds a lot more relaxing." Zac crossed his arms behind his head.

"We should prepare." Kieran rolled up the map and tucked it under his arm as he stood to leave.

"One more day here." I yawned.

"No, we get the job done." Beau shook his head.

"Of course, YOU would say that." I glowered.

"Every day we give them is another day to grow their army." Beau added. " I know Rael, he's not wasting this time, he knows we are up to something now." He explained.

"Well, we should all get to bed." Ele yawned.

Torin scooped her up in his arms and carried her out of the room effortlessly and up the stairs to their room.

"They've really hit it off." I smiled at Astrid.

"I like him for her." Astrid smiled.

"Yeah, well as long as he eats the food provided and not my best friend." Kieran added.

Luca smiled as he and Kieran headed to the room that they had decided to share. They seemed to be sharing quite a lot lately, so I guess swimming around naked was no bother to them.

Astrid eyed me as if she knew what my thoughts were. "I wonder?" She whispered to me.

"Have to be!" I smiled back.

"Explains why he and Eleanor never hit it off!" Zac added.

"Ohhh!" Beau gasped.

"I think they are just enjoying all the world's pleasures." Astrid straightened and became a little more serious, but the wine had clearly hit her, she was more giggly than normal and more handsy so I put Zac between us so he could help her to their room.

"Our turn." Beau grasped my hand.

"Just a minute!" I smiled as I grabbed a plate and stacked it full of food.

"Are you seriously still hungry?" Beau asked.

"I might be hungry in an hour." I shrugged.

"I saw a supply closet on the way back in, I might raid it for clothes that don't make me feel like a Fae." Beau said.

"You are a Fae." I squinted as I ate a fig from my plate.

"If this is how the Fae dress, then I don't want it." He laughed.

"Back to the leather jackets and pants?" I arched my brows.

"Is that how you like me?" He asked.

"I like you naked." I laughed.

He moved closer to me and slapped my ass making me spill some food off my plate.

"You might have to bend over and pick that up!" He teased.

His hand pinched a handful of my dress as I bent over, and he pulled up the rest exposing my ass to the cool breeze that whipped through the natural open-air windows. I swatted his hand afraid someone might see up.

"Relax, everyone else is doing the same thing right now." He pressed against me as I stood upright, and he forced me into the wall. His hands creeping up my thighs and squeezing handfuls of me.

I wrapped my arms around his shoulders dropping the plate of food.

"If you bend over again, I'm fucking you right here." He laughed.

"Take me to bed!" I kissed him.

He picked me up and carried me to our chamber and placed me on the bed. The stream glistened as the water danced against the wind that gently swept over it, mirroring the candlelight and reflecting beams of shimmering golden strobes around the cave-like room.

I laid back on the bed as Beau undressed before me, his gaze drifting over the water, lost in thought. The moonlight bathed him in silver, illuminating the scars that carved their history into his skin. Now a deep maroon under the glow, they stretched long and wide across his back, their texture impossibly smooth—like silk over old wounds, a haunting contrast to the violence that had put them there.

I rose and stepped toward him, the cool night air wrapping around us as I slid my arms around his waist. My lips brushed against the raised ridges on his shoulder blades—the place where wings should have been. The place they had been stolen from. A shiver passed through him, though he said nothing. I knew the weight of this moment, the truth lingering in the air between us.

It sickened me to know my own father had done this to him. That his cruelty had taken something so sacred and left behind only scars and silence. And worse—how it had changed them both, twisting their fates together in ways neither of us could escape.

He swung an arm around me and pulled me to face him, we stood there a moment in the peace of the harp being strummed from levels above us.

"I could stay here forever." I squeezed my eyes closed as I rested my head on his bare chest.

"I won't fight you on it." He began to brush the sleeves of my dress off my shoulders, and he gently grazed his knuckles over my nipples.

"I thought we were meant to be preparing for tomorrow." I gasped as his hand reached up my thigh and suddenly my skin prickled excitedly.

"Do you want me to stop?" He whispered as his fingers teased the opening of me.

"Fuck no!" I pulled his face to mine and I kissed him passionately till he was carrying me to the bed.

He stretched my legs open, and he slid between me, slamming his length deep inside me. I gasped with every thrust, each time threatening me with an eruption of sensations that would make me buck and scream.

Beau held one thigh against his ribs and stuffed a pillow under my ass as he pressed his free hand on the lower part of my stomach, trapping my g spot as he pounded me hard and fast. Soon, I was quivering against him, the hairs on my body sprung to attention and the quaking I craved surged through my body. Beau grabbed my other thigh now and he pounded relentlessly as he reached for the same feeling. He wasn't far behind me, and he pulled away and let himself cum over my stomach.

"Shit!" He puffed.

He fell to the bed and lay beside me, and I rolled into him and pulled a blanket over us.

"Not so fast, we need to pack." He grunted.

"UGHH!" I groaned while throwing the blanket over my head.

Beau scuffed my hair playfully, threw his legs over the side of the bed and got up to clean himself and then he began rolling up supplies that had been left in the room for us.

CHAPTER FOURTEEN

ASTRID

It was the next day, and Zac was still packing a bag with the warmer clothes Draven had gifted him. I began rolling the thick jacket and tied it to the top of his bag as he pulled on the clothes he'd wear for the journey.

"I wish I was coming." I said.

"Me too." He moved forward and kissed me.

"We should go eat." I opened the door and headed down the hallway to the stairs and finally, we reached the dining room.

Everyone was here already, we had overslept. There was a spread of salads and breakfast foods, and Zac was quick to pile a plate, and he took a seat between me and Kieran.

I was worried about how this journey would go, I didn't doubt their individual powers but the harmony between them was barely holding on by a thread. Aliera sat in front of me, and we shared the same worried glance as Ele also added her own worries through a long stare.

Ele walked over and handed Aliera a small bag. "Here, not that *you* need it, But maybe Kieran or Beau." It was a bag full of labeled potions and tea leaf blends.

"Thank you." Aliera stood up and hugged her.

"Take care." Ele said softly.

"I wish you were coming." Aliera sighed. "Not sure I can trust their mood swings." She raised a brow playfully as she glanced between Beau and Zac.

"I'm not mad about staying back and frolicking on the pools here." I laughed.

"I'm extremely jealous." Aliera smiled.

Beau and Zac were wrapping food into leaves and placing them into secondary bags. They were both armed and their swords on their backs collided every time they got too close to each other and Kieran's stress levels could be seen rising.

Luca and Torin had unexpectedly started talking, a surprise to all of us given Torin's violent history with Tecrit. But Torin was not what any of us had assumed. Beneath his imposing frame was a man of quiet strength, his kindness hidden behind the walls that others had built around him. His size betrayed him, making people believe he was a monster when, in truth, he was anything but.

Ele had seen through him from the start. She was utterly smitten, and it was clear he felt the same. Watching them together, seeing the ease with which they fit, brought a rare sense of peace. I was glad they would have this time in Lexia, away from the battles and the burdens of war.

Torin's identity was no secret to Cleo or Draven, yet they welcomed him without hesitation. More than that, they seemed relieved to have him here. His knowledge of the Durgun was invaluable, but beyond that, his presence itself carried a weight—one that felt like the shifting of something long unresolved, something that, perhaps, was finally beginning to heal.

The time it would take the others to travel to and from Sonsuz would be enough to rally Lexia's army. Cleo was already making preparations, her leadership unwavering. She was older, her silver-shaded hair always intricately braided over one shoulder, a quiet testament to her wisdom and experience.

Draven, younger than Cleo, carried the marks of countless battles. His dark hair did little to hide the scars that marred his skin—a map of the wars he had fought. Though Fae possessed exceptional healing abilities, their wounds never truly vanished; the scars remained as reminders of survival. His wings were unlike any I had seen—colossal, surpassing his height, their tops horned to a sharp point. Once covered in sleek, pristine feathers, they were now worn and scaly from the relentless loss of plumage. The once black feathers were now off-white scales, their hue had been forever stained with the colors of war.

He was a warrior who had fought time and time again, and his very presence carried the weight of every battle he had endured.

Kieran was the first to sling his bag over his shoulder, his expression unreadable as he nodded to those of us staying behind. Aliera followed suit, adjusting the strap of her pack before exchanging a lingering glance with me. Zac and Beau secured their bags over their swords, their movements measured, their focus already shifting toward the journey ahead.

Together, we stepped out of the bathhouse, the comforting warmth of the steam fading as the crisp air met our skin. A carriage stood waiting, its polished surface gleaming under the morning sun. The small group of guards flanking it remained poised and vigilant, their armor catching the light as they prepared to escort our companions through the heart of the city.

"Draven, I'd like to go with them to the bridge if that's okay." I said to him.

"You may, the guards will bring you back." He nodded.

"They aren't going with them all the way?" I asked.

"No, nobody enters the Sonsuz without a purpose." He explained.

I smiled back and raced to the carriage before it left, and I jumped in beside Zac. "Draven said I can come along just to the bridge." I said as the carriage began to move forward.

"Still another day with you." Zac held my hand, and I rested my head on his shoulder.

Kieran was on the other side of Zac. Beau and Aliera sat across from us. Aliera was going through the bag of potions from Ele and Beau was sharpening his hand blades.

"I hope you don't have to use those." Kieran said as he watched the way Beau would glide the blade over an old stone.

"I expect not, but always good to be prepared." He sighed.

"You've been in that position a lot?" Kieran asked.

"Almost everywhere I go." He answered. "Comes with the territory I guess." He added.

Kieran fumbled through his bag and counted out the eggs twice making sure he hadn't miscounted them.

"If they are hatched, will they fly to Azra?" Aliera asked Kieran.

"I'm not sure, my people have never hatched eggs like this before. Usually, the older women would help rear the babies, they can be quite a handful." Kieran smiled.

"How long will it take to hatch them?" Zac asked.

"The tree is a being of magnificence, it will choose." Kieran answered.

"How does it choose?" Aliera asked.

"Some kind of deep divination." Kieran rolled his eyes as I was about to dive deep into a plethora of information nobody seemed interested in.

"Ughh, yeah." I sighed.

"Go on…" Aliera smiled.

"Before this was all a simmering war, Titans, Fae, and Farkli used to get along, our powers combined created the eternal tree for times of need." I explained.

"Is that what Antoli is?" She asked.

"Sort of, Antoli was responsible for caring for the greatest powers in the Dunya. When the Titans abandoned it for the war the castle sealed itself off from the world. It's not just a castle, Aliera. There's a lot about Antoli the Titans never told anybody." I explained.

"So, what's in there?" She asked.

"Nobody knows. Could be nothing." I shrugged.

"Guess we'll find out soon enough." She said as she repositioned herself.

The ride over the cobblestone paths was rough and by the end of the day when we reached the bridge, I began to regret that I'd chosen to make the return trip.

Draven had flown to the bridge with Starlette, and they led us to a beautiful boat with lanterns and a small cabin onboard to shelter them from the crisp night air.

"See you soon." Aliera hugged me.

"Be careful." I hugged her back.

Kieran and Beau hugged me farewell also, they both towered over me. Zac waited till last, he wasn't as tall as Kieran and Beau, but he was just the right height for us to kiss with me on my toes.

"Please don't be a pain, I love you." I smiled through a kiss.

Zac laughed. "I promise I won't kill Beau." He joked.

Beau laughed as Aliera squeezed at his hand. Kieran was already on the boat as Draven loosened off the ropes.

"Come on!" Kieran said excitedly.

"Why are you so excited?" Zac grunted as he stepped onto the boat.

"We're going to the Sonsuz Forest, nobody goes to the Sonsuz." He exasperated.

"And for good reason. It's off-limits. Be respectful and Let Aliera do the talking." Starlette smirked.

They stepped onto the boat, Draven lingering last as he used the immense strength of his left wing to push them off from the dock. I stood at the edge, watching as their boat shrank into the distance, swallowed by the creeping darkness and the frost that began to settle around Starlette and me.

Without a word, we turned back toward the carriage, the weight of their departure pressing against us. The ride back to Lexia was quiet, Starlette drifting into sleep as the steady rhythm of the wheels lulled her into slumber. I remained awake, wrapped in a thick cloak, my gaze lost in the night sky. The heavens stretched wide above us, painted in swirling hues of deep blues and purples, streaked with greens and golds. Our three moons loomed closer now that we had returned to Lexia, their soft glow casting a spectral light over the land. Beyond them, other worlds floated in the abyss, distant yet visible, unreachable yet ever-present.

The carriage halted outside the bathhouse just as dawn broke, the golden light spilling over the horizon. Starlette stirred at the sudden stop, blinking drowsily as she took in her surroundings. I bid her farewell with a quiet nod before stepping out, the crisp morning air biting against my skin.

Inside, the shared dining room was already stirring with life. Ele sat at the long wooden table, tearing into a sliced loaf of bread, thin cuttings of ham arranged neatly on her plate. The scent of warm food curled through the air, but it wasn't hunger that drew me forward—it was her. As I approached, she looked up, her eyes catching the morning light, something unspoken passing between us before a small, knowing smile touched her lips.

"You look famished." I smiled at her as she whipped her head around.

"You startled me!" She shrieked.

"Sorry, I just got back and was looking for some food." I explained, trying to let her know I wasn't spying on her.

"How's Torin." I asked.

"He hasn't tried to eat me if that's what you're getting at." Her eyes followed me around the table.

"Good to know. You seem moody?" I sat across from her.

"I promise I'm not." She put her head down and ate her bread.

"You know I'm your sister if you want to talk…" I started.

"I can't bring him home, can I?" She stopped me.

I shook my head from side to side. " I don't think that would be a good idea." I sighed.

"What do I do?" She asked as she stuffed her mouth with ham.

"Is it that serious already?" I asked.

"I think so." She nodded.

"Let's get through this war first. Maybe it'll change how people see him." I tried my best to be encouraging.

"I hope so. I can't figure out where in the world he fits in after this." She sighed.

"Maybe we find a new place." I reached for her hand and tried to give her hope.

"Do you think we could?" She asked.

"I think anything is possible. Let's just take it a day at a time." I squeezed her hand.

Torin appeared in the doorway, his eyes still sleepy, his hair a mess with only pants on.

I grabbed my plate of food and smiled between them both. "I'm going to try and get some sleep." I stood up to leave and Torin smiled kindly on my way out.

As I ascended the stairs to my room, the soft strains of the harp drifted through the halls, its melody delicate and soothing, promising a peaceful sleep after my meal.

I didn't mind the nights away from Zac. He often went hunting with Kieran, leaving me time to immerse myself in my lab. Some of my best potions had been crafted in the solitude his absence allowed, the quiet granting me the focus I needed to refine my work.

Still, I worried for him. Beneath his bravado, he was a good man—kind in ways he never let others see, though his bluntness made it difficult for him to win people over. I hoped that in time, he and Beau might find common ground. Perhaps the journey to Sonsuz would give them the chance to forge something beyond grudging tolerance—something that resembled friendship.

CHAPTER FIFTEEN

ALIERA

We sailed north into the cold night air, the stars distant and sharp above us. Keiran, not handling the chill as well as the rest of us, retreated into the cramped warmth of the tiny cabin. Zac sat silently at the bow, gently warming the water around us with flickers of fire dancing at his fingertips. He stared ahead as the boat sliced through sheets of ice, the frozen shards cracking and drifting aside in our wake.

Draven and Beau took turns paddling, their movements steady and strong, gliding us forward through the dark waters. The cold bit at our faces, numbing our fingers, but no one complained. Zac's subtle warmth kept us just above freezing, and the quiet camaraderie between us made the journey bearable.

By dawn, we reached a lonely dock, its wooden planks slick with ice and glistening under the pale morning light. The forest behind it loomed still and silent, heavy with snow. There was no welcome, no path—only the unspoken challenge of the wild ahead, the dense forest was capped in snow.

"How are we going to make it through that?" I groaned.

"Patience." Draven replied.

Beau and Kieran tied the boat to the dock as I chipped ice off the side of the vessel, but my efforts were useless. The ice was frozen solid and not coming away easily.

"ZAC!" I whined.

"Step away." He heated his hands over the side panels just enough for the ice to fall away from the wooden frame but not hot enough to ignite it.

"How about the dock now?" I asked, pleased with his efforts.

"NO! NOT the dock." Draven interrupted.

"What if one of us slips over on the ice." I pestered him.

Draven walked to my side, grasped both of my hands, and flew me to the land where the dock began, and he then set me down.

"As a wind wielder, I'm surprised this is something you can't do on your own." He titled his head.

"I've not had this power long, I'm still learning." I said as I looked at my hands.

"It's in here." He rested a hand on the side of my head.

"I'll keep working on it." I nodded.

Kieran was holding the bag with the eggs when Draven took flight, gliding effortlessly through the crisp air to retrieve him. He landed gracefully, setting Kieran down gently beside me.

Beau refused the help, opting instead to carefully scale the icy dock. Zac followed, both of them moving with deliberate caution. Their boots slipped slightly on the frost-slick surface, and for a breathless moment, they caught one another—hands gripping arms, faces too close, tension flaring in their eyes. The moment passed quickly as they broke apart and they finally reached Kieran and me, saying nothing, but their silence spoke volumes.

"I'll wait for you here." Draven said.

"You're not coming?" Beau asked.

"The less in attendance the better. The Suz Fae aren't big on unannounced guests." He nodded. "Once you're in, you'll be fine." He assured us.

I looked at the others as we stepped into the unsuspecting forest. At first, it was nothing more than ordinary trees, their trunks dusted with thick snow and branches creaking under the perpetual weight of winter. But as we journeyed deeper, the world around us began to change.

The snow faded away, revealing a path unlike any I had ever seen—a winding trail lit by towering crystals, their glow pulsing softly like a heartbeat. Giant mushrooms loomed overhead, their caps casting colorful shadows, while glowing pixie lights hovered in the air like floating lanterns. Streams wound alongside the path, their waters alive with tiny, luminous creatures darting between the rocks, casting playful ripples across the mossy banks. Up ahead, a delicate bridge arched gracefully over a glimmering stream, leading us toward the capital of Sonsuz.

Tiny pixies buzzed around us now—round faces beaming, large eyes wide with wonder, and smiles as bright as starlight. They spoke in rapid whispers, their language melodic and strange, as they twirled through the air. They took an especially keen interest in Beau, swarming around him with delighted giggles as he batted them away in frustration, muttering under his breath. The more he swatted, the more they seemed to adore him.

I smiled to myself, the magic of this place settling around us like a dream, alive and watching.

"Don't do that!" Kieran grunted.

The pixies oooh'd and ahhh'd, their delight evident as they caught wind of the tension. They giggled among themselves, their twinkling voices like wind chimes in a breeze. One particularly bold pixie made herself right at home in my hair, wrapping it around her tiny glowing form like a shimmering burgundy gown as she nestled onto my shoulder.

"Gorgeous." I murmured, glancing over at her. She beamed at the compliment and she gave a delicate and theatrical bow.

"Are we going the right way?" I asked.

She nodded with enthusiasm, pointing through the thick of the forest and dramatically motioning to suggest the long journey ahead. Then she turned to Beau, her small arms flapping as she tried to mimic wings, her expression filled with curiosity.

"Fly?" I asked, brow furrowed.

She smiled wide and tilted her head at Beau, clearly wondering why he wasn't using wings to travel. I leaned in and whispered gently to her, "No wings."

She gasped, her tiny hand flying to her mouth as she looked at Beau in wide-eyed alarm. Quickly, she knotted herself back into my hair, tucking in tightly over my shoulder as if the revelation had startled her into silence.

"Should have brought Luna. She'd eat these little pests." Zac muttered, swatting at the air as the pixies circled his hands. They were drawn to the red veins glowing with heat, curious and unbothered by his irritation.

Beau chuckled, a rare moment of shared amusement. "She really would."

"STOP IT! They're just curious." I snapped, turning on both of them with a sharp glare.

A chorus of delighted ooo's echoed around us as the pixies giggled, clearly pleased with the chaos they had stirred up. They zipped through the air like sparks, twirling and clapping in celebration of my defense.

"They're annoying." Zac grumbled, crossing his arms as a pixie tugged at his sleeve, undeterred.

But even he couldn't fully hide the twitch of a reluctant smile tugging at the corner of his mouth.

"Not too long to go." I said, nodding toward the structures carved into the mountainside, half-wrapped in mist and sunlight. Homes of the Fae clung to the cliffs, their elegant balconies blooming with hanging plants that shimmered like glass in the light. As soon as the residents noticed us, a gentle buzz of excitement rose in the air, wings fluttering and voices calling out softly in greeting.

Between the homes clinging to the cliffs, waterfalls spilled gracefully into the river below, their silver ribbons catching the sunlight as they danced through the mist. The bridges we crossed arched elegantly over the flow, crafted from pale stone veined with glowing crystal, each step echoing with a soft hum of magic.

The sound of the water was soothing, a melodic contrast to the growing flutter of wings and soft chatter that swelled around us. The Fae had noticed our approach. They peered from balconies draped in flowering vines, their eyes alight with curiosity, their greetings carried on lilting voices and shimmering laughter.

As we moved toward the heart of the city, the towering crystal formations that had lit our path gave way to towers of wax and flame. Thousands of candles—tall and slender, some twisted like braids or carved into patterns of stars—lined the palace steps. Their golden glow flickered in the shifting air, warming the smooth marble and casting soft halos across the entrance.

The palace stood ahead, quiet and grand, carved into the mountain itself. Its open doorway beckoned, not just with light, but with the unmistakable pull of something ancient and powerful, waiting to be awakened.

The pixies flew away now and perched on the bridge's handlebars, their wings glinting in the shifting light. Smaller Fae began to drift down from their balconies, hovering gracefully in the air as the great doors to the city slowly opened.

At the heart of it all stood the Tree—an enormous, awe-inspiring presence with a colossal trunk that I could only assume was part of the same living being. Its sprawling, leafy branches stretched so wide and strong they brushed the mountainside, forming a natural canopy over the entire city.

It was adorned with offerings from the Fae: delicate flowers, radiant jewels, glowing crystals—treasures hung lovingly from its limbs like sacred ornaments. The castle, along with a large portion of the city, was seamlessly built into the Tree's massive structure, as though it had grown to embrace and protect everything within it.

It was not just a city. It was a living sanctuary, ancient and eternal.

We stood still as six figures flew through the great doors and landed beside us in a sudden, synchronized sweep abruptly beside us. They were guards, swift and silent, and without a word, they linked their arms through ours. In a blink, we were airborne, soaring over the water, beneath arching branches heavy with blossoms, through the laughter of children darting between sunbeams. The world blurred into color and wind until, just as abruptly, we landed inside the castle.

The doors shut behind us with a quiet finality, sealing away the vibrant magic outside. We were ushered into a throne room that pulsed with quiet grandeur. At its center stood a towering statue of a female Fae, carved in a moment of raw desperation. Her arms reached forward; her face etched with emotion so real it stole my breath. I paused, caught in her silent cry, until the guards urged us onward.

At the far end, two thrones rose above a marble staircase, and upon them sat the rulers of this realm. The woman was a vision of nature itself—vines and leaves cascading through her hair, her skin like pale, silken bark, and eyes ancient with knowledge. She radiated beauty that was both wild and serene, and the longer I looked, the more her presence unfurled in delicate layers that captivated me.

Beside her sat a man who embodied the forest's strength—tall, broad-shouldered, with antlers arching from his crown-like branches reaching for the sun. Gold threaded through his hair and into the contours of his face, accentuating the regal fierceness in his gaze. His golden hair was braided into four thick ropes.

They watched us with anticipation, and though neither spoke, their attention settled on us like sunlight through ancient trees— warm, unwavering, and impossible to ignore.

Beau grabbed my hand and pulled me tight beside him and Zac stood on my other side. They had found their common ground as they communicated to protect me over everything.

"I am Thane, and this is Teresina." He turned to the woman beside him and smiled proudly.

"I'm Aliera, this is Beau, Zac and Kieran." I introduced us all.

"What's in the bag?" Thane asked.

Kieran stepped forward. "With your permission, Azra has begged we hatch her eggs beneath the tree." Kieran's voice was shaky as he pulled out each egg and he laid them on the ground before Thane and Teresina. The eggs fit perfectly within his two hands, each covered in stunning scales like an artist had made them. It was the first time I had seen them in such clear light. The eggs shimmered with scales of deep sapphire, molten bronze, and glistening emerald—as if forged by time, starlight, and fire. The etchings that adorned their surfaces were mesmerizing, curling in ancient patterns that pulsed faintly with magic, dazzling as the light immediately gleamed from misshapen scales and patterns.

"Azra is alive?" Teresina gasped.

"She resides in the tunnels beneath the mountain." I stepped forward away from Zac and Beau. There was something so alluring about Teresina, that I felt an immediate trust between us as she picked up the smallest egg and cradled it gently in her arms.

"And why are the rest of you here?" Thane asked.

"Can you not feel their power, Thane?" Teresina asked as she circled me now with the egg still in her grasp.

"A Titan!" Her eyes glowed a subtle green as she reached for my hand and a whoosh of air flowed between us. "Air is your power." She smiled. Words didn't come out, but I nodded like a small child as I acknowledged what she had said.

She moved to Zac next and her hands crisped as she reached for his hand, and she pulled away with a smirk on her face. "You're a spicy one." She giggled as she shook off the embers.

"ZAC!" I snarled.

"I'm just demonstrating." He hissed back.

"Enough!" Thane snapped his gaze between us now as he stood up from his wooden throne and approached. He was tall and intimidating and his eyes were now on Beau.

"And you?" He asked.

"I'm just here to protect them." He answered.

"Who sent you?" Thane questioned.

"Draven and Cleo." I answered.

"Then you are not here for protection." He seemed to sniff at Beau now as he paced around him.

Thane flicked aside the hair that concealed Beau's ears, his expression shifting as he took in the truth of what stood before him. His chest rose sharply, awe flickering in his eyes. Teresina was quicker. She stepped forward and gently touched the tips of Beau's ears, then let her hands trail down his sculpted cheekbones. With delicate purpose, she tugged down his jacket, her palms resting over the small, protruding bones along his back—bones that told them everything they needed to know.

She sank to her knees, her breath sharp as tears spilled freely. Her sorrow filled the great hall. Thane, eyes blazing, gripped Beau's shirt and tore it from his body in a rage not meant for Beau himself. The sight of the scars, the evidence of what had been done to him, made even the air seem to tighten.

"THIS IS AN OFFENSE!" he roared, the sound echoing through the vast hall. The very walls vibrated with the force of it, and from all around, Fae began to gather. They filled the high balconies carved into the walls, beneath the open ceiling where starlight streamed through the branches of the great tree above.

Chatter died instantly. Silence spread like wildfire as Thane spoke again, his voice ringing with fury and finality. "Anyone who harms a Fae is an enemy. We do not tolerate the torture of our kind. You will have justice. You will have revenge."

His hand came to rest on Beau's shoulder, a solemn promise in his grip.

My breath caught. My skin went cold. That promise wasn't just for Beau—it was for all of us. And still, all I could feel was the weight of my own blood in my veins, the knowledge settling like stone.

My face flushed—My father.

A lump swelled in my throat as I sank to the floor beside Teresina, her quiet sobs still shaking through her as grief and truth wrapped around us both.

"We will not wage war over this." Teresina stood and challenged Thane.

"If we cannot protect our people the outside world will come for us next!" Thane belted his voice so everyone could hear.

"Let them come." She wiped her face and stood from the ground, a single egg still in her hand and she packed the bag with the other eggs, and she disappeared into the depths of the tree and Kieran followed not letting the eggs leave his sight.

Thane stood staring at Beau for a moment longer as he glowered over the abomination that hatched his back.

"Tell me who did this boy." Thane commanded.

"Rael…" It wasn't exactly a lie, but I feared Thane's response if he knew it was a Titan.

Granted our father was lower in status. He didn't possess powers like my siblings and I. It was always assumed that our powers were a lot more sorcery-linked than Titan but the Titan in us gave them a unique strength, amplified their strength. Another abomination to the Dunya.

"The *human* king, the generational warrior. The Fae deceiver. The greedy. I could go on!" He growled at the thought of him. "You will have what was stolen from you." Thane gripped Beau's forearms, and the crowds cheered as Thane lifted Beau into the air and they disappeared so high into the trees I couldn't see them anymore.

Guards escorted Zac and me into a banquet hall where Fae, similar in appearance to Teresina, brought us food and showed us to a large, shared room with basic beds with one large round table in the middle.

"What are we doing here!" Zac kicked a chair over.

"We are here to give their people hope. To let them know we will support them in this war. We play a role. KEEP YOUR COOL!" I lowered my eyes at him as I thrust him into a chair with a swing of my arm.

Zac swallowed hard as he fell into the chair and I sat in the one beside him. "That's not fair, I can't hurl flames at you." He groaned.

I smiled and shrugged.

"Now what?" He asked.

"We wait…" I grunted.

Chapter Sixteen

BEAU

Thane carried us through the vast, interwoven canopy, soaring along the natural bridges formed by thick, ancient branches. The air shimmered with soft light filtering through the leaves, casting golden beams across our path. We dipped lower, weaving through a maze of limbs and moss until we reached the entrance of a massive, hollow trunk that glowed from within, its pale light pulsing like the heartbeat of the tree itself.

At the opening, a narrow staircase spiraled downward, carved directly into the wood. Thane stepped ahead, his movements sure and silent, and I followed. The descent was long, the air growing warmer and richer, the scent of earth more robust with every step. My legs burned, numb from the strain, but I pressed on.

Deeper and deeper we went, until the stairs gave way to a chamber nestled in the roots of the great tree. The soil rose around us in gentle curves, radiating a comforting warmth. It felt alive—ancient and sacred. The silence here was profound, like the world itself had paused to let us pass through something eternal and revered.

"I'll stay with you here in this place while you endure this." Thane said softly, his voice tinged with sorrow. There was pity in his eyes, and it chilled me even with the warmth of the chamber wrapping around me.

"Endure what, Thane?" I asked, my voice barely a whisper.

He held my gaze for a long moment before replying. "You will see. I suggest you drink this." He handed me a steaming cup of tea, the aroma floral and unfamiliar.

"What will it do?" I asked, hesitant.

"It should help with the pain."

He swallowed hard, then pushed open the heavy wooden door before us. A wave of golden light spilled out, bathing the hallway in warmth. I stepped inside, and my breath caught.

Before me were the five eggs—not as I had known them, but ablaze with magic. They pulsed with a fiery brilliance, their shells glowing and fractured, fine cracks spidering outward in slow motion. The heat in the room was thick and alive, humming with energy as if the air itself held its breath.

They were hatching.

And I could already feel the ache of what was to come.

I sipped the tea, the warmth trailing down my throat with deceptive gentleness. Thane gave me one last look—solemn, steady—then closed the heavy door behind me, sealing me inside the golden stone chamber.

The heat crept in first, slow and searing. My back ignited in flame, and the old, hatched wounds split open now, raw and unrelenting, covering me in my own blood. The warmth of the room slithered into my bones, and I collapsed onto the soil-covered floor, my body thrashing in agony.

My ears rang and muffled, blocking out everything but the sound of my own ragged breathing. My teeth ached down to the roots, my gums bleeding as if rejecting their shape. Every bone in my body seemed to shift and crack, redefining itself with a brutality I had never known. I felt my form unravel, pulled apart, and stitched back together by something ancient and unmerciful.

Time lost meaning. Pain was the only constant. Sleep didn't exist here—only the cycle of burning and breaking. The tea dulled the edge for mere hours, but when it wore off, there was nothing but the raw, unfiltered torment of transformation.

I was on fire when my hands formed callouses and my nailbeds thickened. Every nerve screamed, every shift in my body a reminder that I was becoming something more—or something I had once been. My vision sharpened, clarity cutting through the haze like a blade, and my hearing locked onto Aliera's voice as she pounded her fists against the sealed door, her cries muffled but frantic.

Kieran and Aliera were begging for my release when the worst of it struck. My back cracked, splitting into four jagged surges of pain as my spine shifted, bones fracturing and reforming to make room for what was coming. Wings—not the ones I remembered, but new, colossal, and wild. They burst from me in a violent bloom, tearing through skin and muscle, expanding with terrifying grace.

These wings dwarfed even Draven's. They rose in chaotic arcs, massive and dark, scaled forearms folding outward like a second pair of limbs. The fingers were thick and black, sharp at the tips, while the mainsails stretched wide and fearsome—a deep, violent blue, veined with pulsing black ribs. The membranes shimmered red in the golden light, a fierce tapestry of fire and shadow.

I wasn't just Fae again.

I was something ancient. Something more, something new.

The eggs had hatched now, though one hadn't survived. The air still trembled with lingering magic when the four hatchlings gathered around their sibling's lifeless form. Without instruction, they set the body aflame, honoring it in the only way they instinctively knew. Smoke billowed, thick and silvery, as the door blasted open and Aliera appeared, framed in wind and light, her hair a storm around her and her eyes glowing white with power.

Kieran dropped to his knees as the dragons waddled out first, unsteady on their legs but filled with life. Each one was nearly the size of Luna, their scales glittering like newly forged metal. They puffed out playful bursts of flame, circling each other in mock combat before rushing toward Kieran, recognizing his scent like it had been etched into their very being.

Scales now coated parts of my chest, my shoulders, and the length of my back, glinting faintly beneath the haze. Thane looked utterly drained, the weight of what had transpired etched into the lines of his face. He pulled me into a tight embrace, voice caught in his throat. As he stepped back, his gaze swept over me in awe. He shook his head slowly, circling me, trying to comprehend everything I had become.

"How?" He pondered aloud.

"The infant died. You have the essence of Fae, but also the dragon now." Teresina looked over me now.

"What?" I asked, but I was exhausted, it was taking everything I had left to concentrate on her words.

"A dragon has guarded you once before. Now you will guard her remaining children." Teresina explained.

"Azra knew not all the eggs would survive. It's okay." Kieran assured me.

"You look so different." Aliera paced around me touching my wings and shoulders.

"I'm still me, I think." I grasped her forearm.

"You can make it a little less confronting, you'll learn. Most of us like the full appearance though." Teresina closed her eyes and in a few seconds her skin that was once bark melted into smooth velvety skin, her vines turned to hair, and she was just as stunning as before but appeared more human-like.

"You try." Thane stood beside her and crossed his arms as he watched me.

"What do I do." I asked.

"Just want it." He nodded.

I reached for the version of myself that felt less distant, less intimidating. As the shift settled, my wings shrank to a more manageable size, and the tightness in my skin eased, no longer straining against the weight of what I had become.

Aliera sank into my arms without hesitation, her presence grounding me in a way nothing else could. She pressed her lips to mine, soft and warm. I wrapped my arms around her, holding her close. In that moment, nothing else mattered. She was the comfort I hadn't known I was still aching for—the warmth that softened the storm within me.

"I thought you'd die in there." She kissed me.

"Told you!" Teresina elbowed Thane.

"It's really great and all that you got your terrifying wings back and became some dragon king or lord, but these guys are hungry!" Keiran said anxiously as the dragons circled and snapped at each other but never at him.

"You are going to have your hands full." Zac laughed.

"Take them for their first flight!" Teresina encouraged Kieran.

"Can they fly?" He asked.

"There's only one way to find out." She smiled.

Each dragon latched onto a limb of Kieran's—one to each arm, one to each leg—and in a sudden burst of chaotic flapping, they took off. Kieran let out a wild scream that echoed down the long passageway, not so much from fear as from sheer disbelief.

"I'm flying!" he shouted, limbs flailing as the dragons carried him out of the tunnel and into the open air.

They burst through the canopy like a firework, sunlight hitting their scales and casting rainbow reflections through the leaves. The treetops whipped past in a blur as Kieran soared above the forest, dangling, his laughter now mixing with his yells.

"Put me down! No—wait! Higher! No, LOWER!"

The dragons shrieked joyfully, clearly enjoying the ride just as much as he wasn't sure he was. And though he kicked and flailed and cursed, there was no denying the exhilaration on his face as they spiraled higher, twisting and diving through the clouds like a flock of overenthusiastic kites with a very loud, very unwilling passenger.

It was chaotic. It was ridiculous. It was absolutely magnificent.

"Can I get a lift too?" Aliera smirked at me.

"I haven't done this before, are you sure you trust me?" I asked.

She wrapped her arms around me as I scooped her legs into my arms, the weight of her grounding me just as the thrill of flight surged in my chest. I let the scales ripple back across my skin, wings unfurling with a familiar rush. With a deep breath, I flapped hard and slow, the way I had once coached Azra, feeling the strength return to every muscle.

My feet left the ground in a burst of power, wind curling around us as we lifted into the air. Below, Thane and Teresina watched with pride, their figures growing smaller. Zac, ever stubborn, chose to take the long trek up the dark staircase, his footsteps echoing faintly behind us.

We broke free from the passage, soaring into the open canopy where thick, winding branches stretched across the sky. The treetops whispered as we passed, and ahead of us, the ice mountains shimmered beneath the sun, stretching endlessly across the horizon like a frozen sea of silver and light.

The wind roared around us, and I tightened my hold on her. She laughed against my shoulder, the sound bright and wild, and in that moment, we weren't just flying—we were free.

"How does it feel?" Aliera asked.

She smiled and traced the scales on my bare chest with her fingers. "It's the flying thing." She wiggled her fingers at me as a joke.

"I feel unstoppable. Complete." I said, my voice low, still raw from everything that had brought me here. "I don't know if it's because I just survived an inferno to reclaim my wings, or because you continue to take my breath away."

I held her in my gaze, letting the words settle between us. She didn't look at me. Not yet. Her eyes were fixed on the horizon, where the mountains stretched endlessly, and beyond them, Antoli—quiet, distant, tucked into the furthest western corner of the world we knew.

The wind tugged gently at her hair, the golden light catching in the strands as if the sun itself couldn't resist reaching for her. And still, she stared, her longing so palpable it softened something in my chest.

I smiled as she rested her head on my shoulder, and we watched birds fly around us as they took a keen interest in my wings.

"Was it really that bad?" She asked.

"It was like I melted and then was reborn through fire. Excruciating." I explained.

"I'm glad you're okay." She kissed my shoulder.

"How long was I down there?" I asked.

"Five days. I waited in the castle with Zac for the first three, but Kieran refused to come up without the eggs and I began to worry about what Thane had done with you." She sighed.

"I guess this is why Draven sent me. He knew this would happen." I said.

"Fae aren't too forthcoming with information I've noticed." She laughed.

"Are you having a stab?" I smiled.

"You were always a little hard to get to know, in the beginning." She replied.

"What does the end look like for us?" I asked.

"I guess we find out one way or another." She pushed up to stand ready to leave the peak of the trees.

I stood beside her as she sat to rest on a branch and my wings closed around us.

"I'm not letting either of us die. I get you for a lifetime. That's all I want. Thane can have Rael's head." I pulled her into me and kissed her as I cradled her legs, and we flew down to the city.

Aliera screamed playfully at the speed as we swept through wind barrels that she had manifested in front of me, we played with the pixies who enjoyed the wind sliding with us. Soon Kieran and the baby dragons joined, and Kieran panicked as he almost slammed into us.

We landed swiftly in front of the main doors where the guards gasped at the sight of me and kneeled. Kieran landed next with the four baby dragons around him, and he threw them each a hefty lump of meat to consume from a bucket a servant had brought to the gates for the dragons.

"We should go back to Lexia." Aliera spoke.

"Where's Zac?" Kieran asked.

"I guess we have a whole night to wait. He's walking out." I laughed.

"Too proud to ask Thane for a lift." Kieran laughed back.

"Sounds about right." I added.

Teresina appeared in the doorway and summoned Aliera to her quarters while an elderly woman came to meet Kieran and me.

"It's been a lifetime since I saw a dragon. They are big and strong!" She said excitedly.

"You've seen dragons before?" Kieran asked.

"I am the Drake Hoca." She smiled. "I knew their mother." She knelt before the dragons.

"You're not a Fae?" I was surprised.

"No, I'm like you." She looked at Kieran. "I'm Farklian, but I served the Titans and their dragons." She said proudly.

"You must be ancient!" Kieran exasperated.

"I'm the oldest being in the forest, except for the tree." She smiled.

"You saw the Titan war?" I asked.

"I did and I saw thousands fall from the sky to their deaths because of what your great-grandfather's greed did to him. Greed is a sickness that affects generations, the more you have, the more you want. But you are different, you have what you want." She whispered.

"How do you know who I am?" I stepped forward.

"It's common knowledge. We can smell the Varsilian in your veins." She confessed. "Be careful Beau, Fae have the same greed as the humans. What they seek in Antoli is not magic, it's a weapon. One that should not be unleashed." She warned.

"What is it?" Kieran asked as his eyes narrowed on the Hoca.

"Irmak…" she was breathy and so quiet I wasn't sure I heard her correctly. But Kieran's face lost all of its color and soon he was on his knees weakened from the shock.

"There are others?" He asked.

"And Caxia who terrorizes the shores, she is a water drake." She explained.

"A drake?" I asked.

"A young or inexperienced dragon…childish." Kieran explained.

"Hopefully when the time comes, she'll fight on our side." I added.

"These young dragons will stay here in the Sonsuz to learn and grow." The Hoca explained.

"Can I stay with them until they are grown?" Keiran asked.

"We hoped you would ask that, would be nice to have a fellow Farklian around." She smiled.

"Ele is going to kill you." I said with wider eyes.

"She's busy with Torin, she'll understand. Tell Luca I'm the ultimate wingman now." He laughed.

I nodded as I walked in through the main doors to the large castle and up the stairs to where a room had been prepared for me. I ran a hot bath to clean off the sweat and steam my body had endured over the last few days. My skin felt hot and sticky as I dumped buckets of freshly boiled water into the polished wooden tub with gold fixings.

The room had a large open window, with green draping vines that grew in through the aperture and clung to the roof. The room was lit by a mix of candlelight and natural light. I lit the fire beneath the tub, heated the water, sprinkled scented salts and soap shavings into the water, then found a sea sponge to scrub myself with.

I closed the doors to shut away this open part of the room and disrobed what was left of my clothes. I smelt of ash, smoke, and death. Death of my old self, death of my old body. This was a new and improved version— I hoped.

Chapter Seventeen

ALIERA

Teresina walked me up the stairs to hers and Thane's room. She sat me at their private dining table where she offered me cakes and a platter of sweet delights.

"Do you think we can avoid this war, Aliera?" She asked me.

"I would like to, but the mages have created armies for war. I don't see another way." I sighed.

"Hmmm." She pondered. Her skin was barky once more and her thin vinelike hair gleamed in the sunlight that beamed through the window as it bounced gently in the soft breeze.

"We could strike a peace bargain…" I started.

"What does Rael want most of all?" She asked.

"Me…" I sighed.

"You?" She asked.

"Can I call you Sina?" I straightened as I brushed crumbs from an orange cake off my chin.

She smiled and nodded in response.

"Sina, Rael found out he had Titans living in his city, my parents thought the closer to danger, the further away from harm, but that wasn't the case. I was only ten years old when my family gave themselves up trying to keep me safe. My mother spelled our home and for fifteen years I lived as quietly as I could. But Rael found out I wasn't just a whisper and sent his assassin, *Beau* to kidnap me. But Beau is his bastard and his claim to the throne is strong. Rael's legitimate sons aren't warriors, they aren't respected at court the way Beau was." I began.

"How was your family found?" Sina asked.

"Zac worked in the armory, he was caught wielding fire in his hands.' I explained.

"He's reckless, even now." She sighed.

"Rael wants me to breed a new stronger leader to take over for him when he dies." I added.

"But you fell inlove with Beau." She smiled.

"And it's something he's struggled with 'cause he feels like Rael wins this way too." My eyes became glassy.

"Beau is an intelligent man, a good man." Her eyes gleamed.

I nodded as I fussed with my hair. "We have to kill him, and all the anarchy he stands for." I reached for her hand, and she nodded softly.

"I'll fight with you air wielder." She smiled.

"Air or wind?" I pondered playfully.

"Your power is so much more than you know. With air, you can control all the elements." She became excited now.

"I have a lot to learn and no time to do it." I pressed my lips into a thin line.

"It will come to you when you need it." She assured me. "Rael will have his war, and we will send the Sonsuz warriors. This will be the last war the Dunya will see!" She added.

"Thank you." My lips curved into a weak smile.

"Beau is three doors down." She stood from her chair, and we walked to the door as Thane went to open it from the other side.

I bowed my head respectfully and quickly darted down the hall, the whole way feeling their eyes on my back. I swung open the door. Beau's clothes were tossed on the floor. The doors to the bathroom closed and I barged through them eagerly looking for him. He sat upright with his wings out of the tub and his knees bent up so he could fit.

"You look squished." I laughed. I walked forward and gazed into the tub. "And that water is filthy." My eyes bulged.

He splashed his dirty water on me and hurled a sponge at me next. "Hey! Constructive criticism, go easy." I giggled.

I picked up the sponge and knelt beside the tub and began to scrub Beau's shoulders. They were bigger now, covered in thin scales that thickened and became smaller the closer they got to his wings. They would need more flexibility and movement when in flight.

I scrubbed gently between the scales, and he moved his arm as he still figured out the comfort of his movements.

"It's a whole new body." He sighed.

"Are the wings heavy?" I asked.

"Strangely they feel weightless, they are a lot different to the ones I was born with." He said.

"What were they like?" I asked as I made my way over his chest with the soap-lathered sponge.

"Smaller, black feathers. Nothing at all like these." His hands tried to demonstrate the size difference.

"I like these." I traced my fingers over the blue leathery wings, and they shined brightly as the sunlight gleamed through them.

"It's going to take some getting used to; sleeping should be interesting." He raised them up and down.

"Will we leave tomorrow?" I asked.

"Once Zac gets back, I think we should leave." Beau answered.

"He might be back by nightfall." I narrowed my eyes.

"Then we'll leave tonight." Beau said.

I pulled the plug from the bathtub. "Better get ready then." I stood up and flung a towel at Beau as he climbed from the bathtub.

I walked out of the bathroom and began gathering my things, there wasn't a lot. I'd barely unpacked so much as a pair of boots since Sina had been so accommodating while Beau was in transformation. It was beautiful and peaceful here in the Sonsuz. The Fae were curious but friendly and they had spoilt me with gifts, and gowns, braiding my hair, and feeding me the most wonderful food. I wasn't ready to leave.

"We should get Kieran." I said as Beau walked through the door, his wings out, his ears slightly pointier than before and all that stood between us was a towel that Beau made look tiny.

"He's staying." Beau cautioned over the words.

"WHAT!" I flicked my eyes up.

"We met with the Hoca. He needs to stay here with the baby dragons to learn how to train them." I explained.

Ele and Astrid…" I began.

"Ele and Astrid know this about him. His purpose in life is to serve the dragons and this is where it's safe for him to do so." Beau sighed.

"Does Sina know?" I asked.

"I wouldn't be surprised if it were her idea." Beau said.

He was right. Sina was reluctant to go to war, I couldn't imagine her wanting to send four immature baby dragons into a war full of Dreadwolves, Mages, and Durgun. This war would be worse than anything that came before it. There were more moving pieces now, more races, and everyone had something on the line. Draven knew what was in Antoli, he had to, why else would he want it so badly? But Irmak could only be controlled by a Titan, I couldn't understand his angle. Unleashing Irmak as a Fae, he was just as likely to kill Draven than align with him.

The dragons' screeches echoed all the way up to the castle, followed by the rhythmic whipping of their wings as they searched for something near the windows. I poked my head out through the tangle of vines just in time to see Kieran dangling a leg of raw meat from a window three levels above us. The dragons flapped harder, fighting against the gusting wind, their wings slicing the air with desperate force. Still too far, they began to tire.

The largest of the hatchlings, determined but clearly struggling, reached out with his claws and latched onto a thick vine for support, clinging to it as the others hovered uncertainly behind him, waiting to follow his lead.

I sat with my legs out over the wall now. I closed my eyes and summoned a gust of air through my hands and with it, I lifted the closest dragon to Kieran.

"That's cheating." He grumbled as the dragon snatched the food from his hands.

"You're teasing them, this is so high up!" I snickered.

From where we stood in the castle, the Fae below looked like ants moving through sun-dappled streets. I gathered the next gust of wind and sent it upward, guiding the three remaining dragons as they rose effortlessly toward Kieran, who stood several levels above us, dangling more food from the balcony. The dragons landed one by one, talons clicking against the stone as they perched and devoured their meal—first roasting the meat in bursts of flame, then swallowing it nearly whole.

Beau appeared silently at my side, settling beside me at the window. His wings glowed in the sunlight, stretched behind him like panes of blue-blown glass, delicate and powerful all at once. He plucked a few grapes from a bowl, popping them into his mouth one by one. When the last one was gone, he glanced at me with a quiet smirk before diving out of the window without warning.

My breath hitched as he fell, wind rushing past with a howl—and then, at the last second, his wings unfurled in a graceful snap. He caught the air with practiced ease and soared upward, circling the city below. Sunlight shimmered off his hair as it whipped behind him, his ears fully exposed for the first time, proud and unapologetic. He looked free—utterly and impossibly free.

"FLAP!" Kieran yelled.

Beau soared toward us, his enormous wings slicing through the air as he hovered effortlessly above the ground. I summoned a gust of wind, swirling it around him, lifting leaves and dust in a spiraling dance. The dragons immediately responded, their excitement palpable. With a burst of energy, they lunged into the sky, mimicking Beau's every movement.

They glided first, wings outstretched in perfect imitation, then flapped with growing confidence. It was breathtaking to watch—they whipped past unsuspecting shoppers, swooped under arched bridges, and skimmed their wings across the river's surface, sending up shimmering sprays of water.

In a matter of moments, Beau had given them their first flying lesson. And they had taken to the skies they were born for.

"He's a natural." Thane said from behind me.

I swung my legs back into the room and stood before Thane. He was peering out the window and not looking at me as I moved aside for him to have a better view.

"He is." I smiled as I hovered around.

He turned to me now. "We will meet you in Orman in a week's time." He bowed his head.

"A week?" I asked.

"Is there a problem?" He asked.

"No, it's just so soon. I thought we'd have more time." I said as I looked into the sky where Beau played with the baby dragons, he looked so happy. He never looked so at peace with himself.

"I can't explain the feeling." He followed my eyes out the window to where Beau sat in a branch with the dragons.

"Freedom." I smiled. "This is what it is to have a taste of freedom. To not have to hide or be ashamed of what we are." I said.

"Neither of you should have ever had to live like that." He sighed.

I smiled politely as Thane left the room, then wandered back to the window, leaning against the cool stone frame. Below, I caught sight of Beau landing on the bridge, his massive wings folding gracefully as he met Zac, who already seemed completely enthralled with entertaining the dragons. Kieran had disappeared from the window above, and the air was quiet again.

Feeling the weight of exhaustion press against me, I retreated to the bed, hoping to steal a few precious moments of rest while Zac prepared. This was, without question, the most luxurious bed I'd ever had the pleasure of collapsing into—a far cry from the makeshift sleeping arrangements back in Varsili. There, beds were little more than hollowed platforms, often missing proper padding, the absence of furs turning rest into a test of endurance. Here, the mattress welcomed me like a cloud, and the blankets were heavy but deliciously soft.

I burrowed beneath them, adjusting the mountain of pillows around me, flicking my hair over the edge so it wouldn't get trapped beneath my shoulders. A breeze slipped in through the open window, fresh and cool, brushing against my face like a whispered lullaby. There was nothing else I needed in this moment, and I let my eyes fall closed.

Sleep claimed me fast, but it hadn't lasted long. A shadow swept across the room, dimming the golden warmth of the afternoon sun. A sudden chill followed.

It was Beau. His enormous wings filled the window frame, blotting out the light.

"You're blocking my sun!" I growled, squinting one eye open and waving my hand lazily in his direction.

He didn't move—typical.

"We're ready to go." He sat on the bed next to me, he rubbed my shoulder gently trying to bring me out of sleep.

"You suck!" I pulled a pillow over my face.

"Get up." Zac ripped the blankets from me now.

I sat up in the bed and yawned and Beau rubbed my back. "Sorry." He kissed the side of my face.

I leaned into him, and he gave me a moment to gather myself while Zac paced about the room impatiently.

"We have to go now?" I sighed.

"If you like I can fly you out." He smiled.

"What about me?" Zac huffed.

Beau shrugged his shoulders and laughed. "I'm sure Thane will oblige you." Beau teased.

"I don't know how I feel about being carried by such a big masculine man." Zac rearranged himself and puffed out his chest.

"You'll be fine. Or maybe Sina?" I laughed. "She's about the same size as you." I giggled.

Zac had always been sensitive about his height. He wasn't short by any means, but every male was still taller than him and he hated it.

"I think I'll enjoy the walk through the forest." He huffed.

"Maybe another time, time is of the essence." Sina said from the doorway. In her hand, she had an envelope addressed to Cleo. "If you wish I'll fly you through the forest, Zac." She smiled cheekily.

"You can go with Beau if you like?" I offered.

"No thanks, I've seen the way he carries you, he might try to kiss me." He laughed.

"I'm sure the smell of embers and ash will remind me not to." Beau shook his head.

Kieran entered the room with the baby dragons and the Hoca. I pulled myself off the bed and went to hug Kieran. "You'll be missed. But I understand this is your calling." I smiled.

"Tell Eleanor I hope things work out for her and Torin. I hope things work out for all of you." He raised the side of his mouth into half a smile.

But we were going to war, there was a chance some, if not all of us would die and that's where he hesitated.

"I'll tell her." I smiled.

I watched as the baby dragons tackled each other, threatening one another with smoke clouds, and a few sparking embers, knowing they weren't meant to have firefights indoors.

"You look like you'll have your hands full, you're a dad now." Zac punched him in the shoulder playfully.

"Okay, enough of the pleasantries, it's time to go." Beau said as he fought with his backpack. "How the fuck do you do this!" He growled.

"Breathe! Now pull your shoulders in. Relax and feel your wings getting smaller, they'll become more of an armor on your body if you want them to. The pack won't be a problem when you learn how to control your body." Sina smiled as she guided him through the process.

Beau did as she said. It took some time, but it worked, and he was ecstatic. "So, I can sleep like I used to." He beamed.

"How do you think we sleep?" She laughed.

"Upside down from branches like bats." I snickered.

"There are those who are more entuned with nature, the possibilities are limitless." She said with grace, and I bit my tongue as I tried to swallow the cheeky comment I had made.

"Okay, let's go!" Beau grabbed my shoulders and squeczed gently.

I turned and smiled at Beau as he grabbed my hand, and we walked down to the throne room where Thane waited to say farewell to us. Zac was in front of us with Sina and he looked nervous and darted me a cheeky unimpressed expression.

"He's going to let her take him." I whispered to Beau.

"Good, I don't want to wait for him when we reach Draven." He whispered back.

Thane came over to us, clasping our hands with a firm nod before guiding us through the castle doors. Outside, Pixies and Fae lined the walkway, tossing petals into the air, their laughter chiming like bells as they celebrated our departure. The petals shimmered in the sunlight, catching the breeze as they drifted down around us.

Beau flared his massive, dragon-like wings, their iridescent membranes catching the light and casting a brilliant blue glow across the stone pathway. Gasps rippled through the crowd. Faces turned to one another, marveling at what they saw—a winged form unlike anything they had witnessed before. Even the baby dragons rose from the ground, fluttering around Beau in excitement, chirping and squealing as if eager to be part of his farewell.

At a short distance stood Sina. Her wings flared in response, more luxurious and mesmerizing than Beau's—delicate and satin-like, shimmering with every movement. They buzzed like dragonflies, rapid and effortless, lifting her with grace and control. She slung a saddle-like harness over her neck and shoulders, then scooped Zac into it in one smooth motion. He looked like a child on a tree swing, gripping tightly as she lifted off the ground.

They shot into the sky, slicing through the trees. Zac's wild howls echoed through the forest, alternating between joy and alarm as Sina darted through the canopy with impossible precision, never once hitting a branch. His laughter trailed behind them, growing fainter as they disappeared into the emerald expanse.

"Your turn." Beau laughed.

"I don't need a saddle." I smiled as I wrapped my arms around his neck, and he wrapped his arms around my legs and waist.

He flapped hard and fast and pushed off with his feet and soon we were airborne, and I waved with one free hand to the pixies who had guided us to the city.

Beau was faster than Sina, we caught up quickly, and soon we overtook them as we entered an unofficial race back to the dock. Sina whipped through trees and Zac screamed a lot more as he dodged trunks and branches by shifting his weight in the seat.

The dock was in sight now and the lantern on the boat was still flickering as Draven warmed his hands against it and sighed with relief when he saw us approaching.

He waved out as Beau landed and Draven's jaw almost hit the wooden planks as he circled around Beau. Draven reached out to touch what was before him.

"I knew you'd be healed, but this! THIS is exciting!" His voice became higher as he jumped with enthusiasm.

Sina landed beside us and Zac tumbled from the saddle seat. "You're a terrible driver!" He growled at Sina.

"I got you here in record timing!" She laughed as she removed the saddle and threw it at him. "Souvenir of our time together." She giggled some more.

"Teresina." Draven's jaw dropped once more and soon he was kneeling.

"Draven, please get up." She reached for his hand.

"It's been so long." He sighed with relief. "You look well." He smiled as he looked her up and down.

"I am well, good of you to send us some visitors." She smiled.

"I knew they would please you. I never thought I'd see this though." They spoke of Beau as if he weren't here.

"We lost a dragon life in the hatching, the essence went into the healing. I've never seen anything like it. He's magnificent." She began circling with Draven now and Beau became annoyed.

"Perhaps we should go." I interrupted.

"I have this for you." She handed Draven the letter. "It's a contract for war, we will fight alongside you." She nodded.

"This is more than I could ask for." He smiled.

"It's not for you, it's for the Dunya. If Rael and his flying pets aren't contained, we will have a real problem eventually. This ends now." She became serious.

"And Antoli?" He pressed.

"You intend to release Irmak, or something else?" She asked.

"Zac is a Titan without a dragon, Aliera already has a claim to Azra. Irmak can help us win this war with fewer casualties." Draven said firmly.

"Zac is a fire wielder, and you wish to align him with an ice dragon?" She laughed.

"We don't have too many options." Draven's eyes narrowed and Sina straightened.

"Umm, hello. Zac doesn't know anything about this." Zac said childishly in the third person. "What if I don't want a dragon?" He pressed.

"You want this one, trust me." Draven smiled wickedly. "Where is Kieran?" Draven asked.

"He's staying in Sonsuz to raise the baby dragons with the Drake Hoca." I explained.

"A Hoca? You have a Hoca?" Draven glared at Sina.

"The only safe place for a Hoca now is in Sonsuz, we don't exactly advertise it." She scowled.

"Dragons were extinct a year ago…" He took in a deep breath.

"And now they're back, with Titans!" Her eyes glowed an icy shade of blue as she looked between me and Zac.

Draven bowed his head one last time, stepped into the boat, holding it steady for me, Zac, and Beau.

Sina waved as she disappeared into the dense forest and we began to row, but we weren't rowing back to Lexia. We were going further north.

"Where are we going?" I asked after an hour.

Draven tossed each of us thick furry coats and hats as we rounded a bend. A colossus castle of black stone and squared edges came into view. It was covered in old and new layers of snow, ice, and dirt. It had been abandoned.

"It's so big." I gasped.

Draven landed the boat on an old jetty and tied the boat to the only existing post. I stepped off first, Beau stuck right behind me, but Draven stopped him.

"No, only the Titans can enter here." He said as he pointed to a silvery pathway. The stones that pathed the way were untouched by the snow as if they were heated from below.

"I'll be safe with Zac." I kissed Beau's cheek.

"If anything happens to her, I'll skin you." His eyes narrowed on Zac as the horns on his wings crept over his shoulders in a threatening way.

"Like to see you try." Zac said menacingly.

I pushed Zac off the boat and stepped over him as he brushed off the snow he landed in. "Come on!" I grunted.

My boots clicked with every step up the stone path. It wavered and rounded up the castle until we were on the highest point, and

I could see the demolished port and a lake of ice surrounded by trees, the ocean was now nothing but icebergs that thrashed against the shore.

"Do we knock?" Zac questioned.

I sighed as I shook my head.

"It's abandoned, idiot!" I scoffed.

I looked for a doorway but everything about the building told me there wasn't one. "Do you remember when we were little, and what mom would tell us?" I asked Zac.

"Chime the bell and the door will open." Zac replied. "But what bell?" He added.

"That one!" I pointed to the shelter on the roof of the building.

"There are no more stairs, do we scale the stones now?" He grunted.

"SHUT UP!" I snapped. "Let me focus." I said as snow whipped past my face thrashing my hair around me.

I closed my eyes and imagined the wind circling the Castle. The bell was frozen in its place as I pounded it with cyclonic booms, every thud cracked the ice weakening its hold on the singular large bell.

"AGAIN!" Zac shouted.

One final whisp was all it took. My hands filled with the power of the wind, my hair was on end now, and my eyes blurred as I unleashed one final gale on the shelter. The whole structure collapsed sending the bell to our level and the clapper pounded violently one single time into the mouth of the bell before my feet.

"WOAH…" Zac's jaw dropped.

A split second had barely passed when the stones of the castle folded inwards, the halls were lit up with blue flames and we entered cautiously. We followed the long corridor until it opened onto a behemoth of a room, it was foggy with clouds that cleared with every step we took towards the thrones. There were many and they were all of equal size.

"There's another hallway." Zac said as he pointed to the right. "What are we looking for?" He asked.

"I guess a room or cell. Something big enough to contain a dragon." I assumed. "Then again, this whole place is like a prison, there's no way out unless you're a Titan." I muttered under my breath.

"Will he eat us?" Zac gulped.

"We are immortals, we can't be killed unless we're beheaded and even then, you have to know how to dispose of the body." I grunted.

"Is that what you did to Mason?" His eyes darkened.

I slapped his face hard. "You weren't there, you have no right to keep holding that against me." I pulled away.

"No, I wasn't. And I'm one brother down because of it." He rubbed his face.

"Why do you do this?" I became angry.

"What?" He asked.

"Become so unbearable that nobody can stand to be around you!" I hissed.

"I don't know." His face paled. "Maybe because everyone hates me for what I did, it's why Mom left me in Farkli, and probably why she didn't come back." He sighed.

My eyes were wet at the idea of it, but I was frozen. A scraping against the stone echoed and my hairs stood on end. Zac backed into a wall, and he held my hand in his.

"I'm sorry, you're my baby sister and all I've done is wreak havoc on your life." His eyes watered.

"There'll be a time for this conversation. But I don't blame you, Zac. I hope that means something." I squeezed his hand.

"It means a lot." He smiled.

The scrapping continued and a gurgling crackle from the throat of a dragon ghosting the hallways as I felt the coolness of his breath light up my skin.

"He's coming, you need to show dominance. He won't be like Azra." I whispered.

Zac nodded and readied himself by warming his hands. He stood in front of me like a shield as the dragon came into sight and slithered into the room, his presence making it look miniscule.

Zac looked at the dragon, and for a long, tense moment, they simply stared at one another. Then, without warning, the dragon opened his mouth. Zac stepped forward, arms outstretched, and he pulled the flame directly from the dragon's throat. It flowed into him, coating his entire body in brilliant, majestic blue fire. With unwavering resolve, he continued walking forward, cloaked in flame.

Irmak was immense—easily two, maybe three times the size of Azra. His scales were a striking, icy blue that shimmered like frozen crystal, and his eyes glowed with a piercing blend of white and blue, sharp and ancient.

"I've come to claim you." Zac said, his voice catching at the edge of emotion.

Irmak turned his attention to me now. I stepped forward, needing to show him what I was—a Titan. I raised my hand slowly, offering it for him to scent. His enormous nostril, larger than my entire head, hovered over me as he inhaled. The force of it tugged at my hair, and then—he sneezed.

The blast knocked us off our feet, hurling us backward and slamming us into the far wall. The castle groaned in protest, stone cracking as a cloud of dust rained down over us—so much for a graceful first impression.

"Ouch." I groaned as I pressed my hand into my back and moved Zac's foot away from me.

"IRMAK!" Zac called.

The dragon whipped his head to Zac and looked at him from a sideways perspective, so his ear was near us.

"We need your help, and we need you to be okay with working alongside the Fae." Zac said cautiously.

Irmak's eyes darkened and narrowed as he turned to face us head-on.

"Please trust us. We would never hurt you." I sighed.

He nodded as I approached. I rested my hand on a single scale on his cheek and I felt the slight adjustment of his head as he nodded gently and pressed his eyes closed as a tear squeezed from the crevice of his eyelids.

"He's afraid." I said softly.

"Can you blame him? We're asking him to work alongside the same race that almost wiped out his race." Zac softened and came closer to touch Irmak.

"I know how you feel." He whispered.

"This can't be it, what else is here that everyone in the Dunya wants a piece of?" I pondered between the three of us.

"Maybe we should look around before we leave." Zac said.

I agreed with a nod, and we followed the hallway Irmak pointed to with his nose. It seemed endless. Room after room locked, some with more complexity, some just a simple key.

"Should we bust one open?" Zac said.

I shrugged unsure of what to do. Until I came across a door with the figure of a harpy on it. "Zac, look at this." I said as I traced the carving with my fingers and blew off the dust.

My hand stretched out and turned the doorknob. It was locked. "Blast it!" I turned to Zac.

"This one isn't locked." He turned the handle of the door across from mine and it opened.

The room was offensively bright, crammed to the brim with jewels, gold, dragon scale fashioned armor in abundance, and arrows made of Priontine with Sunfire.

"These are priceless…" I gasped as I held up one of the arrows, it was taller than the height of my whole body and extremely heavy.

Zac was sizing up armor against his body and filling his pockets and bag with jewels.

"We'll never get this all out of here." I looked around mesmerized.

"Just take what you can carry for now, we'll come back. You should take this, it'll fit you." He smiled as he handed me a breastplate made of dragon scales.

"We should go, Draven and Beau are waiting for us." I said as I collected as much armor as I could carry.

"We should take some of the gold." Zac said.

"No, look at it. It's not from the Dunya and it isn't gold. It's Stormcopper." I said.

"That's from a whole other realm, Aliera." Zac looked panicked.

I dropped the bags I had and looked through the jewels. I examined the two black and clear jewels and recalled something similar from a book our mother had shown me, a single copy from Farkli she had kept with her.

"Gloomstone and Pure Lustre. Zac, these aren't meant to be here. Do you remember Mom's apothecary book? The deep green one—it had a section on the realms. Tierra Hundida and Cypra the city of Vacia Isla. I think these jewels are from one of them." I said.

I sprinted down the main hallway, scanning the insignias carved into each door—a Harpy for Tierra Hundida, a Siren for Cypra. But the hall was expansive, there were more doors, more creatures. My heart was racing as I found a door with a Foogal etched into the wood. I pulled a Storm Copper coin from my pocket and pressed it into the hollow of the Tierra Hundida door. At once, the door warped, sucking inward like a collapsing vortex, and a powerful gust of wind slammed into me, stealing the breath from my lungs.

When the wind finally settled, the world beyond the doorway came into view: a sprawling city spread out beneath me, unlike anything I'd seen. An enormous aviary loomed in the center, large enough to hold a hundred beings. Harpies prowled and hovered around the outside of its bars, their wings twitching restlessly, their sharp eyes watching from the shadows as if daring anyone to come closer.

It wasn't just any door; it was a door to another realm. It was alive—wild and waiting.

Before I could do anything, Zac grabbed me and pulled me back and the wind slammed the door shut.

"There are people in there! They're in that cage!" I yelled.

"ALIERA! It's another world—we need to help ours first!" His voice cracked with urgency as his hands cradled my face, grounding me in the storm of my thoughts.

"We will come back for them." he said, softer now, his eyes locked on mine. "But I need you to help me. I can't do this without you."

For a heartbeat, I searched his expression, the weight of everything crashing down in my chest. Then, slowly, he exhaled and sat back, releasing me with a quiet resolve.

He was right. And I hated that he was.

I nodded as I pulled myself up the wall and pushed myself off my back. "Okay, let's go." I pulled my hair to the side and Zac secured the smaller arrows from the armory onto Irmak with ropes.

We climbed onto Irmak's back, his scales glittering like ice beneath the fading light. With a deep breath, I summoned the cyclonic winds, the air crackling around us as I reached out to the ancient bell. The sound rang out in a low, haunting chime, and the ceiling of the castle groaned as it slowly opened. Irmak pushed through with a powerful thrust of his wings, barely squeezing past the narrowing stone.

Once free, he roared with triumphant fury, his colossal body soaring into the cold air above Antoli. He was breathtaking—a creature carved from sky and storm, his icy-blue form almost indistinguishable from the snowcapped mountains stretching behind him. Then, with a flick of his wings, he let loose a thunderous beam of blue heat, scorching a path through the sky as if to announce his return to the world.

He was showing off, reveling in the freedom he'd been denied for too long.

"Go, Irmak!" Zac shouted, grinning wide.

Irmak dipped low, skimming over the frozen coastline of Antoli. His wings sliced through the frigid water, shattering icebergs with ease as he plunged just low enough for his talons to skim the surface, sending geysers of sea spray into the air.

He moved like a force of nature—untamed, unchallenged, and completely alive.

Draven clapped from below, a grin stretched across his face as Beau took flight, his wings carving through the air with practiced ease. He rose to meet us, catching the wind in a graceful arc. But Irmak spotted him, his instincts sharp and immediate.

With a guttural roar, Irmak lunged—massive and swift, his throat filling with a deep, thunderous fury. Beau twisted midair, ducking low and weaving with agility, narrowly avoiding the blast of heat that followed.

"HE'S FRIENDLY!" I shouted, my voice carried by the wind.

Irmak huffed in response, the sound more growl than breath, clearly unimpressed by my declaration. He turned and descended, wings folding as he landed with a seismic thud. The ground cracked beneath him as his talons crushed what remained of the once-lush forest path that had led to the castle—now just ash and ruin beneath his weight.

Beau landed as I jumped down from Irmak, but Zac stayed in place. "I could get used to this." Zac smiled. Irmak grinned and anxiously trotted his feet in place, he was eager to leave.

"This is Irmak. Irmak, this is Draven, the leader of Orman's armies and this is Beau—my boyfriend." I smiled as Beau wrapped me in his arms and then his wings.

Irmak took a great interest in Beau, lowering his massive head to inspect him with slow, deliberate breaths. His nostrils flared as he sniffed at Beau's wings, the shimmering membranes trembling under the weight of the dragon's curiosity. Beau, visibly nervous for the first time, stood still and closed his eyes, surrendering to the moment.

Irmak leaned in closer, the icy wind of his breath ruffling Beau's hair as he inhaled his scent. Then, with surprising gentleness, he brushed his snout against Beau's shoulder—not with suspicion, but with a sense of familiarity, like he was greeting someone he recognized from another life.

It was a moment of unspoken understanding between ancient power and reluctant heir, one that neither of them fully grasped, but both seemed to accept.

"I think he likes you." I said sarcastically.

"I think he recognizes the infant's essence in you. You were essentially reborn into your new form." Draven smiled.

"We should get back to Lexia." Draven said.

"I agree, the faster the better." Zac smirked.

"Race ya!" Beau sneered playfully at Irmak.

"Aliera, can you send the boat back?" Draven asked as he warmed his wings.

"I can try." I shrugged.

I closed my eyes and focused on the boat, picturing it drifting down the river, carried by the current and wind, heading for the outpost where the Fae soldiers would be waiting. I could almost see it gliding through the mist, silent and steady—a final message carried by the water. The wind then swept the boat away out of our sight and Beau scooped me into his arms.

"Let's fly!" Irmak broke the earth below him as he pressed off and lifted into the air, Beau close behind him and Draven beside us.

"THIS IS AWESOME!" Zac shouted.

We all smiled as the wind swept around us, the same gust that carried the boat now making our flight smoother and faster. The journey felt effortless, and in less than a day, we arrived at the outpost. Draven raised a hand in greeting as the guards swam out to intercept the boat, and I held the wind steady, guiding it gently into their reach.

It wasn't long before we were back in Lexia. Zac led Irmak to land on the eastern side of the castle, where the pale sands stretched out like silk and the sun still hung warm above, casting golden light across our skin.

Curious Fae rushed to the shoreline and gathered on balconies and towers, eyes wide as they caught sight of Irmak. He was radiant here, his massive form impossible to miss, his icy scales catching the sunlight and scattering it across the castle walls like shards of mirrored glass.

He was wary, but cautious not to show his temper. Astrid ran out with Ele, Torin, and Luca. Zac leaped down and caught Astrid in a hug.

"I was not expecting all of this." She was exasperated as she approached Irmak, and he let her touch him.

"Woah and WOAH! Beau?" She looked at me.

"I wish you could have been there." I said as I hugged her.

"You guys have been busy." Torin said as he approached Beau.

"They did most of it." He smiled at me and Zac.

"Umm, you only writhed in pain and flames for days on end, but sure we did it all." Zac laughed.

"Where is Kieran?" Ele asked.

"Ugh, he stayed in Sonsuz. He is helping to raise and train the baby dragons." I explained.

Torin hugged her and kissed her forehead. "You'll see him again, even if I have to take you there myself." His hug looked warm and comforting, he had care in his eyes, and he wiped her tears, and I began to see what she saw in him.

CHAPTER EIGHTEEN

BEAU

We camped that night on the beach with Irmak. Cleo, Jace, Starlette, and the other leaders came to greet us, their faces lit with relief and wonder. They had arranged a feast to be brought down to where we slept. The Fae had set up elegant canvas bell tents with fully padded beds, each one turned toward the sea, offering a perfect view of the moons and stars above.

I climbed into the big bed with Aliera and stared at the sky through the open flap of our tent. It was peaceful. Music drifted down from the city, soft and joyous, a celebration of Irmak's arrival. Street parties erupted through Lexia, and fireworks lit the night in bursts of gold and silver.

The air grew cold as the sea breeze rolled in, curling through the tents and tugging at the edges of our blankets. Zac, ever practical, arranged logs for a fire. Irmak barely coughed—a low rumble in his throat—and a surge of blue flame roared to life, crackling with heat and casting a brilliant glow across the sand.

"That's cool." Ele smiled from the opening of her tent.

"Nice score." Luca said from his tent.

We were all lying with our heads out now staring into the sky and talking amongst ourselves.

"We're just going up to the bathhouse to freshen up." Astrid had a wicked grin on her face as she said it. Her hand was in Zac's as he tried to pull her along.

"Sure, go freshen up." Ele teased.

"Just cause you've had company in your bed all week." Astrid retorted. Ele went red and Torin froze at their exchange.

"Go and have some fun, you've been miserable moping around all week without him." Luca interjected. Astrid flashed him a smile, she squeezed Zac's hand, and they ran up to the city.

Aliera was ruffling through her bag. She pulled out some items, walked over to Ele's tent, and sat on the ground outside, but she kept her hand closed.

I stood up and joined her as I became curious.

"Ele, can you take a look at something for me? If anyone can identify these accurately, I think it's you." Aliera said as she opened her hand.

In her palm, she held an off-gold coin, a black jewel, and a clear jewel that captured the light around us.

"Where did you find these?" Ele's mouth hung open as she looked at the pieces.

"We found them in a room in Antoli." Aliera answered.

Ele looked worried. "This is Storm Copper, it's from the underworld of a human planet called Earth.

"An underworld?" She asked.

"Doomed to live in shadows and haze. It's an evil world, but some good prevails." She explained. She flipped the coin that had a stamp of a harpy on one side, and a cage on the other.

"That's the world I saw." Aliera said.

"You opened a door to a world?" Ele asked.

"Zac helped me close it straight away." She replied.

"Don't ever do that again." Ele became firm as she sat up. 'Any other open doors I should know about?" She asked.

"No, we didn't have time, but Zac saddled Irmak with arrows made of Priontine, they were cast with Sunfyre." She said.

Torin got up and looked over the pile of arrows as big as his leg. "These are smaller than I expected." He remarked.

"These ones were forged for Fae, not dragons." Draven spoke.

Ele played with the two jewels in her hand. "This is Pure Lustre." She smiled. "It's a drop of moonlight that falls into the Philyreian sea. How did they get this?" She gasped.

"Why is that hard to get?" Luca asked.

"Philyreia is a vast sea within the realm of the Vacia Isla." she said, her voice low with urgency. "Tierra Hundida—it's a separate realm entirely, with its own rules, its own dangers. Vacia Isla is the sister island to the Harpy continent. Someone's been hopping into other worlds." Her expression shifted, panic flickering in her eyes. "Pure Lustre falls to the deepest parts of the Philyreia sea. Only a Siren can catch it." she whispered. "And trust me—you don't ever want to come face to face with one of those." She added.

"Well, I'm glad they aren't inhabitants of the Dunya." Luca exhaled.

"What's this one?" Torin picked up the black jewel and it heated to his touch. "OUCH!" He dropped it on the bed, and it cooled instantly.

"That's Gloomstone, it detects and exposes lost souls." She smiled up at him. "I've never seen one in person, or seen it work!" She sat up on her knees as she pressed the cooled gem into her hands.

"So, Torin's a lost soul?" I asked.

"He is, he's had his humanity stolen from him. It doesn't mean you're bad, but it will do the same with anyone who has undergone any sort of transformation." She explained.

I picked up the stone and instantly it scalded my fingers, and I dropped it into the grass. "That hurts!" I blew at my fingers.

"Told you so." Torin muttered.

"Keep that thing away from me." I furrowed my brows as Aliera picked it up without effort.

"Scared of a little rock." She teased as she juggled it in her hands.

I narrowed my eyes at her, and she pulled me back down. "Where is it from?" She directed her questions back to Ele.

"Cloplands, the Cyclops lands." she said with a sigh, pulling in a deep, heavy breath. "Before the Titans were known as Titans, they were called Giants. That's why the ruins are so massive. But over time, as their bloodlines mixed with other species, they became lesser—smaller. Still enormous to us, but not what they once were." She began.

"Peace didn't always exist between the Giants, or Titans as we now call them. There was a village of Giants in the north, vile and twisted. The others tried to destroy them, but all their magic could manage was to disfigure them—to make them unmistakable, wherever they went. Giants with a single eye." Ele explained.

"They still had access to Antoli, and they stormed the castle, driven by revenge. That's why they were banished through a realm door. The adults were never found. And their children…" She paused. "They were cast into Tierra Hundida."

"What made the stones?" I asked.

"Gloomstone are their solidified tears, it helps them find each other when they heat on someone who has lost their soul. But they aren't specific to the Cyclops, they work on anyone with a broken soul. " She sunk her chin.

"That's sad." Torin sighed.

"Did you find anything else?" Ele looked to Aliera for more.

She shook her head. "No, we didn't have time." She sighed.

"There was so much in there." She beamed.

"Some things are best left." Ele held Aliera's hands and locked her gaze.

Aliera forced a smile, and I could feel resentment in her tone as she spoke. "I know." It was a lie.

"We should all get some rest. We are training tomorrow." Draven said as he rolled over in his bed and flicked his curtain closed.

Aliera and I headed back to our tent, and we settled in for the night, as did the others.

Sleep was nearly impossible that night, a cacophony of snores rising and falling in strange harmony between Luca and Torin. I tossed and turned, the sound relentless, until I finally gave in and slipped quietly out of the tent. The cool night air whipped against my skin as I wandered down toward the shore.

The sea was calm, its dark surface rippling under the moonlight, and in the distance, the lights of Korsan shimmered like scattered stars against the dark silhouette of the isle. At first, it looked vibrant—alive, even—for such a late hour. But as I focused my improved, renewed vision on the isle, my chest tightened at the revelation.

It wasn't lanterns burning, the light flickered too wildly, too high—The cliffsides were ablaze.

Flames cascaded down the rock faces like waterfalls of fire, licking at the edges of the forest, consuming everything in their path. My breath caught. The entire isle was in flames, and the night air carried the faint scent of smoke and something far worse—the acrid sting of destruction.

Korsan was burning.

Torin snuck up behind me. "You could smell it too?" He asked.

"No, I don't have a dog's nose." I laughed and he nudged me. "But I have sharp Fae hearing." I added.

"There's trouble over there." Torin said as he looked out over the isle.

"Want to go for a look?" I asked him.

"Only if you promise to carry me like you carry Aliera." He joked as he held up Zac's saddle from Teresina and laughed.

"I think I like you." I said as I pulled the harness over my arms and neck.

"Don't tell Aliera." He teased.

I shook my head and laughed as I secured the harness and Torin sat in the swing-like seat and held on for dear life. "Don't drop me, I hate the sea." He begged.

"Then hold on tight and hope you don't weigh too much." I said as I thrust us off the ground and into the air.

Torin yelled almost as loud as Zac until I shushed him. "Be quiet!" I growled.

We flew low and slow to avoid detection, hugging the cliffsides that radiated such intense heat I feared the red ash below would ignite on contact. Instead, we descended toward a lower ridge, where the terrain softened. A small patch of green clung to life there, protected by the surrounding stone—the only surviving oasis. We landed quietly, grateful for the cover, and for the fleeting sense of safety it offered.

"The cities being sacked." Torin became angry as he watched women and children fighting for their lives as their husbands and fathers stood no chance against the marauders.

"I see that, but by who?" I said.

"They've got to be with Rael." Torin angered. "Let me at them!" He held my gaze.

"Can I trust you to control it and turn back?" I asked as I unsheathed my jagged sword ready to support him.

"I promise. I wouldn't do it if I didn't think I wouldn't come back for Ele." He said.

"Cute!" I rolled my eyes.

"Fuck you." He chuckled back.

"Let's go save some people, pup." I snickered.

He shook his head at me as his fangs protruded from his gums, hands morphing into massive paws tipped with dagger-sharp claws. His chest expanded with a deep, guttural snarl that echoed off the cliffside, drool trailing from his jaw as his transformation completed. Then, without hesitation, he launched himself down the slope.

I soared above him, covering from the air as he tore through the raiders, shredding them into pieces so mangled they were beyond recognition. The scent of blood and smoke filled the air, but I stayed focused, scanning for survivors. As he fought below, I darted through the chaos, doing everything I could to help the families flee to safety.

Torin was fast, ruthless, and brilliant to watch. He moved like a storm unleashed; a weapon of mass destruction born for the anarchy of war. And I was proud to fight alongside him. For every ten that came at him, I only needed to take three—not because they were easy, but because he made it look that way.

Once I knew he was holding his ground, I took to the skies. Wings slicing the air, I soared over the raiders' ships. Barrels of oil rained from my hands, crashing onto their decks. I ignited them with a single strike of flame, and the fire surged upward, roaring as high as the cliffs. The ships burned in violent succession, and smoke filled the sky, drifting westward like a dark banner of warning.

Then Irmak appeared overhead, drawn by the scent of smoke curling through the air. Zac, riding with fierce determination, guided him down to the red-hot ash smouldering along the cliffside. With a thunderous roar, Irmak unleashed his flame, incinerating every visible threat with ruthless precision, his heat casting waves through the scorched air.

While pandemonium erupted around us, I raced through the streets, ushering families into safety and striking down the last of the invaders. The firelight danced across my blades, each movement accurate, each breath focused on survival.

But it didn't take long. The battle broke as quickly as it had begun.

Most of the raiders dropped their weapons the moment Torin prowled into view. Even on all fours, he towered over them, a monstrous force wrapped in muscle and menace. He snapped and snarled, his fangs glinting in the firelight, and the raiders crumbled into sobbing heaps, too afraid to run. Just one look at him, one growl, and they understood: even a lick from him could tear flesh from bone.

They yielded, broken by fear before blood—his very presence promised devastation.

"Torin…" I warned. He looked back at me and grunted in a playful tone. I'm sure if a Dread could laugh, he just did it.

He rose slowly, towering above the crowd of trembling raiders. They dropped their weapons, hands raised, voices cracking with pleas for mercy. His body shifted, bones snapping and muscles realigning as he morphed back into his human form. Naked, bare feet pressed into the blood-stained earth; he stood completely exposed—but not vulnerable.

He radiated power, even now. Vicious and unrelenting, he stepped forward, eyes locked on one raider who had dared to raise a blade against him. Without a word, he knelt, bringing himself to the raider's level, and bared his teeth in a slow, deliberate snarl.

His claws remained partially formed, curved and gleaming in the firelight. He lifted one hand and placed it on the man's chest, just enough pressure to remind him how close he was to death.

"Next time." he growled, his voice like gravel. "You won't get the chance to beg."

The raider sobbed, paralysed by fear, but no further punishment came. The message was clear—Mercy had its limits.

"Who sent you?" His growl was low and husky.

The man cried uncontrollably until Torin pierced his throat with his claw.

"That's enough. Keep two, we kill the rest." I ordered.

Zac and Torin took their own pleasure in the kills. Both were drenched in blood once they were done. The ground was soaked in puddles of their massacre.

"We'll take these two back to Lexia." Zac said as Irmak hovered over and clawed each of them through their shoulders and violently flew them to Lexia once Zac had climbed back up to his neck using scales as a staircase to reach the top.

The humans emerged from the few remaining homes only after Irmak had flown away. Shaken and displaced, they stepped cautiously into the ruins of their village, where ash floated like snow and flames still licked at fractured beams. The air was foggy with smoke and silence, broken only by the soft sounds of grieving.

They moved like ghosts through what remained, searching through the rubble for pieces of their past. Homes were no longer recognizable—only charred memories of what once was. Their women bore the weight of unspeakable trauma, eyes vacant and haunted. Their men, bloodied and broken from defending their families, stood dazed in the streets where they'd been beaten.

It was devastation. Absolute and merciless. And still, amidst the ruin, they clung to one another.

"We can't leave them stranded on this island like this. All the ships were torched, they'll never survive." Torin turned to me.

"How do you propose we get them to safety?" I asked.

"Could we go back and bring a ship?" He questioned.

"We have to try." I agreed.

Torin climbed back into the saddle, and we flew back to Lexia where Irmak could be seen on the beach from a distance breathing fire onto one of the hostages.

"Idiot." I grunted as I landed beside Zac.

"They had cut their own tongues out on the flight over." He looked me in the eyes.

"You didn't think maybe to check them for weapons first?" I glowered over him.

"I don't do this for a living. Unlike you, assassin." He scowled at me.

"ENOUGH!" Aliera snapped as she raced for us.

She looked between the three of us and at Irmak who was covered in grey soot. "What happened?" She asked.

"We saw flames building up from Korsan, Torin and I flew over and it was being raided, we helped." I shrugged.

"You helped?" She looked at Torin and motioned at her face as if it were messy to warn him that he was covered in blood.

"We couldn't just let those people be murdered." Torin answered as he straightened up and tried to wipe away the dried blood.

"Go and clean yourself up." She ordered.

Astrid appeared as Torin was walking back and her eyes narrowed on Zac. "Joy riding with the only dragon we have in the dead of night? A WHITE FUCKING DRAGON, ZAC!" She screamed.

"They needed help!" He replied, but he didn't dare raise his voice as Astrid and Aliera stared at him with daggers in their eyes.

"Speaking of help, it's still in flames and those people need somewhere to go." I added hesitantly as I avoided eye contact with Astrid.

Astrid rubbed her tired face with both hands as Cleo approached with guards.

"We saw the flames, I have a ship heading over now." She nodded. "Where are the hostages?" She asked.

"There." I pointed to the two piles of crisp ash still smoking from their dragon encounter, red embers floating in the sea breeze.

"Well, that's not helpful." She groaned.

"They had cut out their tongues." Zac rolled his eyes as he repeated himself.

"Less attitude from you." I teased as the girls all walked away.

"I saved your ass!" He punched me softly.

"And I'm grateful." I pushed him with one of my wings and he staggered.

"We make a pretty good team me, you, and Torin." He said proudly.

"Little taster before the big war." I sighed as I sat on a boulder and the sun began to rise. "You know that wasn't just a raid, that was planned by Rael. He doesn't care who he ruins, as long as he gets what he wants." I sighed.

"And he wants my sister." Zac sat against me on the boulder and leaned into my wings.

"She can't come to the frontline." I said.

"Pffft! Good luck telling her that." He laughed.

"I'm serious, if they catch her, they'll do unspeakable things to her. How do we convince her." I sighed.

"Ele can make a tea to knock her out, it'll have to be strong to take out a Titan for a significant amount of time though. And it still won't be long enough." He looked at me sadly.

"I just want to protect her." I confessed.

"You love her." He patted my shoulder.

I bobbed my head as I rubbed my forehead, elbows on my knees and my legs wide.

"I'm glad, I know we don't always see eye to eye, but this we can agree upon. She doesn't go to war." Zac said.

"And what if none of us come back?" Ele spooked us from behind.

"DAMN IT! You scared us." I shrieked.

"Answer the question." She said as she sat with us on the boulder and leaned into my other wing.

"I haven't thought that far, but I'm hoping we can leave the Dunya in a better way than it is now." My cheeks flushed with heat.

"Can you make a tea to knock her out for a while?" Zac asked.

"She'll kill us all if she finds out." Ele wasn't convinced.

"Do I have to tell you what Rael will do if he captures her?" I felt like I was on repeat by this point.

"No, I know what he'll do. But he'll expect you to hide her, Beau. Like you've said in the past, he isn't stupid. Maybe the safest place for her is with all of us." She shrugged.

"A Fae, two Titans, two Sorceresses, a Dread, a dragon, a legion of Fae warriors from all three cities. We will protect her." Ele leaned into my wings and by now I was supporting both her weight and Zac's.

But she was right, we had power on our side, we had the army, the leadership, the dragon. I was overthinking it. I hoped.

"Okay, but we all stick together. Zac, stay close." I narrowed my eyes at him.

I got up, and they collapsed into each other as I walked back to the tent where Aliera had already climbed back into our bed. I slipped beneath the blankets beside her and exhaled, trying to let sleep reclaim me.

The camp had quieted. Luca had wandered up to the bathhouse for breakfast, and with his absence came the gift of silence. No more snoring, no rustling, just the soft hush of the sea in the distance and the warmth of Aliera pressed gently against my side.

For the first time in days, it felt like peace.

Chapter Nineteen

ALIERA

It was after midday when we woke to the sound of tents being pitched on the grass above the shoreline. The rhythmic thud of mallets striking wood echoed through the air, accompanied by the rustling of canvas and the low murmur of voices as men worked to build temporary homes for the displaced families of Korsan.

Beau yawned beside me, then wordlessly pulled me into his arms, his body warm against mine. With a sleepy sigh, he wrapped his wings around us, shielding us from the world. The light filtering through his iridescent sails bathed us in a soft sapphire glow, casting rippling patterns across our skin as if we were underwater.

For a moment, we stayed like that—safe, hidden in our cocoon of quiet, stealing a few more heartbeats of peace before the day truly began.

"We should help." I whispered as I brushed the hair from his eyes.

"We should, shouldn't we?" He bobbed his head up to kiss me long and softly.

"Let's help get the tents set up and then we can disappear up to the bathhouse." I smiled through a kiss.

"What about Irmak?" He asked.

"Are you worried someone will steal him?" I teased.

He laughed. "Okay, good point."

Beau's wings released us, and I pulled on my clothes and stretched as I opened the flap to our tent. "Ugh, it's bright." I hissed as the sunlight.

"TOLD YOU!" Beau grunted as he pulled on his pants and strapped his weapons back on his body.

We walked out through the now expansive camp. There was a food station, a medical station, a place for laundry, another for children to play and somewhere to collect linens and clothes. It was a full rescue mission, and it occurred to me that none of these people would have survived had it not been for Beau, Torin, Zac, and Irmak. I looked up at Beau as he gazed around at the fine processes that it took to get these people somewhat comfortable again, even though so many grieved the loss of loved ones. Everyone had lost someone, this was only the beginning of rebuilding for them. Brick-and-mortar homes would be a long way off.

"You are wonderful." I stopped at his side and held his hand in both of mine as I rested my head in his strong arms.

"Huh?" He asked.

"You helped these people." I smiled.

He nodded unintelligibly barely taking in anything I said as he watched a grown man crying beneath a tree with a woman in his arms and he made a beeline for him almost knocking me down.

I hung back a little while he went and sat with the man. I fetched a plate of food and a pitcher of water and brought it over. Beau was on the ground with the man now crying over the body of the woman. She was dead, she had been dead for some time.

Beau's eyes watered, there was a sadness in him I hadn't seen before as he comforted the man. "I'll help you bury her." Beau offered.

"She deserved more." The man cried.

I poured a cup of water and handed it to the man who was polite and took it, but he placed it in the sand beside him and didn't drink it.

"There'll be a ceremony tonight for all the dead. I overheard the women at the food tent speak about it." I explained.

He wiped his tears and kissed her sunken face. "Her body already so cold and stiff." He cried.

"We should bury her soon." Beau said gently.

The man nodded as he stood up, he was strong enough to lift the body alone and he carried her to the place where they would do a mass cremation for all the bodies that the families were able to retrieve.

"I'm going to kill him…" I growled.

"Who?" Beau asked.

"Rael…" I said as I looked into the masses of people, most were nursing an injury of some kind. Children who had been beaten blue but still found joy in playing because they were saved. Today they got to play on the beaches of Lexia. Lexia was a dream city, the only Fae city that adopted humans in need.

In the distance there were always Fae hard at work building permanent homes for these people, Fae worked so quickly that it would only take a few months to complete. But it was still months exposed to the elements, piecing together their lives as best they could. Grieving the loss of family, homes, and belongings.

"I'm so in awe of your people." I said to Beau.

"My whole life I was made to feel ashamed of what I was, told to hide my ears, clipped of my wings. I've seen nothing bad about them at all." He became angry.

I reached up and held his face in my hands as my fingers traced the points of his ears. "You're out of there now, and soon he'll be gone. You're mine now, not his." I assured him.

"Don't be so sure." He stroked my face. "What happens next won't be easy. Promise you'll stay close to me, if not me then Zac, Astrid, or Torin." His request felt more like an order.

"Since when do you like Zac?" I snickered.

"Since he's your brother, I trust him to protect you." He winced.

"I promise I'll stay safe." I assured him.

A horn blew from the castle and the guards rallied everyone into the city square. Beau and Zac went looking for Cleo or Draven and I stayed with the crowd in the square as the keeper of the city made an announcement.

"Our dear townsfolk, I have a message for you." He cleared his throat. He was nervous as his hand with the letter shook.

"As you know, there has been a war now for many centuries, but Lexia has been able to avoid the conflict with strong borders and patrols. But the time has come for us to aid Orman, who is losing the battle against the Varsilian tyrant. A new age of mages have created armies strong enough to end our way of life. If we don't act now, we fear the worst for our people and humble way of life.

People of Korsan, you have experienced the torment of war already. Those unable to fight will remain in Lexia where your skills will help us win the war in other ways." He exhaled hard and stepped away from the podium and chatter amongst the people grew louder.

"We aren't warriors!" One man shouted.

The crowd agreed and the masses began to protest. "I've been to those war camps. I've seen what the mages did to their soldiers. I will not fight against monsters!" Another yelled.

"Yes, you will." Draven approached the stand.

"Why, what safety can you guarantee us?" Another questioned.

"Have you not seen the dragon outside the walls?" Draven laughed.

"One dragon!" A man yelled.

"MY DRAGON!" Zac stepped up to the stand now and Beau was behind him. His huge hulking wings were more enormous than ever, his shoulders splayed for the entertainment of the city, and I couldn't help but blush as he winked in my direction.

"Who are you?" a woman hollered at Zac.

Zac didn't say a word—he showed her. His eyes ignited with red-hot flame, the heat rolling off him in waves so intense that Beau instinctively stepped back and Torin shielded his face with his arm. Fire surged around Zac, engulfing him in a blaze of pure fury. He summoned a fireball the size of his body and raised it high above the crowd, the flames roaring and writhing with power. Heat rippled through the air and sweat beaded on every brow. The crowd held its breath.

Then, with a sharp clap of his hands, Zac extinguished the fireball. Smoke hung in the air, deliberate, a lingering warning.

He turned his gaze to me, and I met it with a nod. I pulled back the hood of my cloak, twirling in a dramatic flourish that drew a murmur from the crowd. My hands rose skyward, and I reached through the smoke to summon the wind. A gust funnelled down through my fingers, lifting the smoke into a spiralling column above the city. The sky darkened as I called in the clouds, coaxing rain to follow.

Together, we reminded them who we were—and what we could do.

"TITANS!" A woman screamed with excitement.

The crowd cheered as I released a small sprinkling of rain and I walked forward to where Zac stood, Torin by his side clapping playfully.

"What else?" A man asked.

"My turn or yours?" Torin looked to Beau.

Beau smiled and tilted his head at Torin to take front and center.

"Wait!" I pressed my hand on Beau's chest and looked at Torin. "I don't think we should give away *all* of our tricks at once. You might scare them." I cautioned.

"If we don't show them, we risk them mistaking Torin for one of Rael's dreadwolves." Beau said.

"There's a lot more to be afraid of than me." Torin rested his hand on my shoulder.

"You're truly, okay? You're not going to feast on the city?" I cautioned.

"I promise. If I do, you can kill me yourself." He winked.

"Don't underestimate me." I smiled.

He stepped aside and moved to the podium in front of the crowds, where people were still murmuring among themselves. Children huddled together in the throng—some Fae, some human—clearly overwhelmed by the rising tension in the square.

"Move the children away!" I called to the guards. Then, turning to Torin, I added, "Wait." He nodded in agreement, his gaze softening. The little ones didn't need this burned into their memories.

The guards guided the children to safety, and I let out a breath, giving Torin a thumbs-up.

He stepped forward, and silence fell.

Torin possessed a natural authority—not just because of his immense frame, but the calm confidence in his expression. His dirty blond hair hung in tousled waves, his beard full and rough, and his piercing blue eyes scanned the crowd with gravity. Women looked at him as if he were a myth made real: a warrior from Sonsuz, a soldier from the Fjord, something ancient and enduring.

But that image shattered the moment he placed his hands on the podium—and crushed it.

Claws burst from his fingers, splintering the wood as his body surged in size. His jaw extended, reshaping to make room for rows of lethal fangs. His eyes bled orange, glowing with an intensity that clashed violently with their ocean-blue hue. The transformation overtook him, his muscles swelling beneath his skin, bones cracking and reforming. The remnants of his clothing fluttered to the ground in torn shreds, and in their place, a thick coat of wiry light brown fur enveloped his towering frame.

Now, he loomed above us all—no longer the gentle warrior, but a creature of fearsome power.

Torin was no myth—he was a reckoning.

"DEMON!" A man yelled.

"No, he's not a demon." Beau spoke to the crowd, his wings still spread and a catch in his throat that alarmed me to worry.

"He's not like the other Dreadwolves. He is good." I explained.

Luca sighed in the back and Ele linked his arm with hers as she offered him comfort.

Torin morphed back now, and I was relieved as he addressed the crowd's concerns.

"I'm not like the others. Rael and his mages tortured me and experimented on me. But I got away." He said as the crowd listened with intent.

"Everyone here has a reason to fight. And if you don't know someone who was hurt by him then fight for your own freedom, the freedom to see the Dunya and visit cities you wouldn't have before." He said.

"I'll fight with you, for you, for us all!" He threw his fist into the air and the crowd roared with him.

"Well, I think we found our public speaker." Astrid smiled as she stepped up beside me.

"They love him!" I giggled.

"Didn't see that coming." She laughed.

"RUDE!" Torin strode past us and laughed also.

"And what about him?" The crowd pointed to Beau.

"I'm just another Fae." He answered.

The crowd didn't press any further as they accepted his answer.

"You're not just *any* Fae." I said as I walked over to him.

"They don't need to know my roots." He brushed my hair from my face.

"That's fair." I nodded.

Draven stepped forward, flanked by guards, and began handing out tokens—each one a symbol of purpose, a path forward for those who had survived. The tokens came in four distinct colors, each representing a role within the effort to rebuild and defend.

Blue tokens were given to those who would remain in Lexia. They were assigned to tend the land, nurse the wounded, care for the young, and keep the city functioning. Most of these went to women and older children, their quiet strength forming the backbone of a recovering society.

Red tokens were reserved for sailors and those with knowledge of the sea. Anyone who had expressed interest in naval work or had experience with ships received one. They would patrol the coastline, supply distant outposts, and help maintain contact between cities.

Green tokens marked those bound for combat. Many were Fae, agile and fierce, but several young humans joined them as partners, riding tandem with Fae warriors to increase their effectiveness. Draven, impressed by the ingenuity of Teresina's sling. He had ordered thousands more to be crafted, arming this new force with tools that could turn the tide of battle.

Yellow tokens were rare and carried weight. These were reserved for leadership—Draven himself, Jace, Beau, Torin, and Zac, though Zac had no desire to command anyone but Irmak. Still, his strength demanded recognition. Cleo and Starlette, fierce and unyielding, would remain in Lexia to guard its border, the final shield between the capital and whatever darkness still lurked beyond.

With each token placed in a waiting hand, a new future was claimed—not just for the city, but for the people who had chosen to fight for it.

For those of you with red and green tokens, meet tomorrow at dawn for armor and weapons. Everyone scattered quickly back to their homes as we stood in the square, which was actually an oval with the representatives of the realm.

"Cleo, would you please care for Luna?" I asked as Luna crouched by my side fully aware that something big was happening.

She gave me a pitiful look and then looked down at Luna and held her hand out for her. "I'll keep her safe." She said as she knelt at Luna's height and did what she could to befriend her.

"She's a very good girl." Beau knelt down with her now also and hugged her as she licked his face. "I wasn't sold on you at first, but you quickly changed my mind." He brushed through her thick black coat. She barked at him playfully and they tackled him on the ground.

Luna stopped and looked between me and Beau, then Zac and Astrid as if she were asking a question. "If it were safe we'd bring you." Zac knelt to hug her next.

"This feels like goodbye." Astrid wiped tears from her eyes.

"Don't say that!" Torin nudged her.

Torin had quickly bonded with Luna after the first initial standoffs. He was the only one who was able to communicate with her in a meaningful way, even though it wasn't a full understanding, he just got her.

"Kieran left a gift for you all at the armory, come and see." Starlette announced.

We all looked at one another with a puzzling confusion at what the gift could have been. We followed Cleo and Starlette as they led us to the armory. Draven and Jace stayed back strategizing attacks and coordinating plans. The most southern point of Lexia was a large harbor with what was once trade ships, but now those large trade ships that had been banked for so long had been turned into warships. The last of the supplies were being taken from the armory and mills past us on wagons as we walked the long distance.

"This is far." Zac groaned.

"We've walked further." Torin laughed.

"You don't know far." Beau grumbled.

Torin rolled his eyes playfully as he bit into a crust of bread while we rounded the corner of the armoury. The plasterwork on the doors was stunning—two Fae figures sculpted in mid-draw, their bows forming the handles. The cornices were carved in elegant patterns of ocean waves, flecked with glimmers of precious metals I didn't recognize, catching the light with every step we took.

"Is that Bastion in the ceiling?" Ele asked Cleo.

Cleo turned to Ele, visibly impressed by her knowledge. "Bastion mining is forbidden now, but what was once found has been forged into the very walls of Lexia. Every now and then, the plaster peels away, and you can catch a glimpse of it—glinting through like a secret the city never quite forgot." She smiled, a trace of reverence in her voice.

"That's how you've kept Lexia out of the conflict for so long." Astrid spoke.

"I guess it's wearing off." Cleo pressed her lips into a sad line. "Come! There's much more to see in the armory than Bastion." She added.

We walked through the forge, where countless Fae worked in harmony—melting precious metals, shaping blades, and weaving magic into their weapons. The air shimmered with heat and enchantment. Cleo led us down a long corridor lined with glass cases, each displaying intricately forged weapons and armor, their surfaces glowing faintly with embedded spells.

At the end of the hallway, she opened a door that led into a smaller, more secluded storeroom. Unlike the others, which were arranged in cozy, open nooks for admiration, this room was set apart—quiet, hidden, and closed off from the bustle of the forge.

The space inside was stark white, almost ethereal, glowing with soft reflections of bastion stone embedded into the walls. Light filtered through high windows, casting golden shafts that danced through the gaps in the vines draping the exterior of the building. The room felt sacred, as though the weapons stored here held a purpose far beyond war—meant for something rare, something extraordinary.

"Before you left for Sonsuz." Cleo said, her eyes moving between me, Beau, and Zac." I had a quiet meeting with Kieran. We both suspected Sonsuz would become his new home, and I offered him the chance to gift you each something before the departure. But he had something else in mind."

She paused, a proud smile tugging at her lips. "He brought me a bag of elder dragon scales."

Beau's expression shifted with recognition, the memory flickering to life—the two of them gathering the shimmering scales in the tunnels beneath the ruins, the echo of their laughter carried by the stone, the dust of ancient earth rising in their wake.

The moment was quiet, but warm, like the scales themselves still carried the heat of the dragons who had shed them—a gift not just of power, but of memory.

The forgemen and weavers had outdone themselves, crafting armor worthy of kings and heroes. Cleo opened a tall cupboard, and inside, displayed on mannequins sculpted in our likenesses, were the most breathtaking suits of armor I had ever seen. Each piece gleamed with precision and power, and for Beau, there were even wing shields that capped his horns, enhancing their formidable edge.

Cleo summoned the weavers, who entered with quiet purpose and began dressing us in the armor tailored for each of us.

Mine was forged from deep blue dragon scales. They started by fitting me into a suit of supple leather, surprisingly lightweight despite its appearance. Then came the armor—chest and back plates moulded to fit, followed by guards for my forearms and thighs. Despite the intricate layering, I could move with ease.

The others were suited up also, their armor reflecting their essence—Zac in bold red, Torin in midnight black, and Beau in a blue similar to mine to match his wings. Together, we looked less like warriors and more like legends pulled from the pages of a forgotten myth.

"Woah. Try and stab me!" Zac punched at his chest.

"Gladly." Beau drew his sword, the jagged one we all feared.

"NO!" Astrid stood between them.

"Just kidding, we're cool now." Beau winked.

"Your antics alone will get us all killed." She hissed at Zac. "And I expected better from you!" She snarled at Beau.

Ele's lips tightened in a downward smile as she watched on anxiously over Astrid.

We were then instructed to undress and redress one another, a practical exercise meant to ensure we knew how to properly handle each other's gear in the chaos of battle. It felt oddly intimate, stripping away layers of armor piece by piece, then carefully replacing them—checking straps, tightening buckles, smoothing down clasps. Taking off my armor hadn't been high on my list of priorities, but if it kept Cleo satisfied, I was more than happy to comply.

It took hours more to arm everyone. Cleo handed us each a quiver and then showed us a range of arrows we could select to fill it. Wooden, thick with a hooked point. The only way out was pushing it all the way through. Emberleaf, a metal that caught fire as soon as it was shot, Emberleaf was rooted with magic, the same magic that burned my ancestral lands to ash. The point of the arrow was skinny but deadly, so thin you wouldn't even feel it pierce at first. Glass arrows that would shatter on impact and kill from the inside out, one of the more insidious weapons. Eclipse thorn was next, a metal so lethal it poisoned your blood without even dipping it in a toxin. Then there were the arrows Zac, and I had found in Antoli. Forge with Priontine they could only be shot with an equal bow which Cleo only had one of. Antoli arrows shot with the corresponding bow would kill ten men at once and never missed their target.

"Ration those arrows." Cleo said as she handed me the bow.

"ME?" I gasped. "I've never used a bow and arrow, I'm not your girl." I pushed it back into her.

"You'll learn." She didn't take no for an answer.

"I'll teach you." Ele smiled.

"No, really! Why me?" I ignored Ele and grabbed Cleo's arm, startling her.

"Because Aliera. You'll be the only one able to get close enough to Edi and Wren." She sighed.

"They're alive?" Whispered.

"Yes, and none of these arrows will kill them, but they will slow them down. You don't feel your power like your father, but your strength will surge through the bow." She said quietly as the others busied over knives and swords after selecting handfuls of arrows to equip their individual quivers.

"They're on Rael's side?" I asked.

"After so many years I can only assume they feel a sense of belonging at the very least." She explained.

"My father?" I asked.

"I know nothing of General Gray, if he is alive, he has been well hidden." She sighed.

"I need Azra." I looked at Zac.

"NO!" She gripped my arm and pulled me away from the others. "Azra has never been to war, she has never seen battle…" She spoke.

"YES, SHE HAS!" I yelled.

"When?" Cleo crossed her arms.

"She helped Beau and I in Tecrit to defeat the Dreadwolves and Mason." I explained.

"Did you…You know?" She used her hands to animate a beheading.

"Of course." I groaned.

"I'm sorry you had to be the one to do that." She sighed.

"He was lost." I sighed also.

"Let me talk to Draven about Azra." She said.

"Talk all you like, she's not your dragon to decide for." I pursed my lips.

"Aliera, you are young, new to your powers, and inexperienced in battle and I doubt you can control a dragon who has very rarely flown." She narrowed her eyes on me.

"I've flown her." Beau interrupted.

"YOU?" Cleo looked mortified. "A Fae on a dragon?" She laughed.

"I saw it, she let him, and he helped her. Without Beau, she would have never even got off the ground." Astrid interrupted.

Cleo was confused as she sat on a velvet stool in the hall. "This is unheard of." She looked at the ground.

"I'm sure it will never happen again, she needed me to get her to Aliera." Beau assured her.

"Gather your weapons of choice, we have a battle to fight." Starlette ordered as she exchanged glances with Astrid.

Everyone was on edge. No one said it aloud, but it was clear in the way we moved, the way we avoided each other's eyes. Torin wouldn't stop eating, tearing through portions like they might vanish. Ele fussed over herbs and potions, checking her satchel so many times it bordered on obsession. Beau and Zac were locked in their own rhythm, sharpening weapons in silence—even the spikes on Beau's wings, their edges gleaming beneath the torchlight.

I finally managed to sort my knives and arrows, laying them out with methodical care. Ele had been patient with me, guiding me into a field to practice my aim with both the bow and throwing knives. She was a good teacher—steady, clear, and endlessly kind.

By the time twilight fell, the city began to glow. Lights sparked across rooftops and lanterns floated into the sky as the war feast began. Every home was provided rations to last the week, a hopeful gesture that this wouldn't be our end.

In the castle, a banquet was laid out on two crescent-shaped tables, the spread nothing short of lavish. Bowls of fresh fruit, platters of roasted meats, warm breads, cheeses, and vegetables arranged with artful precision. Lexia was rich in so many ways—in beauty, in heart, and certainly in food. Even on the brink of war, they hadn't forgotten how to nourish their people.

We sat at a table away from Draven and the other leaders, it was nice to feel like ourselves and be able to talk without the words of war being spread between us.

"Got any plans after this?" Beau kissed the part of my neck beneath my ear.

"I was hoping you'd take me back to the bathhouse and we could lay beneath the stars and listen to the gentle harp one more time." I nuzzled into the crook of his neck as I inched my chair closer to his.

"I'd love to." He wrapped his arm around me.

The evening felt like a blur, I felt engaged in conversations with the people who had become my nearest and dearest, but I also felt like I was floating in and out of consciousness.

Torin and Ele were the first to leave the banquet, Ele had been emotional all night and worried for Torin. The crowd in the hall was so thick we barely noticed them slip out the doors. Zac and Astrid were next, Luca leaving with them to head back for a somewhat decent sleep.

"Ready to go?" Beau asked as I yawned.

"Let's go." I said softly as we walked out of the halls, eyes on us as Beau scooped me up like he always did and flew me away to the bath house. The wind was cold and teased the bottom of my dress up my thighs, tickling my legs.

"Promise me we'll find our way back to each other." I clung to him tighter.

"It'll take a whole army to keep me away from you." He said as we landed on the steps to the bathhouse.

"And me from you." I stood on the higher step and for the first time I could reach his face without being on my toes, so I snatched a kiss in the quiet of the lonely street.

Beau pulled us through the doors and down the hall that led to our room. It was lit up with white and blue lights, the water was warm and inviting as always and I undressed him with my eyes as he stood before me, his eyes low and sultry as they scanned me.

"I don't know if I can." He sighed.

I tilted my head, and he knew I was asking why.

"If we do, it feels like I'm saying goodbye." He dropped his chin and sat on the bed.

I sat beside him and rested my hand over his huge thigh. "Is it so bad if we are…just in case?" I softened and tried to stop tears from rolling down my cheeks.

He pulled my face into his palm, and I threw my legs over him as he cradled me into him. "Gods protect the man who takes you away from me." He stroked my neck and kissed me with all the passion he could muster as he climbed over me now and tore the clothes from my body.

He kissed every inch of me as I kicked off my shoes and greedily pulled at his pants until he sprung with excitement for me. We were naked now and he picked me up, his strong arms under my thighs as he pressed into me and I rested my hands on his scaled shoulders as he pounded me gently, slowly, and lovingly against the cold wall that sent shivers down my spine. It made me hungrier for the warmth that was building inside me even more as I ached against Beau's body. His lips were all over me as I felt the warm liquid between my legs seep down my thighs as he thrust harder now, and I shook from his pleasure.

He held me against him as he stepped into the warm water, and I leaned back into the pool as my nipples hardened against the cool air from lying on my back. He hovered over me and gently sucked at them as I gazed up at the way the light of the moons lit up his majestic wings.

I stood up in the pool and climbed into his lap, pulling my wet hair to one side and I brushed the few chest hairs he had into patterns, and he smiled down at me.

"You're the only thing in this world I've ever wanted." He grinned.

"You didn't know that a year ago." I smiled.

"But a year from now if you're all I have I'll be a happy man." He replied.

"So will I, but I will think of this place often." I snickered.

"Would you like to live here?" He asked.

"I think so, it's so different to everywhere else we've been." I pondered.

"We can keep exploring, build something of our own if you want to." He smiled.

"You don't want the crown?" I circled my hand over my head like a halo.

"No. Varsili should vote for their next King. Hopefully, someone kind and peaceful." He sighed.

"Do you know anyone?" I asked.

"I've always thought Creed should take Varsili, I like Nixon." He said.

"Maybe when we win this war it can be proposed to the people." I said.

"*Maybe*, let's win first." He kissed me as he put me down and began washing himself.

"Will you leave tomorrow?" I asked as I began to tear up again.

He heard the hitch in my voice and pulled me into him and he exhaled long and hard. "I don't want to leave at all." He sighed.

"I'm sorry, I'm not making this easy." I sighed as I splashed my face.

"I will see you off at the docks and I'll be flying just ahead of you patrolling until we round up to Orman." He explained.

"Within my sight, right?" I asked.

"I'll have Torin with me and Zac on Irmak. I promise I'll be in good company." He kissed me.

I nodded as I tried to be okay with the logistics. "Thane and Sina will be arriving tomorrow also." He assured me.

"Those waters into Varsili are bad though. There have been so many wrecks." I said.

"I know, don't worry, Draven isn't sailing into Varsili. We have enough Fae to bring the war to them." He explained.

I couldn't wrap my head around thoughts of war right now. My head throbbed from crying too much, my body heavy with exhaustion. I climbed out of the water, wrapped myself in a towel, and crawled into bed. Beau followed, quietly drying off before slipping in beside me. He threw his arm over my waist and pulled me close, his warmth grounding me in the moment.

The thought of losing this—losing him—was unbearable. We hadn't had long. What we had felt sudden, like something wild and fleeting. And yet, it had already become everything. He was everything I had ever known, my first real friend, my first *everything.*

CHAPTER TWENTY

BEAU

I woke to the sound of harps once more, Aliera in all her beauty sprawled in the bed with her shiny hair tangling with mine. Bells sounded as the sun rose and I could hear Zac protesting all the way from his room.

"Rise and shine, baby." I kissed Aliera's perfect pouty lips, and she wriggled beneath the sheets and pulled me back down with her.

"Can you braid my hair?" She muffled.

"I don't know how." I laughed.

She pushed off the blanket and sat upright. "It doesn't feel right that we won't be back here tonight." She grunted.

"No argument from me." I agreed as I stood up and pulled on the first layers of armor we were issued.

"You look hot in tight leather." Aliera teased as she woke just as I was tucking my manhood into the armor designed just for the men. "Interesting." She smiled.

"Draven slipped them to us." I rolled my eyes.

"No, I'm happy about it." She shrugged.

She stood up still perfectly naked and began dressing also. Her clothes slipped on like a glove and her plump ass looked damn good in black shiny pants.

"Fuck, turn around or I'm going to have to fuck you again." I squeezed my eyes together.

She walked over to me, her breasts still exposed, and her hair splayed over them. "Do we have time?" She asked.

"NO!" Astrid pounded her fist into the door.

"Buzz kill." I sulked.

"I'm coming in so cover it up." She counted to three and pushed the door open just in time for Aliera to cover her breasts, wrestling her top on.

"You have awful timing!" I groaned.

"Says you." She grimaced as she began to brush Aliera's hair back into a tight braid over her shoulder and then Aliera did the same for her.

"It's weird seeing you two with your hair back." Zac peeked into the room.

"It is!" I agreed.

I started securing Aliera's armor for her and Zac did mine as I worked away. Astrid was always ready first. She had that boss energy about her. Luca was running down the stairs and Ele was shouting at Torin to hurry.

"Have you all got everything?" Astrid asked as she counted the arrows in her quiver.

"Use those wisely." Zac said as he watched over her.

"I can't help but feel like this is the last time we'll all be together." Astrid sighed.

"Don't think like that." Aliera sat beside her and leaned into her shoulder.

Ele sat on the other side and the three of them wrapped their arms around each other.

"You three, under no circumstances get off the ship unless it's to dock in Orman. Got it?" Torin stood beside me and Luca as Zac looked over everyone's armor.

"STOP! We aren't fighting today." Luca swatted him.

"Yeah, just making sure you know what you're doing." He shrugged.

Everyone stood up and we left the room and headed outside into the street. It wasn't peaceful and quiet anymore, it was chaos. Carts and wagons were racing through the streets full of supplies from armor and weapons to food and clothing.

"This is really happening." Ele gasped as she froze in front of the carriage.

"You can stay!" Astrid grasped her shoulder and held her face. "You're no use if you're afraid." She added.

"No, if you're all going then so am I. I'll be fine, you're going to need a healer." She forced a smile.

Torin stepped into the carriage first and Ele followed and sat close beside him.

"Want a lift?" I pulled Aliera aside and flapped my wings.

She smiled and nodded. "Meet you guys at the east dock." She said into the carriage and then came running back to me.

It wasn't the usual flight, the skies were full of Fae flying around running errands in preparation for the next few days, maybe even hours.

Clouds moved faster when the skies were busy with Fae. The windswept faster across our faces, the rain spat a little harder the higher we went, and the clouds felt heavier the darker they became. I didn't need to see Thane or Sina to know they had the left, the clouds did that for them. Dark grey rain clouds traveled from the north in an easterly direction, and it began to rain hard just as we touched down at the dock.

"GREAT!" Aliera shouted over the sound of the rain.

Her long braid now dripping wet as she hid in a shelter trying to dry herself off by shaking like a cat out of water.

"We should have taken the carriage." I squeezed out my hair.

"It was sunny an hour ago." Aliera grumbled.

"The weather is manipulated by the movement in the sky." I explained.

"All of the Fae? Rael will know we're coming? We've lost the element of surprise." She sighed.

"Not yet, I need to find Draven." I grabbed her arm to pull her along with me as I looked for Draven around the docks.

"I think that's our ship, The rest seem to be loaded and waiting." I said.

Carriages began to arrive as Jace and Starlette called out from the ship docked in front of us. They waved for us to come aboard.

"Is it a long journey?" Aliera asked as she sucked in a deep breath as her feet were about to leave the ground.

"We'll be there before nightfall." I assured her.

She stepped up into the ship and Starlette took her for a walk around and showed her the stations as Draven walked onto the boat and we watched as Zac's carriage arrived.

"Thane's left Sonsuz?" I said to Draven.

"They left this morning. They will be there before nightfall.

"Are your people ready?" I asked.

"Beau, my people are always ready. They have been the shield of the realm for too long." He sighed.

"Let's hope this ends quickly." I nodded.

Everyone was onboard now, and the ship's captain began steering us out of the marina and into open water. The sea shimmered beneath the afternoon sun, each wave catching the light.

In the distance, a mass approached from the north—not clouds, but something far more vibrant. It rippled across the sky like a living rainbow, shifting with a mesmerizing grace that pulled the clouds along in its wake. The wind carried with it a hum, subtle and melodic, as if the very air recognized the arrival.

It was the Fae.

Wings of every shade sparkled in the sunlight, casting stunning patterns across the horizon. Their formation moved as one, fluid and unbroken, a tide of color and magic sweeping through the sky. It wasn't just a sight—it was a promise, a presence, a living force descending from the heavens.

It wasn't long till we could see the ash clouds still smoking on Korsan as we sailed off its coast around midday, the rain had subsided now.

I approached Draven over lunch, slipping into the seat across from him as the ship swayed gently beneath us. He glanced up, the sea wind tugging strands of his hair loose from their braid, and nodded in greeting.

"You have a moment?" I asked.

He motioned to the food between us, an invitation to speak freely.

Most of the Fae weren't with us—those who sailed today were mostly human, or the few Fae who had been rescued from Korsan. Their absence weighed on the ship like a silence that couldn't be shaken.

I leaned in, lowering my voice. "What are your plans? When we dock, when we finally make it to the coast—what happens next?"

Draven didn't answer right away. He tore a piece of bread and chewed thoughtfully, eyes fixed on the endless blue horizon.

"We hold the line." he said finally. "And if we can, we push it. But first—we survive the landing."

The words settled like anchors between us, heavier than the calm around us let on.

"This is a sizable army, but when will the Fae join us?" I asked.

"Now." He smiled as he pointed to another movement of shadow in the distance from Lexia. "If the Fae move before the ships, he'll see us coming. We still need the element of surprise. "They should arrive at the same time as Thane." He explained.

"How many ships?" I asked as I looked out over the ocean.

"Two hundred, and that includes trade ships, galleys, and battleships. It's not enough, but we hold the sky." He smiled.

"The Dreadwolves." I said.

"We can take them." He smiled.

"Have you ever fought one?" Torin walked over.

"No." He sighed.

"They are fast, relentless, be on your guard always. They attack at night when you see nothing coming." Torin explained and he took a seat beside me.

Aliera looked afraid as she began to pick at the overgrown eyes of a raw potato. Ele was eating grapes and Astrid had been sharpening her knives the entire sailing. Starlette was sitting with Luca as he told her about Tecrit, she took a keen interest in his home, it was one of the few places in the world she had never seen, it was so hidden from the rest of civilization, an untouched sanctuary.

We soon passed the rougher seas and were able to see the Ormanian docks in the distance as the ships slowed. As we approached most of the ships dropped their anchors for the night, we wouldn't be sailing to the cliffside before morning with nowhere to dock the ships.

"Our ship will disembark." Draven said as lanterns from the shore waited for us.

We stepped off the ship after a day of sailing and Luca kissed the ground the second his feet touched the ground.

"See, we're okay." I said in a low voice to Aliera.

"Hold me up, I have sea legs." She wobbled.

I stood still while she regained her balance against me and soon, we were following a group of soldiers into a castle away from the city.

"It's safer here for all of you." Draven explained as he shut the doors behind us. It was me, Zac, Torin, Luca, Starlette, Astrid and Aliera. We had about ten guards with us as we looked around the castle and found rooms in the darkness and then we went back into the main room to bid farewell to Draven.

"I'll see you all tomorrow." Draven said as he opened the doors.

"Is the city safe for you?" I asked.

"I'm not going to the city, I'm going to meet Thane and Sina, the other Fae. They will all stay in those other castles. Abandoned long ago by the lords and ladies of Orman." He sighed.

"It'll be over soon, and they'll come back." I assured him.

Draven turned and the guards closed the doors as he flew into the night back towards the shipyard.

"I don't like this." Astrid said as she looked around the castle and two of the guards nodded to agree.

"Neither it's too quiet. Why isn't the city loud?" I grabbed one of the guards and pressed him into a wall and threatened him with the horn of one of my wings.

Aliera grabbed my scaled shoulder and begged me to relax.

"The city is always quiet." The guard gulped.

"Why?" Astrid stepped forward.

"Cause there's no one left." Another guard said as he pulled off his helmet.

"What do you mean there's no one left?" Aliera became fierce.

"This war didn't start when you decided to join, it's been going on for years." He huffed. "If you think you can beat whatever their mages send next then I respect your bravery, but that's not enough. We were all brave once too." He sighed.

I looked at Zac, and he tilted his chin to acknowledge what I had planned.

"NO!" Aliera pushed Zac.

"Hey!" Zac growled.

"No sneaking out, you are not leaving us here in a dark castle." She hissed.

"Why are you yelling at me? It's his idea." Zac pushed back.

"Please…" She turned to me.

"I can't sleep if I don't know what's out there." I sighed.

"WHAT'S OUT THERE?" Astrid punched one of the soldiers.

"WHAT THE FUCK, LADY!" He rubbed his jaw.

"There's something fishy going on here." Torin said as he sniffed at the air. Luca took his queue and listened closely at the windows.

"The roof?" Ele asked.

Aliera grabbed her hand and together they ran up the stairs to the roof. We were all behind them when they opened the door to a rooftop dining room that had been tossed and strewn all over the rooftop.

"I thought he said it was abandoned?" Luca gulped.

"Looks like it was targeted." Astrid picked up a broken glass.

"I think I'd feel better if you called Irmak." Astrid said to Zac.

"He's coming in the morning once everyone else has arrived." Zac rubbed her back.

"They're arriving now." I pointed to the sky as a draft blew in.

Thousands of Fae began to land on the shores, all being directed to the other castles in the north that were so much bigger than this one. This was a taller skinny castle, but we had the advantage of being higher and able to spy.

"Maybe we should go to bed." Zac yawned.

"Shhh." I grunted as I listened for any signs of chatter.

Aliera watched me closely trying to read my expressions. "Nothing?" She asked.

"It's weirdly quiet, even with the Fae here. It's too quiet." I sighed.

"Varsili is a long way away, maybe we're just all on edge." Astrid said.

"I hope you're right." I nodded.

We all walked back down the stairs and agreed to stay together for the night. Dragging mattresses and blankets into the largest room, we made a nest of comfort in the quiet gloom and barricaded the door as best we could.

The guards chose to remain outside, insisting they'd keep watch, though four of them were already asleep by the time we returned. They were young—barely more than boys. I doubted there was much they could do to protect us if danger came. They were kids playing at bravery, not warriors forged by battle.

CHAPTER

TWENTY ONE

ALIERA

It was the middle of the night when I woke suddenly. Everyone around me was sound asleep, their breathing steady, a few even snoring softly. The room was quiet, save for the occasional creak of wooden doors disturbed by the sea breeze and the distant hush of waves beyond the walls.

A sharp urge pulled me from the warmth of my blankets—I needed to pee. Careful not to disturb anyone, I gently pulled away the chairs that had been stacked against the door as a makeshift barrier. Each scrape felt like a shout in the silence. I paused, heart pounding, then slipped through the door and padded quietly down the dim hallway toward the bathroom.

The air was cooler out here, tinged with the scent of salt and old stone. Shadows stretched long beneath the moonlight spilling through the windows, and for a moment, everything felt suspended—still, waiting.

I kept walking, the soft patter of my bare feet the only sound accompanying me through the quiet hall.

"Wait for me!" Ele whispered. "I'm desperate to go but I didn't want to go alone." She laughed silently.

"I get that." I smiled as we held hands and walked down the dark hallway to a room with only moonlight, torn curtains, and no running water.

"You go first." I said to Ele.

She sat on the low wooden toilet seat and the violent rush of her pee echoed through the room. "Slowly!" I shushed her.

"Sorry, it's about to get worse." She clenched her teeth. I fought the silent laughter as I blocked my eyes and nose, and she unleashed hell on that toilet.

"I'm never eating that many grapes again." She heaved as she held her stomach through the violent cramping.

"I'd be ever grateful." I joked.

"Find me something to wipe with." Ele pleaded through the next cramp.

I looked around the room for something she could use, and I tore away a piece of the curtain.

"Here." I handed her the fabric, and she began to carefully wipe herself. She was finally finished, and I covered my nose and squeezed my eyes closed as I took my turn on the toilet, the seat now warm.

"I swear I just got a splinter on my ass from this seat." I winced as I shuffled.

Ele laughed as she walked over to tear off a part of the curtain for me. She approached the window and ripped at the fabric that let in more moonlight now and suddenly she screamed.

"ARGHHHHHH!" I felt the heat from her scream electrifying through my body as I pulled up the tight suit and jumped up as fast as I could as the glass from the window shattered inwards and a Dreadwolf forced its way through the small opening of the broken window as it snapped its fangs at us viciously and we screamed at the top of our lungs.

"HELPPPP!" We screamed in perfect unison.

I yanked a dagger from my waistband and lunged, driving it toward the beast just as it tried to force its wings through the shattered window. Its limbs thrashed in frustration, wings catching on jagged glass. Blood streaked the frame as it continued to shove forward, slicing itself open with every desperate movement, refusing to retreat.

But it wasn't alone, I could hear others outside the window now pushing it through.

"TORIN!" Ele screamed as she jumped up and raced for the hall.

I jumped up just before it got through the window, and I slammed the door shut and tried with all my might to hold the door closed.

"HURRY!" I yelled.

I held the door as long as I could, but I wasn't strong enough, there were more on the other side now.

"MOVE!" Torin roared, his fangs bared and bleeding as his voice thundered down the corridor. I stumbled backward, heart pounding, pressing myself against the wall as Zac's fists ignited beside me, casting flickering firelight across the stone. The castle walls glowed with the warning heat of battle.

Torin kicked the door open with a splintering crack. Inside, chaos reigned. Four Dreadwolves snarled and snapped, the window shattered behind them, shards of glass glittering across the floor. Blood streaked their matted fur from a dozen cuts. One of them, hunched over the toilet, looked up with glowing eyes and turned its attention straight to me.

Zac launched a barrage of fireballs, the flames crackling and lighting up the chamber. One blast scorched past Torin, singing the edge of his shoulder, but Torin didn't flinch. He charged forward, a blur of muscle and fury.

Beau stormed in next, his wings folding back into his spine to give him room. With graceful brutality, he cut down two Dreadwolves in a sweep of steel and blood.

But more were coming.

I turned and sprinted down the hall, feet pounding the floor, until I reached the guards' quarters. They stirred sluggishly, half-awake and disoriented.

"Get up!" I shouted. "We need you now!"

Behind me, the battle still raged, the sound of claws on stone and fire on flesh echoing through the castle.

"WE NEED YOU!" I shook each of them.

They all cowered in fear as they heard the sound of howls and gnashing teeth.

"ALIERA?" Astrid was looking for me.

"Stay close! They're coming from the roof too." She said as she leaned into the door that led to the stairs.

"We can't stay here." I held her hands.

"YOU! Need to hide." She held my face.

"I can't leave you." I squeezed her.

"Get Ele, I have an active power." She faced the door, and her eyes flamed as her hair raised off her back and her skin crawled with embers.

Luca was ready with his bow and arrow now and he stood at Astrid's back ready to take anything she missed.

"They're coming." Ele raced to us as she saw the light from her sister. "We have to go, Astrid." Ele pulled at her, but the touch burnt her hand.

"ARGH!" She screamed as skin melted from her fingertips.

The castle walls began to tremble, fractures spreading like veins through the stone as the chaos in the bathroom spilled violently into the hallway. Zac and Astrid stood at the center, flames flickering at their fingertips, casting wild, dancing shadows across the blood-slick floor.

Torin emerged from the fray, drenched crimson, his breath heavy as he stalked over the mangled remains of the Dreadwolves he'd torn apart. His eyes glowed with lingering fury, claws still half-formed, chest heaving with the remnants of battle.

Beside him, Beau. He flicked the blood from his twin blades, splattering it against the cracked wall before dragging a cloth across the steel, his expression unreadable.

The fight wasn't over, but for a moment, the corridor held only the sound of dripping blood, scorched stone, and the quiet thunder of hearts still racing.

"We're not done yet." Astrid said as she used her hands to heat the door before her and the stone caved inwards crushing the Dreadwolves who lined the stairwell, but the door burst open and soon more of them dropped in from the sky.

"WHERE IS EVERYONE?" Ele screamed at the guards.

"They're all too far away." One cried.

"WELL, FLAP YOUR FUCKING WINGS AND GO GET SOME HELP." She yelled.

I knew I was useless in this moment. Any power I used would only smother the flames Astrid and Zac had ignited. Their magic blazed with purpose, synchronized and deliberate, while mine would have been a gust of interference, untempered and in the way.

So, I held back—silent, watchful—my hands clenched at my sides as the heat from their combined power surged around me. The walls pulsed with light; the air crackled.

Beau threw his spare sword at me and drew the other for himself. "Thank you." I said.

A pack of Dreadwolves descended the stairs, snarling and ravenous, their claws skittering over stone. Above us, others clawed at the roof, tearing it open bit by bit, shards of timber and tile raining down. Astrid stood her ground, a force of fury and precision. Each time one of them lunged, she struck with deadly grace, and each Dreadwolf she felled collapsed just feet from where we stood, their bodies forming a protective ring around us.

The air was thick with the stench of blood and smoke, and still, she fought—relentless, untouchable.

"We need to move." Luca said as he shot an arrow between the eyes of another Dreadwolf.

"AGREED!" Beau said.

Together we all went back into the main room of the castle where the guards were fighting to get the doors open.

"It's locked!" They argued.

"ASTRID! MELT IT." Beau ordered. She ran to the door and melted it instantly.

I began to wonder if she was just as powerful as Zac—maybe even more. But I reminded myself that Zac possessed abilities she couldn't begin to comprehend. Still, she was a force in her own right. I had never seen her like this before—a weapon of sheer will and fury.

The door crumbled beneath our weight as we burst into the open air. Above us, Fae had taken flight, their wings glinting in the sunlight as they spotted the flames rising from our castle. They descended swiftly, armed and ready. In moments, they reduced a hundred Dreadwolves to ten.

And then Draven struck down the last one.

Relief swept through the crowd like a tide. Shoulders dropped, breath returned, and the air finally felt safe again.

"They know we're here." He panted.

"Now what?" I said.

"I don't know." He said as he drank from a canteen.

I leaned on Beau, seeking balance, when a sudden, searing pain tore through my shoulder. Warm blood spilled down my arm as a lone Dreadwolf swooped from the shadows, its claws sinking deep into my flesh. Before I could react, it lifted me off the ground, wings beating furiously as it carried me high into the night sky.

A scream ripped from my throat, raw and desperate, echoing into the darkness. Below, Beau reacted instantly. His massive, gleaming blue dragon wings unfurled in a blur, slicing through the wind as he launched into the air, his eyes locked on the creature stealing me away.

He wasn't alone. Draven and countless others stood behind him, a wall of strength and fury, while ahead of me, more Dreadwolves descended as we neared the ocean's edge. I raised my hands to the sky, summoning the winds with a whisper and turning the clouds a deep, menacing grey. A deluge poured down in sheets, drenching the skies.

Thunder cracked above us, sharp and unrelenting, shaking the air as lightning split the sky. The rain pelted the Dreadwolves, soaking their fur and weighing down their wings. Their screeches were drowned by the storm's roar as they faltered mid-air, their vision obscured and flight disrupted.

The ocean raged below us, its waves crashing against the rocks in sync with the fury of the sky. The storm was mine to command, and I unleashed it with everything I had.

"LET ME GO!" I grabbed my knife and sliced violently at the claws with my one good arm.

The Dreadwolf fought through the tremors of weather I had summoned.

"MORE!" Beau yelled as he flapped harder fighting off the Dreadwolves that tried to hold him back. Dreadwolves and Fae were falling from the sky now, into the ocean below us and they didn't come back up.

"I said, LET ME GO!" I screamed, summoning every ounce of strength left in me. With a desperate lunge, I drove my blade across the Dreadwolf's stomach. A sickening tear followed, and its insides spilled out in a torrent, drenching me in warmth and blood.

The beast howled, faltered, and plummeted from the sky, dragging me with it into the chaos of the violent sea below.

I hit the water hard, the salt immediately stinging my shoulder as I fought to find the surface, but I didn't know which way I was swimming through the storm I had summoned. Then I felt a pulse violently strike my head and then I saw black.

CHAPTER

TWENTY TWO

ALIERA

I was dry when I woke, not in my armor, not in Orman.

I was in a dungeon, and in front of me stood my brother Wren who I barely recognized. He was pale, his eyes blue like the sea and if not for his white, blonde hair I might not have recognized him at all.

"Wren?" I choked.

He didn't say a word, he just looked at me like I was a stranger and then I was surrounded by mages, and Rael. He had a sickening smile on his face, and he clapped like a small child as he whacked Wren on the back like a good boy.

"Oh, Aliera! I've been so looking forward to meeting you." He snickered.

I turned my head away as I tried to stop myself from crying. He grabbed my chin and pulled my face to him. "Oh, I see why he took you. You are a beauty." He stroked my cheeks with his icy fingers, and I shuddered at the frost his touch left upon me.

"LET ME GO!" I pulled at the chains that locked me down.

"They are enchanted. Don't bother." He laughed.

"How do you know they work on me." I growled.

"They worked on him." He pointed at my big brother, my blank brainwashed brother who I had missed every single day for the last fifteen years.

There was an ache in my chest as I burst into tears as the truth struck me. Mason hadn't chosen his path, he was just another experiment.

"I'M GOING TO FUCKING KILL YOU!" I tore at the chains.

"Oh, she's feisty!" Rael smiled.

"You have no idea." I muttered.

"How is my boy, Beau?" He asked.

"You're a monster!" I hissed.

"Oh, that. That wasn't me, that was him." He pointed to a tall man in the back of the room.

I lowered my eyes and glowered at Rael. "My father?" I asked. He nodded.

"Did you poison him too?" I asked.

"I didn't need to. He's obedient, as you know." He smiled.

"Commander, please come. You must wish to see your little girl." He teased.

He paced forward, tears spilling freely down his cheeks as he dropped to his knees, reaching trembling arms through the narrow bars. A thick collar clung to his neck, its metal stained with dried blood, and the skin beneath was a roadmap of old and fresh scars. A vicious mechanism designed to wound him every time he moved.

It hissed faintly, blades embedded within its structure slicing into him again and again, a cruel punishment for even the smallest motion. His rapid healing, once a gift, only made the torture endless. The wounds would close, then open anew, over and over, as if the collar was determined to strip him of his very existence.

But still, he reached.

"DAD!" I cried, but I couldn't hug him either.

"GET AWAY FROM HER!" Rael kicked him in the back of the legs.

"What is that around his neck?" I growled.

"That is collateral." Rael replied.

"Sorry." My father stood upright and apologized as he looked between me and Wren. The blades slicing a little deeper now. He seemed normal, just as I remembered him. Rael hadn't messed with his head, not yet.

"Now, I need more of *you*." He smiled at me.

"I will never bear your children." I screamed.

"You won't have to, I can't wait that long anyway." He snapped his fingers and mages approached, unlocked the cage and Wren held me down. Rael made my father watch everything.

Bowls were placed beneath my elbows and deep cuts were slashed along my veins and blood poured for a few moments until I healed.

"I will have a never-ending army!" Rael celebrated as he stared at the bowls filling with my blood, and I became lightheaded.

Wren opened another caged door and pulled out a man just as pale as him, his teeth had been filed into blades, but his movements weren't violent or erratic like I had expected. He wasn't in his own body, his soul was gone— he was a Durgun.

"What did you do to him?" I said as my eyes flickered, and a mage poured water into my mouth that tasted of algae.

"I'm hoping your blood will help complete the process, a creature of the night that can move in the day. The Dreadwolves are great for long distances, but they are useless to me during the day, I never know where they've gone or when they'll be back." He babbled.

He scooped a cup of my blood from the bowl and pressed it to the mouth of the Durgun that sat in the chair not three feet from me. Rael forced the cup to his mouth until his color changed, his eyes lit up and suddenly his veins became black on the surface of his skin and his nails thickened like a callous and sharp like a cats.

"So far, so good." A mage smiled from beneath the hood of their cloak.

Everyone stepped back and Wren pushed our father into his space and the Durgun thrust itself to its feet and snapped its teeth at my father who blocked all the attacks with his forearms. The Durgun was still no match for his strength. But he was an impossible enemy, my father landed blow after blow and broke bones. Rightly that man should have been dead, but he kept attacking until a mage stepped in and sliced his head off with a black blade and that's when he stopped coming, the blade— Gloomstone.

The head was severed and burnt all at the same time, killing the Durgun. Rael clapped.

"MORE BLOOD!" He smiled.

"Take mine!" My father begged. "Let her go." His chin hit his chest as I watched the wounds on his chest and arms slowly heal.

"You're not a woman." He smiled at me.

Rael walked through the dungeon and up the stone stairs that led into the heart of the castle, his boots echoing with every step. Behind him, the mages continued their relentless work on me—

feeding me, offering sips of water, then bleeding me. This cycle repeated for days, an unending rhythm of care laced with cruelty.

All the while, my father remained locked in a cage. But it was no true prison. The only thing that held him there was the threat of decapitation should he move too far, too fast. The bars could never truly contain a being like him—unless he allowed them to.

I was never left alone. Heavy chains bound me, their pale shimmer betraying their true nature: aetherium steel. Older than any living race, aetherium was not forged but found, remnants from an age when Giants walked the world. Each link was impossibly light, like spun silk, yet utterly unbreakable save for Bastion.

And so, I remained—bound by relics of a forgotten era, a prisoner of both time and blood.

CHAPTER

TWENTY THREE

BEAU

I dove into the ocean after her, but so did another. It wasn't a mage or a Dreadwolf. It was another Titan—not Zac, and not like any Titan I had seen before. This one moved through the water as if they belonged to it, as if the ocean itself bent to their will.

With effortless grace, they reached Aliera and pulled her into their arms, vanishing with her into the deep. Down through the darkest, coldest parts of the sea, out of sight, out of reach, out of hope.

I swam until my limbs gave out, until I could no longer tell which way led to the surface. I searched until the salt burned my eyes and my lungs begged for breath. Draven and Thane had to drag me from the waves, but I fought them, furious and heartbroken.

Eventually, they left me alone—perched on the skeleton of a shipwreck, drenched and shaking, staring out at the vast, unfeeling sea as I tried to gather what remained of myself.

I wasn't the only one burning with fury. I saw the inferno Zac had unleashed on the shores of the small isles scattered off Orman— a blazing testament to his anguish. His pain echoed across the water, raw and unrelenting, each flame a cry for Aliera. He ached for her with a helplessness that twisted in my chest like my own.

We knew she wasn't safe. She was deep in danger.

And the only path to Varsili led straight through an army of Dreadwolves.

"I WILL COME FOR YOU!" Zac's voice shook the earth, rippling the waters, and creating a surge that even the fish couldn't bear. His hands touched the waters as he heated the ocean, fish and creatures that dwelled below rushed to the surface trying to escape the heat. Then he appeared, he wasn't the same Titan though— it was Edi.

He walked over the water like he was born to do so, the waters around him cooler as fish seemed to shield him. Then I realized they were carrying him over the water.

"Zac, the outcast." His voice was deep and echoed over the sea and gave it so much more gravity.

"Edi, the asshole." Zac growled.

"Still a pathetic annoyance I see. Always putting our little sister in danger!" He mocked him.

Zac's rage swept over him in blue flames and suddenly Irmak was flying overhead and landed behind him, fierce and ready to crisp anyone who attacked. The Dreadwolves were gone now; retreated for the daytime.

I stood up on the shipwreck and Thane had landed on the port side of the ship I was on with Sina. Draven was closer to me as we watched closely with our sharp sight as Irmak threatened to incinerate Edi in one sweep of icy blue heat.

"We should go to them." I said as I watched Ele patching up Luca on the shore. Torin standing guard over them with Astrid.

"Not yet. We see how this plays out." Draven stopped me.

"Irmak lowered his neck, his throat thickened with heat as his scales stretched, and his jaw opened, a glowing blaze of blue flames left his body, and he attempted to scorch Edi.

But Edi was knocked out of the way by something bigger, longer, and scaled. As white as Irmak, she slithered wingless through the swells. Her body was more elegant than a land dragon, but dragon she still was.

"Caxia." Sina gasped as she moved to watch closer.

"This is not good." Draven's voice hitched at the surprise.

"That's the same beast that scavenged the shores of Varsili." I added. "But she's a lot bigger now." I gulped.

Caxia thrust herself onto the land and slithered closer to Zac and Irmak now, Edi not far behind her.

"RUN!" Astrid screamed at Zac.

Zac climbed Irmak's back as Irmak breathed flames at Caxia, but she was too fast and followed him beneath the water with ease, she was agile and terrifying as she thrust herself out of the water hundreds of feet into the air and she tried to attack Irmak when he dipped closer to the ground or sea.

"let's go!" I said as she swam closer to the shipwreck we stood upon.

I spread my wings and launched myself as high into the air avoiding not only her teeth but the firestorm she was unleashing over the Bays.

There were hundreds of Fae hovering on the shores now watching on as Caxia showed no restraint, she followed every order Edi gave her. Irmak circled in a safe space over the lower seas that became a sight for dead ships.

Caxia weaved her sleek body through the muddy and mossy wood. The planks were cracking and snapping beneath her weight as she launched up into the air in an attempt to attack Irmak one more time.

"GET OUT OF THERE!" Astrid screamed.

I flew to the shore of Orman and landed on the cliffs where Torin was guarding Luca and Ele and Astrid was visibly distraught.

She raced to me and grabbed my shoulders. "BEAU, TAKE ME TO HIM!" She demanded.

"He's tiring her out. He knows what he's doing." I said, trying to calm her down.

"She's going to kill them, if she doesn't Edi will." She cried.

"You think he'll kill his own brother?" Torin asked.

"Have you been paying attention?" Ele scowled at him.

"I thought that was my thing." He shrugged.

Ele stood up with Astrid and together they backed me into a corner. "Beau, without Irmak we aren't getting close to Aliera. Edi is playing with him and Zac is taking the bait!" Ele hissed as she pushed me with her palms.

"You got a plan?" I said to Astrid.

The skies began to darken with grey clouds so low I could fly up and touch them. "NOW!" She punched me.

"I hope you know what you're doing." I grabbed her around the waist and lifted her into the air. I flew as fast as I could, and Thane had sent a handful of his best Fae to aid me in Astrid's mission.

"THERE! GO LOWER." Astrid shouted up at me.

"You want me to put you down?" I asked.

"DO IT!" She growled.

"You're insane." I lowered to the island of rocks she had pointed at.

"I'm counting on it." She sighed as we set down amidst the skerry of rocks.

"What are you going to do?" I whispered.

"If my history is correct. There's a volcano here, or there was. If I can wake it up and Irmak can Lure Caxia here we have a shot at destroying her and Edi." She explained.

"Are you sure that will kill her?" I asked.

"Yes, but I'd feel better if we had an Eclipse Thorn for insurance if we can even impale her." She sighed.

"I'll get one, Sina and Draven had all the quivers of arrows." A Fae soldier said, and he quickly flew back to the shore.

I felt the droplets of rain spit on us from the sky as the clouds became darker and I could only see Irmak's shadow flying around now as Caxia's white body skimmed the surface of the sea, buckling the waves and causing mini tsunamis on all the surrounding shores with every big movement. She was far longer than Irmak, her face slim and feminine.

"We need to do this now before the Dreadwolves wake from the darkness." Another soldier panicked.

"It's the middle of the day?" I furrowed a brow. Then I heard the howls and cries of hungry Dreadwolves and the Isle of Deniz which was once a trading post woke with terror as the Dreadwolves rose to the air and snapped their ugly muzzles at one another.

"Whatever you're going to do, do it NOW!" I growled at Astrid.

Her hands were red with fire, her skin melting away and a small hole in the rocks began to bubble with red hot lava.

"ASTRID!" I yelled as I raced to help her.

"NO, IT'S NOT ENOUGH!" She yelled back as she visibly began to pour her magic into the licks of flames that would catch on anything flammable around the hole, it grew every second, but every second it took, we lost a little more of Astrid.

Her hair was on fire now and her face was black and cracked like coal and the lava surrounded her legs. It rose and poured around her and she became the liquid flames she had summoned.

"ASTRID!" I felt Ele's screams from miles away as she watched on while her sister sacrificed herself. Torin was trying to stop Ele from jumping off the cliff and swimming to us.

And then Astrid muttered words in another tongue with a voice so deep it couldn't be her own. The lava and stones lifted her into the air like a beacon for Zac. Lava completely seized her body now. I was hovering in the air when the rock formation rose from the depths of the sea and they suddenly split. The cracking of the earth rupturing in the sea caught everyone's attention. Zac swooped in low and beelined for Astrid as he finally had sight of what was happening. Rage filled his eyes as he dipped desperately to save her, but even Irmak couldn't bear the heat from the volcano as it rose from the sea bigger than ever before.

Zac circled nonsensically and then Caxia sprung from the sea. Irmak used his tale to knock her into the Pyre and Edi along with her. The weight of molten rock encapsulated them, and Irmak breathed one last fiery inferno over Caxia.

The Fae collecting the quiver arrived just in time and shot two arrows of Eclipse thorn into Caxia and Edi.

Zac leapt down into the pit of flames with no consequence, and he slit his blade violently across Edi's neck removing his head from his body.

"We need to bury that." I lowered.

He squared his eyes at me and tossed the head over his shoulder and into Irmak's mouth and he indulged himself in a feast of Titan head.

"YOU!" Zac pointed his blade at me, and I flew higher.

"I DIDN'T KNOW WHAT SHE WAS PLANNING" I yelled. "Zac, I swear to you."

Zac sunk into the lava, clutching the few surviving tresses of Astrid's vibrant red curls.

"I'm nothing without her." Zac cried.

"Zac, we have to get out of here." I urged as the Dreadwolves flew in closer to us and the army of Fae pressed against them in our direction.

"ZAC!" I yelled.

His eyes filled with fury, and he stood up in the liquid inferno.

"WATCH OUT!" One of the Fae shouted as the Dreadwolves closed in around us.

Zac didn't hesitate as he summoned the lava into outstretched arms of their own and threw them up into the air, wrapping them around Dreadwolves, and pulling them into the growing volcano. The sky was now painted with red hot embers and ash, and the blackened clouds began to reflect the violent stain of red, a reminder of what this had cost us.

Starlette had flown over with Draven to collect Zac while Irmak did all he could to hold the shore of Orman. The sea below him was now a marine graveyard of crispened Dreadwolves.

Thane was guiding Sina up into the sky with an army surrounding her as she spun, whipping the clouds to nothing and clearing the sky of the weather. Only the smoke cloud remained as the volcano continued to grow from the ocean.

The remaining Dreadwolves retreated back to the coast of Varsili, and they vanished into the city as daylight once again appeared.

I flew up into the sky with Sina and Thane as they composed themselves and acknowledged my worry.

"They shouldn't be in the city." Sina gasped.

"There's a lot of innocent humans in Varsili." I nodded.

"Then we help them." Thane nodded and he quickly turned and flew for the city.

"HEY, CAN I GET A LIFT?" Torin yelled up at me.

"Sorry." I dropped to the ground and landed hard on my ankles.

Torin tossed his length of rope around me and saddled in.

"Come with me, Eleanor." Sina smiled.

But Ele was hysterical in the seconds it took to say her name. Her sister was her whole world, she'd already lost her best friend to a life that was unpredictable.

"I don't want to go anywhere, with any of you." She cried.

"Ele…" Torin stuttered as he left the saddle and walked towards her.

"I can't do this." She cried into him.

"I know, you don't have to go anywhere you don't want to." He held her and stroked her hair.

"We need her." Sina whispered to me. I nodded as I agreed with her. Her healing powers were unmatched and that didn't even account for her potion abilities.

"It feels like my heart is exploding." Ele dropped to the ground and grasped at her chest.

"What can I do." I knelt beside her to offer her my support.

"Did you know?" She spluttered.

"She told me nothing, Ele. I wouldn't have let her do it if I knew." I sighed.

"Typical Astrid." She laughed through her grief and sobbed soon after.

"I know it's unfair of me to ask anything of you right now, But there are innocent people in Varsili, and we need you." I begged.

"She would help." Ele nodded.

"I promise you I'll end this." Torin kissed her forehead as she leaned into him for support.

"Can you carry us both? I'm not leaving her side." Torin looked at me.

"Those big dragon wings better be good for something." Thane smiled.

"Come on then." I nodded. "Hold on, there'll be more sway with more weight and I'm going as fast as I can." I grinned.

Torin scooped Ele into his arms, and she clung tightly to his body while he held onto the ropes, and we took off high into the air. Sina and Thane were flying below me just to be certain neither of them fell.

Irmak flew beside me with Zac on his neck, but he didn't make eye contact with any of us. He sped directly for Varsili, but we'd lose daylight by the time we arrived.

An army of Fae was at our backs, and the sky buzzed with the sounds of different wings flying to rescue Varsili — and Aliera.

I knew they wouldn't kill her, but what they would do to her was what truly frightened me. The fighting over the Orman and Deniz bays had lasted days and nights.

Chapter

Twenty Four

ZAC

I was going to save my little sister and then raise Varsili to the ground. I had never felt pain or fire like I felt now, and I knew this was the beginning of the end, there was no place to arrive now, Astrid was my home, and the keys meant nothing without her. I refused to live a life alone from this point forward. Being alone and feeling alone were two very different feelings. This was grief — the final act of love.

As I rode Irmak to the coastline of Varsili I could hear the screams of the humans below us. Darkness fell upon the city and Irmak crushed the roof of a castle and I stepped down from Irmak, scale after scale, then into the rubble and onto the street that led to the castle where Rael had my sister.

Beau landed beside me with Torin and Ele. She glanced at me, her face a complete puffy mess, but she pulled in a deep breath as she took in the destruction around her. Draven with Jace landed next with Thane and Sina and soon all the Fae lined the city, and the Varsili guards began to fight against our armies.

Luca ran towards me. "I need your help to open the gates." He puffed.

"The gates?" I asked.

"Come!" He started running off and I raced after him.

The Fae soldiers were fighting the guards at the gate before us and I sprung to the rooftop to see what they were guarding against. I was ecstatic to see Tecritians on the other side, with a barge trying to pound the first gate in. The wood cracked with each blast of weight and soon they broke through.

Luca scaled the wall and pulled up a man from the other side. An older version of Luca. "You came!" Luca hugged him.

"Couldn't let you have all the fun." Elio smacked him on the back. "I liked killing those things." Elio laughed.

"This is Zac. Aliera's brother." Luca introduced us quickly.

"Another Titan. Handy beings to have." He reached out and hugged me.

An army of Tecritians were flooding through the first gates. We couldn't see it, but you could hear it. It was still quite a distance away from where we stood but the gates were enormous, and by the sounds of it never or rarely had opened, at least on this side of the city. The rust had built around the hinges causing the crackling that became eerie for most to endure. It must have taken a hundred men to open those doors— or one Titan.

I dreaded everything about anything that came next. While those around me were excited like Elio, frightened like Ele, or hungry for revenge like Beau. I felt numb, I had nothing left to fight for. I could live another thousand years, and it was the thought of what I was living without.

I felt the pang that should have been a pain as I hit the ground, the Dreadwolf standing over me snapped its muzzle at my face. I gripped the bottom jaw with one hand of the flying beast and the top with my other hand and tore in separate directions, the weight of the monster collapsed on top of me.

"ZAC!" Luca rushed towards me.

"I'm fine." I took his hand and stood as the anarchy and wrath of the Dreadwolves descended and Fae warriors became engulfed in a war so old they might not even know what it was they fought for.

I cast flames and fires down the street into the Dreadwolves as Tecritians and Fae finished them off. Beau was running for the castle, and I chased after him with a hoard of Dreadwolves on my tail, but Irmak backed my escape and sent a flume of flames in their direction, but they attacked him from the sky.

"BEAU!" I said with a crackling volume in my chest.

He didn't turn, he was on his own journey now and I wasn't sure which he coveted more—revenge or love.

Still, I followed him around the back of the castle to a dark entrance, Irmak was left behind now, caught up in the fighting.

Beau pushed a heavy iron door open and slipped through but held the door open for me as he waited in the entryway.

"What's first?" I asked.

"Aliera." He nodded.

We were strictly business now, I knew what happened wasn't intentional, but I was far from rational. Even though it all made sense, I knew Astrid and that what he said was the truth of it. But he was the last to see her alive, to touch her. It should have been me. And I'd never be able to forgive him for robbing me of that.

We took the staircase up to the grand hall, but it was empty. The whole castle was empty, but it didn't *feel* empty.

"This way." Beau's eyes darkened and he pulled in his wings, so they didn't graze the walls. "Be ready for anything." He looked at my hands as he pulled out his sword.

"Where are we going?" I asked.

"The dungeon. Where the mages usually are." He sighed.

"Should we get back up?" I gulped.

"Zac, you are the backup. It doesn't get much better than a flame-wielding Titan." He grabbed my shoulders like he was giving me a pep talk.

"Right! We got this." I nodded.

"I know your combat experience is limited but just think of Astrid and how mad or sad that makes you and project it on everyone down there that isn't your sister." Beau added.

"Don't do that. Too soon." I growled.

"I'm truly sorry." He sighed.

"I know, but it doesn't bring her back." I replied.

We walked towards a door disguised into the walls of an unsuspecting hallway and Beau pressed a combination of stones that let us enter another hidden room that was pitch black.

I flamed my hands and hanging on the walls were corpses of the dead past experiments of the King's mages. "The mercy of King Rael." Beau scoffed as he looked at each creature as we skimmed past them to reach the long winding staircase.

It wasn't screams we heard as we descended the spiralled stairs—it was the sound that came after screaming became impossible. Beau halted just beyond view, keeping to the shadows as we watched from a distance. Mages moved briskly between curtained sections of the room, carrying buckets filled with a thick, dark substance. The groans that slipped from behind the sheet were raw and broken, the kind that lived in the throat after all strength had been spent.

Beau's eyes scanned the chamber with razor focus. In the dim back corner, obscured by shadow and iron bars, stood a cage. Inside it, slumped and silent, was General Gray.

My father.

"What is he doing here?" I slumped back.

Beau looked at me and used his fingers to sign for me to go to him and he would inspect behind the curtains.

I crept silently behind the shelves, weaving through the shadows cast by flickering flames beneath glass beakers and softly bubbling potions. The long laboratory table was cluttered with tools and vials, their contents glowing faintly in the dim light. A second room adjoined this one, its door perpetually ajar. The constant draft from within slammed against the walls with rhythmic bursts, each gust loud enough to mask my careful footsteps as I moved unnoticed through the gloom.

He saw me now, my father. He tried to tell me to leave as he pointed to a collar around his throat, but I was already so close I could touch him. "I'm getting you out." I whispered as I pulled at the bars.

"No, get your sister!" He whispered.

I looked over to the curtained space where Beau had gone and fresh blood sprayed over the curtains just before Beau tore them down. The curtain dropped to the ground.

Aliera lay on the table, so pale I barely recognized her—if not for the familiar fall of her hair. Her skin held none of its usual warmth, and it sent a chill through me just to look at her.

She wouldn't know about Astrid. Not yet. They had grown so close these past months, finding comfort in each other in the quiet moments between chaos. The thought of her waking to that loss broke something in me.

I reached for her hand, unsure if I was offering comfort or searching for it. Either way, I stayed beside her, willing her to come back to us.

Beau worked to cut her free, but mages surrounded him and then Wren was in front of me. "You really think we'd leave two Titans unwatched." He snickered.

"You mean three, right? You're still one of us, or are you brainwashed like Edi and Mason too?" I growled.

He didn't answer as he turned to walk towards Aliera and Beau. Rael was descending the stairs now and he had an excitement as he looked over at Beau.

"Wow! You really have exceeded all my expectations." He smiled as he stood just feet from him. I tried to pull the bars to my father's cage apart before any attention diverted to me.

"It's no use, go help, Beau. He will need you." He squeezed my hand. "I'm so proud of you." A tear escaped his eye, and he urged me to go.

"Another gift?" Rael sneered as he watched me walk towards them.

Four mages stalked from behind me now as I stopped beside the table with my almost lifeless sister. She was choking back water being force-fed to her by another mage.

"Leave her." I growled as I held her hand.

"NO TOUCHING!" Rael growled as he walked towards me.

"Now you must be something extra special! I hear you're the one who got away. The fire wielder your mother was protecting." Rael smiled.

"Protecting?" I asked.

"But that's not the point! You're here now and I have use for you!" Rael galloped around the room like an insane person before stopping beside Beau and he traced his wings without invitation. Beau turned and struck him with his fist in a heated rage, Rael dropped to his knees with no emotion in his expression.

"You can kill me, I'm a mere human. But this is my legacy." He waved his arms up and down over Beau.

"I'm nothing like you!" Beau kicked him but the mages threw potions to make him disorientated.

"You'll never get your father out of here without me." Rael laughed as Wren helped him up.

"Can he be saved?" I pointed my Gloomstone dagger at Wren now.

Wren was emotionless as he stood there like a pawn in a game. All personality was lost from him.

"Try it." Rael pressed as he observed my dagger.

The mages closed in around us as I threatened Rael. But then the door to the cage clicked and Gray was pushed towards us by guards. We were vastly outnumbered even if Aliera were able to fight.

I looked at Beau and he knew what I was planning. He pulled himself together, jumped over to Aliera, and wrapped her in his wings as I ignited everything in the room. The mage's potions exploded, and Rael walked through flames that should have killed him.

"You really thought I wouldn't be prepared for you." He laughed.

"HE DRANK HER BLOOD!" Gray yelled.

The mages all raced for the stairs as I faced off with Rael. Gray stood by my side with death wrapped around his throat.

"Beau, I believe you are owed a debt." Rael shouted as he looked at Gray.

"It's not his debt to pay." Beau growled back.

"But if we're talking debts, you also owe him a debt." Rael danced around words as the flames dissipated beneath his steps.

"What are you talking about?" I asked.

"Oh, he didn't tell you?" Rael laughed. "He's the one who executed your mother." He smiled.

"WHAT?" Gray growled.

"Yes, she was sent back from Farkli to Creed, Jace sent her to the war camp to aid me in healing all those terrible experiments so we could spare a few souls. But she was putting them out of their misery instead, so Beau disposed of her once he knew she was Gray's wife. The perfect revenge for clipping his wings." He explained.

"Jace is involved, where the fuck is Nixon?" I growled.

"Probably in that room that like the rest of Creeds warriors." He shrugged as the door pounded from the force behind it.

Aliera's healing had begun to kick in now and she was able to stand, still pale and weak as she glowered at Beau and his heart sunk in his chest as she took a step away from him.

"I'm sorry, I didn't know." He confessed.

"You've made a mess of things haven't you." Rael scolded him.

"You've made a mess of things!" I slashed the Gloomstone blade across his throat and Beau raced to hold him down.

"KEEP GOING!" Beau ordered.

I forced the blade down through his neck until it was completely severed from his body.

"DAD!" Aliera screamed.

The collar had tightened around Gray's throat now and it kept tightening. His fate was tied to Rael's.

"How do we get it off?" She cried.

"We don't." I cried with Rael's head still in my hand.

"WREN!" Beau shook him violently.

He was frozen and I handed Beau the Gloomstone blade that burnt Wren with just a slight touch.

"NOOOO!" Aliera screamed.

"HE'S GONE, ALI! He's not Wren anymore." I cried.

"Help me get this off him." I begged as I pulled at the collar slicing through my fingers.

"It's not going to come off. Get out of the city!" Gray pleaded.

"We can save you." Aliera kneeled beside him as she wept.

"NO! It's my time." Tears leaked from his eyes now.

"How can you ask me to leave you." She cried.

"He's a good man, Aliera. He's full of mistakes, but he learns, and I can see he is hurting. That means something." He choked as the blades broke his flesh deeper now.

"I CAN'T HOLD IT!" I yelled and Beau dropped to the floor and gripped the other side of the collar. Together we were able to hold it long enough for the skin to heal a little.

"You're delaying the inevitable." Gray sighed.

"I'm so sorry for all I've done." Beau cried.

"It's me who has hurt you." Gray gripped his wrist. "What I did to you as a boy, you exacted your revenge. I don't blame you." He squeezed.

"GO! There is still a war to fight, and a snake in your camp. Kill Jace!" Gray ordered.

"I can't watch." Aliera kissed his cheek and said goodbye before covering her eyes and together Beau and I released the collar.

The snap was loud, and it felt like a bomb had gone off in the dungeon as the hinges on the doors loosened from the impact.

"He's gone." I grabbed Aliera and hugged her tight.

"Deal with him!" I ordered Beau as I pointed to the Wren.

"DO IT! It's what you do." Aliera's words were cold and callous, and I felt pity for Beau as I watched him decapitate my last brother.

The doors broke open and the Durgun flooded into the chamber. Beau picked us up and lifted us into the air of the chamber. With what anger I had inside me I scorched what I could from the height of the room as Beau thrashed with horned wings at the singular window to get us out.

It broke open and he flew us to the gates where only a handful of Dreadwolves stood against half of our other armies.

"WHERE THE FUCK ARE YOUR PEOPLE?" I rushed at Jace and pounded my fist into his cheek, and he hit the ground hard, the impact shattering the stones beneath him into dust.

"What are you doing?" Starlette tried to stop me.

"HE BETRAYED US! HE SOLD US OUT, DO YOU SEE ANYONE FROM CREED HERE?" I roared.

"Where are they, Jace?" Thane became enraged.

"They're coming." He laughed as hordes of Durgun burst through the streets, Durgun that were once the villagers from Creed.

"IRMAK!" I called.

He was injured badly, but he stood on the rubble with me and offered his protection as he filled his throat with fire once more as they approached us. The Fae flew into the air for the advantage and Aliera refused Beau's protection as she walked to stand beside me.

"Together." She held my hand.

"I'll flame, you disperse it." I nodded.

Irmak ignited the street, but there was nothing left to burn, everything was black and bloodied now. Any sign of human life had disappeared.

CHAPTER

TWENTY FIVE

ALIERA

Beau hovered as close as he could without getting scorched by the flames, his wings carving through the smoke with each glide. Ele stood poised on the wall beside Torin and Luca, their eyes locked on the mayhem below. I was surprised to see Elio here, along with the warriors from Tecrit, their weapons gleaming beneath the haze of battle. The sight of them brought a flicker of hope—a reminder that we weren't alone in this fight.

I searched the battlements, my heart tightening when I couldn't spot Astrid. But the battle had struck on several fronts. She was powerful, more than capable, and likely holding another part of the wall. Protecting those who couldn't protect themselves.

"They're moving fast!" Sina yelled, her voice sharp over the roar of battle as the Fae from Sonsuz notched arrows to their bows, wings flaring with tension.

The Durgun surged from the shadows—their white, soulless eyes gleaming, blackened veins pulsing like ink beneath their skin. They moved like humans, but there was no humanity in them, only the eerie coordination of the dead controlled by distant magic.

"NOW!" Zac's voice was a command that echoed over the city.

Irmak roared in response, the massive dragon rearing up as his wings beat once with thunderous force. Flames erupted from his mouth in a blinding wave, sweeping across the field to engulf the first line of Durgun. Their shrieks were lost beneath the fire's fury.

Zac unleashed a blaze into the swarm of Durgun, scorching them in a sweeping arc of fire. But the gates now stood unguarded, and Durgun from the war camps and Creed had slipped into the city undetected. Without pause, Zac summoned flames from the Emberleaf arrows, each one igniting a Durgun into a burning beacon. I joined him, and together we harnessed the heat, channelling it into cyclonic winds of flame that spiralled through their ranks. The winds roared through the swarm, a fiery tempest that turned the tide of the battle, if only for a moment.

"DRAGON!" a Fae shouted, the warning sharp above the chaos. But it wasn't Irmak—he was already with us, grounded but alive. Then I saw her.

Azra.

She dove from the sky in a hot blaze, wings cutting through the smoke. She landed beside Irmak, nudging at his wounds with a rumbling growl, urging him to fall back. He hesitated, then backed away, settling on his haunches to recover.

Without hesitation, I ran to Azra and swung up onto her back.

"Let's do this!" I shouted. It was my turn now, grinning as I leaned into the familiar curve of her neck.

With a powerful surge of her wings, Azra lifted us into the sky. We soared above the burning city, the wind stinging my eyes, the scent of smoke and blood rising in waves.

Below us, the castle loomed. Durgun spilled from its shattered doors like a dark tide, relentless and soulless.

"Give them hell!" I roared, and Azra answered with a deafening cry. She dove at such an angle I feared I might fall from her neck.

Azra unleashed a torrent of flame over the castle, reducing it to rubble and burying most of the Durgun beneath the crumbling stone. The tide of their assault broke in an instant, their momentum halted. But I didn't stop. I directed Azra toward the remaining threats still pouring in from the Varsili countryside.

The war camps were the worst—densely packed with Durgun, a writhing mass of mindless violence. Even the inn where I had once stayed with Beau, a place once filled with warmth and quiet, would be now overrun.

This was no isolated battle. The entire country trembled under the weight of the invasion. And we weren't finished yet.

The sky turned darker still, any trace of light devoured by a thick veil of shadow and the oppressive black aura radiating from a new horde of mages that emerged from a distant quarter of the ruined city. Their eyes glowed white, vacant and twisted, stripped of will. The last of the Durgun fell into formation, parting to make way for the mages, while the remaining Dreadwolves soared overhead, circling the fractured remnants of Rael's former castle like vultures.

Beau stood at the forefront, unwavering, his gaze locked on the gathering storm as the mages began to summon something darker than anything we had faced. The air pulsed with unnatural energy, tendrils of light piercing through the ash-choked sky. Then the ground erupted. The Durgun were flung like rag dolls, tossed aside by the force of something monstrous clawing its way from beneath the earth.

The land shuddered violently. Without hesitation, the Fae launched into the air, wings flashing in the dim light. The dragons rose with them, echoing the urgency, their roars splitting through the thick, suffocating dark.

Zac's eyes ignited, flames dancing within them as heat rippled off his skin. His knuckles cracked, and fireballs surged to life in his palms. The Durgun grew more frantic, snarling and thrashing as I swept my arms forward, sending gusts of wind slicing through them like blades. The wind struck fast, razor-sharp blades, cutting down the twisted bodies that stood in our way.

They were just pawns, meant to distract us.

But above us, Thane soared. Wings spread wide, he rose above the battlefield, scanning the trembling ground below. And then he saw it—something massive stirring in the rubble, something not yet fully formed but pulsing with power.

Something being born.

"SHADOWBORN!" He yelled with all his might.

Beau whipped into the air, Azra at his back. Zac mounted Irmak and together they rained dragon fire upon the entity.

"IT'S NOT DOING ANYTHING!" Zac yelled as Dreadwolves swooped for him. Azra caught a Dreadwolf in her jaws and hurled it into the dark pit. But more attacked and Dragons fought Dreadwolves with teeth and claws before my eyes. Azra was fast, it was obvious she had been practicing in the ruins since she had left Tecrit.

The Fae descended into the pit now using all their knowledge, agility, and elemental powers to conquer the enemy Shadowborn, but it wasn't enough. It had no physical form, it was a sucking pit of dark magic that grew bigger, stronger, and more powerful with every single body that fell into its darkness.

I threw a cyclonic blast at the Mages throwing them away from the protection of the Durgun and Dreadwolves. They scattered, but Torin licked his fangs as he settled his score from the months of torture he endured at their hands. His fangs and claws tore through them, he was faster than I could have ever imagined, and he had me on his side slowing them down.

Sina and Thane made quick work of the remaining Mages who attempted to flee, their strikes swift and merciless. Overhead, Draven commanded the Fae, launching coordinated attacks against the Shadowborn, their weapons glinting with enchanted light, but each strike came at a terrible cost.

The Shadowborn retaliated with waves of black energy, violence that lashed out in every direction. The darkness tore through ranks of Fae, dragging their screaming bodies into the pit below. Each soul consumed only seemed to make the creature stronger, its form growing darker, more immense, more impossible.

Draven didn't falter. He called for the next wave, his eyes locked on the heart of the beast, even as the battlefield trembled beneath them.

"What are we going to do?" I asked, my voice trembling as Beau landed beside me, his wings folding with a snap. Torin took position at his side, grim-faced and ready. Ele stood firmly at my other side, and Zac stood before us all, seething with fury.

"That's it!" Zac roared, raising his fists into the air. Flames erupted from him—not ordinary fire, but Titan fire, so intense it burned an eerie, brilliant blue. He lifted into the sky, hovering with raw power as the blaze poured from his body in a massive shockwave. The fire rained into the pit below, a furious storm meant to consume.

The creature shrieked, thrashing wildly, its limbs lashing out in all directions. It lunged at Zac—but not in desperation. The fire hadn't weakened it. Not even close.

Now it crawled from the pit, oozing over the rubble and the fallen, its body shifting like an enormous octopus, all tendrils and hunger, gliding toward us with terrifying purpose.

Torin swallowed hard, his voice barely audible over the chaos. "We're fucked."

Beau dove straight at the creature, driving his jagged blade into what should have been its head—but there was nothing solid to strike. The blade passed through it like mist. It was barely more than a shadow, a writhing cloud of black smoke.

And just as we dared to believe the worst had passed—that the Dreadwolves and Durgun had finally been beaten back—the ground trembled with the low, haunting echo of distant howls. They were coming again. More of them. An entire wave flying in from the countryside.

"We're all going to die." Ele whispered, her voice breaking as tears welled in her eyes.

"NO! We're not dying today. But I need you up there with Irmak—do what you do best. Patch him up with whatever potions you've got. Without the dragons, we're finished. We need them to burn every last one of those Dreadwolves to ash." I commanded, my voice sharp with urgency.

Torin cleared his throat pointedly. "Ehem!" he coughed, raising an eyebrow.

I shot him a glare. "You're different!" I grunted.

Just then, Beau landed beside us, his wings flaring wide with a thunderous snap. His muscles were taut with strain, the scales along his back streaked with blood. His eyes burned—no longer Fae, not quite human, but something deeper and more primal. More dragon than anything else now.

"Your eyes!" Torin gaped.

"You should see yours when you're all Dread." Beau replied with a crooked grin.

"No, he's right. You're different." I said, stepping closer.

I reached for his hand—his nails were more like claws now, thick and calloused with razor-sharp ends. His teeth, too, they were sharper and more animal than before.

"I think that little baby dragon gave you more than just her wings." I added, awe lacing my voice.

Thane swooped overhead; eyes wide as he caught sight of what was unfolding.

"No time." Beau said, turning toward the sound of wings.

Dreadwolves were pouring over the walls, dark shapes blotting out the sky. Beau launched upward, scaling the stone like a predator reborn. He tore into them with a savagery that left nothing but ruin in his wake, his transformed body moving with lethal grace.

Elio and Luca sprinted to us, urgency written in every line of their bodies. They skidded to a stop before me, panting.

"You gotta do that thing again." Elio said, breathless.

His eyes were wide, not with fear, but with a hope that burned as fiercely as the battle rising around us.

"What? What thing?" I asked.

"It's breathing, Aliera. Watch it." Elio grabbed my chin and turned my face toward the Shadowborn.

I stared at the beast, horrified as it consumed the dead—and then the living—with ravenous hunger. It lunged skyward, snatching unsuspecting Fae from the air, its gaping maw endless and wild.

A storm built inside me.

I stepped forward, hands raised, and I called the wind to me. My hair whipped violently around my face as the sky darkened. Thunder cracked above as I summoned the sky to permit me the power of unspoken rage. Zac appeared at my side, flames roaring from his palms. Together, we wove air and fire into a furious cyclone, whipping through the city skies in a storm of blazing fury.

The creature paused, retreating toward the chasm from which it had emerged—but the pit was now clogged with rubble. I drew the air from around it, forming a vacuum. The Shadowborn let out a shriek—a sound that tore through the night, jagged and monstrous—as it writhed in the suffocating storm.

And still, we pressed on.

At first, I didn't think it would work. The creature still absorbed the fire, greedily swallowing it as if nothing could touch it. But then—suddenly—there was nothing left to consume. Every ember, every trace of life-giving essence had vanished from its reach.

It began to choke.

A desperate, rasping sound echoed from deep within as it thrashed violently, clawing at the sky above us, then crashing down toward the scorched earth below. The air trembled with its fury, but the fire that once fed it was gone. It was unraveling.

And we watched, breathless, as the impossible finally began to fall apart—it was suffocating.

"NOW!" I shouted.

Zac together with Irmak and Azra roared exploding flames on the beast and soon it took on a solid form. Beau dropped from the sky and impaled it with a small unassuming Gloomstone blade.

"GET BACK!" I shouted at Beau.

A deafening explosion erupted from the Shadowborn, the blast wave tearing through the battlefield like a scream from the underworld. Beau was caught at the center of it, flung backward through the air. His wings, once majestic and shimmering blue, were shredded—red membranes ripped apart, edges torn and tattered like silk burned in fire. Blood streamed down his back where scales had been violently stripped away, leaving raw, exposed flesh.

He hit the ground hard and didn't move.

"BEAU!" I screamed, my voice cracking with terror. Torin sprinted toward him, Draven and Ele close behind, their eyes wide with horror. I stood frozen, the world around me spinning in silence.

And in that stillness, my heart clenched so hard it felt like it might break. He wasn't just hurt. He was broken—but I couldn't lose him.

It was gone, they were all gone. There was nothing left but bodies and stone.

"It took out all of them." Zac looked around as he stood there in the dust beside me.

"They were all connected. I wouldn't be surprised if the shadow was their life source. That's usually how mages worked. They need an anchor and what better anchor than something that can't be physically harmed." Sina explained.

Smoke swirled as the sun rose and the stench of burnt flesh began to simmer in the early morning heat. Blood soaked the earth where we stood, and the once stone paths everywhere were now unsteady.

"We need to incinerate this place, that way we are certain it's done. Care to do the honors?" Starlette asked Zac and looked up at Irmak and Azra.

"Let's get the wounded out of here first." Ele interrupted.

We had lost more than half of the Fae armies. More than what we had expected, then it dawned on me— where was Astrid?

"Where is Astrid." I pulled Zac's arm.

His eyes welled and his chin dropped. " She didn't make it." He whispered under his breath.

"WHEN?" I screamed.

"When you were being held by Rael." Beau answered as Draven helped him to stand.

"She saved everyone. We would all be dead if she hadn't woken the volcano." Sina answered.

"I don't understand." I puffed. " What volcano?" I asked.

"I took her, I didn't know what she was planning but she begged me. Caxia was after Zac and Irmak, it seemed like the only thing I could do was to listen to her." Beau panted his confession.

"How did she die?" I asked.

"She infused her fire magic into the volcano, she stood in the lava to make it erupt. It was the only thing that could take out Caxia." Sina was quick to jump to Beau's defense.

I collapsed to the ground, the pain in my body roaring to life after being drained again and again over these endless days. Exhaustion gripped me, but it was the silence—the sudden absence of enemies—that made the ache worse. The loss of my sister-in-law hit me like a wave, stealing the air from my lungs.

I turned to Zac. He hadn't said a word. And Zac's silence was never empty—it was heavy, dangerous. His eyes locked onto Beau, and I saw the shift in him. Grief evolved into rage. His body tensed, muscles bulging, his form beginning to swell with fury. Irmak mirrored his emotion, steam curling from his nostrils as the dragon hissed low and threatening.

Azra stepped forward, wings flared, placing herself between Beau and whatever storm was about to break. Her chest rose, wings flapping, and her throat rumbled with a warning cry. She was ready to defend him—ready to burn the world down if it meant keeping him safe- she wasn't just mine anymore, her child's essence was within Beau now, and she would destroy anyone to protect that legacy.

"NO! Enough death for one day!" I shouted, leaping beside Azra to the place between Zac and Beau, my body trembling with the weight of everything unraveling.

"He killed our mother, and he lied to you about it! YOU WANT ME TO GIVE HIM MERCY?" Zac's voice was ragged, fury spilling from him in a storm of spit and grief. His jaw clenched; his shoulders hunched forward like a beast cornered by heartbreak.

Tears welled in my eyes. "He still saved me..." I whispered, my fists pounding against Zac's chest as the pain finally cracked open.

"And then he killed my wife!" Zac screamed, his voice cracking mid-sentence. The strength drained from him all at once, and I caught him as he crumpled, his knees buckling beneath the weight of sorrow.

He wept in my arms, the sound of it piercing through the stunned silence.

Nearby, Ele sobbed into Torin's shoulder, her own grief a quiet echo of ours. Sina stayed focused, her hands steady but her expression drawn, working tirelessly to mend Beau's tattered wings. Her every movement was a silent prayer—that something, anything, could still be made whole.

"I don't deserve your forgiveness. If my life ending brings you peace, it's yours to take." Beau said, his voice low, broken. He sighed, the weight of everything settling over him.

My head snapped toward him, and the tears I'd been holding back spilled freely. "NO." I cried, my voice cracking under the strain.

"Zac, please don't." I begged, my throat raw and tight. I pressed a bloodied hand to my mouth, trying to hold back the sobs clawing their way out of me.

Zac's eyes darkened. "You choose him?" he growled, rage simmering just beneath the surface.

"I know it doesn't make sense." I said, tears streaking down my face. "And I know he kept the truth from me. But if you kill him, you're killing all the good parts of me too." My voice trembled. "Please. He's done more good than bad." The tears dripped from my chin, and I made no effort to wipe them away.

Beau struggled to his feet, unsteady, pain etched into every movement. He took a step toward us, his body trembling.

Zac raised a hand. "That's close enough." he snapped, voice razor-sharp.

"Aliera, I..." Beau said, his voice catching. He looked at me with eyes full of regret, sorrow, and something else—hope. Then he choked on the next word, unable to speak past the lump in his throat.

I reached for him, even as Zac stood between us like a wall of fire and fury.

"Did you know the whole time who she was to me?" I pleaded, my voice barely more than a whisper. "Please don't lie..." My body trembled, caught in the storm of emotion. Everyone's eyes were on us, in a moment that should have been so private and intimate, I was so exposed.

Beau's eyes shimmered with grief. "Once I learned who you were, it didn't take long to piece it together, but I was already so taken by you. I didn't plan to fall for you—I tried not to love you." A tear carved a path through the dried blood on his cheek. His truth was honest, raw and unsettling.

"Say the word and I'll turn him to ash where he stands." Zac said coldly, hovering just behind me, a flicker of fire in his voice.

My heart tore in two, pulled between the past and what could never be. Beau had saved me, loved me, cared for me in ways no one else ever had. I saw it in his eyes—the regret, the longing, the quiet surrender. It was as if he were capturing this moment.

He reached for me, and his fingers brushed mine. The callouses on his skin were familiar, grounding, heartbreaking.

"You have to leave, Beau…" I whispered, squeezing his hand with trembling resolve. His eyes closed, and he nodded slowly, broken, but with understanding.

"I love you, and if there's ever a time we can find our way back to each other, I'll be waiting."

Tears streamed down his cheeks now, and I sobbed as he flapped his torn, bloodied wings. With a final glance, he lifted into the sky, his silhouette vanishing against the clouds. Sina and Thane soared after him, their figures disappearing into the horizon.

I turned to look at the city—what was left of it. Once vibrant, now reduced to ash and rubble. My knees gave out, and I collapsed beside Zac, my chest heaving with exhaustion.

"What now?" Ele asked softly.

"We ended a generational war." Zac said, exhaling deeply. "Now? We go wherever we want."

"Where is that?" I asked, wiping tears from my cheeks.

He paused, his eyes scanning the skyline as smoke curled through the air.

"I'll never return to Farkli." he murmured. Then, more to himself, he added, "Maybe Antoli."

And we sat in the ruins of a world that had finally stopped fighting, uncertain of where to go next—but knowing we were free to choose.

I stood and walked toward Azra, who was still eyeing Irmak with quiet vigilance. "You're safe to enjoy the sky now." I said softly, brushing her cheek with my fingers. "Keep him safe for me." I whispered just so she could hear.

Beau had been Azra's first rider—the one who taught her how to soar. Though he was never truly hers, they had bonded in a way that defied title. And now, with the essence of one of her children coursing through him, he was part of her. She would guard him fiercely.

Azra looked at me with gentle eyes, her massive body relaxing as she leaned into my touch. In that stillness, in that shared breath, we exchanged the quiet ache of goodbye.

Ele and Torin stepped up beside me, each running a hand along Azra's warm scales.

"Where will you go?" Ele asked, her voice tender, laced with uncertainty.

"I think I'll stay in Lexia for a while, I'd like to see Luna again." I said softly.

"We'll go with you." Torin nodded.

"You don't want to go home?" I asked.

"It's not home without Astrid." She sighed. Zac sobbed behind her, and I felt his heartache more than anything now.

Luca and Elio walked over to say goodbye. "Take care. Don't be a stranger, you are always welcome in Tecrit." Luca said, pulling me into a hug.

"I wouldn't dream of it." I replied, forcing a smile through the ache of parting.

Elio joined the embrace, his arms wrapping around both of us. That familiar, infectious energy radiated from him—an undeniable zest for life. He squeezed me tight, lifting me slightly off the ground, and I couldn't help but laugh through my tears.

It was a farewell wrapped in warmth, and for a moment, it made the goodbye a little easier.

The Dunya was finally at peace, but I had never felt more broken. I had lost all of my brothers. Zac would never be the same, my parents were both gone, and Beau... Beau was gone too.

I was right back where I started—alone in the streets of Varsili. The one place I swore I'd never return to. The ache in my chest settled deeper as the quiet crept in, broken only by the sound of birds slowly returning to the city.

"I'm going through the door..." I whispered, eyes fixed on the sky, on the wings above me, trying to find meaning in their effortless flight.

"The one in Antoli?" Zac asked, his voice low, careful.

"There are people in there, Zac. Something terrible was happening. I could feel it." I sighed, the weight of it all pressing down.

"Let's go then, I've got nothing better to do." he said with a steady nod, no hesitation in his voice.

"We're coming too!" Torin called, looking to Ele, who answered with a silent, resolute nod.

Together, we turned toward the unknown—not because we were whole, but because we still had something left to give.

We all climbed onto Irmak and soared toward Antoli. The flight was swift on dragon wings, swifter still with the wind at my command. I shaped the currents beneath us, guiding our path with precision as the world blurred beneath.

The roof of Antoli had caved in, and the once-grand halls now lay exposed to the sky. Snow coated the stone, hardened into a slick sheen of ice. I climbed down the rubble carefully, my boots sliding as I sought steady footing. Behind me, Zac lifted his hands. A slow, steady warmth pulsed outward as flames sparked, melting the frost and ice, bring Antoli back to life. Lanterns along the corridor flared for the first time in centuries, casting flickering light on the cold stone. Antoli breathed again.

"We should find weapons." Ele said, her voice echoing slightly in the long hallway. She tugged at locked doors, one after another, her fingers scraping frost from the handles.

Then came a soft click.

None of us had touched the old black door that opened. It stood at the end of the long corridor, untouched by time except for flecks of Bastion embedded in its wood, now glinting like embers in the lantern light.

We stared, breath caught, as the door creaked inward on its own.

"That was creepy…" Torin gasped.

"You're a Dread, and you think that's creepy? Have you seen yourself?" Zac laughed.

"I like Beau better than you." Torin scoffed.

My heart sank at the sound of his name. Azra had followed us, she became uneasy on the roof as she crumbled stones beneath her.

Then wings battered down around us and suddenly the light of the world was blocked out and Thane approached with Beau.

"You can't go in there." Thane protested.

Torin walked over to hug Beau as if it had been months, but it had barely been a day. I wanted to hug him too, and hiding behind Ele was all I could do to stop the wave of emotions from controlling my actions. But I was still mad, Zac wasn't wrong. I was just torn.

That same door was right next to me, the one covered in Harpies. I pushed it open, and I peered in once more, this time seeing a different perspective. It wasn't the aviary now; it was a field of tall grass, and a human girl was falling from the sky into the perpetual night. Without a second thought, I threw myself through the door, lunging to save her. Her screams pierced the air, raw and desperate. Behind me, I could hear their voices, shouting my name as they faded into the distance.

Then the weight of Beau's wings thundered after me, the sound of his descent like a promise not to let me fall alone. A heartbeat later, Torin's howl echoed through the darkness, wild and unrelenting, as he followed, but once I crossed the threshold, everything vanished. No faces, no light, no familiar ground. Just the echo of screams swallowed by the dark, and the silence that came after.

I couldn't see anything. Not her. Not them. Only the void and the cold rush of air around me, as the world closed in.

The End.

VANESSA JOYCE

To be continued in

Book 2:

Home of the Harpies